FERN MICHAELS

Promises

ISBN-13: 978-0-373-60599-6

PROMISES
Copyright © 2008 by Harlequin Books S.A.

The publisher acknowledges the copyright holders
of the individual works as follows:

NIGHTSTAR
Copyright © 1982 by Fern Michaels

BEYOND TOMORROW
Copyright © 1981 by Fern Michaels

HARLEQUIN®
www.Harlequin.com

Printed in U.S.A.

CONTENTS

NIGHTSTAR

CHAPTER ONE

WHOEVER coined the phrase "Blue Monday" had certainly known what he was talking about, Caren Ainsley thought morosely from her desk in the typing pool of Rayven Cosmetics. It was raining in New York City proverbial cats and dogs, and had been for several days. The rent was due in two days, and if this weather continued, she wouldn't be able to make her class at the community college where she was enrolled in a secretarial course.

Impatiently, Caren brushed at a feather of hair that kept eluding the tight bun at the back of her head. She frowned and her glasses slipped down on her nose. Darn it, when were her contacts going to be ready? She frowned again. Even if they were ready today it would be another three weeks before she could save the money to pay for them. She brightened momentarily when she visualized the day she would get them and then, voilà, she would be an instant beauty with gorgeous men throwing themselves at her feet. She would also get a new hairdo, of course, to go with the fantastic job she would have once she had finished her secretarial course in a few weeks.

A new life, sort of. Off with the old Caren and on with the new. She shouldn't be thinking about that now, not with all the work sitting unfinished on her desk. It was Secretary Week, or so the sign hanging in the outer office said. With all the secretaries at Rayven Cosmetics out to a fantastic lunch, she was holding down the fort, along with her supervisor, Maggie Bryant.

"Caren, stop what you're doing and come with me," ordered an agitated voice from behind the partition in the long typing-pool room. "Hurry, please."

"What is it, Miss Bryant? Did I do something wrong?" Caren asked in a fearful voice.

"Good heavens no, child. On the contrary, you've done something right by taking that secretarial course. It's going to pay off for you right now. Listen to me carefully, Caren. As you know, all of the secretaries are attending the company lunch in their honor, but right now there's a board meeting going on, and Marc Rayven just called down for a secretary to sit in. I'm giving you your chance for promotion, Caren. I've seen your stenographic skills, and I know that you're the fastest typist, not to mention the most accurate, in the pool. If you do a good job now, you might be able to move up to a better position instead of looking elsewhere for a job once your course is finished. You have to hurry. Mr. Rayven is not known for his patience, and you know all about his assistant, Moira. If you're even moments late, she would have no compunction about slicing you to ribbons—in front of all the board members," Maggie Bryant said in somber tones.

"But, Miss Bryant, I've never met any of those people. I'm not sure I'm good enough or fast enough to handle this. Are you sure there isn't someone else?"

"Caren, there is no one else. Look around. You know the other girls will be out longer for lunch today. And the only reason you didn't go to the park to eat was because you didn't want to go out in the rain. If you give up this lunch hour, I'll allow you to leave an hour early this evening. Or another day for that matter. Please say you'll do it. I think you can handle it," the older woman said firmly.

"But…but look how I'm dressed. If I had known, I would have worn a suit or something," Caren protested.

"You look tailored and that's all that matters. A navy blue skirt and white tailored blouse is fitting in any office. Don't worry, I spoke with Mr. Rayven myself and told him I was sending you, and I explained that you were almost finished with your course. I recommended you so highly, Caren, that you can't let me down now."

"All right, I'll do it, but I'll have butterflies in the pit of my stomach the whole time. I need a steno pad and some sharp pencils. Walk with me to the conference room, Miss Bryant?"

Caren took a deep breath and stared at her reflection in the window. She looked plain—plain and neat. She brushed back a stray wisp of soft brown hair from her brow and nudged her heavy-rimmed glasses back on her nose. Horror of horrors, her hands were shaking. How could she take dictation? She couldn't. Yes, she could, and she would! She was at the head of her class, and if Maggie Bryant had faith in her ability, that was enough for her.

Another deep breath. Marc Rayven. She was actually going to sit at the conference table and take down his dictation and notes of the meeting. Wait till the other girls in the typing pool heard this. Handsome, debonair, and don't forget, dashing, she told herself; Marc Rayven, president and chairman of the board of Rayven Cosmetics, was all these things.

The profile she had read just a few short months ago in the Sunday supplement said he was a thirty-five-year-old genius and well on his way to building an empire in the cosmetics industry. The article had hinted at a new, top-secret line of cosmetics that would either place Rayven at the top of the business or at the bottom. The article had gone on to cite quotes from the other prominent figures in the industry, and Caren had been amazed to find Rayven described as "ruthless," "mercenary," a "playboy," and in other terms far less complimentary.

"Here you go, Caren, three fresh pencils and a brand new steno book. Hurry, you have only a few minutes. I want you in there before the meeting gets under way. Make me proud of you, Caren," the older woman said fondly. With a last gentle pat on her shoulder, Maggie withdrew, leaving Caren to stand alone in front of the closed conference-room door.

Moistening her dry lips, Caren knocked softly and then took a step backward. Moira Evans opened the door, her patrician features haughty and aloof. "You must be Miss Ainsley. We've been waiting for you." She made it sound like "we" had been waiting for *hours!* Caren glanced around. The board members weren't seated and Marc Rayven was not in attendance. Caren's head went up a little higher as she stood quietly, waiting to be told where she was to sit. She was getting a headache. The perfume Moira Evans was wearing was not going to sit well with Caren. It was overpowering, heady to the point of being sickening. She knew it wasn't a Rayven perfume. Rayven perfumes were all subtle, yet alluring, and they didn't overpower the way Moira's scent was doing.

"Sit here, Miss Ainsley," Moira said, motioning to a chair next to the head of the table.

Caren quietly advanced across the room to take her assigned seat at the long conference table.

Moira Evans dismissed Caren with a nod. "Ladies, gentlemen, please be seated. Marc, Mr. Rayven, asked me to get the meeting under way. He's going to be a few minutes late as you can see."

Chairs were pulled out from the incredibly long, polished table as the board members took their seats. Cigarettes were lit, pads and pencils shifted from one spot to another. Muted conversations wafted through the high vaulted room as Caren made herself nearly comfortable in the plush high-backed chair at one end of the gleaming table. In spite of her resolution to appear efficient and experienced, Caren's eyes began to wander from the soft celery-green carpet that practically swallowed your ankles when you walked on it to the even softer-colored celery-green walls that rose majestically to the fifteen-foot ceilings. A corner office, it had two walls of wraparound glass; through filmy yards of draperies, these walls displayed an exquisite view of New York's East Side. Along the other two sides of the rectangular room were low white sofas and before them stood heavy, square, glass cocktail tables. The only splashes of color came from the Manet paintings hung above the sofas, illuminated by their own gleaming brass lights.

Moira Evans stood at the head of the conference

table waiting until the members of the board realized that she was not going to speak until she had their undivided attention. Caren had to admire the woman's poise as she stood there, still as a statue, eyes flashing, mouth grim. Eventually, the room stilled.

Caren waited expectantly, her pencil poised, ready to begin her notes of the meeting. There was no doubt in her mind that Moira Evans belonged in a cosmetics firm. The woman's makeup was perfection and the expensive Halston suit she wore molded her slim form perfectly, its willow gray outlining her incredibly slim figure. Every jet-black hair was in its place, swinging freely about her face and ending bluntly just above the snow-white collar of her Oscar de la Renta blouse. Every male eye in the room was on Marc Rayven's assistant; Moira knew it and preened beneath it. The woman nodded her head to acknowledge the silence and prepared to speak from a sheaf of papers held in her manicured hand. It appeared to Caren as though this was Miss Evans's grand moment, a moment she had anticipated and relished. She was going to bring a meeting to order in place of the company's president.

Suddenly the conference-room doors swung open as if some unleashed hurricane had made landfall. A whirlwind entered in its wake in the personage of Marc Rayven. He waved airily at the assembled board and motioned with one hand for Moira to stand aside.

What a pity, Caren thought uncharitably, Miss Evans's grand moment dashed to splinters by the entrance of a hurricane.

Marc Rayven was imposing, an electric personality. He threw himself into his chair at the head of the table. "I'll take it from here, Moira." His voice was clipped, cool, professional. For one instant Moira stiffened and Caren expected her to defend her position at the head of the table. Apparently, Miss Evans thought better of it and gracefully took her seat across from Caren.

Rayven shuffled his papers and then lifted his head to stare at Caren. He frowned and Caren's heart fluttered. "You must be the secretary."

"This is the girl who'll take the minutes of the meeting, Marc," Moira said coolly as she stared straight into Caren's eyes.

Caren's shoulders straightened. "My name is Caren Ainsley, Mr. Rayven; I'm from the typing pool." Caren spoke quietly, surprised that her voice was so confident.

"Now I remember; Maggie spoke to me about you. I won't need you after all. But take a seat just in case."

"Thank you, Mr. Rayven." Caren melted when he smiled down at her. It was almost as if the room were empty and they had a secret between them. It was that kind of smile, she decided.

As he prepared his notes, Caren watched him. He was handsome, more so than his pictures in the society columns. How aptly named he was, with his hair the black of a raven's wing. And his eyes were deep blue, almost turquoise. A definitely handsome combination, she mused. Evidently, Moira thought so too because Caren was receiving the most malevolent look she had ever received in her life. And that look could mean only one thing. *Moira Evans saw Marc Rayven as her special property.*

Caren relaxed. Moira Evans couldn't do anything to her. Not here in this conference room or outside it either for that matter. She didn't know how she knew, she just knew that Marc Rayven would protect her. Whoever the journalist was who had said he was ruthless didn't know this Marc Rayven. So much for profiles in Sunday supplements.

Leaning back in his chair and tossing the stack of papers he was holding onto the shining surface of the table, Marc Rayven spoke. "Let me begin by saying that this is not a formal meeting. I would prefer at this time to consider it a sort of open discussion." He waited for comment. When none was forthcoming, he continued. "I say that we go with the enfleurage method for the new perfume line. I know," he said holding up his hand to quell the disagreements, "it's the most expensive method, but this is a one-of-a-kind perfume. If we use distillation, we'll end up selling it to the dime stores. I want all of you to think along the lines of an entire line—from cosmetics to toiletries to perfume—all bearing the same name. I want this scent on every woman in America. I want them talking about it. I want it blitzed from one end of the country to the other. After we do that, we'll tackle the foreign markets, but this is an *American* perfume, made by an *American* manufacturer and at this time we're aiming exclusively for the *American* woman. A woman like Caren Ainsley." His gaze fell on her and something in it warmed her cheeks. "We're going to give the American woman," he continued, "a line of her own—cologne, toilet water, lipsticks, bath powders, and oils.

"You other ladies," he said, addressing the female members of the board, "can afford to pamper your-selves with expensive French perfumes. But it's time we began to think of the average American woman. She's got as much right as the rest of you to want a scent that's within her means. And I plan to give it to her. Let's kick it around a little. What we want is a perfume with sensitivity, a perfume that wears for all seasons. Most of all, we want a scent that becomes a woman's own the instant she puts it on."

"That's impossible, Marc," one of the men at the other end of the table insisted.

"At one time I would have agreed with you, but not now. My chemists have come up with something I think is going to blow this industry sky-high. I have here a sample and I want all of you to test it. Tell me, ladies and gentlemen, if you think we have the right mixture of spice, wood, floral, and fruit all rolled up into one. A complete line. Dollars in your bank accounts. Not just perfume, an entire line."

Caren watched in amazement as Marc Rayven bent down to his attaché case to withdraw a small, slender vial. Tenderly, he removed the cork stopper and inhaled deeply, then passed the vial to Moira, who sniffed and passed it along, too. There were murmurs of appreciation and approval.

The man sitting beside Caren passed the vial to her. Cautiously, she sniffed and then sniffed again. "It's beautiful, I've never experienced anything like it."

Marc lapsed into thought for a moment, then slapped his palm on the conference tale. "That's it! Did you hear what she just said?" He inclined his head in Caren's direction. "She said she'd never experienced anything like it! This is more than a perfume! It's an *experience!* An experience I have decided to call Nightstar. Our promotions will say: Nightstar— an experience."

"Now wait a moment, Marc," came a sober, dissenting voice from the far end of the table.

"Burgess?" Marc addressed the man. "You have a problem with the name of Nightstar?"

"No, no, it's a lovely name. Perfect as a matter of

fact." The elderly gentleman smiled and bowed in Caren's direction. "As I see it, the problems still exist in reaching the American woman."

"Burgess, as head of our internal publicity department, your word carries weight with me. Why don't you just spit it out. What's your problem?"

The slim gray-haired man whom Marc Rayven called Burgess straightened his shoulders and addressed the board. "It's a wonderful idea. The problem, as I see it, exists in promotion. If Rayven Cosmetics sticks to the perfume and *only* the perfume, there is no problem in having our campaign ready for the coming Christmas season. Christmas being the most popular time of year for buying fragrance. Gifts and—"

"Just get to the point, Burgess," Marc interrupted.

"The point is, *in promoting the perfume,* we can hire a high-fashion model to do our advertising. *In creating a whole line for the American woman,* a high-fashion model just wouldn't go down, if you know what I mean. She would be associated in the public's mind with money, designer labels, and unfortunately, expensive toiletries. These will be mundane, affordable items; and yet the products require the glamour these models portray. It would take months to map out the kind of campaign that would deliver the message that this scent is for the average American woman. For the secretaries and the housewives and even for the little shop girls who'll sell the stuff. That would take a great deal of thought and, quite frankly, Marc, I don't believe there is anyone who could conceive of such a campaign. Others have tried and failed as you well know. It would be easier to get Mickey Mouse elected President."

Marc sat back in his chair, his sun-bronzed hands running through his hair while he considered Burgess' words.

When he lifted his head, he stared unflinchingly down the table at Burgess. "I agree with you completely. But you see I have no intention of using high-fashion models. I don't see some scrawny woman with good bones becoming the identity of the American woman. We need an amateur!"

"Marc, that's impossible and you know it! *All* the companies use professional models. Professional people. We have too much at stake to use anyone but a professional who knows her business. I'm afraid we're going to have to go with the perfume only. Perhaps at a later date—" Burgess said confidently, knowing Rayven encouraged his executives to speak their minds; and it was an informal meeting.

"No way. I say we go with the whole line. I believe in it. I'm telling you that the Nightstar line will be accepted by American women. Loved by them. *If* we take one from their ranks and make her our Nightstar spokeperson. We *can't* use the same old approach. Women have to *believe* that Nightstar can make them be the women they want to be." His turquoise eyes flew around the room and landed on Caren, who was watching him wide-eyed. "Take Caren here. Who is she? A typist in a company pool. But who is she when she goes home at night? Who does she dream of becoming? And the same goes for the women who work at home. Who do they want to be? That's the message that Nightstar has to convey. 'Be the woman you've always dreamed of being… Nightstar becomes *You*....'"

Caren was listening attentively. Marc Rayven seemed to know so much about women, all women. He even knew about her. He knew that in her fantasies she was never a typist. No, she was a slave girl kidnapped by a handsome sheikh…Scarlett O'Hara…Shakespeare's Juliet….

"We all know you've always had a flair for advertising, Marc, but you must see it is not feasible to install a complete Nightstar line. This has got to be thought out thoroughly."

Marc glared down the table looking at each and every individual board member. "Do you want Nightstar or don't you? Either we go with the complete line or it's 'no go.'"

"But where will we find the production company? The models?"

"*No models.* We need Miss Jane Doe. Nightstar will become *her* perfume, *her* image, *her* fantasy."

Burgess spoke up again. "Marc. Be reasonable. All that Jane Doe stuff makes good copy, not good sense. Of course you need a professional model. You can't just take a girl off the street and make her your Nightstar girl."

"If I believe in this line, I can. Can't you see, if we use a model, someone whose face has been seen in every fashion magazine in America, how are we going to convince women that they *too* can be a Nightstar girl? No, we need someone who's an unknown…. We need that girl off the street." Marc Rayven's eyes raked every face in the room, resting inordinately long on Caren's. "We don't have to find a girl off the street," he said softly. "The girl fresh out of the typing pool would do just as well. Miss Ainsley," he said firmly, "how would you like to become our Nightstar girl?"

Gasps filled the room. "Marc! You can't," Moira Evans cried.

"Have you lost your mind?" said someone from one end of the conference table.

"Make sense, man." Burgess sighed, exasperated.

"I haven't lost my mind…. I am making sense. Why not?" Rayven defended. "She's a woman, isn't she? She has two arms, two legs…. Her figure is trim and neat—"

"But her hair!" a female member moaned.

"And those glasses—"

"It will never work."

Caren was dumbfounded and then paralyzed as she listened to the rousing protests directed at Marc Rayven. They were picking her apart as though she were an object, not a woman with feelings.

"She must be twenty-five or twenty-six, at least. Too old."

"We need someone with a sense of style…."

On and on they found her faults, leaving her flushed, stricken, breathless. Oh, God, if she could only crawl under the table and hide until they all went away. She didn't want to be the Nightstar girl…. She wanted to finish her course at the community college and find a nice job somewhere.

"She has no sense of style. Marc, we need someone who can bring something to Nightstar—"

"And *I* say that the Nightstar line can make a woman anyone she wants to be," Marc Rayven thundered. "And I say we go with Caren Ainsley."

"Marc, be reasonable," Moira's voice cajoled. "Call off the joke. Tell everyone you've been joking."

Silence pervaded the room. Moira Evans was giving Rayven an out from his ridiculous idea.

"I *am* being reasonable. Caren is the kind of girl we see every day. She's not a beauty queen. She's a hard-working, levelheaded girl. Just like the kind of girls and women who will buy Nightstar—the kind of woman who can't be fooled. I know she's not perfect. If she were, she'd be one of the professional models I definitely do not want for Nightstar. We're going to prove that we can make a silk purse from a sow's ear."

Caren looked up. Had Mr. Rayven said that? Had he called her a sow's ear? Horrified at the thought of being so demeaned, her shoulders stiffened and a hot flush of anger stained her cheeks.

"Do I have to remind you all that as president and chairman of the board, I own the controlling interest in this company? Your affirmative votes would be most welcome, but they are not necessary. Anyone who so chooses can offer his stock in this company for sale. I'll be glad to take it off his hands at current market prices."

Hush was the only word that came to Caren's mind. It was so still one could have heard a pin drop on the thickly carpeted floor.

"If Miss Ainsley agrees, she will be our new Nightstar girl." Marc Rayven left his place at the head of the table and stood beside Caren. He took her hands in his own and looked down into her face. His remarkable blue eyes melted into her own; her breath came in little gasps. She was frightened, embarrassed. She wanted to run, never to see the inside of Rayven Cosmetics again. But Marc Rayven's hands were holding her, and he was looking down into her face. There was such a silent persuasion there, a hope. How could she, after all she had heard, agree to his wishes? She knew that the others felt his scheme would fail. Could she play such a major part in that failure? Could she be the Nightstar girl? It could mean the end to her financial hassles and provide an escape from the humdrum to life in the fast lane. Before she realized what she was doing, she nodded her agreement.

"Caren Ainsley, you are our Nightstar girl. From this moment on your life will change. Your dreams will come true."

Caren was stunned. The board members were looking at her with respect, if not approval. Was Marc Rayven making a joke at her expense? One glance at Moira Evans's face told her the head of the cosmetics firm was deadly serious. It couldn't be. This just couldn't be happening to her. One moment she was Caren Ainsley, typing-pool worker, and the next she was the Nightstar girl.

"But I only came in here to take dictation. This is so sudden—"

"Forget the dictation. Miss Caren Ainsley, I'm going to take you out to lunch and buy you the biggest steak on the menu. Now, this minute. Get your coat and while you're at it, quit your job. You were just promoted. Tell Maggie to get in touch with me later this afternoon."

Caren left the board room in a daze, Moira Evans's eyes stabbing her every step of the way. The minute the door closed behind her, she ran as if the hounds of hell were at her heels. She wanted to run away from Rayven Cosmetics—run so far she could pretend she'd never heard the name Nightstar, run away from Marc Rayven who could make her agree to change her whole life.

CHAPTER TWO

SOME of the girls in the typing pool were jealous at the news, others were genuinely happy for her. Lunch with the gorgeous president of Rayven Cosmetics! Lunch with Marc Rayven!

"Yes, she's leaving us!" Maggie Bryant cried happily. "She's going to work for Mr. Rayven himself. Isn't that right, Caren?"

Caren nodded, still too stunned to speak.

"You'd better hurry, child, run along to the washroom and powder your nose. You said Mr. Rayven didn't want to be kept waiting," Maggie said, literally pulling Caren away from her coworkers.

Caren found her voice. "I don't believe this is happening to me. I simply don't believe it! I'm going, Miss Bryant, but I'll be back after lunch and give you all the details."

"Fine, fine. Hurry along now; you really can't keep Mr. Rayven waiting, and your nose is on the shiny side," Maggie responded as she thrust open the door that led to the corridor. "Just a minute," Maggie said drawing Caren aside. "I think you should know the office grapevine has it that Moira Evans has her cap set on being Rayven Cosmetics' first lady, and the way things have been going lately it looks to be more true than untrue. In short, honey, Moira wants to be Mrs. Marc Rayven. Any way you look at it, you are going to be a threat to her. Be careful," she admonished in a tight little whisper.

Embracing Maggie, Caren then raced off to the lounge area. She stopped momentarily as she fished around in her handbag for lipstick and compact. She was off to the side unable to see into the area where the washbasins were. She would think about Maggie's words later. She heard voices and running water. At first, she paid no attention to the voices, and if the truth were known, she simply didn't want to come down off that fluffy cloud she was on to hear everyday words.

She, Caren Ainsley, was going to be Marc Rayven's Nightstar girl, and that definitely took her out of the humdrum. She blinked when she happened to hear her name mentioned and then smiled. News of her promotion had traveled quickly.

"I don't know why Marc did what he did. But that ugly duckling has no more of a chance of being the Nightstar girl than Maggie Bryant. I was there, remember? I had dinner with Marc last night and he was boasting to me, boasting mind you, that he could convince the board that he could find the most wretched excuse for a woman and make her into his new Nightstar girl—with the proper promotion and buildup. But I didn't take him seriously!"

Caren's world literally crumbled at her feet. The voice belonged to Moira Evans. Marc Rayven couldn't have said those things. He just couldn't have said them!

A second voice seemed as questioning as Caren felt. "Moira, that's an awful thing to say about anyone. You make it sound as though Mr. Rayven *handpicked* this girl to be his victim. I can't believe Mr. Rayven would say something like that. I'm sorry, I just don't believe it."

"Well, you'd better believe it, Lorraine. If you want proof, just ask little Miss Four-Eyes if she took down one word of dictation. Not one squiggly line," Moira said triumphantly. "Marc said it himself when he told the others that she, the typist or whatever she is, was just what he was waiting for. He set her up. The whole board knows it and so do I. The little dummy fell for it, too."

Caren was stunned. She had to get out of here, out of this lounge area, before Moira Evans and her secretary came out of the powder room. There was no way she would allow that Evans woman to see what her callous words had done to her.

Quietly, Caren opened the door. She would quit her

job all right. She would quit Rayven Cosmetics altogether and go somewhere else. How could that man make a fool of her like this? The words from the Sunday supplement ricocheted in her brain. *Ruthless, mercenary.* Ruthless people trampled over other people and paid no attention to their feelings. Mercenary people were concerned with money night and day. Ruthless and mercenary. Tears rose to the surface. She had to get out of here. Run! her mind screamed. Don't let him humiliate you. Moira Evans wouldn't say such brutal things without truth. Or would she?

"Here you are. Maggie said you were powdering your nose. You look fine, Caren," Marc Rayven said gallantly.

Now, what was she going to do? She couldn't run now; she felt too ashamed, too humiliated, and all the girls on the floor were waving and giggling. Even Maggie wore an ear-to-ear grin. She had to go through with the lunch, but she didn't have to take the job. She knew how to say no. She looked up at the tall man towering over her and forced a sickly smile to her lips. "Yes, I'm about as ready as I'll ever be," she answered in an even tone that surprised even herself.

"Then we should be on our way. I called down to have the doorman have a taxi waiting. No point in taking my car out of the garage. How does the Russian Tea Room sound to you?"

Caren had heard of the elegant restaurant, but had

never been fortunate enough to eat there, either as someone's guest or on her own. New York City boasted many fine restaurants, but the Russian Tea Room was supposed to be somewhere near the top of the list. How she would have enjoyed it if she hadn't heard Moira's hateful words.

"A penny for your thoughts, Caren," Marc murmured as he helped her into the back of a Checker cab.

"I'm sorry—I was thinking of something. What was it you asked me?" she said leaning back in the leather seat.

"I asked you how the Russian Tea Room sounded to you?"

It seemed to Caren that there was a slight edge to Marc's words. "I think it's fine. I've never been there, but I have certainly heard of it. Isn't it a little late to get reservations?" Caren asked peering at her watch.

Caren was pleased that her escort suddenly wore a sheepish look. "It is, but I called ahead and pulled a few strings. We won't have a problem."

"You just called ahead and everything was arranged? Just like that?" Caren asked in amazement.

Marc Rayven grinned. "Actually, there was a bit more to it than that, but it doesn't matter as long as everything's set."

Caren flinched as the Sunday supplement swam before her eyes. Playboy, rich playboy. Rich playboy escorts ugly duckling to famous restaurant. Why not?

Why should she care what he thought of her? Imperceptibly, she drew away from him, more aware of him as a man than anything else. Suddenly, she felt confused. He didn't seem to be the kind of man who would say the kind of things Moira said.

"Are you always this quiet, Caren? By the way," he continued, not waiting for her to reply, "call me Marc. I really feel as though we're going to get to know each other very well. I wonder why that is?" he mused.

Caren's defenses rose. She wouldn't answer that or any of the other questions he asked. She shielded herself; the person who did that didn't get hurt. She knew instinctively that the man sitting next to her could hurt her—hurt her badly if she allowed it.

Marc Rayven whisked Caren from the cab and into the restaurant so fast her head was spinning. She watched with an amused expression as Marc spoke with a tall, dark-haired man. He motioned to the top floor and Caren heard the words "by the window." Within seconds they were seated at a table overlooking busy Fifty-seventh Street.

Caren ordered white wine and Marc ordered Scotch and soda. They sipped, eyeing each other. "Why do I keep getting the feeling that you don't approve of me?" Marc asked in a cool tone.

"I can't imagine why you would think that," Caren replied bringing the glass to her lips.

"I have a habit of doing things very fast. I've done so all my life. I make a decision and then I follow it through to the end. Some of my competitors frown on what they call my 'unorthodox methods' but they have never failed me as yet."

They made small talk, each eyeing the other warily, or so Caren thought. What in the world did he think she was thinking? Better yet, what was *he* thinking? Was she supposed to be all bubbly and excited? Evidently. And now when she was keeping a low profile, he couldn't understand it. Ugly duckling! Somewhere between the wine and the end of the appetizer, Caren made up her mind to go through with Marc Rayven's plan for her. Why not? She didn't have anything to lose. If he wanted to consider her some kind of test case, some kind of guinea pig to practice on, why not let him? As long as he paid her more than what she was making in the typing pool, it was all right with her.

"Have you always worn glasses, Caren?" Marc asked bluntly. "Let me see what you look like without them."

"I've worn them for the past several years. In the beginning it was just to read or study, but yes, to answer your unasked questions, I do need them to see. I ordered a pair of contact lenses several weeks ago, and I expect them any day now," Caren said evenly, striving to keep her tone neutral. She removed the square, dark-rimmed glasses and stared at Marc Rayven.

"Your eyes are incredible, just the perfect shade of lavender. Did you know Elizabeth Taylor has eyes the same color as yours?"

Caren smiled in spite of herself. "That was a superb compliment. You could have said I had eyes like Elizabeth Taylor instead of the other way around."

Marc grinned. "Now that you mention it, I see what you mean. I don't know Elizabeth Taylor, but I do know you. It seemed natural to say it that way."

"Whatever," Caren said sipping at the wine.

"Tell me, Caren, do you have any ties keeping you here in the big city? We will probably need you to go on the road to help promote the line and I want to know now if there will be any kind of difficulties."

Caren forced her tone to be neutral. "I'm quite alone. My father was in the military, but he died a year ago. I have no other family. I'm world-traveled, if that will set your mind at ease. I see no problems, do you?"

"No boyfriends who will gnash their teeth if you desert them?" His blue eyes challenged. Was it her imagination or had the man's tone softened somewhat?

"No one in particular, if that's what you mean. I didn't know men gnashed their teeth; I just thought women did that when they got angry. At a man, of course." Caren smiled.

"Then it would appear we're in business. You will shortly become Rayven Cosmetics' Nightstar girl.

Tomorrow morning, you're to report to me; and Moira Evans, my assistant, will see to your transformation."

Caren swallowed hard. She knew somehow that it would be Moira.

"I would like to ask a question. What does an assistant do? I'm referring to Miss Evans." She couldn't bring herself to say Moira's name to the man sitting across from her.

"Quite a few things as a matter of fact. For the most part she's a buffer between me and others. She has not only a feel but also a flair for the cosmetic business. She had her own boutique for a good many years. She has very good business sense and she's been a good friend and sounding board."

She couldn't keep sipping at the nearly empty wineglass. What to do with her nervous hands? This time there was no mistake; there had been a fond note in his voice when he said Moira was a good friend. Playboys always had gorgeous girls around, she thought glumly.

"All in all, she's fairly close to being perfect. It's strange how she can almost anticipate my needs."

Caren nearly choked. "Are you saying she's without faults? I never met anyone like that." This time there was a definite edge to her voice. Marc Rayven sensed it and his eyes narrowed.

"Let's just say she has a few imperfect character traits."

"And I'm the ugly duckling you're going to transform into a beautiful swan." Caren grimaced as she plunged her fork into the thick steak she didn't want and knew she couldn't eat.

Caren watched, fascinated at the way Marc cut his steak. He had strong, square, capable-looking hands. She wondered if they would be gentle if they ever got close enough to touch her. A bright flush stained her cheeks, and she was glad Marc was intent on his food and didn't notice. She couldn't get out of line, think things that would never come into being. He was offering her a job and she was accepting it—pure and simple, a job. Nothing would come of it. Not if her intuition was right about Moira Evans's possessive eyes when they fell on Marc. And always remember, she cautioned herself, that I am the ugly duckling. I must never lose sight of that. And last of all, but not least, Moira would always be in the wings reminding her, lest she forget.

EACH SECOND that brought Caren closer to the Rayven Cosmetics firm left her feeling more trapped. Why was she going through with all of this? Why was she subjecting herself to Moira's sure-to-come insults and Marc Rayven's desire to turn her from an ugly duckling into a beautiful swan? *Hopefully* a beautiful swan.

Rayven Cosmetics was less than half a block away

when a strong gust of wind snatched her crushed-velvet beret from her head. Giving her hat up for lost, she braced herself against the buffeting wind and hurried for the door that would lead her to her new duties.

She felt the light touch on her shoulder and then heard the words. For a moment she did not comprehend who was doing the talking and touching. "Your little hat gave me a hell of a time, but I'm a kite flyer from way back. I was right behind you when that wind blew up and I saw it go sailing. I leaped into the air and there it was, right on the end of a street sign."

"Mr….Mr. Rayven. You didn't have to do that. I wouldn't want to make you late. I gave up on the hat. But thank you," Caren muttered, not certain what else she should say to the tall man grinning down at her.

"Of course, I had to do it. I couldn't leave a lady in distress now, could I? And I'm not late for work. Did you forget? I'm the boss." He gave her a devastating smile. "Actually, I walk in the morning. There's something about greeting each day with a brisk walk."

Caren lengthened her steps to match the long-legged stride of the man walking alongside her. She couldn't believe the twist her life was taking. Here was the president of Rayven Cosmetics talking to her as though they were old friends. Sure they were, she thought cynically. All he was interested in was promoting his cosmetics and keeping on the good side of her.

A small warning system in Caren's brain went off and the smile died on her lips. Over and over it repeated the message. He's not interested in ducklings, just swans who can make pots of money for his firm and make him *numero uno* in the cosmetics industry. Well, she didn't have to go along. During her transformation she would have to do as she was told in order to earn her pay. Outside of the office and the glamorous salons, she would let him know she saw right through his little plan—thanks to having overheard Miss Evans in the lavatory.

Caren hadn't realized she had ceased walking until the feathery light touch startled her for a second time. "Do revolving doors hold some kind of terror for you?" Rayven's cool voice demanded. "Is something wrong? I've been speaking to you, but I don't think you've heard a word I said."

Caren stepped into the opening, and before she realized it, she was standing next to Marc Rayven. At best, it was cramped. A flush stained Caren's cheeks when she stared up at Marc and noted the strange look on his face. "If I could bottle the color on your cheeks, I would make a fortune."

Caren flushed a deeper crimson. Why was she forever doing such stupid things? Now he was looking at her as though she had two heads. Two-headed ladies didn't do much for the cosmetics business. He was probably sorry he had made such a hasty decision in hiring her. If ever there was a time to say something brilliant, this was it. Moira would know exactly what to say and just how to say it. On the other hand, Moira would never, never, under any circumstances enter a revolving door with someone else. Caren could almost hear the musical tone, "But darling, one simply doesn't do that! Infants, toddlers, perhaps; adults never but never, darling."

Caren forced a sickly smile to her lips. "I guess I wasn't thinking or watching where I was going." It sounded lame and she knew it. Marc Rayven's face still wore that strange look.

"If you're sure you're all right, I'm going to leave you here." He seemed genuinely concerned. "I'm meeting someone in the coffee shop."

A second later she felt a careless kind of kiss on her high cheekbone. Not exactly careless, to her it seemed more insolent. Annoyed at herself and even more annoyed with the Nightstar King, as she now referred to him in her mind, Caren stalked off to the waiting elevator and marched inside, her face a vivid scarlet.

Caren fixed her gaze on the overhead number plate and wished the pesky elevator would go on forever. Sooner or later it was going to stop at the thirtieth floor, and she would have to get out. A frightening feeling of dread was making her feel all trembly and weightless. Was any job worth all of this turmoil? Was Marc Rayven worth all this heart fluttering? A Nightstar girl should be in control. It was too late to worry now. The elevator door was opening with a silent swoosh and then she was standing in the reception area, feeling like a lost lamb. Squaring her shoulders, she announced herself to the receptionist. Then she affixed a grim, tight look to her mouth and marched down the corridor to where Moira Evans awaited. "And the lamb goes to the slaughter," Caren muttered to herself.

Moira was a commercial artist's dream in her burgundy dress. To Caren's inexperienced eye it looked like nothing more than sheer handkerchiefs sewn together with the points hanging and swishing sensuously about her elegant knees. A wide gold braided belt and a slender gold chain were her only accessories. Caren was impressed. It was also evident that Moira was not impressed with her new protégée. She gave the appearance of dusting her hands and looking helplessly about. Caren could almost read her thoughts. "Whatever am I going to do with this infant?"

A devil of impishness perched itself on Caren's shoulders. "Mold me, Miss Evans, into the Nightstar girl. I'm all yours."

Moira Evans moistened her glossy lips, which were just a shade lighter than her dress, and stared at the slender girl. Her voice was arrogant, haughty. "There's just *so* much I can do! Follow me, please."

She dresses like a model and walks like a model. If she can turn me into a close second, perhaps I won't dislike her so much, Caren thought with feeling. But do I *really* want to be like her? She answered her own question. Of course not. I just want... Actually, what I would like to have is her beau. Such an old-fashioned term. Marc Rayven could hardly be called a beau. He was Moira's man. They were an item, a thing, according to the grapevine and Maggie, and there must be truth in it because Maggie didn't indulge in idle gossip. Her warning to Caren echoed clearly. They appeared to have a relationship other than the one that went on in the office. Surely they didn't live together! And if they did, what business was it of hers? The only way it could be her business was if she made it her business and that was the one thing she had no intention of doing.

Moira's tone was curt and cold. "Wait here," was the command.

Caren seated herself primly on a vivid orange chair and waited. Just where did Moira think she was going to go? she wondered tartly. She liked this whole situation less every moment. Caren watched as Moira stood inside the doorway, talking in soft whispers. Every so often she waved her hands in a languid kind of gesture to emphasize a point she was obviously trying to make.

Whatever she was trying to do, the man seemed to object. From time to time he glanced in Caren's direction, and then shook his head negatively.

The gold leaf on the door said the salon was operated by Jacques Duval. It was the makeup salon, evidently the one all the models used. Caren watched in alarm as Jacques stepped back a step and finally nodded his head. Apparently, he was finally agreeing to whatever demand Moira was making. Agreeing, but not liking whatever he was agreeing to do. Moira's face was now wreathed in smiles as she made her way back to where Caren waited, but not before she pecked Jacques on the cheek.

"I'm leaving you here in Jacques's capable hands. He'll call down for me when he's finished with you. Mr. Rayven wants hourly reports on your progress." Her pale blue eyes glittered and her handkerchieflike hem swirled angrily around Moira's legs as she stalked from the salon's tiny foyer.

Caren inhaled deeply. Now she was in someone else's hands. Hourly reports! A sigh caught in her throat as she awaited Monsieur Jacques.

AT THE END of three hours, Caren felt as though she'd been pushed through a gristmill, but she did notice a sense of excitement begin to well up in her at the astonished looks of the people who were "doing her over." They all, with the exception of Jacques Duval, seemed to be enjoying her transformation into Rayven's Nightstar girl.

Although she had barely moved a muscle that morning, she felt achy and exhausted. First order of the day had been a body massage, a steam bath, and then another massage; after which her eyebrows had been painfully tweezed and reshaped. Then a facial with soothing creams and astringent herbs. A manicure, a pedicure, and on and on. She was pushed this way and that. A dressmaker came in to measure her and take her sizes. The couturier who had been consigned exclusively to Rayven Cosmetics clicked his tongue and made disapproving noises as each inch of her was noted on his pad. And once he had actually had the audacity to step over and pinch the flesh at the back of her arms. "This must go!" he had scolded. "Kevin Germaine creations are conceived to enhance the body—not to cover fat!"

Caren blushed vividly. She had never considered herself "fat." Not by any measure. "Young lady, you must lose one complete dress size. At least eight pounds. Until then, there is nothing I can do and I shall inform Mr. Rayven as much."

Caren's blush deepened and changed from shyness to humiliation to know that Marc Rayven would be told she was "too fat." Her defenses rising, she turned on the slim, silver-haired Mr. Germaine. "I am not fat! I wear a perfect size ten, and if that's not good enough for you or for Mr. Rayven, that's too bad!"

Immediately, Kevin Germaine's attitude changed to one of grudging respect. "No, no, Miss Ainsley. It's only that if you were to be just a few pounds thinner it would be so much more flattering to you. Please, forgive me if I spoke out of turn—"

A bell sounded and three young girls in pink smocks glided over to Caren and handed her a plate with assorted raw vegetables and a cup of herbal tea. "Miss Ainsley, why don't you go into the office and stretch out? There's no one to bother you and you can rest up from this morning's ordeal. We won't be back to hassle you until around two o'clock," one of the girls offered.

Caren sighed. It sounded too good to be true. A whole hour and a half to just nibble on the rabbit food and stretch out. No poking, no prodding, no snipping or brushing. She was exhausted, she admitted to herself.

It was an elegant, sumptuous office by any standards. Bright green carpeting swirled around Caren's slim ankles; she felt as though she were tripping through a summer meadow. All she needed to complete the feeling was a sprinkling of wild daisies and a few butterflies.

She had never known there were so many shades of green. All in all, it was one of the most restful rooms

Caren had ever seen. Light filtered through pale, wheat-colored draperies and the furniture was antique white in French Provincial styling. Long, deep divans lined the walls and pastel-tinted watercolors brought out the light greens of the furnishings. Whoever belongs in this particular office must have a great deal of trouble concentrating on work, she thought. It is so reminiscent of the great outdoors or of city parks in the summer.

Caren walked around the restful office touching one object after another. She was just admiring what appeared to be an intricate telephone system when she heard Marc Rayven's voice. Startled, she whirled around to see if he had just entered the room. He hadn't. His voice was coming over the contraption that passed for a telephone. Caren's face wrinkled into a frown—a definite no-no, according to the makeup specialists in the salon. Besides, when one eavesdropped one never heard anything good about oneself. She should turn the machine off, but how? Most machines had an off button somewhere. Not this machine. Twelve buttons with initials over them. What if she pressed one and Rayven's voice sounded all over the building? A horrible thought struck her. Was this the president's office? Was this sea-green meadow Marc Rayven's office? She shouldn't listen to what was being said, but she wanted to know. Any self-respecting, red-blooded female—and she was one—would want to know what Marc Rayven was saying.

Jacques Duval's faint French accent was minimal as he spoke quickly, almost too quickly, Caren thought. "You're sure, Mr. Rayven, that you want me to follow Ms. Evans's orders exactly?" Was there a touch of defiance in the Frenchman's tone or was it Caren's imagination?

Marc Rayven's voice purred dangerously over the wire. "Exactly, Jacques. How is the transformation coming along? Are you molding the raw material into a length of silk?" Not waiting for a reply, Rayven continued. "Jacques, I'm staking my reputation and my company on this line of cosmetics. No mistakes, no errors of any kind. You're to follow Moira's instructions to the letter. I know it's a kind of sow's-ear-silk-purse thing, but I have the utmost faith in your ability. That's one of the reasons you're the head of the salons. By the way, just out of curiosity, how is our girl taking to this experiment? She is cooperating, isn't she?"

Sow's ear! Experiment! He thought of her as "raw material." Well, Mr. Rayven, just you wait till you see the finished product, she thought angrily. Jacques's voice continued to flow. "Miss Ainsley is very cooperative. I can't say I would do the same if I were in her position. I'm following Ms. Evans's orders to the letter. I certainly hope the both of you know what you're doing. You know, Mr. Rayven, it's times like these that I think I should be selling used cars. I just might do that one of these days."

"Duval, you're talking in riddles. If that's a hint for a raise, why don't you just come out and ask for one instead of telling me you want to sell used cars."

"I don't want a raise. Selling used cars is at least an honest business. When a customer comes in, he knows the chances are ninety to ten that he's going to get a lemon. Here the girl goes to the slau— Never mind. Look, Mr. Rayven, if that's all, I have to get back to the hair salon and work on Denise. She's modeling at three and clients don't wait for Jacques Duval."

"Look, Duval, if something is bothering you, why don't we have a drink after work and talk it out. I'll bring Moira along and we'll discuss it."

"You talk to Moira, Mr. Rayven. I talked to her this morning, and it was enough to last me for the rest of my life. I'm doing my job and that's all that matters or should matter to either of you."

Caren perched herself on the end of a forest-green chaise and stared at the silent box on the desk. Neither Marc Rayven nor Jacques Duval had said good-bye.

Outrage and anger ripped through Caren at what she considered total disregard for her feelings. She wasn't a piece of merchandise; nor was she a convenience item. Something was going on. Her pulses hammered at the thought that whatever that something was, it boded ill for her. Moira seemed, according to Duval, to be behind whatever it was, but with full authority from Marc Rayven. What was going on? It must have something to do with the new Nightstar line of cosmetics; and if that was true, then it was going to affect her in some way. Sow's ear, raw material! Of all the colossal nerve! and she had gone into the same revolving door with him. Him! Harrumph!

Caren literally flopped down on a grass-green recliner and toppled the raw vegetables onto the floor. The stalks of celery were barely noticeable on the green carpeting. The carrots made a vivid splash of color to Caren's eyes. She ignored both as she sipped at the cold herbal tea. This whole thing was a mistake—a mistake that it was too late to correct.

Caren's back stiffened and her shoulders squared. Whatever was going on, whatever Moira had planned for her, she would fight. She was going to be the best Nightstar girl that Rayven Cosmetics could want. If the stunning Moira was really jealous of her, as Caren suspected, that was her problem. I'll handle my own problems in my own way as they come up. Sow's ear, huh? She would show *him* and Moira Evans as well. From this moment on she was going to be Grade-A silk all the way.

CHAPTER THREE

"You must be exhausted," Jacques Duval said quietly. To Caren's ears it sounded more like a statement of fact than a question that required an answer. "You're a pleasure to work with," Jacques complimented. "So still and uncomplaining, and with excellent bone structure, I might add." His faint French accent was a pleasure to her ears, and he smiled at her into the mirror in front of which she was sitting.

With a snap of his fingers he summoned a young woman in a pink smock. Murmuring something in French, he gave the girl instructions. In turn, the young woman picked up a brush from the nearby vanity and began to brush Caren's brown hair back off her face into a severe, sleek chignon.

"Oh, Jacques," Caren said hesitantly, "I don't think this style is right for me—"

"*Non, non, chérie*…it is only for the photographs. Soon, we will decide on the proper haircut and style… For now it is only for the photographs."

"Oh, I see," Caren said quietly. Did he or didn't he like her? Jacques seemed to go out of his way to be polite, but that was it. He made little small talk and he stared at her when he thought she wasn't looking. All in all, Caren was uneasy in his presence. The overheard words on the telephone system rocketed around in her brain, making her frown.

"Never frown. Do you want the number eleven engraved on your forehead?" Jacques demanded suddenly.

Caren apologized. "I guess I was thinking of something and—"

"You don't have to explain, Caren," he replied shortly. Then he repeated something in French to the girl who had just finished her hair. Picking up a soft, flat brush, Jacques dusted Caren's face with the specially blended face powder he had mixed for her that morning. "Now, Caren, if you will come with us, we will take you to the photographer."

Gulping, Caren did as she was instructed, pulling at the ties of the soft gray wrapper that she had been instructed to wear. On her feet were soft, flat-heeled slippers, and she felt decidedly undressed having nothing on beneath the wrapper except her panties.

Obediently, she followed Jacques, who was carrying a tray of makeup, down the hall to a dim little room containing all manner of lights and reflectors that varied from something resembling little umbrellas to sophisticated photographic equipment.

The girl who had brushed her hair back was following behind, brush in hand, and Jacques told her to close the door behind her. From out of the depths of darkness came a voice. "Jacques? Have you brought our little Miss Nightstar?" The owner of the voice stepped into the light.

"Caren, I would like you to meet Bill Valenti, our house photographer," Jacques introduced them.

Bill Valenti was a young man dressed in ragged jeans and, of all things, saddle shoes. His pale face revealed young features and light blond hair that fell onto his shoulders. "How are you holding up, Caren?" the man asked. His friendly manner set Caren at her ease.

"I'm hanging in there, Mr. Valenti." She smiled.

"Bill," he corrected. "Please call me Bill, okay?"

"Okay," she said, relaxing still further. There was no threat in his manner, none of Jacques' imperiousness.

Leading Caren over to the platform and into the lights, Bill assured her, "Now, Caren, I want you to relax. I don't want you to stiffen up or worry about how these photos will come out. They're only for our use. For Jacques to study to decide on the perfect hairstyle for you and, of course, your makeup. I want you to think of the camera as your friend. And it is."

Caren looked around her at the frightening equipment, at the glaring lights, and was not comforted by his words. Like most women, she felt the camera lens was a critical viewer, ready and able to pick out each and every flaw and to reveal them to the world.

"You're a very pretty girl, Caren. The camera will see that. And if you think of my lenses as friends, they will be kind to you. Do you think you can do that?" he asked kindly.

Caren gulped and nodded her head. "I'll try, Mr. Val—Bill."

"Good." He smiled boyishly, his eyes meeting hers for the first time. "Good heavens, I wish we were filming in color. Those eyes! Remarkable! They're going to be a challenge—" He broke off in midsentence and clapped his hands. "All right, everyone, clear the room. Miss Ainsley and my lenses need some time to form a friendship."

From out of the shadows several people stepped forward and headed for the door. Caren blanched; she had had no idea there had been so many eyes behind those cameras.

"Jacques, you may stay of course. Everyone else, clear the set."

Feeling like a butterfly at the end of a pin, Caren perched on the high stool, aware of her near nakedness beneath the thin gray wrapper. The lights were so bright she felt they would penetrate the soft material and reveal her.

"Now, Caren, I want you to watch what I'm doing with the lights. I want you to see everything; nothing must be a mystery. You will come to know each key light by name; each reflector will become your counterpart. There is no mystery to photography, and once you learn that, the film will capture the woman inside you, Caren. A warm and lovely woman—"

Each word Bill Valenti spoke relaxed Caren still further until she was able to take an interest in the adjustments he was making with the equipment.

"Now, as I was telling you, this is black-and-white film. My intention is to reveal the light-catching surfaces of your face and, of course, those hollows and curves that create shadows. On film your face will become two dimensional, not three. We'll be able to judge your best side, your best features—and, of course, those that we must play down."

Caren frowned.

"Smile, Caren. Even the most beautiful models in the magazines have some feature that is less than flattering in two dimensions. But I'll tell you their secret. They become friends of the camera. They form a relationship; you might even say they have a love affair."

All the while Bill Valenti was talking, Caren could hear the whir and snap of the automatic shutter, the eye that would judge her. But she was so engrossed with what Bill was saying, the little stories, the gossip he was revealing about well-known personalities he had photographed, that she simply forgot the discriminating eye of the camera.

"That's great, Caren. Now, we want to see what that glorious long neck of yours looks like through the lens. Would you open your wrapper, please."

Caren flushed, flustered. She couldn't; she wouldn't. She would never, never...

"Caren, don't be a silly little girl; Bill only wants you to drop the wrapper off your shoulders," Jacques's voice reassured.

Feeling like a foolish child, Caren loosened the neck of the gray wrapper, dropping it over her shoulders, her hands clutching the material together over her breasts.

"That's perfect, Caren. Perfect. Now, look this way. That's right, right into the camera. It's your friend, remember?"

Obediently, Caren gazed into the camera, hearing the whirring and the snap of the shutters. Again and again Bill snapped her image, capturing her first from one angle and then from another. All the while his voice soothed her, encouraged her.

Bill Valenti murmured something to Jacques who hurried over to dust Caren's face with powder to remove the shine. She felt as though she were melting, dissolving beneath the glaring lights. But somehow, they warmed her too, filling her with their radiance.

Her back was to the camera; she was glancing over her shoulder, her eyes downcast as per Bill's instructions. She thought she heard a sound behind her, but was unable to see.

"That's right, Caren, look down. We want to get a profile shot. Okay, now drop your wrapper a little farther, that's right—"

Suddenly, a hand touched her, roughly pulling her wrapper up to her shoulders, covering her. A deep, recognizable voice thundered, "What the hell do you think you're doing? The both of you?" Marc Rayven's tone was murderous, causing the blood to curdle in her veins.

"Caren, cover yourself up," he ordered, pulling the wrapper up still farther.

Caren was almost afraid to turn around, to see his face. From his tone she knew it must be black with rage, his eyes spewing fire.

"Listen, Valenti, I sent this girl in to you to get preliminary photos, not for a centerfold layout!"

Stammering with confusion, Bill Valenti protested. "Since when is a bare shoulder a 'centerfold layout,'" he demanded. "I don't tell you how to run your business, so don't tell me how to run mine!"

"And you, Jacques, I placed Caren in your hands," Rayven continued, ignoring Bill's statement. The rage in his voice vibrated through the room, bouncing off the walls and coming to rest somewhere near the top of Caren's head. She hated this feeling that she was the cause of the argument, the reason for the man's pounding anger.

So it was that she was startled by the sudden gentleness of his tone when he spoke to her. "Caren, I want you to go back down the hall and get changed. You're through for the day."

Unable to lift her eyes to his, Caren scooted off the stool and headed for the door, before Marc Rayven could resume his tirade. But she wasn't quick enough. His voice thundered again.

"What the hell do you mean by pulling a stunt like that, Bill? Haven't you any decency?"

"What's gotten into you, Marc? Since when did you become a prude? You never took on this way with any of the models, and you know as well as I that there was a lot more skin showing than just a bare shoulder and back—"

Something inside of Caren bristled and became rigid, stiffening her spine and freezing her feet to the floor. Pulling the wrapper around her and tightening its belt, she whirled around to face Marc Rayven.

"Stop it this instant!" she demanded hotly, causing the three men to stop and stare at her in amazement. "You can just stop it!" Her eyes were burning through Marc Rayven, incriminating him. "I am not a child, Mr. Rayven, and I certainly have a very high standard of decency. I can assure you that I was not offended or asked to do anything that would compromise that decency. Mr. Valenti and Mr. Duval have been perfect gentlemen. I am not such a babe in the woods that I need Victorian protection from you, and I am affronted that you would think I want to be the Nightstar girl so badly that I would do anything I would be ashamed of." Caren's face burned. Had that been her voice shouting? Had she really said those things to Mr. Rayven? She could feel Bill's and Jacques's glances bouncing back and forth between her and Marc Rayven.

"What did I tell you, Marc?" Bill asked. "Even Caren thinks you're making a fool of yourself. What's gotten into you anyway? I've never seen you like this."

Caren glanced at Jacques and wondered at the knowing look on the Frenchman's face.

Marc Rayven stood his ground. "Drop it, Bill. That's a wrap for today. Jacques, take Caren back to Makeup with you." His tone was tightly measured, refusing to give an inch. Suddenly, he turned on his heel and brushed past Caren and out the door, leaving her with the impression of electrically charged air and a vague scent of his cologne.

Down the hall in Makeup Jacques removed the tight rubber band from Caren's hair and ran his fingers over her scalp soothingly. As he worked, his face was screwed up in a frown.

"Jacques, don't frown. Remember the number eleven." She tried to make light conversation.

Jacques was having none of it. "Mr. Rayven acted very strangely before, Caren. Do you know why?" he asked, his eyes meeting hers in the mirror.

"No, I have no idea…. Actually, I'm ashamed of myself for speaking to him the way I did. I know he was only looking out for my welfare—"

"*Non, non, chérie,* it was more than that." Jacques gave a typical Frenchman's shrug. "I want to reassure you that Bill Valenti is a master of photography and he seems to like you, Caren. He would never compromise you." The frown returned again, accompanied by a look of confusion in the man's eyes and a downturn at the corners of his mouth.

Suddenly, Caren wondered if Jacques was trying to tell her that although Bill Valenti would never compromise her, he himself would. Pushing the thought away as being foolish, Caren managed a smile into the mirror.

"I'm leaving now," Jacques told her. "I'm certain you are happy to be done with this place for the day. By the way, Caren, it really is nice working with you compared to some others around here. I mean that as a compliment."

"Thank you, Jacques, you're very kind. I was told you're the best in the business, so I'm just doing what I'm told. I trust you to do whatever is best for me," Caren said simply.

"That's a mistake."

Caren whirled around and was stunned at the miserable look on the Frenchman's face. "What's a mistake?" she asked, her tone puzzled.

"Trusting anyone. Still, you're young. You have much to learn about people, I'm afraid." The silver wings in his dark hair framed his darkly troubled eyes. Even the short clipped beard gracing his chin seemed to droop a little.

Caren frowned again, she couldn't help it. "Jacques, I was talking about trusting *you*. Trusting you to do whatever is best for me in my transformation into the Nightstar girl. You have such an excellent reputation. Why shouldn't I trust you? I don't understand. Did I say something wrong? If so, I'm sorry." She was babbling and she knew it. Why did Jacques look like this? What was wrong with saying she trusted him?

A look of panic settled over the makeup artist's face. Why? Caren wondered. Better to leave it alone. Something was going on; that was obvious. Sooner or later she would find out what it was that was bothering Jacques and she would deal with it at that time. For now, a simple good-night should close everything for the day. Tomorrow was something else. "I guess I'll see you in the morning then. Good night, Jacques."

"Good night, Caren," Jacques said just as quickly.

With a last glance at Jacques, Caren left the room

and started down the long corridor decorated in gay, colorful murals, toward the bank of elevators. Her mind was buzzing with questions. Questions that no one, it seemed, wanted to answer for her.

Yesterday she had been just another girl in the typing pool and then, suddenly, she was picked to take dictation at the board meeting and her whole life had changed.

Yesterday there had been direction to her life. She had had it all planned. She was going to finish her course at the community college and then apply for a better job, preferably right here at Rayven Cosmetics. Now, nothing was the same. Now, she was going to be the Nightstar girl instead of an executive secretary.

Yesterday she had known who her friends were: the girls in the typing pool, several friends she had made at college, and most of all, Maggie Bryant. Now, there was no way of knowing her friends, and Jacques had just told her not to trust anyone.

Her path to the elevators took her past the door to the photographer's studio. Remembering the scene Marc Rayven had created behind that door made her quicken her step. She still couldn't believe she had stood up to him that way. He was wrong, that's all there was to it, she thought hotly. He had practically accused her of compromising her morals and had accused Jacques and Bill Valenti of being unscrupulous. In her soul Caren knew nothing could be further from the truth. It was true that when Bill instructed her to loosen her wrapper she had panicked. But that had only been for a moment, until Jacques explained exactly what Bill wanted. Centerfold layout, indeed! Marc Rayven, you have a dirty mind!

The express elevator stopped and Caren entered the lonely, brightly lit cage and made the descent to the ground floor of the Rayven building. She shuddered at the sight of the revolving door, waiting a full minute till there was no one in sight before she gave a push and sailed out into the soft, evening air. She really didn't want to go home. A walk. Hadn't Marc Rayven said a brisk walk in the morning was a great way to start the day? Well, maybe it worked that way at night too. A brisk walk home to get her adrenaline flowing and she could sit through four hours of inane chatter on the television shows.

As she stepped briskly along Third Avenue, she again thought of Marc Rayven. Only moments ago she had been thinking of him as a dirty-minded man and here she was taking his advice about a walk. Unconsciously, a smile broke out on her face.

Bill Valenti had been startled and amazed at Mr. Rayven's reaction to a little bit of skin. Hadn't he even said that he'd never known the Lipstick King to behave that way before?

Something inside Caren told her that whatever her

original reaction had been to Mr. Rayven's stormy behavior, it was provoked by some protective instinct toward her. Inwardly, she knew she forgave him for the scene he had created. Something inside her told her she would forgive Marc Rayven practically anything.

As she walked, head bent against the wind, Caren's thoughts were jumbled as were her emotions. She jammed her hands into her raincoat pocket, intent only on what she was thinking. Marc Rayven was a very handsome man. She was attracted to him. She felt a flush creep up her neck as she imagined what it would feel like to kiss the tall dark-haired man. The word fantastic came to her lips. Just fantastic.

Moira Evans whirled her way into Caren's thoughts as she waited for the red light to turn green. How many times had Marc Rayven been kissed by his assistant? Plenty…hundreds…thousands… Hrumph, Caren snorted inelegantly. She had kissed a few men in her time, too. So what? But they were boys compared to Marc Rayven. This was where a girl mentally separated the boys from the men and grew up a little herself. An image of Marc Rayven's shoulders floated before her. She imagined that they could blot out the world if he bent toward her with the intention of kissing her. A smile tugged at the corners of her lips. Of course, she would have to be sitting down in that particular fantasy.

The light finally changed and she entered the crosswalk with the others who had been waiting to get to the other side of the avenue. Her busy thoughts spiraled once again. And that glorious warm golden skin of his. How would it be to touch—no, caress—those tawny muscles of his on some secluded beach out of sight of prying eyes? Marvelous. The grin tugged again at the corners of her mouth. So far, she had one fantastic and one marvelous to contend with. For the first time in her adult life her emotions were in a turmoil. She had stirred the simmering pot and now it was about to boil. When that happened you turned down the flame and added a lid. Not so easy, she mused as she stopped to peer into a shop window. When she continued onward, she couldn't remember what she had looked at.

Did Marc Rayven really think she was a gawky schoolgirl? A sow's ear? That hurt—wounded actually. While she might not be bleeding, she definitely felt cut to the quick, not to mention humiliated. How was she going to face him the next time she met up with him? She wasn't flashing and beautiful like Moira, but she did have endurance. And most important, she was a survivor.

What bothered her more than anything, she thought to herself as she waited for another light to change from red to green, was that Marc Rayven was using her. Using her for his own personal gain. The cosmetics business, like the garment industry, was a dog-eat-dog business, and in order to survive and make a fortune, everyone expected you to cut other people to ribbons. Emotionally, Caren knew she could not afford Marc Rayven in any way, shape, or form.

Already, after just a few days, she was becoming short tempered, fearful, and jealous—alien emotions to her. And Marc Rayven seemed to be the catalyst. He was responsible for all these new feelings, all these faint stirrings within her. And when he got what he wanted he would discard her like an old tube of lipstick and she would be left an emotional cripple. He used people. He went after what he wanted and he got it regardless of what or how people felt. She was people. How could he be so nice to her on the surface and say she was a sow's ear to Jacques? He and Moira must have a grand time talking about the ugly duckling, she thought morosely. Soon, the ugly duckling was going to be a beautiful swan if things went the way they were supposed to, and then look out, Moira Evans and Marc Rayven!

Caren slowed her pace. She was almost home. Another two blocks and she would climb the three flights to her apartment, make something to eat and watch the early news. Why did she have to be such an introvert? Introverts, with a lot of help, could be extroverts. She made a mental note to work on that starting the following morning.

Her key in the lock, Caren heard the phone ringing

shrilly inside. For some reason, she didn't remember the bell being so loud, so demanding. She closed the door, locked it behind her, and then took her time walking over to the end table. She picked up the beige receiver on the seventh ring and said "Hello."

"Caren?" A slight hesitation as Caren's heart fluttered wildly in her breast. "Marc Rayven here." Not bothering to wait for a reply, he continued. "I know this is short notice. Moira was scurrying all over the building trying to find you, but you had already left. I would like it if you could be ready to go to a party this evening. I'll pick you up at nine. You can be ready, can't you?" Again, he didn't wait for a reply. "This is an important event. Some of the best in the business will be there. You could consider this a sort of preview, so to speak."

Red-hot anger shot up Caren's spine. She'd just bet old Moira was scurrying about looking for her. She and Marc Rayven with their hourly reports. If they knew where she was every hour, why couldn't Rayven's right hand find her? Because she wasn't looking, that was why. And now this…this…Lipstick King—the nickname he had earned when he'd launched the line of lip glosses that had made him famous—was telling her he wanted to take her to a preview. She *was* the preview. She was the one who was going to get a good going over. People were going to pass judgment on her.

She wasn't ready yet. How could he do this to her? She was tired. Sow's ear!

"Are you saying you want me to go to a preview or that I am the one who is to be previewed?" she asked coldly, her hand trembling on the tightly clutched receiver.

"A little of both." The friendliness was gone, replaced with a cool authority.

"I'm very tired, Mr. Rayven. I just this minute got in the door and I was looking forward to a quiet evening. Perhaps another time."

The cool tone was now frigid. "Perhaps you didn't hear me, Miss Ainsley." Before it was Caren. "I said I would pick you up at nine. A suitable dress is being sent by messenger. It should arrive within minutes. Wear it. I took the liberty of getting your address out of the personnel file, so I know where you live. I heartily endorse punctuality."

A suitable dress! Well, why not? After all, she was considered a sow's ear. Tacky, in plain English. And why not take her address out of the file? After all, he owned the company and did pay her. Rank certainly did have its privileges. Of all the colossal nerve! She should tell him what to do with his dress, and when he arrived in his custom-made car with the French horn, she should simply refuse to answer the door.

"I'm sure you can't be so tired that a refreshing

shower wouldn't do wonders for a person," the frigid voice said clearly.

Caren's tone matched his. "Is that the same as taking a brisk walk in the morning?" Not waiting for a reply, she rushed on before what little outrage she had deserted her. "At the orientation meeting this morning I was told that an itinerary would be given to me and that I would have ample notice to prepare before any appearances. This evening's preview does not fall into line with your previous instructions. In short, Mr. Rayven, this sow's ear is not ready to go public. The moment I turn into pure silk I am yours to do with as you see fit. Until that time you will have to make other arrangements. Do I make myself clear?"

"Perfectly. I'll pick you up at nine. Be waiting." The line was dead.

Caren replaced the phone and stared at it. The dull buzzer sounded a warning that someone was pressing her worn-out bell in the small lobby of the apartment house. She picked up the phone, pressed six, and spoke harshly. "Yes?"

"Abrams Messenger Service. I have a package for a Miss Caren Ainsley. Shall I leave it or bring it up?"

"I really don't care what you do with it," Caren snapped. "Take it back where you got it from."

"Miss, I can't do that. My boss would fire me. If you don't want to come down for it and you don't want me to bring it up, I'll leave it with the super. You can send it back, but do me a favor and use another messenger service. We have a good reputation. We deliver anywhere in the city and that's our motto. How is it going to look?" the unseen voice whined.

"All right, all right, you can bring it up. Just leave it by my door." Again, Caren replaced the receiver and stood staring at it. She was only committed as long as she accepted the dress box in her hand. For all she cared, it could sit outside her door forever.

The phone shrilled a second time. She really would have to get it checked. "Caren," a sweet, syrupy voice all but cooed. It was Moira Evans. Funny how things changed. Now, she was Caren. Several hours ago she couldn't remember her name. "Darling, I've been trying to call you and track you down for just hours. There is this preview you simply must attend this evening. I realize this is very short notice, but you were…you were just gone. Marc—Mr. Rayven—feels it is imperative that you attend. I do, too, of course. It's just that you were… Wherever did you disappear to? I, for one, think it was very thoughtless of you not to tell anyone you were leaving. But that is neither here nor there," the throaty voice continued. "You must be ready and available at nine sharp. Mr. Rayven will be picking you up on schedule. And, I must warn you, he is punctual. Of course, I will be with him. I detest tardiness myself."

Caren stuck her tongue out at the phone in a childish gesture. Now what was she to do? She really had no choices, no options. She had to go. Her decision made, she unlocked her apartment door and picked up a snow-white box tied with a vivid purple bow. She hated purple. She imagined Moira wore purple a lot.

CHAPTER FOUR

THE GOLD-LEAF LETTERING on the snow-white box read "Albert Nipon," and although Mr. Nipon's creations were definitely out of Caren's financial league, she recognized the name of the famous couturier.

Almost reverently, her fingers untied the satin bow and from out of the pale blue tissue paper she withdrew what had to be the loveliest after-six dress she had ever seen. It was white; more than white, pure white. The most pale lavender beading at the neck and sleeves was repeated at the uneven handkerchief hemline. It was exactly right for her; this she knew instinctively. The white would enhance the pale ivory tones of her skin and those beads would pick up the color of her eyes.

Once again, her eyes fell to the box. There was something more. Her fingers touched the finest silk lingerie bordered with wide bands of Holland lace. It was exactly right to go under the opaque silk dress. Shoes! Scandalous slippers with modest heels, held on to the foot by an ingenious placing of slender straps.

As she shook out the dress and held it up to herself, something slithered down and fell onto her feet. It was yards of a wide self-belt that could be wrapped cummerbund-style around the waist. Caren decided at once that she would forgo the belt and allow the dress to skim lightly over her figure, presenting the lines of the creation without encumbrance.

Lightly, she stepped over to the mirror to see the dress against her face. Ye gods! Her hair! Jacques had cut it and it was freshly shampooed, but that had been the extent of her hairdressing that day. Jacques had been more concerned with her bone structure and skin tones than her hair. He had told her that the next day would decide what would be done with it.

And Moira, Moira had known. She *had* to have known! Hadn't she received hourly reports on Caren's progress? Marc Rayven was a man; he wouldn't give consideration to the fact that her hair was hanging in dull brown hanks. But Moira would and she would want Caren to embarrass herself.

Quickly, Caren went into the tiny bathroom and surveyed her face, scrutinizing it. Her makeup was still perfect, still bearing Jacques's master hand. But her hair!

It had been cut to a shorter length than she was accustomed to wearing and would be difficult to manage. She just knew that her blow dryer and curling iron would help matters only slightly. It would be possible to take a bath so her makeup wouldn't be ruined, and her fingers and toes were freshly manicured; but what about her hair?

Caren's eyes fell on the kitchen clock. Less than an hour to get ready. Another of Moira's ideas, she was sure. But then again, if she hadn't dawdled on the way home, she would have given herself more time.

No sense crying over it. She had to think of something.

Caren experimented, pushing her hair this way and that, finding each attempt most disappointing. In a flurry of panic she raced out once again to the living room.

Her shaking fingers grabbed up the wide belt. Crossing her fingers for luck, she shook her hair back from her face and began wrapping the belt around her head. Frowning, she examined her attempt and then brightened. The tiny glass beads along the edge of the belt fell flatteringly along her hairline, softening its severity and accentuating her features and Jacques's masterful makeup artistry. She had never attempted anything so sophisticated before and felt a little self-conscious. But she reminded herself that she was the Nightstar girl and sophistication and style would be required of her.

Feeling much more self-assured, she hurried once again to the bathroom and ran the tub, making certain to leave the door open so the tiny room wouldn't fill with steam and cause her makeup to streak.

Forty minutes later Caren was dressed. The silk slip felt cool and luxurious against her skin. The dress was perfect, no doubt altered according to the measurements that had been taken of her earlier that day. Even the shoes felt as though they had come from her own wardrobe and fitted perfectly.

Her concern was centered on the head covering she had designed. Turning her head this way and that, she began to feel more confident about it. The belt had been yards long, meant, no doubt, to be wrapped several times around the waist and then to fall in long ends to the hemline. Instead, she had centered it across her forehead and crisscrossed it in the back, bringing it up over the top of her head and crisscrossing it again, repeating this several times until her entire head was covered. Finally, taking both long ends, she fashioned them into a soft knot resembling a rosette. This she secured over her right ear with pins. The resulting effect was sophisticated and exotic, the little drooping beads falling symmetrically across her brow and tickling her pleasingly.

Suddenly, the doorbell buzzed. A quick glance at the clock. Fifteen minutes early! Wasn't that just like Moira? Hoping to catch her at a disadvantage in front of Marc Rayven. Smiling to herself, Caren picked up her house key and slipped out of her apartment. She would meet them downstairs and save herself reason for apologizing for her small, sparsely furnished apartment. As she closed the door behind her, she once again heard the impatient buzzing of the bell. Darn that Moira!

Flouncing down the three flights to the door, Caren's feet felt as though she were walking on air. She looked stunning and she knew it. She was going to stand up straight and keep her chin up. Mr. Nipon's dress wasn't going to be wasted on a bumbling little schoolgirl. She was a woman and she looked her best, better than she had ever looked, and she was going to show the world she was aware of it.

When she opened the door of the vestibule, it was not Moira Evans's finger pressed impatiently on the buzzer to her apartment; it was that of Marc Rayven himself. When he turned at her entrance, she could have sworn she saw his jaw drop. The appreciative look in his eyes gave her further confidence and she preened. A sow's ear, was she!

"Mr. Rayven, how nice of you to come early," she said, with just a touch of sarcasm in her tone.

"Actually, Miss Ainsley," said Moira Evans, stepping out from the other side of the vestibule, "we arrived early in case you needed any help dressing."

"Yes, Caren. That was Moira's helpful suggestion," Marc interjected. "But as you can see, Moira, Caren is perfect—just perfect."

Caren felt Moira glaring at her. It was evident to her that the woman was hoping to catch Caren with her hair down and rushing around like a madwoman trying to get her act together. Alien and dangerous feelings rose in Caren as she smiled sweetly at Moira, taking pleasure from the stiff set of her shoulders. "How nice of you to think of me, Miss Evans. But as you can see, I did the best I could all by myself. I haven't needed anyone to wait on me since I was a little girl." She felt her smile broaden and her words were sugary sweet. Moira had attacked her self-respect by indicating that Caren was incapable of making herself presentable enough to be seen in public.

Marc seemed oblivious to the hostility between the two women as he opened the outside door to usher them out. Men, Caren thought hotly. World War III could be going on right under their noses and they wouldn't notice it. They all thought their own sex had a monopoly on doing battle. When would they realize that it really was the female of the species who was deadlier than the male?

It was Caren's arm that Marc tucked under his own as they went down the front stairs, leaving Moira on her own to teeter on her incredibly high heels. It was Caren who was helped into the front seat of Rayven's Mercedes, leaving Moira to struggle into the backseat. It was at this point that

Caren noticed the shiny black satin of Moira's skin-tight sheath dress. The long tight sleeves and figure-hugging bodice showed her pencil-slim figure to perfection. Against the white of Caren's dress, the black made Moira seem sensual and sexy, almost vampish, an effect that Caren was almost certain Moira had planned.

"We're going to a preview of a new film and all of New York will be there, including photographers and columnists. That's why I felt it was important for you to attend. You understand, there will not be a formal announcement made at this time of our new Nightstar campaign and the part you play in it. It's enough for now for people to wonder who this pretty new face is. Understand?" Marc spoke quietly as he drove, addressing his remarks to Caren and from time to time glancing over at her, a strange new light in his eyes.

"I understand," Caren answered, knowing without being told that anyone new whom Marc Rayven was seen with was automatically newsworthy. "So you don't want me to say anything about Nightstar if I'm asked."

"Right. Just smile that dazzling smile of yours and act mysterious. Think you can handle it? I'll be right there at your side; I'll help fend off some of the more pointed questions," he assured her.

"I understand, Mr. Rayven."

"Marc. You must call me Marc." His hand covered

hers, as it rested on her lap, and squeezed it meaning-fully, causing Caren's heart to leap to her throat.

Moira, in the backseat, was oblivious to the intimate contact between the two up front and she commented stridently, "Of course, it will be Mr. Rayven at the office, Miss Ainsley. Understood?"

Before Caren could answer, Marc's voice thun-dered, "I have just told Caren to use my first name and that's the way I want it, Moira. Both at the office and outside the office."

"Marc...I just...well, it's always been your policy not to fraternize with the help, I just thought—"

"Don't think, Moira. And besides, Caren is not 'help.' She's my Nightstar girl." Marc squeezed Caren's hand again.

"Do you think she can handle it tonight? About re-maining mysterious, I mean. You know that any woman you're seen with creates a stir. What do they call you—New York's most eligible bachelor? What I mean is, Miss Ainsley doesn't know how to deal with this segment of society—"

"That's enough, Moira," Marc said wearily. "All Caren has to remember is not to say anything about working for Rayven Cosmetics or the Nightstar campaign. You can handle that, can't you, sweetheart?" Sweetheart! Sweetheart! From a sow's ear to sweet-heart! Instantly, Caren pulled her hand away, dropping the keys she had quickly grabbed before she had left the apartment. She didn't have an evening bag that would go with Mr. Nipon's creation, so she had thought it better not to take one at all.

"What's this?" Marc asked picking up the jangle of keys from the seat beside him.

"My keys. I...I didn't have a bag to go with the dress—"

"Moira, take a note. I want Caren to have a complete new wardrobe—from soup to nuts. Understand? Nothing but the best."

"But I...really don't need—"

"Nonsense. I've admired the tailored suits and dresses that you've worn to the office, but now it's time for you to be wearing designer labels. Okay?"

Of course it was okay! It was especially okay since he had mentioned that he'd noticed her at the office and the clothes she'd worn. It was extra-specially okay since he'd just said he admired her taste.

The keys still jangled in his hand and he slipped them into his tuxedo pocket.

"My keys—"

"I'll keep them for you, Caren." He took his eyes off the road long enough to look over at her and smile that bewitching smile. "I'll give them back when I take you home."

"Home," Moira was heard to mutter from the backseat. It was evident the woman was positively seething. "I'd say that was a pretty questionable neighborhood, if you ask me."

"Oh, really?" Marc asked, looking straight ahead at the traffic. "I thought it was all right. It reminded me of the neighborhood where my first apartment was. I was pretty independent when I went to college," he said aside to Caren. "I wanted to try my own wings and leave the family fortune in the bank where it belonged. I took a loft in the Soho district with a couple of friends, and I still think those were the best days of my life. I loved it. All the world seemed to pass right by the front door, and many of the friends I made were artists and writers. Happily, some of them are very famous and successful today. I still count them among my friends."

Somehow, Caren couldn't quite see Marc Rayven as the "poor little rich boy" but something in his tone made her heart go out to him. She was about to ask him about some of his well-known friends when Moira interrupted.

"Oh, Marc, you make it sound so romantic and it wasn't that way at all and you know it! Remember the days when there was little else to eat except canned spaghetti and chicken noodle soup? That wasn't all that much fun."

Caren's ears perked up. Had Moira known Marc

since their college days? That would make her somewhere in her thirties? She was surprised as she had always thought Miss Evans was only a little older than herself. Surprise dissolved away into a curious kind of jealousy that Moira had shared an experience with Marc that was obviously close to his heart. Jealous? No, she denied, it *had* to be something else! How could she be jealous of a man who had called her a sow's ear?

Marc was silent and Moira, suspecting she had said the wrong thing, began to amend her first statement. "Actually, though, it was rather fun. Marc," she said excitedly, "remember the time your English Lit professor was going to fail you if you didn't pass the exam? And remember how we stayed up all night for three nights helping you cram? And remember how we all waited outside the lecture hall for you to finish your exam, and remember the party we had afterward?"

Marc laughed, a deep booming sound. "Yes, and I also remember how you spent a whole day preparing all my favorite foods and how angry you were when I fell asleep, too tired to eat."

"Ooh, you used to make me so angry!" Moira laughed, a deep, throaty, sensual sound that vibrated through Caren's very being. They talked so intimately, had so many memories to share. A disquieting thought occurred to Caren. From the sound of their conversation, it appeared Marc and Moira had lived together. Again that curious worm of discontent rolled around in her innards. Was it possible they still maintained that relationship and kept it secret from the office? No; she negated the thought. Otherwise, the society columns would link Moira Evans's name with Marc's. Moira wasn't the kind of woman to share her man with another woman. And besides, if their relationship was an intimate one going back over the years, why weren't they married by now? From the signals Moira was sending, Marc's continuing bachelorhood was definitely not her preference. So it had to be Marc who wasn't serious about Moira. The little worm of discontent stilled and a pervasive sense of well-being took its place.

COMING out from the dark theater into the bright lights of the lobby, Caren felt blinded. The film was being soundly acclaimed as a work of genius; voices echoed its praise all around her. Caren sighed. Perhaps there was something wrong with her, but she hadn't been able to follow the film. Its meaning was all a mystery to her. She supposed she was behind the times, but she still preferred the sharp wit of a Tracy and Hepburn film or the schmaltzy melodrama of a romance between Clark Gable and Lana Turner. Even those old Charlie Chan movies gave her more pleasure.

Moira was speaking to several people and uttering words like "divine" and "inspired." A hand took Caren by the arm and led her away from the milling crowd exiting the theater. All around her were the scions of society; it was rumored that Jacqueline Onassis was somewhere in the throng. Marc's voice sounded alarmingly close to her ear. "Remember what we discussed in the car. And yes, you loved the film."

"Look this way, Mr. Rayven!" a voice from the perimeter of the crowd called. Both Caren and Marc looked in the direction of the voice as flashbulbs exploded.

"Marc! How nice to see you again!" a woman in a stunning creation of rainbow silk called out. In her hands she carried a miniature tape recorder, the trademark of Cassandra Phillips. The woman's shrewd eyes slid over Caren speculatively, but to Caren's credit, she lifted her chin and met the woman's challenging gaze, a sweet smile stretching her lips.

"Cassandra. I should have known you would be here." Marc grinned. "No preview is complete without you and your recorder. I suppose you want to know what I thought of the film?" he asked, looking at the small recorder she carried in the palm of her hand.

Caren recognized the name Cassandra and knew that this was *the* Cassandra Phillips, the society columnist for the *Daily Journal*. The woman beamed at Marc and then transferred her pointed gaze to Caren. Imperceptibly, Marc's controlling hand on her arm pushed Caren into the foreground. He had instinctively known the columnist was not interested in his critique of the film; her curiosity was centered on the beautiful creature on his arm.

"Never mind the film, Marc." Cassandra smiled. "Everyone knows it will be a raging success." Still her eyes had not left Caren. "Are you going to be rude, Marc, which is so unlike you, or are you going to introduce me to this charming young lady?"

"Of course, Cassandra, may I present Caren Ainsley."

"Ainsley. Of the Newport Ainsleys? No? My dear, you're positively ravishing. Without turning around I can tell you that every male eye in the room is on you."

Caren flushed and murmured a response to the compliment.

"Marc, where did you find this enticing beauty? Tell me, my readers will be delirious at the new face in tomorrow's early edition. Would you mind if I borrowed Miss Ainsley for a few moments to get some pictures?"

"Not at all; I'm sure Caren would be delighted."

Cassandra turned to Caren. Her eyes clearly recognized the designer dress. "Nipon creations photograph well." It was Caren's turn to smile.

Cassandra stared a moment longer at Caren as though she couldn't quite make up her mind about something. "Marc, do you mind if I introduce Miss Ainsley around? Instead of single I think I'd rather have group shots. My readers will think it more exciting. Perhaps one or two of you together, but I can't promise that you'll see them in print."

"You're the expert, Cassandra," Marc said gallantly.

Cassandra steered Caren toward a group of people on the other side of the room.

From that point on, everything became a blur. She was meeting people whose names she had read in the newspapers and magazines—news correspondents, actors, actresses, television personalities…. They all asked her many questions, some pointedly inquiring as to her background, where she worked, what her plans were. Deftly, she avoided giving direct answers to their questions, hedging where she could, but mostly giving short answers and turning the conversation around to ask them about their own lives and work. All the while Cassandra stood nearby, her palm holding the miniature recorder extended. Flashbulbs popped and cameras clicked continuously.

Miraculously, her maneuvers worked. The best way to talk to someone was to talk about *them,* not herself. From Cassandra's approving glance it was clear that Caren was a success.

Marc, with Moira in tow, rescued her from the crowd. She was aware that her picture was being snapped constantly, but it wasn't until several reporters, pen in hand, broke through to her and demanded, "Miss Ainsley, how does it feel to be Marc Rayven's new Nightstar girl?" that she felt the blood drain from her face. How had they found out? Who? How?

From the black looks Marc was bestowing on her it was clear he believed she had spilled the beans. But she hadn't!

A frown of displeasure settled on Cassandra's face. Her shrewd gaze traveled swiftly to Marc Rayven. Instantly her hand-held recorder was placed in front of Marc as the reporter demanded, "How long did you think you could keep this secret, Mr. Rayven? Is Nightstar the name of a new line of cosmetics? Tell us all about it," the reporter pleaded. "What can the women of the world expect from Rayven Cosmetics in the weeks to come?"

"Actually, we were hoping to keep it secret until we formulated our entire campaign—" Marc began, his eyes piercing Caren's like knife points.

Cassandra turned back to Caren. "My readers will want to know your feelings on the matter, Miss Ainsley. My column could help you immensely." Again her long slender arm shot out, the small cassette held firmly for all to see.

Flabbergasted, Caren glanced wildly around. Her eye fell on Moira who was displaying a forbidding expression. Before she could answer, Marc seized her by the hand and literally dragged her out of the theater and ordered his car to be brought around immediately.

Outside in the brisk night air, she stood beside him, waiting for the Mercedes. Moira, breathless, joined them. "I thought we had it all clear, Miss Ainsley. You were not to say anything about—"

"But, Marc, I didn't! I swear—"

"It seems as though your little Miss Ainsley couldn't wait for her fame and she spilled the beans. I hope you don't think you can hold us up for more money on the Nightstar contract just because your face will be splashed over every newspaper in New York!" Moira threatened the astonished Caren. "Just remember, you're nothing but an insignificant typist and we can always find someone really deserving of the assignment—"

"That's enough, Moira," Marc stilled his assistant with a deadly calm voice. "Why don't you catch a cab home? I'll take Caren home."

Moira's mouth literally flapped open. Then she resumed her composure and stared at Caren as if to say, "Now you're going to get it!"

When the Mercedes was brought around, Marc helped Caren into the car and hopped behind the wheel. They had driven several blocks before he spoke to her.

"That was a foolish mistake on your part, Caren. I thought I could count on you to follow orders."

"You're not going to believe me, Marc. But I honestly didn't say anything! I have no idea how they found out! I was talking—no, listening, and suddenly those reporters began flashing my picture—"

"I want to believe you. I know you're not sophisticated like those people back there. I know how they can get things out of a person and the word is out before you know it—"

"No, Marc, I definitely did not tell anyone! I'm not a child, even if I'm not ultrasophisticated. I should know whether or not I said anything, and I didn't. Mostly, I was getting them to talk about themselves."

"They could only have known if you told them! What's done is done and we'll have to go on from here. I don't want to hear another word about it. You've said enough for one night!"

Caren bit her lips, silencing herself. If she were three years old, she would have thrown herself on the floor of the car and kicked and screamed and cried her eyes out! But she wasn't three years old and she had to sit here like a grown-up and take it.

When they were almost back to her apartment, Marc's anger seemed to have dissipated. "I must say you made quite a conquest in Cassandra Phillips. And she's one tough cookie. She's been around for so long, she can tell a phony just by looking. You handled yourself quite nicely and I'm proud of you. That sector of society can be a sea of sharks when they want to be.

But they certainly seemed to like you. Even before they found out about Nightstar—"

"You just passed my house," Caren interrupted coldly. "Stop here and let me out."

As instructed, Marc pulled over to the curb. The car was still in motion when Caren opened the door and leaped out. Without a backward glance she ran to the brownstone where she lived. The devil take Marc Rayven and the devil take Nightstar. She didn't like being called a liar and that was exactly what he had done!

Blinded by tears, she scaled the high steps to the front door and pushed against it. When she was between the doors in the tiny vestibule, she realized that her key was in Marc's pocket. Damn! Damn! It was late. Her face was streaked with tears! She didn't want to face the superintendent of her building and make all kinds of explanations. Not now. She wanted to hide away from the world, curl up in a ball, and lick her wounds—wounds inflicted by Marc Rayven.

Her knees were shaking so badly they threatened to give out under her weight. Back against the wall, she slid down onto her heels, curling her head to her knees and covering it with her arms. Silent sobs tore at her throat. I won't cry! I won't cry! she scolded herself.

The door had opened so silently that she hadn't heard it. Suddenly, strong hands were pulling her to her feet and gathering her into waiting arms. Marc pressed her face to his broad chest and soothed her with small, tender caresses.

"Caren," he whispered, "I came to bring you your key. I didn't mean to make you cry—"

"I'm not crying! I...I'm just...tired."

"I'm a beast. Tell me, tell me what a beast I am," his voice was soft, softer than she'd ever heard any man's voice. His hand cupped her chin, lifting her face. "I'm sorry, Caren. Say you forgive me," he whispered; then his mouth covered her own.

Her protests were only momentary. She felt herself go limp in his strong embrace. Hungry lips pressed on hers and her confusion welled as he pulled her closer and closer into his powerful embrace. Imperceptibly, his lips became more demanding and his hands molded themselves down her spine, pressing her into his lean, hard body—his body that was as unyielding as steel.

Disconnected thoughts of running, seeking shelter, finding safety from this man assaulted her. But he was creating a dizziness in her head, fogging her thoughts, robbing her of any will, save his own. And he willed her to respond, demanded it.

His kiss became gentle, tender, his lips clinging to hers. Their breaths mingled and Caren felt herself become warm and supple against him. Against her own will, her senses reeled and soared, making her dizzy, making her want more; she pressed herself closer, always closer.

A riot of emotions whirled through her; seizing her in their grip and arousing in her wants and desires she had never known. The dark, tiny vestibule became the top of the world and she spun and turned in an orbit of Marc Rayven's making. The cracked and painted ceiling became the dome of the heavens, its nightstars gleaming brightly against the velvet black of the universe. And when her knees threatened to buckle beneath her, his arms held her, supporting her, taking her with him on a flight to the moon where desire would be fed by passions. Caren became a willing passenger; her ticket was stamped "One Way" and that was up, up, up. A need ignited within her, a need she had never known she possessed. She wanted Marc Rayven. She wanted his touch, his caress, his kiss. And when his lips upon hers hinted at unexplored heights of passion, she wanted to chart those realms with him.

Her arms wrapped around his neck, her fingers grazed through the thick, curling hair at the back of his head. She could feel the sheer strength of his body against hers, could sense the needs rising within him. In spite of herself, because of herself, she wanted to answer those needs.

Roughly, Marc put her away from him. Confused,

she gazed up into his face, unable to read the spectrum of emotions she saw there. Suddenly, the night air felt cold upon her cheek. A faint sense of abandonment and desolation fell over her like a gossamer veil. Unable to speak, too stunned by his sudden unexplained reaction, she could only look at him questioningly.

"I didn't mean to do that. It was only when I came in here and found you crying—"

"I wasn't crying…. Why, why did you do that?" she insisted, her voice a harsh whisper.

"Why did I kiss you?" he asked, his familiar insolence and arrogance returning.

"I should slap you, kick you, do something. You had no right to call me a liar! You had no right to kiss me that way!" Her instinctive self-preservation was returning. But it felt empty and hollow compared to the feelings he had aroused in her.

Marc Rayven's face hardened into lines carved from granite. He picked up her hand and dropped her keys into it. "I kissed you, Miss Ainsley, because I wanted to see if your mouth was as good for loving as it is for telling company secrets."

Without another word, he turned on his heel and left the tiny vestibule where he had given Caren a glimpse of the heights and depths her passions could reach. He left her alone, confused, and angry. She could deal with those emotions, she told herself as she let herself into the apartment building. What she couldn't deal with was the humiliation she had suffered since coming to know that…that…Lipstick King—Marc Rayven.

CHAPTER FIVE

CAREN sat quietly, allowing Jacques to work on a new shade of makeup blended especially for her. The Frenchman seemed as preoccupied as she herself was. From time to time she watched him as he risked a glance in her direction out of the corner of his eye.

She still hadn't recovered from the night before. Marc's effect on her consciousness was almost tangible and she found herself looking endlessly into the mirror to see if the imprint of his mouth was still on her lips. Last night had opened her eyes in more ways than one. First, she now felt confident that she could hold her own in the upper crust, Marc Rayven's social stratum, the echelon that being the Nightstar girl would thrust her up to.

Secondly, she knew there was a traitor in their midst. And more likely than not, that traitor had been wearing a skin-tight black satin Givenchy.

And last, but not least, she learned that Marc Rayven could transport her into worlds she had never known existed.

Caren admitted to herself that she did have a competitive spirit. She didn't like being made a fool of by Moira Evans, and she was determined to do something about it. She was also determined to throw herself into this Nightstar business and make the best darn Nightstar girl Marc Rayven could ever want. She would prove Moira wrong if it was the last thing she did on this cold, cold earth.

"What do you think of this shade of mulberry for your eyes?" Jacques asked, making her blink and come away from her thoughts.

Caren shrugged. "You're the expert. What do you think?"

"Just a little lighter," he said, turning his back on her and deftly adding a smidgen of white powder to his pot of feathery dust.

Caren remembered Moira's proprietorial air concerning Marc—her attempts to malign Caren in Marc's eyes. Not that she had needed to do much, Caren decided, remembering his remark about a sow's ear. It was clear to her that Marc had been trying to prove a point to the members of the board when he'd chosen her to be the Nightstar girl. And since making that foolhardy decision on the spur of the moment, he now found himself stuck with it.

Still, hadn't he told her last night that he had noticed her and admired her style of clothing? Don't be a silly, she told herself. That was just her old competitive spirit rising again, trying to give her confidence. But someday, she promised, someday she would make Marc Rayven eat those words about a sow's ear.

As she watched Jacques, Caren thought of the expression on Moira's face when Marc had suggested she take a cab home and that he would take Caren home. Sheer hatred, deep and pure, had been written on her features. Any ninny could have seen it—and Caren was no ninny.

"I think we're ready to try this out now," Jacques said with brush poised in midair.

Caren leaned back in the velour chair, much the way she would have done had she been at the dentist's. She felt rather than saw Jacques stiffen at Moira's words.

"You *do* want to darken that mulberry shade, don't you, Jacques? We want this little pigeon to be perfect now, don't we?" Moira said sarcastically.

Now, where had she come from? Caren moaned inwardly. Why couldn't Marc's assistant wait until the end of the hour to check on things? Every time the black-haired, sleek-figured woman was within ten feet of her she felt as though she were trapped in a fishnet and would never get free.

Caren opened her eyes. Jacques had indeed stiffened. As a matter of fact, he was positively rigid and

Caren, from her position in her sky-blue chair, could see his normally firm hand tremble a little.

"Impossible! This particular shade of mulberry wasn't meant for someone of Caren's coloring. Any fool with an ounce of sense could tell you that!" Caren had never heard Jacques's voice so angry, so enraged. He had spoken through tight lips, barely controlling himself.

It was Moira's turn to grow rigid. Her voice was the stab of an icicle when she replied. "Are you insinuating I'm a fool?" Not waiting for a reply, she continued. "Because if you are, you can pick up your salary at the cashier."

Caren thought the Frenchman was going to ignore Moira's comment as he bent over to brush the soft powder against her eyelid. Instead, he brushed lightly and then turned, his movements perfectly controlled. "*Marc Rayven* hired me and *Marc Rayven* will have to fire me. However, that is neither here nor there at this moment. I just might take you up on my resignation. But," and his voice suddenly hardened, "not before I transform this young woman into the Nightstar girl. Don't tempt me, Moira, because you might come to regret it. Do we understand each other?"

Moira's face flushed to the same shade Jacques was holding in his hand. For a split second Caren noticed that Moira Evans was actually a very ugly woman with her face contorted in rage. However, Moira recovered quickly and with a last angry look at Jacques, she stalked from the room, her spike heels tapping on the tile floor.

Now, what was *that* all about? Caren wondered as she leaned back against the chair. She was disappointed when Jacques offered no explanation for the scene she had just witnessed.

Ugly duckling, sow's ear. The words kept ricocheting around in Caren's brain as she remained dutifully still while Jacques worked on just the right shading and toning for her skin. Twice he wiped the mulberry shadow from her eyes till he had what he called perfect shading.

Caren felt herself slipping into a light sleep and gave a small start. "I'm sorry," she apologized.

"No problem," Jacques said, moving back a few feet. He stared at Caren from first one angle and then another. "I think we're going to see a big difference in this batch of photographs. Yesterday was a sort of trial-and-error session. Rayven will be pleased, you have my word." His tone was impersonal and cool and it surprised Caren.

"I didn't see the pictures yesterday. Neither Mr. Rayven nor Moira said anything last evening to me about them. How bad were they?" Caren asked fearfully, imagining the worst.

"Bad," the makeup artist said curtly. "It was my fault. I was off my feed yesterday, and any session with

Moira Evans automatically makes me do my worst. For whatever good it is, you have my apologies."

"Accepted." Caren grinned.

Jacques merely nodded. "Rayven is going to be in the studio when they photograph you. I'm not sure about Moira. Can you handle working with the boss watching?"

"I don't know," Caren said honestly. How was she to act when she looked at him and remembered the feel of his arms and his lips? And if Moira was there, it would be worse.

Jacques shrugged again. "Rayven is a nice guy. As a matter of fact, he's one hell of a guy. He's fair. Always remember that." Suddenly, his tone softened. "You must think this place is weird, and I can't say that I blame you. Trust me. You really can, you know. Just do your job and go home. That's the best advice I can give you at the moment. Don't allow yourself to become involved with the inner workings of this company. If you should, for some reason, suddenly find that you have a problem, or something comes up that you feel threatens your position as the Nightstar girl, go to Rayven. And remember, he's fair. He'll listen."

Caren was stunned by Jacques's words. Was he trying to warn her about something and taking the long way around in telling her? Why couldn't people just say what they meant and leave it at that?

Evidently, Jacques was not expecting an answer to his remarks for he had already begun to pack up his pots and brushes and was making notations on the colors and shadings he had used on her. An "Okay, thanks for telling me," was all Caren could manage.

"Don't mention it, *chérie,*" he said warmly, looking up from his notepad to glance at her in the mirror and smile. "They are expecting you in the hair salon in fifteen minutes. Before you go, there is something I want to try."

Caren nodded and watched as Jacques picked up a skein of hair that was variegated shades of blond. He began to pick through the colors and was holding them up to her face.

"Oh, no, Jacques. I don't think…I don't want to be a blonde!"

"No, no, *chérie.* You are by nature a brunette. *Never* would I suggest anything so drastic, so artificial. But look here. See?" He was holding a hank of hair just shades lighter than her own against her face at the temples and hairline. "See the way the slightly lighter shade enhances those fabulous eyes you have? And see what it does for your skin tones? I was only suggesting a streaking, much the way the sun would lighten your hair. See?"

Caren had to admit that the difference in hair shades was only slight, but the effect was astounding. Now why hadn't she herself ever thought of that? "You're a marvel, Jacques, and I do trust you."

"*Oui, chérie.*" He smiled, making his perfectly manicured mustache lift in humor. "Now, I will call in an assistant to cleanse your face and then I will take you to the hair salon myself. I will put you into the hands of a protégé of mine, Henri. Okay?"

"Okay," she agreed, liking Jacques more today than she had yesterday.

"Good, I will leave you now, but I will be back in a few minutes." Picking up several implements from his vanity table, he exited the room and Caren could hear him calling for an assistant to attend to her.

A harried-looking girl, carrying a portfolio under her arm, entered the room. Immediately, she began to apply cold cream to Caren's face, removing all traces of Jacques's artwork.

"Couldn't we just leave the makeup? It seems so senseless to have Jacques go to all that trouble to apply it again later."

"Oh, no, Miss Ainsley. Mr. Duval has given express orders that you were to have nothing but a moisturizer on your skin when you sit under the dryer. The heat would spoil the makeup anyway and it would also drive impurities into your skin," the chatty assistant explained. "And I also happen to know that Mr. Rayven himself has given Mr. Duval express orders that nothing, absolutely nothing, be allowed to destroy your peaches-and-cream complexion. So many women positively ruin their complexions by improper cleansing—" The girl continued, but her words were falling on deaf ears.

Caren's thoughts were centered on this new information. Marc Rayven himself had given the order that nothing should destroy her peaches-and-cream complexion? That seemed an overstatement. While she had never had skin problems, she had never considered her complexion peaches and cream. But Marc Rayven had! It would seem he had noticed much more about her than she had ever dreamed. Yet something didn't fit. How could a man who admitted he had noticed her figure and clothes and now, she discovered, her complexion, and had admired those features make a remark about a sow's ear?

"Miss Ainsley…Miss Ainsley?" The girl was pulling Caren away from her musings. "Would you care for a cup of tea before Mr. Duval takes you to the hair salon?"

"Yes, that would be lovely."

"I'll get it for you immediately. I'll be right back."

When the girl had left the room, Caren noticed the portfolio she had brought into the room sitting on the vanity. Spying her name printed on the front piqued her curiosity and she leaned forward and picked it up. The label stated that it contained photos—the photos Bill Valenti had taken of her the day before.

Curiously, Caren opened the portfolio and withdrew the eight-by-ten glossy prints. What she saw almost made her gag! It was her own face, or was it? It was barely recognizable! She looked hard, a painted lady—if "lady" could be used in the loosest terms. There were deep shadows over her eyes and in the hollows of her cheeks. Her hair, being sleeked back as it had been, added no softness to the jaded look. Even her lips gleamed darkly in the black-and-white photos, making her appear vampish. She stared at the photos, hardly believing she was looking at herself.

Caren was sick inside. Her innards churned and nearly bolted. She hadn't looked like this when she had walked into the studio; what had Bill Valenti done to her? Maybe there was something wrong with the lighting. Astounded eyes fell on the photos of her bare shoulder, her face tilted down, profile to the camera. Looking up into the mirror, her hand smoothed across her cheeks. There were no deep hollows there; why had the camera picked them up?

Behind her she heard a voice. Jacques Duval. She saw him frown when he saw the pictures opened on her lap.

"Oh, Jacques. This is terrible! This isn't me! I hardly recognize myself. What did Bill Valenti do to me!"

Jacques's shoulders slumped. "It wasn't Bill Valenti, *chérie,* it was me."

"You? But why…how? I didn't look like that when I walked into the studio to have my photos taken!"

"*Oui, chérie.* You did. Only you couldn't see it because you do not see in black and white and the camera did. Even Bill Valenti could not see it through the lens. It was done with varying shades of tints…. No matter how it was done, I, *chérie,* betrayed you." Jacques lowered his head, ashamed.

Caren gasped, astounded by the man's revelation. Suddenly, a thought struck her and she almost cried. "Jacques…last night…at the premier, newspaper photographers—"

"*Non, non, chérie,* that was an original part of the plan, but I couldn't go through with it. Remember, I touched up your face after the hot lights. I corrected my…my sin."

"Original part…what plan?"

"Let it go, *chérie.* You were sabotaged, but not today. No, not today!" he said vociferously, raising his hand and beating on the back of the chair she sat in, his anger making her quake.

"Say you forgive me, *chérie.* Please…I could not go through with it."

"But who put you up to this?" A sudden thought occurred to her. Had Marc Rayven, realizing his error

in making her the Nightstar girl ordered Jacques…?
"Jacques, just tell me, was it Marc Rayven?"

"No! Never! I swear, *chérie*. It was planned so
Marc Rayven would think himself a fool to have
chosen you—"

"Say no more, Jacques. I'm not a child and I can put
two and two together. This is what Moira Evans and
you were talking about when I came up to Makeup
yesterday, isn't it? And that was why she came in here
today, to be certain you were continuing with the plan."

"Oui," the Frenchman said sadly. And then raising
his head with dignity, he looked her straight in the
eye. "But Jacques Duval is not an evil man, *chérie*. Nor
will I succumb to threats any longer. As long as I am
with Rayven Cosmetics, I will be your slave. I will
protect you and give you the best of my talent. Please,
chérie, forgive a fool."

Caren's anger abated. He was so contrite, so sincere,
he went straight to her heart. Tenderly, she lifted her
hand and placed it on Jacques's bowed head. "I forgive
you, Jacques; and I need you. Today is another day and
we will put this behind us. I only ask one favor. If Mr.
Rayven has not seen these photos yet, I would like it
if he never sees them."

"There is no need to protect me, *chérie*. I will throw
myself on his mercy—" In his agitation, Jacques's
French accent was becoming more pronounced and he

was revealing his Frenchman's penchant for being melodramatic.

"No, I don't want Marc to see these pictures. And as far as protecting someone, I'm not—I promise you. It's just a simple matter of learning the rules, Moira Evans's rules. And knowing the rules is a big part of winning the game." A slow smile spread over her face and soon Jacques was smiling, too.

"Mademoiselle is the most generous, most beautiful—"

"No, Jacques." Caren stopped his words with a raised hand. "The mademoiselle is your friend."

IN THE hair salon Jacques hovered over her like a mother hen. Each and every hair that Henri wrapped in aluminum foil was inspected by Jacques himself. Henri, another Frenchman, had listened attentively to a long diatribe in his native language, and when he approached Caren it was with profound respect.

Diligently, Henri worked, lifting tiny sections of hair around her hairline and the nape of her neck with the tail of his comb. Much discussion took place between himself and Jacques before Henri applied the foamy bleaching solution to each minuscule section of hair and wrapped each in strips of foil.

Timing was all important, Henri told her as he time and again checked the process. At last, Jacques, looking over Henri's shoulder, agreed with his protégé that the shade was perfect.

Quickly, Caren's head was over the sink and Henri removed the individual strips of foil, washing the bleach off before it could touch the rest of her hair.

Shampooed and rinsed, Caren gazed into the mirror seeing hardly any difference. "You cannot see the change so much when your hair is wet, *chérie*. But I assure you, it was well worth the inconvenience. When dry, your hair will seem to have lights of its own. And before the camera, it will soften your features, so."

"I believe you, Jacques." Her eyes met his in the mirror. "I'll always believe you." Remarkably, the Frenchman blushed.

When Henri had set her hair in huge rollers and tied a net around the whole works, he placed her under the dryer. Jacques solicitously brought her a plate with a delectable and appetizing array of fresh-cut vegetables and a yogurt dip accompanied by a cup of beef broth. "After your lunch the manicurist will attend you. If you need anything, anything at all, you are to ask Henri. No one else, do you understand, *chérie?* I have told Henri about my sin and your generosity. I assure you, he is now as devoted to you as I am."

Caren flushed, but accepted Jacques's statement and proffered lunch. She wouldn't think about those photos taken yesterday, and she wouldn't think about Moira Evans. That little bridge would be crossed when she came to it.

FORTY-FIVE minutes later, her lunch consumed and her nails freshly painted a subtle shade of mocha, Caren sat before Henri's mirror.

"What is troubling you, mademoiselle? Has not Jacques warned you about frowning? Don't you like what you see?"

Caren laughed. "It's not that, Henri. And yes, Jacques warned me about frowning. It's just that I don't think I've looked at myself in the mirror as much in my whole life as I have in the past two days."

"Ah!" the Frenchman soothed. "At least you have something very pretty to look at." He gently removed the rollers from Caren's hair and picked up his brush. Again and again, the soothing bristles stroked through her hair, taking away that tight-scalp feeling she always experienced when sitting under a dryer. Again and again, the brush ran through her hair, brushing it forward, brushing it back.

"Now, shake your head, mademoiselle. Like this, so your hair lifts away from your face. That's right."

Marveling, Caren watched as the light caught her hair. There were indefinable streaks so subtle they reminded her of how her hair had looked when she was a child and had spent the summer in the sun. And the haircut she had had the day before had added fullness and body; no matter which way she tossed her head, her hair fell in exquisite lines framing her face. "Is that me?" she asked incredulously.

"*Oui,* mademoiselle. It has always been you."

The warmth in Henri's voice brought color to her cheeks, but it was Jacques's wholehearted praise of her and his protégé's work that broke her into laughter. Happily, she followed Jacques back to the makeup room where he applied his tints and powders according to the notes he had made earlier. When he had finished, Caren had a hard time believing she was seeing herself. Not that the artistry of the Frenchmen had changed her—rather they had enhanced her, making her look vital, alive, and most of all, really pretty.

Jacques had been right. That particular shade of mulberry was perfection. She could see how if he had added a few grains of the darker color as Moira had wanted, she would have appeared gaunt. He had done a superb job, and she now felt more confident than ever. She still had that photographic session to get through with the handsome Marc Rayven in attendance, but she wouldn't let herself worry about that. Today, she had made great gains. Jacques and Henri were her friends, and she now knew the role Moira Evans had intended to play in her new career as the Nightstar girl. As she had told Jacques, now that she knew the rules, she had a better chance of winning the game.

As she walked down the hall to Bill Valenti's studio, Caren was aware that her knees were shaking. She had to admit to herself that she was not looking forward to the working session. In fact, she was dreading it. Again, doubts assailed her, punishing her. Why did she keep having these wide mood swings, these vague stirrings that had no name?

The thought of Marc Rayven sitting on his perch somewhere in the darkness as he watched the photograph session was curdling her innards. She remembered the fury the day before when he had misinterpreted Bill Valenti's reasons for baring Caren's shoulder. In spite of her embarrassment, she had to admit that his protective instincts had thrilled her.

What would he be thinking today as he watched her pose? Would he remember how she had felt in his arms? Would his flesh tingle the way hers did when he thought about the touch of her lips and the way she had responded to him? She shook her head; not likely. She had only to remember his parting shot when he told her he wondered if her lips were as good for loving as they were for lying.

Suddenly, it all became clear to her. If she had had any doubts she didn't have any now. It was Moira who had revealed the information about the Nightstar line and Caren's role as the Nightstar girl. Another thought occurred to Caren. Moira had known that news photographers would be present, snapping pictures. News photos were in black and white. How smug Moira must be feeling, assured that those photos would be published making her look like...like the jaded harlot that had appeared in the photos Bill Valenti took that day. She had had no way of knowing that Jacques, feeling guilty about his part in Moira's plot, had corrected the makeup before she had gone home. The girl who appeared on Marc's arm at the preview would be as pretty as Jacques could make her.

Marc! A horrible thought struck her. Here she had been, little fool that she was, hoping that Marc would remember the kiss they had shared the night before. What if he sat through her photo session comparing her to Moira? If he did, how would she, Caren, fare? Second best?

"I don't want to be second best!" she muttered to herself.

"I, for one, don't blame you," said a cool, masculine voice in her ear.

Caren swung about sharply and fell right into Marc Rayven's outstretched arms. Marc's eyes seemed to be mocking her, and yet they were alive with something akin to speculation. He was making fun of her and enjoying it. Damn you, Marc Rayven, she seethed inwardly. If she had any delusions about the previous evening and its meaning to the handsome cosmetic king, they were shattered. She was just a means to an end. He was using her to prove a point to the members of the board in order to get them to back the Nightstar campaign.

Caren felt her eyes narrow as she stared up at the man towering over her. "You know what they say, you can't make a silk purse out of a sow's ear. I guess it goes with second best, that kind of thing."

Marc's eyes were slits as he stared at her before striding off. He made no comment, but his jaw had tightened and Caren noticed that his powerful hands— relaxed only seconds ago—were now balled into tight, angry-looking fists. He was gone. Even his walk looked angry, Caren thought as she rounded the corner that would take her into the photography studio. It was evident that he knew just what she was talking about. The truth hurts, doesn't it, Mr. Rayven? Sow's ear, my foot. Indignation welled up in her as she made her way over coiled electrical wires and skirted hard wooden chairs.

It was a large studio. There were none of the comforts of the other studios and salons in the Rayven building. This was a working area with as little clutter as possible. Every conceivable light and tripod made seemed to be on the round stagelike platform. Scenery was piled haphazardly against every wall as were folding chairs. A large, stainless-steel coffeepot with a red light glowed from one corner of the room. It was perched precariously on a lopsided wooden chair with two slats missing from the backrest. A faint aroma of some flowery scent hung in the air. Caren sniffed, unable to name the elusive scent. It wasn't the Nightstar collection, of that she was sure.

Voices from the end of the room next to the lavatory reached her ears. She peered out against the lights, but couldn't distinguish any forms. The saccharine-sweet sound of Moira's voice seemed to hang in the still air of the studio. Jacques said something, his accent unmistakable. She waited, drawing in her breath, for Marc Rayven to say something. He must be there.

Quietly, she seated herself, straining to hear the words from the far end of the room. Drat, only the tones could be heard; the words were indistinguishable from where she was sitting. To Caren's untrained ear Jacques sounded defensive, Moira petulant, and Rayven downright angry, but controlled. Her back stiffened when she heard the word "infant" bounce off the walls and come to rest at her well-shod feet. They were moving now in her direction, speaking normally of everyday things—things she was evidently allowed to hear. As if I care, she murmured under her breath.

"It might be a good idea if Caren attended the

meeting this afternoon. I suggest, Moira, that you cancel it and reschedule it for 5:50. Nothing is ever solved or settled after a three-martini lunch. The ad men will be there so we might as well make use of everyone's time. We'll get good ideas, fresh approaches, because each of us will be doing our best in the short time we have. In other words, Moira," Marc Rayven said coldly, "everyone wants to get home as quickly as possible after a long working day, and the only way to do that is to come through in the time allotted. Make it a full hour meeting. This way everyone can still catch the commuter."

Caren said nothing as she watched the little byplay between Moira and her boss. Her model's face was impassive as she seated herself next to Caren and crossed her legs, deliberately hiking the skirt she wore to well above her knee. With the slit on both sides of her skirt, Caren didn't know why she bothered. She was no prude, but halfway up the thigh was a bit much. Evidently, Marc Rayven thought so, too, as he stared pointedly at the silky expanse of leg. Moira fidgeted a moment and then demurely pulled down her skirt and uncrossed her legs. She folded her hands primly in her lap and smiled innocently at the assembled men. Caren felt a grin tug at the corners of her mouth. She erased it, but not before Marc's eyes twinkled down at her. His expression clearly said: there is a time and a place for everything.

The camera session was grueling and brutal. When it was over, Caren had a healthy respect for the gorgeous cover girls who made it all seem so easy. She was exhausted from all the twisting and turning, the perching, the languid poses that must look natural. Henri and Jacques were always at her elbow as one series of shots went into the next. The costume changes were made at breakneck speed, leaving her trembling and shaky as she emerged from behind the dressing screen.

Raggedy Ann, she thought as she flopped onto one of the hard wooden chairs when the photographer called it quits. Caren removed one spike heel and then the other. A sigh escaped her as she massaged her weary feet. A single tear gathered in the corner of her left eye and trickled down her cheek. Impatiently, knowing it was a sign of exhaustion, she brushed at it and then sniffed. Damn, she had to blow her nose. She sniffed again.

"Something tells me," said an aloof voice, "that you used to wipe your nose on your sleeve when you were a kid, right?" Caren nodded miserably. "Here," Marc Rayven said holding out a snowy square of linen.

Caren felt annoyed. Why did he have such an uncanny knack of showing up at the most inopportune times? She accepted the chalky handkerchief and blew her nose lustily. "Actually, Mr. Rayven, I used to wipe my nose on the hem of my shirttails," she said with an angry edge to her voice. "That was a long time ago, however. Now, I'm all grown up."

Marc Rayven grinned. "I can see that. That you're all grown up, I mean."

He was mocking her again. Well, let him. "I'll return your handkerchief after I launder it."

He was still grinning. "No hurry, but I'll look forward to seeing you under social conditions again."

She must be improving if he was making a half-hearted effort to see her again. No, that was wrong. She was the golden goose, a tarnished golden goose; and she was definitely not going to lay any eggs, golden or otherwise. Carefully, she tucked the square of linen into her tote bag and leaned over to put on her shoes. "It's harder than I thought. I simply was not prepared for this. I think you should know that I'm doing my best, and if that isn't good enough, I'll understand if you want to replace me."

Marc Rayven's eyes narrowed and his face took on a cool, chiseled look. "I wouldn't think of it. Didn't you ever hear that old adage about changing horses in midstream? Regardless of the outcome, we're in this together. If you want to back out because the going is too tough, that's something else."

Together. He had said they were in this together— together, as in Rayven and herself. If he had meant to include the beautiful Moira, he would have said, *all of us* are in this together.

Caren's face stilled. "No, I don't want to back out. I just want you to understand that I am doing my best. I'm not a quitter. My best, Mr. Rayven, is all you can expect from me."

"I think we understand each other perfectly. If we don't get a move on, both of us are going to be late for the meeting. Come along, Caren. By the way, how would you like to stop and have a drink after the meeting? Or are you too tired? I would suggest dinner, but I have a previous appointment."

"How about a rain check?" Caren said pertly. Now, where had she gotten the nerve to say that?

"I hope that doesn't mean I have to wait for a literal rain." The old mocking tone was back in his voice. Caren imagined her turndown was Marc's first rejection by anyone of her gender. Just remember: ugly duckling, sow's ear. How she hated those words.

"I want to stop in the powder room; I'll catch up," Caren said breathlessly, hurrying away from him. Why did this man affect her this way? Why was it suddenly so difficult to breathe?

CHAPTER SIX

IN THE LUSH velvet-and-brocade powder room Caren tossed her tote onto a lime-green chair and then stretched out on a matching chaise. Lord, she was tired. Exhausted was too tame a word for the way she felt. The klieg lights had literally drained every ounce of her energy. She glanced at her watch and saw that she had exactly seventeen minutes to get to the meeting in Marc Rayven's office. Forty winks, forty cat winks. When she had been in school cramming for an exam, all she had had to do was repeat over and over "Seventeen minutes, seventeen minutes," till her eyes closed and then she would wake up right on the dot. It had always worked for her before, even when her alarm had blitzed out on her just over a month ago. It would work this time too; she was sure of it. Her eyes were so heavy, so very heavy. Just seventeen minutes. The thick black lashes fluttered wearily and then lay like gossamer webs on her cheeks.

Caren stirred once and forced her lids open. She still

had seven minutes. How tired she was. Seven minutes more—an eternity at this moment. The feathery lashes closed again preventing her from seeing the shadowy form outlined in the doorway. Had she been awake, she would have seen the triumphant, malicious look on Moira Evans's face as she backed out of the doorway and closed the door quietly. No sound disturbed Caren's deep, even sleep.

The spiky hands of the sunburst clock read 6:50 when angry voices could be heard coming down the hallway. Caren stirred fretfully and rolled over on her side. The chaise was too narrow and she was uncomfortable. Where were those angry voices coming from? Yawning heavily, she struggled to a sitting position trying to orient herself. Fearfully, she stared down at the gold circle on her wrist. It couldn't be! Her stricken eyes traveled to the sunburst clock and she winced as though in pain. It was! The meeting was over and she had missed it. Tears gathered in her eyes. Lord, she was tired. Vitamins—I should have started taking double doses of vitamins, she thought wearily as she grappled for her tote and a comb and brush.

The angry voices were getting nearer. Panic gripped her and she ran into the lavatory part of the powder room. She knew she was behaving like a child, but was unable to stop herself. Quietly, she closed the stall door and then reopened it. She would not hide. Hadn't she just said she was all grown up? Grown-ups were responsible for their own actions. So she had fallen asleep. What could they do to her besides fire her?

Squaring her shoulders, ready to slay the proverbial dragon, Caren thrust open the swinging doors that led to the powder room and was just in time to hear Moira Evans say, "She must be asleep in here."

"On the contrary, Miss Evans, I just woke up. My apologies, Mr. Rayven. I hope you didn't wait too long to start the meeting. I have no excuse; I fell asleep and just woke a few minutes ago. Now, if you'll excuse me, I'll see you in the morning."

Was she mistaken or was that an amused look in Marc Rayven's eyes? Jacques, the photographer, and several distinguished-looking men with portfolios under their arms stared at her. No introductions were made, but then Caren had not given anyone time to do more than listen to her words. As she swept past Moira Evans she said, sotto voce, "If one had a mind to, one might wonder how you knew I was in here sleeping. One might also wonder why you didn't wake me." Without another glance in anyone's direction she was off, striding down the hall to the stairwell. There was no way she was going to stand waiting for an elevator and have to face all those people. Where in the world had she gotten the nerve to do what she had just done? For once in her life she had placed someone else on the defensive. Good, it was a step in the right direction.

The three-inch heels were in her hand as she tripped her way down eighteen floors. She was being silly and ridiculous, but she couldn't help herself. Besides, going down was easier than going up. Let them all wonder where she was and then mark it down to artistic temperament.

Carefully, Caren inched the ground-floor door open and peered outside. Satisfied that no one was about except the security guard, she still waited a full ten minutes before leaving. She whiled away the time considering Moira Evans's remark about her sleeping and the fact that she had opened the door to the powder room. Was it possible that she had seen Caren when she really was sound asleep and hadn't bothered to wake her, knowing that she would later embarrass her in front of the others? More likely than not. It was over and done with and she couldn't do a thing about it now.

Caren glanced at her watch again and then opened the door. She stepped out into the quiet lobby, her heels making the guard look up from his relaxed position behind the desk. She smiled and waved as she pushed at the revolving door.

The brisk evening air swept Caren down the street as she headed for her bus stop. The cobwebs in her brain were cleared by the refreshing winds of early fall.

By the time she reached her tiny efficiency apartment she felt like an evening on the town. Her nap had definitely worked wonders, she grinned ruefully. But at what cost to herself? she wondered as she fit the key into the lock.

The phone shrilled demandingly as she sat down to eat her grilled cheese sandwich. She ignored it.

What's wrong with me? she asked herself querulously. Why am I having so much difficulty handling all of this? Is it because you're falling in love with Marc Rayven and he belongs to Moira Evans? a niggling voice asked.

Caren didn't like the direction in which her thoughts were traveling. There were no answers at the moment. Deftly, she wiped up the crumbs from the sandwich, carried her plate to the sink, and filled it with water. She finished the last of her tea and placed the cup carefully in the hot soapy water. She would clean up later.

The phone shrilled to life again as she stepped beneath the needle-sharp spray of the shower. It was ringing again when she wrapped herself in a faded fern-green terry robe. She padded into the small living room and reached for the receiver only to hear silence. So, they had given up. Persistence always won out in the end.

Caren knew it was ten o'clock because of the news program on television. The fifth commercial was in progress when there was a loud knock at her door.

Caren froze with her hand in a bag of potato chips, her other hand holding a crisp red apple with two bites missing. A wave of panic coursed through her. Her buzzer hadn't sounded. Who could be knocking this late at night? Well, she wasn't going to answer it. A girl had to protect herself, living alone as she did. Police were forever warning single people not to open their doors to strangers. If nothing else, she was obedient, and not dressed for company. How would it look for the new Nightstar girl to open the door looking like a nightmare in real life? It wouldn't. Her decision made, she leaned back and took a third bite out of her shiny red apple. She chewed, unable to swallow the tart fruit.

"Caren, are you home? Caren, it's Marc Rayven. Open the door."

Oh no, it couldn't be Marc Rayven. But it was—she would know his voice if it was projected from the edges of eternity. She really was living under a black cloud, and it was descending rapidly. There was nothing to do but open the door and see what he wanted. Maybe he fired people in person instead of issuing pink slips.

The potato-chip bag scrunched under one arm, the apple in her left hand, she removed the chain and opened the door. She stepped back as Marc filled the doorway to overflowing. Her eyes were angry, her stance rigid as she stared into Marc Rayven's face.

"Yes?" she said coolly, not bothering to invite him into the room.

"Yes what? Yes, I can come in? Just yes?"

"Come in, sit down." Her tone was less than gracious, but she couldn't help it. This was an intrusion on her privacy. He didn't own her, not quite. And this was definitely after business hours.

"Are you going to share?"

Caren frowned. "Share what?"

"Either or. Either the apple or the potato chips."

Was he mocking her again? She couldn't tell. He seemed for the moment just like any other guy that stopped by to see his girl. Only I'm not his girl, she thought unhappily. She flushed and held out the crackly bag of chips.

"Did you have any dinner?" she questioned.

Marc grinned. "Is it that obvious? I *didn't* have any dinner and I'm starved. I know this is an imposition, but do you have anything to eat? I'll do the dishes." The light banter seemed to relieve the tension between them.

Caren laughed in spite of herself. "I think I might be able to manage something. How about an omelet and some sausage?"

"Sounds great. Can I help?"

"If you want to eat, you help," she told him frankly. "You can get the dishes out."

Marc followed her into the tiny kitchen and she

pointed to the cupboard where she kept the plates. As she was frying the sausage and whipping the eggs, Marc helped himself to a glass of milk and pushed the toast down into the toaster. "Ummm," he savored, "smells like breakfast."

"Or it will if you plug in the coffeepot," she told him.

Following her orders, Marc plugged in the pot and sat down at the table. She could feel his eyes watching her as she prepared his meal. Beneath his scrutiny, she burned her fingers twice, spilled grease on the stove, and dropped the butter knife as she was spreading jam on the toast.

"Are you always so graceful, Miss Ainsley?" he mocked.

"Always," she assured him, returning his sarcasm. "Just remember, he who finds complaint finds work. Would you like to prepare your own dinner?"

"Nope. I'd rather just sit here and watch you."

That last remark brought color to Caren's cheeks. Suddenly, she was aware of her freshly scrubbed face—completely devoid of Jacques's artistry—and her nudity beneath the faded green robe. Even her bare feet sticking out from under the long wrapper caused her embarrassment. She should have run and changed almost the minute he arrived, but she hadn't and it was too late to do it now without feeling foolish.

When Caren dished out the omelet for Marc, he

seemed surprised. "Where's yours? You're not going to make me eat alone, are you?"

"Well, you see, Mr. Rayven, the company I work for has put me on this strict diet, and since I've already cheated by eating a sandwich earlier, I think I'll just have coffee while you eat."

"A diet!" he snorted. "That's ridiculous! You're just perfect the way you are. If I'd wanted one of those emaciated fashion models, I would have gotten one. As your employer, I order you, right this minute, to forget about the diet." With great ceremony, he pulled her plate over and pushed half his omelet and a slice of sausage onto it. "And an omelet is never complete without toast. Here, it's the one with extra jelly."

Giggling, Caren happily bit into the toast, dribbling a spot of jelly on her chin. Marc laughed and wiped it off for her.

The rest of the meal was spent in easy camaraderie as they discussed the plans for the Nightstar line, and Caren was very flattered that Marc was truly sincere in hearing her opinions.

After they had drained their coffee cups twice, Marc stood up and began to clear the table.

"What are you doing?"

"I told you I would do the dishes and I meant it."

It was on the tip of her tongue to protest, saying something trite like that was woman's work when she remembered the articles she had read in magazines. There was no such thing as woman's work or man's work either. If you were capable of doing it, then you should do it. "All right then, since you did promise—" she turned on her heel and walked into the living room.

"Would you mind turning the TV set on to the Public Broadcasting System—Channel Thirteen. The Boston Pops Symphony Orchestra is having a gala tonight and John Williams is conducting."

Doing as he requested, Caren sat on the floor in front of the TV. Really fine reception wasn't usual on Channel Thirteen, but she would fine-tune it and do her best. Funny, she thought to herself, when it came to Marc Rayven, she was always giving her best.

The clatter of pots and pans sounded in the kitchen and Caren laughed when Marc walked out to the table to retrieve the coffee cups, wearing the little apron she always kept tied to the refrigerator handle.

"What's so funny?" he demanded.

"You are." She continued laughing. "You...you look so silly—"

"Oh, I do, do I?" A threat was in his voice and in his blue eyes.

"Yes—"

"I'll show you how silly I am." There was a definite threat in his tone now, a teasing menace. His fingers untied the little apron with great deliberateness. Cool blue eyes watched her, measured her, yet there was a hidden bank of fires within them, and Caren was mesmerized by the budding desire she saw in them.

Slowly, step by step, he came toward her, his eyes holding her, hypnotizing her, making it impossible for her to move. Dimly, she was aware of her vulnerability, of her nudity beneath the heavy terry-cloth robe.

He was near her now, near enough to reach out and touch her. She felt herself shrink away from him, yet there was something, some inner part of her that wanted to make her throw herself into his arms and plead for mercy—later, much later.

From her position on the floor she looked up at him, realizing how he towered over her, making her feel small and defenseless. By the dim lights in the room she saw his eyes were alight with desire, the desire he had shown her in the tiny vestibule the night before. His sensually curving lips were grim with a raw hunger, and the stubborn set of his jaw told her that she was facing a power that she was helpless to control.

Even as she shrank away from him, his gaze held her. Slowly, intractably, he extended his hand, compelling her to take it, to allow herself to be lifted to her feet, to fall into his arms. With a will that was not her own, she reached out tentative fingers, allowing him to grasp them in his, allowing him his wish.

His dark hair fell forward over his brow, lending

him a boyish look. Heavy dark brows were drawn together over the bridge of his straight, classic nose. He was a handsome devil and devilish in his desires. His white business shirt was open at the neck, revealing the corded strength of him. As she stood before him, a struggle was evident in his eyes and then, with a deep, broken sound, he seized her and buried his face against her throat.

If Marc Rayven was the devil, then she, Caren, was his advocate. She tumbled into his arms, willingly, reveling in the passion behind his caress. Her body throbbed to the sound of her name upon his lips.

He was an enigma of a man. At once he was tender and at the same time demanding. She realized, with a joyful helplessness, that she was powerless to escape his strength. His will became her own as he evoked her responses with a fiery awakening. His kisses and caresses were inspired; he knew instinctively her little pleasure points where he pressed his lips, his breath hot, scorching her skin, giving her a pleasure she had never known existed for her.

His arms swept her up, his mouth still possessing hers, and he carried her to the wide, chocolate-brown couch. The implications of this movement made her heart pound, made her body quiver with expectation. She should fight, she should protest, but despite knowing what she *should* do, her arms twined around his neck, betraying her. Her emotions were traitorous, succumbing to the wicked power he held over her. In a vague recess of her mind she knew she would be sorry in the morning, but those thoughts were swept away by a wild, pounding need—a need, a thirst, that could only be quenched in the arms of Marc Rayven.

The edges of her robe fell apart, exposing an expanse of creamy skin to his lips, his hands. She throbbed at his every touch as his fingers grazed the hollows of her throat and the gentle curves of her breasts. He was taking her on a journey into the unknown, but as long as he held her, touched her, she was unafraid. She sought the heights his nearness promised, demanded the fulfillment she knew could be hers.

A ringing sounded in her head, sharp and insistent. Again, it sounded, jarring her, making her want to escape it, to hide forever in the arms of her love.

With a strange kind of relieved dismay, Caren realized at the same time as Marc that the ringing was not in their heads, but that it was the phone. With a mournful sigh, Marc lifted himself from the couch and went to the far side of the room to answer it.

"Yes?" he answered angrily, no doubt forgetting that this was Caren's apartment and Caren's phone and that the call could very well be for her.

"Not now, Moira—"

Moira Evans. Of course, Caren thought, pulling the

edges of her robe together, suddenly feeling very exposed and vulnerable and, yes, wicked.

"I didn't think I had to report to you where I would be this evening, Moira, and I *don't* intend to do so in the future. You'd better be calling to tell me about a crisis at the firm; otherwise, I don't want to hear it." He paused, listening for a moment. His simple response was a puzzled, "Oh." He then turned to Caren. "Moira. She wants to talk to you." He held out the receiver and awkwardly, Caren crossed the room, tightening the belt on her robe and pulling the collar up around her neck. Her eyes refused to meet Marc's, refused to lift themselves to look into the eyes of the man she was certain she had fallen in love with, the man who just a moment ago had been holding her in his arms and awakening passions in her she had never dreamed she could experience.

Putting the receiver to her ear, she still kept her eyes glued to the floor. "Yes…yes," she managed with more assurance.

"Is that you, Miss Ainsley?" Moira's nasty voice hissed in her ear.

"Sp-speaking."

Marc had moved away from her. She watched as, never turning for a backward glance, he picked up his jacket and coat from the easy chair and moved toward the door. He held himself stiffly, determinedly, opening the door and closing it behind him. No explanation, nothing. He had just left—gone. And somehow, not knowing how, Caren had the feeling that he was walking out of her life forever.

"Don't talk, just listen," the voice on the phone instructed. "I know what little game you're playing, and believe me when I tell you it won't work. Marc Rayven has no place in his life for a nondescript little typist. He's out of your league. You mean nothing more to him than the last Rayven Cosmetics model he sported around town. I'm giving you fair warning. Stay away from Marc, he belongs to *me*. He always has. Do you understand?"

Crestfallen, feeling abandoned and alone, Caren's eyes tried to bore through the thick wood of the door. If only she could see him, know what he was thinking, she would have the courage to tell Moira Evans where to get off. Instead, feeling defeated, desolate, and rejected, she placed the telephone receiver back on its cradle.

Visions of herself and Marc stretched out on the couch, his hands worshiping her body, his lips promising love, blurred before Caren's eyes. Yes, she definitely understood what Moira was saying. Her face flushed a bright scarlet as she thought about what she had almost allowed to happen between herself and Marc. No, that was wrong. He wasn't Marc, he was Mr. Rayven, her employer—nothing more. Regardless of what her heart wanted to believe, regardless of the white heat her body had experienced, Moira was right; Marc Rayven *was* out of Caren's league.

Her eyes were fixed on the door, still seeing Marc's back turned to her. A silent tear slid down her cheek and touched the corner of her mouth, seeming to cool the warmth where Marc had touched it with his own.

CHAPTER SEVEN

MORE determined than ever, Caren literally put her nose to the grindstone and worked long, exhausting hours in the days and weeks that followed Marc Rayven's abrupt departure. By the minicalendar on her night table she figured that it was seventeen days since she had last seen Marc. Seventeen long, miserable days. She admitted now to herself in the privacy of her bedroom late at night that she loved Marc—for all the good it was going to do her. If she had mattered to him, he never would have left her that night seventeen days ago. One call from Moira and he was off and running like one of those long-distance runners who were always showing up on the evening news programs.

Three weeks to the day of her last meeting with Marc Rayven, Caren woke with a strange feeling. Today was her last day with the commercials. Today was the day the first series of commercials was going to be shown to the Rayven executives and the ad agency. Moira had seemed edgy and out of sorts the night before when she'd reminded Caren to be in the screening room promptly at 10:00 a.m. As if wild horses or the devil himself could keep her away, even if it was her day off—the promised day off that she had looked forward to for the past month. A day to do whatever she pleased. Some luck, she mused as she applied a light layer of makeup in the way Jacques had taught her. Six one-minute commercials. Another hour to discuss the pros and cons and she would be free to do as she pleased. At the last minute she plucked a tiny vial from her purse and dabbed the new Nightstar perfume behind her ears and at the base of her throat. The minuscule cylinder without benefit of a label had been a gift from Marc, sent by him to the studio.

The hastily written note had said, "I believe this small offering is worthy of you." He could have turned that statement around and said she might be worthy of the precious perfume; but he hadn't, and the message had lifted her spirits a little. Still, on the other hand, she grimaced to herself, he could merely have been protecting his investment.

Why, oh why, did she always have to allow such negative thoughts to creep into her mind? Why couldn't she just accept her success and live on a day-to-day basis like all of the other career girls whom she had met in the last weeks? Because success, money, prestige, meant nothing unless you had someone close to you to share the feelings with. And always those hateful words "sow's ear" would ring in her ears reminding her of who and what she was.

One last look in the bathroom mirror that hung on the back of the door and she would be ready to leave. Her weight was stable now, thanks to the high-protein diet the nutritionist had put her on. Personally, she hadn't liked the thin, elegant look she was presenting to the world. And she hadn't felt all that well. The vitamins she was now taking were helping somewhat, but she still felt tired all the time. Visions of food, rich and sweet, tantalized her dreams at night, prompting her to make trips to the refrigerator for celery stalks or carrot sticks. She was a perfect size nine now, and she planned to remain that size.

Caren stuck her tongue out at her reflection and then turned off the bathroom light. Just how well was that perfect size nine going to wear over the next grueling two-month tour of the United States?

All the way to the Rayven building she argued with herself. They had to give her a few days off before the tour started. They just had to. In her heart she knew Moira was pushing her, prodding her, hoping against hope that she would fizzle out and the promotion would go down the drain at the eleventh hour. Well, she had sworn to do her best and that was exactly what she was going to do. Moira could take a flying leap—and where she landed, Caren didn't care.

Marc, Marc, Marc, her mind sang quietly as she rode the elevator to the screening room. Surely he would be there for the preview of the commercials. Could she handle it? Of course. Now that she was the Nightstar girl she could handle anything—almost anything, she corrected herself.

The screening room looked like a miniature theater, and it was full to capacity when she arrived. A sellout performance, she thought wryly as she found a seat in the back row, hoping to go unnoticed. She wanted to sit alone in the darkness so she could look at herself objectively on the giant-size screen. It was not to be.

How could she have forgotten how tall he was or how he made her feel? Her heart thumped maddeningly as Marc Rayven strode down the short aisle to where she was sitting. He stared down at her for a full moment before reaching down for her hand to draw her to her feet. "Front row, center, Caren." She nodded as she followed him down the aisle, not trusting her voice. If it was as shaky as her knees, he would know in a minute what his presence was doing to her.

A veil dropped over her eyes as she took her place next to Marc and Moira. Moira must never know how she felt about Marc. She risked a quick sideways glance at her and was shocked at the expression on her chiseled features. Why was she looking so satisfied, so…so happy? And Jacques, why was he looking so grim and determined? Marc was the only one who appeared to be his natural, cool self. Butterflies fluttered around in her stomach as she prepared herself for the moment the lights went down in the screening room. She forced herself to lean back in the deep scarlet chair and relax. If she was lucky, the commercials would be terrible; Marc would say, "Sorry, it's been a mistake," and then they would all tell her to go home.

By the time the lights came on, Caren was stunned. The commercials were not like she had expected. That captivating, romantic creature on the screen couldn't have been Caren Ainsley! There had been closeups, certainly, and she hadn't had to say a word. She had moved through the scenes as though in a dream; the narrator's deep, articulate voice had done the selling of Nightstar. But she, herself, Caren, had epitomized the essence of the precious perfume.

Looking at it objectively now, she could appreciate the loveliness of the graceful, flowing gowns. Even the old Victorian mansion in one of the commercials had appeared to be a reality instead of a mock-up on the studio's stage. John Williams had composed the music and conducted the orchestra for the background. In another of the commercials, swirls of fog had seemed to lift off the black waters of a New England seaport and waft around her feet. The London Fog raincoat's collar had been pulled high around her neck, and her hair,

Henri's artwork, had been pulled back—only tender little tendrils allowed to escape around her face and neck.

The Nightstar theme was deeply romantic. It was the portrayal of every woman's daydreams. In the film clips Caren was always alone—alone with her Nightstar perfume. But the impression was always given that romance and that special someone were just around the corner, and with Nightstar—and Nightstar alone—romance would find a woman ready and waiting.

Caren's thoughts came back to the present. All around her, voices were babbling; there was much backslapping and high-geared camaraderie being shared. Marc was kissing her resoundingly and telling her that he knew, he just knew, that she was exactly what Nightstar needed.

"Congratulations," Moira said evenly, breaking the spell between Caren and Marc as she held out her hand to Caren. Caren stood still, refusing to accept the handshake. Marc stared first at Caren and then at Moira, seeming to notice for the first time the look of abject fury in his assistant's eyes. At first, Caren thought he was going to say something, and then one of the advertising executives drew him away out of earshot of the stunning Moira.

"Thank you," Caren said quietly, still not bothering to extend her hand. Short of looking foolish, Moira had no other choice but to withdraw her hand and walk away.

Caren watched her weave her way toward Jacques Duval. She waited, watching the expression on Jacques's face change as he waited for Moira to walk up to him. Either the Frenchman was talking through clenched teeth or he was listening to Moira; Caren couldn't tell. Whatever was going on, it appeared to Caren that Jacques was not giving an inch in Moira's direction.

"I'm sorry, that was business," Marc said, drawing Caren off to the side. "Let me say that the commercials were better than any of us even hoped for. What did you think of them?"

Men! He hadn't seen her for weeks, and all he could think of was the commercials. What about the night in my apartment? her mind wanted to shriek. Was all of that a dream? Didn't it mean anything to you? She couldn't say any of those things. Now, she had to play the game. Well, it took two to play any kind of game. She chose her words carefully. "It's just my personal opinion, of course, but I think the commercials prove that you can indeed make a silk purse out of a sow's ear." She was shocked at how calm and matter-of-fact her voice was.

Marc Rayven's eyes narrowed to slits as he stared down at Caren. At best, his voice was chilly. "I don't know exactly what that's supposed to mean, probably one of those womanly remarks that men are not supposed to understand. Now, if you would be so gracious as to give the ad boys a few moments of your time, they want to go over your itinerary for the tour. You leave in three days. Moira has offered to be your traveling companion. I'll meet up with you along the way from time to time to keep an eye on things. Come along," he said, taking hold of her arm. Deftly, Caren shook off his hand and moved back a step.

"Unfortunately, Mr. Rayven, your suggestion, or your order, is entirely unacceptable. I cannot be ready to leave for at least a week. I need time to rest. Your assistant, or whatever she is to you, will *not* be my companion. I am not being uncooperative. If you feel the need to assign me a companion or someone to watch over the image you created, you will have to find someone else. That, Mr. Rayven, is my bottom line— a week. I promised you my best, and I cannot give my best without some time off to get myself back together."

The chilly voice was now frost-tipped as were Marc Rayven's eyes. "You have a contract, and it calls for you to be in Dallas, Texas, at the Neiman Marcus store in three days' time."

"Mr. Rayven, I think you just created a problem for yourself. Please extend my apologies to Mr. Neimen and Mr. Marcus and tell them I cannot possibly be there. My bottom line, Mr. Rayven. And don't put this down to artistic temperament. Put it down to overwork, twenty-four-hour hostility, hunger and sleepless nights."

"These plans can't be changed. If you don't show up or we're forced to change the schedule, the whole damned tour is fouled up. You must honor your contract."

"Mr. Rayven," Caren said hotly, "you may own and operate this company and you may hold your contract over my head all you want, but it won't change things. A week—and without your assistant. My best was all I ever promised you." Now, make whatever you want out of that, Caren thought miserably.

"We'll discuss this later. The agency people are waiting for you," Marc said tightly. "I don't have time to play with your emotional temperament at the moment. My bottom line is you have a contract and you damned well better plan on honoring it. Because if you don't, you'll never work in this city again, and by that I mean you won't even be able to get a job as a salesgirl in the dime store. That's my bottom line." Without another word he strode from the room, a murderous look on his face.

People were staring at her, wondering what she was going to do. Evidently, all eyes had been on the two of them during the heated discussion. Smile, she had to smile and pretend everything was all right. Well, damn it, it wasn't all right. How dare he threaten her! Who did he think he was? Just the creator of the silk purse. And now he thought he owned her. Did he care if she fell on her face from exhaustion? Did he care if Moira was out to get her scalp? All he was interested in was his perfume. Well, she was going to have to make the best of it for the moment or else create a scene that she might come to regret later.

I must have a dual personality, she thought as she talked with the advertising people about her schedule. She smiled, said the right things, allowing them to think she would be in Texas in three days. What kind of gutless wonder am I to do this? she asked herself over and over as she accepted one compliment after another. At the end of the second hour she still hadn't made her intentions known to the agency. Moira was always on the fringes of the group, listening to the conversations and saying little herself.

Caren had six invitations for lunch, all of which she turned down. She was going to stop by the deli and pick up a loaf of sourdough bread, a stick of sweet butter, and a jar of black-raspberry jam, go home and eat the whole thing. After which she would wash it all down with two cans of soda. So there, Marc Rayven.

How could he stand there and talk to her the way he had after that evening they had spent together? Because it didn't mean anything to him, that's how, she answered herself. So much for all of her bravado back in the screening room, she thought as she raced through the lobby on her way home. She knew she was going to do as ordered. Why hadn't she just accepted it and let it go? Oh no, she had to go and give her own ultimatum and make a fool of herself.

And all because her pride was hurt; all because she had fallen in love with Marc Rayven. Fallen in love with a man who didn't or wouldn't return her feelings. The only thing the cosmetics king was interested in was Caren Ainsley, the commodity, who would sell his cosmetics.

All the way home she chastised herself. She was still tearing herself apart when she entered the deli for her treat. Her packages under her arm, her mouth drooling, she walked the rest of the way home, mentally savoring each bite of the still-warm bread under her arm.

The kitchen clock read 2:15 when Caren ate the last slice of the rich sourdough bread. The jam jar contained a half teaspoon of jam. The butter was a thing of the past. One soda can was resting in the trash and the other had barely a sip left.

"I feel like a balloon," Caren muttered to the empty kitchen, "and I feel guilty. It's just that I've been eating that rabbit food for so long I had to get something starchy and sweet or go out of my mind." There was a look of disgust on her face—disgust with herself when she was forced to open the button on her skirt. Gutless wonder that she was, she had given in to her basic urges, the need for food, real food. Basic urges. How wonderful they were when two people agreed. Gut-level basics. Now, she was feeling sorry for herself.

Her lower lip trembled as she remembered the evening she had cooked for Marc and those intimate moments later. Tears gathered in her eyes and slowly trickled down her cheeks. Was it her fault that she was a virginal sow's ear? Was it really? A giggle rose in her throat. That wasn't quite true anymore. Now, she was a virginal silk purse, heavier by at least five pounds since her binge in the kitchen. So I'll just have celery and lettuce with lemon juice for dinner, and I'll exercise for two hours, she pacified herself. Now she would take a nice leisurely bath and then a nap. She would need all of her strength to chew on the celery and for the exercises she would do later.

TEN O'CLOCK the next morning found Caren sleeping dreamlessly in her lonely bed. The beginning of the night had been a torment. Thoughts of Marc Rayven plagued her. Arguments with herself about what she had said and what she should have said rolled around in her weary brain. She had fallen asleep at last, holding the conviction that she should have told Marc Rayven exactly where he could get off, that she would not make her public-appearance debut in Texas or anywhere else, for that matter. She was tired, exhausted, and needed some time to get her act together. Aside from the fact that she wasn't relishing the thought of days at hard labor in front of the camera and making personal appearances, for which she had no background, it was the principle of the thing.

Just who did Mr. Rayven think he was to threaten her that way? Telling her she wouldn't be able to get a job in the local five-and-dime! As if New York was the last city on earth. As if she couldn't move, find a life somewhere else.

It was impossible. Caren Ainsley wasn't the kind of girl to do anything by half measures. Her contract with Rayven Cosmetics was binding. She had signed it. She would live up to it, whatever the cost to herself—and her pride.

When the intercom buzzed, Caren groaned, rolling over between the sheets, clinging desperately to sleep. Wonderful, escapist, peaceful sleep. Again, the intercom buzzed. Again. Again.

Whoever it was, was certainly insistent. Climbing out from under her nice warm covers, she padded into the living room and pressed the button on the intercom. "Yes?" she questioned sleepily.

"Caren? That you? Don't tell me you were still sleeping on a beautiful day like this?" his deep, masculine voice inquired. "Push the buzzer, I'm coming up!"

What was Marc Rayven doing here at this time of day? He should be hard at work in his office, especially after yesterday's viewing of the commercials they had shot.

"Caren? Do you hear me? Push the buzzer, I'm

coming up! I'll give you one more minute and then I'm going to the superintendent." His tone was harsh, insistent, grating on her nerves. The one thing she did not need this morning was another confrontation with the Lipstick King.

"Go away," she managed weakly. "I'm not ready to see anyone."

"You open this door this minute. You hear?"

"Yes, I hear. And must I remind you that today is my day off and I don't have to take orders from you."

"I just want to be certain you're all right. You sound so out of it," he protested, softening his tone a little.

"I assure you I am fine. I sound out of it because you got me out of bed. I was sleeping. And no, I do not feel guilty for spending the morning in bed. I need my beauty rest, remember? Now, go away."

"Open this door! Or else I'll get the key from the super. I'll tell him that I'm your big brother and that I'm worried about you. Or I could tell him I'm your husband and you're my runaway bride. Or I could say—"

Disgusted, Caren pressed the little black button, cutting off his words, electrically opening the door downstairs in the tiny vestibule.

Pushing her hair back from her face, Caren's first impulse was to dash back into the bedroom and brush her teeth, comb her hair, and get dressed. Then she thought better of it. Anyone who came unannounced first thing in the morning deserved what he got. Instead, she padded into the kitchen and began preparing a pot of coffee. She had no sooner snapped on the plastic lid and replaced the coffee can in the refrigerator, than the doorbell of her apartment sounded.

"Who is it?" she called through the door.

"You know very well who it is. Now let me in!"

She snapped the locks and turned the knob and there, before her, was Marc Rayven burdened down with dozens of flowers. "Help me out, will you? I've carried these things for twelve blocks and my arms are about to fall off."

Caren relieved him of three bouquets and watched, openmouthed, as he dumped the rest unceremoniously onto the kitchen table. "I wanted to surprise you." He grinned sheepishly.

"You did, you did." She smiled, burying her nose in the myriad chrysanthemums and daisies intermingled with the sweetest of pale pink roses. She noticed that this was the first time she had seen Marc dressed in anything besides carefully tailored suits and white shirts and ties. This morning he sported a denim jacket lined with sheepskin and faded blue jeans over tall Frye boots.

"I really did get you out of bed, didn't I?"

"I've already told you that. Was the purpose of this visit simply to deliver these flowers? What's happened? Is FTD on strike or something?" she asked sarcastically. If he thought he could buy her cooperation with flowers he was mistaken.

"I wanted to see your face when I gave them to you."

"You've seen it, Mr. Rayven. What else?"

"That coffee I smell. I'm starving. Skipped breakfast this morning."

"I don't believe I invited you, Mr. Rayven."

"But you will, won't you?" He laughed, as arrogant and confident as ever.

"First tell me why all the flowers."

"Because you're terrific. The viewing was a total success yesterday but I never had the chance to congratulate you. Not properly, anyway. Now, where're the cups?"

"Top shelf, right side of the sink. But why so many? Flowers, I mean?"

"Because, Miss Ainsley, you are more, much more than I ever hoped for in my Nightstar girl. You are wonderful and maybe flowers can convey what words can't. Sugar, where's the sugar?"

"On the table, under the roses. And you came all the way over here just to tell me that? And to bring flowers? I don't have nearly enough vases to put them in. They'll die!"

"Do you take milk? Where's your frying pan. I'm going to make some eggs." He removed his heavy denim jacket and tossed it over a chair. "How do you like them?"

"They're beautiful. I've never had so many flowers given to me at one time!" Caren exclaimed, removing a green glass vase from the top of the refrigerator.

"Not the flowers, the eggs. How do you like your eggs?"

"Sunnyside." She ran water from the tap into the vase. "I'm not going to have enough vases. You're incredible! How did you know I loved daisies?"

"Bacon?"

"Don't you think about anything but food? It's in the meat tray, bottom left. And while you're at it, I'll have two pieces of toast. If you're going to undo my diet, might as well go all the way."

"Go get dressed," Marc ordered abruptly. "And dress warmly, it's getting cold just the way the middle of October should. But not too fancy. I just feel like bumming today."

She found her steps taking her to the bedroom to obey his orders, her mind already sorting through her wardrobe for something plain and warm. Suddenly, she stopped dead in her tracks. "Hey, you can't come in here and help yourself to breakfast and then order me to get dressed and even tell me what to wear! Who do you think you are anyway?"

"I'm the guy who's frying your bacon. I'm also the guy who lets you bring home the bacon, if you get my meaning. Now get dressed!"

"No!" She stamped her foot, really angry now. "I will not! This is my home and I'll get dressed—"

The words stuck in her throat. Marc had tossed down the spatula and was stalking toward her. There was a threat in his eyes and a determination about his mouth. "Are you going to get in there and get dressed or do I have to do it for you?" Closer he came, his arms reaching for her. Caren had no doubt but that he would do it, adding humiliation to her anger.

With a shriek that should have brought the house down, she raced into her bedroom, slamming the door shut. Before she realized, she was laughing, boisterously, uproariously.

"And don't forget to wash behind your ears," he yelled through the door. "I'm going to check!"

When Caren stepped shyly out from the bedroom, she was wearing designer jeans that had been part of her wardrobe for a camera sitting and a thick soft yellow mohair pullover. Her hair, streaked by Henri, was tied casually at the back of her head, soft wispy tendrils escaping onto her cheeks and brow. She hadn't applied any makeup except a touch of mascara and a smear of lip gloss. Today was her day off and she wanted to be Caren Ainsley, not the Nightstar girl.

In the kitchen, her breakfast was waiting for her. Also, every available pitcher and deep pot were in use as vases for the meadow of flowers he had brought with him. The air was filled with the unlikely combination of coffee, bacon, and roses.

"Good, you're dressed warm. It's going to be cold where we're going." His voice was approving. "And by the way, Miss Ainsley, did anyone ever tell you that you're perfectly lovely in the morning?"

Caren flushed, the hand holding her coffee cup trembling slightly. Why could this man do this to her? His very presence in the room could set her nerves tingling, turning her into a bumbling idiot. Then the full meaning of his words settled on her consciousness. "Where we're going?"

"You do have three days off, don't you? Hurry up and finish your breakfast. I'll clean up the dishes while you pack."

"Pack?"

"Yes pack, Miss Ainsley. You'll be needing sturdy shoes, we're going to walk through the woods—and a jacket, a thick warm one. And of course, nightgowns and don't forget your toothbrush." He bit into his toast, the sound crunching in the quiet.

"I—I don't know…. Didn't you tell me the tour began in Texas? That's three days from now. I—I wasn't planning on… No! The answer is definitely no! My contract states—"

"Eat!" he ordered. "You are not packing for business, Caren. I'm taking you to my place in the

Pocono Mountains. It's only about two hours from Manhattan. Pennsylvania. You *have* heard of Pennsylvania, haven't you?"

"Yes, of course. But I don't understand."

"Did you or did you not tell me yesterday how exhausted you are? Didn't you tell me you wanted time to get yourself together? Some time for yourself? Well, I've arranged it—and the woods are beautiful at this time of year. You're going to love it. Now eat!"

Chewing on her bacon, Caren watched him as he forked his egg. She wasn't certain she liked the idea of being sent to the mountains. Wasn't she allowed to make any decisions for herself anymore? "I don't want to go. I was planning on staying right here. Do some reading—"

"You can do all that in the mountains. Plus, you can enjoy a change of scene. You can walk through the woods. It's perfect." He challenged her with his eyes, daring her to protest again.

"I—I don't want to go. I won't like being all alone in a strange place—"

"Caren," he said, touching her hand with his fingertips. "You won't be alone. I'll be there with you. Please, I'm asking you. Won't you come away with me? I can promise you'll love it. Or is it that you don't want to be with me after—after the last time we were together?" He watched her; she could feel his gaze penetrate her very being, staining her cheeks pink as the roses he had brought her.

"Please, Caren. It will be good for both of us." How could she deny him anything, this man who could set her pulse racing just by talking to her? The pleading in his tone was a total departure from the way he usually barked commands. Deciding the time had come for her to ignore everything other than what she really wanted, Caren looked up at him. What she wanted, more than anything else on this earth, was to go away with Marc Rayven.

While Caren was in the bedroom packing, Marc, true to his word, was in the kitchen doing the dishes. She couldn't help thinking of what a paradox this man was. On the one hand he was a cosmetics mogul, barking orders, making decisions, running a multimillion-dollar business. On the other, he wasn't afraid to do what some men would call "women's work." There he was this very minute, humming along to the radio and sudsing away bacon grease.

Into the suitcase Caren folded several sweaters and another pair of jeans. A robe and slippers and her favorite talcum powder followed. On impulse, just in case, she added a long black silk skirt, a vibrant blue silk blouse, a gold chain belt, panty hose, and velvet strap evening slippers. She hoped she wouldn't have to wear them, but it was good to know she would have them. Marc's moods were sometimes so mercurial, there was no telling if he would decide to have dinner out at some fancy restaurant. She remembered the casual ease he had displayed when he had taken her to lunch at the Russian Tea Room, even convincing them to stay open past the lunch hour. For good measure, she added a tiny black beaded evening purse. The small makeup kit that Jacques had put together for her contained all the essentials yet was compact and easy to carry. Adding brush, comb, and toothbrush, she snapped the lid on the suitcase.

"Ready? Good girl. That was quick; some women would take half the day deciding on this or that. You're a marvel, Caren." Marc beamed. "Kitchen's all done. Anything else?"

Caren peeked into the kitchen. "You're the marvel, Marc. You really are. You did that in record time. What's your secret?"

"Organization. That's all there is to it."

"No sense in puffing your chest out, Mr. Rayven. You haven't accomplished the impossible, you know. We women do the same little chore day in and day out." There, that should deflate him somewhat. She couldn't allow him to think that cleaning a few dishes was the eighth wonder of the world. Her eye fell on a pot lid still on top of the stove. Before he could stop her, she picked it up and opened the oven door. New York apartments were always short on cabinet space and the oven was as good a place as any to store pots and pans.

The oven door swung open and out clattered a dirty frying pan. Startled, she peered inside. There were the coffeepot, the dishes—

"You didn't do the dishes!" she accused. "You just stuffed everything in the oven!"

"Come on, let's get going." He grabbed her by the elbow and steered her toward the door. "We'll worry about the dishes when we get back."

A last backward glance at the kitchen made Caren cringe. She knew that the "we" Marc spoke of was going to be "she."

Outside the apartment building, Marc's shiny red sports car was parked at the curb—illegally. A stiff white card was stuck under his windshield wiper. "Look, Marc, they've given you a ticket."

"It's not the first and it won't be the last." He shrugged, pushing it into the pocket of his slim, skin-fitting jeans.

"Just a second. I thought you said you walked twelve blocks carrying those flowers. How come your car is parked so conveniently outside my apartment?" She lifted a suspicious eyebrow, liking the way he was squirming.

"How else was I going to gain your sympathy so you'd let me have breakfast with you?" He smiled, his dark hair tumbling over his brow giving him a "Peck's Bad Boy" look.

"You might have tried asking," she said sternly, handing him her suitcase so he could stow it behind the front seats along with his own.

"Next time, I promise. Hop in, it's getting late and I want to show you my woods around the cabin."

The ride was soothing, delectable, but whenever she glanced over to see Marc driving beside her, little shivers would run up her spine. He was so masterful, so confident, handling the car like a pro. Even when the traffic was thick, crossing over the George Washington Bridge, she was completely at ease with Marc at the wheel.

Once outside the metropolitan area traffic was lighter and they spun down the road, the sun streaming through the windshield, warming the interior of the car. Or was it just being so close to Marc that made her feel this way—warm and drugged with contentment?

The mountains loomed before them, the sun touching the gold and red leaves and bringing them to glory. The radio played and they sang along with old familiar tunes, happy to be in one another's company.

Lunch was eaten at a wayside hot-dog stand and they both vowed they were the best hot dogs they'd ever eaten.

It was shortly after two in the afternoon when Marc pulled onto a side road and the sports car hugged the side of the mountain as they made the climb. Caren's ears popped halfway up and still the car climbed, high into the clouds.

When at last Marc pulled into the long, winding driveway, Caren found herself looking ahead, into the distance, for her first glimpse of the house. Marc had talked so glowingly of it during their ride that she was eager to see it.

Around the last curve the house loomed into view and Caren drew in her breath. It was more, so much more, than Marc had told her. It was a house that fit into its surroundings, embracing the woods, becoming part of nature itself. An A-frame, the long sloping roof fell away from the peak and nearly touched the ground on either side, leaving two walls of the house to be constructed totally of glass. Symmetrically, two fieldstone chimneys jutted out of the roof on both ends and a wide, roughly hewn porch graced both the first and second stories. But it was the expanse of glass that caught Caren's eye. Now, with the afternoon sun shining on it, it reflected the beauty of the woods. Golds, reds, oranges, all seemed to become part of the house. And at night, Caren knew, the moon would cut its path across the heavens never escaping the watchful windowpanes.

Caren was silent, breathless.

"I can see you've already fallen in love with it," Marc intoned. "It does that to me each and every time I come here. I find I'm never immune."

"It is beautiful, Marc. You never overstated its charms when you told me about it."

"You wait and see; it will take you at least a full day to absorb the beauty of the place, of the woods. I find that every time I come here my first few hours of settling in are concentrated within the house. It's almost as though the eye can't perceive the over-whelming contact with nature. Then, almost without warning, it hits you, and it seeps into your pores and becomes a part of you." As he spoke he looked out the windshield, and then his hand reached out and touched Caren's. "I like sharing this with you, Caren. I'm glad I convinced you to come."

Marc toted their suitcases inside, Caren following. Immediately, she liked what she saw. There were hardly any inner walls in Marc's house. One living space flowed uninterrupted into another. The living room was starkly furnished in chrome and glass, adding to the feeling of unlimited space. On the polished oak floor was a white shag area rug that united the low-slung forest-green sofa and white occasional chairs. Here the fireplace was the focal point in the room—tall and wide, completely constructed of gray fieldstone with a dark blue slate added here and there for definition.

From this area flowed the dining area, again furnished in chrome and glass and the white area rug. The table sat near the glass wall and offered an unobstructed view of the woodlands. Caren noted there were sliding doors that led out onto the deck for dining outdoors.

In the kitchen, the heart of every home, polished birch cabinets complemented pale butcher-block counters and the accent pieces were in oranges and yellows. Even the refrigerator was enameled in citrus yellow, giving life and cheer. Behind the kitchen, just down the hall, was a doorway that led into the bathroom.

Caren had never seen anything like it outside of magazines. One wall was completely glass and silk shades were attached to the tile floor so that the shades could be pulled up for privacy and still allow the sunshine in. The huge circular bathtub, Caren blushingly realized, was large enough for two people, and the area surrounding it was carpeted in plush melon with accents of turquoise, the color of the pillows strewn around the room. The fixtures were a pale beige and from the gleam of the faucets, Caren wondered if they were gold plated.

Here, too, were sliding doors out to a deck, no doubt for sunbathing. But closer examination revealed a California hot tub. Again Caren felt the blood rising to her cheeks. The total effect of the house was contrived to commune with nature and in that very fact, it was also totally sensual.

"We should have everything we need here," Marc

called to her from the kitchen, "but if not, there's a store about three miles away. Have you been up to the loft yet?"

"No, where is it?" Caren realized she hadn't seen any sleeping quarters. They must be in the loft.

"Out here, up the stairs. Take a look and pick out your bed."

Caren retraced her steps and found the open-tread staircase leading to the top of the house. The loft was just that, surrounding the downstairs on four sides. The railings were waist high and constructed of rough beams. The floor was thickly carpeted, wall to wall, in a heavenly light blue. She frowned when she saw several low beds covered with patchwork quilts, spaced at intervals around the loft. Then she saw the drop blinds separating one area from another, offering privacy.

"It's all open because it conserves heat and it's efficient to air-condition in the summer." Caren was startled; Marc's voice was so close, right behind her. He reached out and wrapped an arm around her. "How do you like my house, Caren?"

"I love it, Marc, I really do." A thought occurred to her. The house was so much like Marc himself. Open, eye on the world, casually elegant. "You designed it yourself, didn't you?"

"You've guessed." He smiled. "Mind telling me how?"

"It's like you."

"You love my house, Caren. Does that mean you love me, too?" The crinkles at the corners of his eyes deepened. His voice was low, seductive, and suddenly Caren was uncomfortable being here alone with him, sharing this intimacy. Or was he just testing her? Trying to get her to commit herself, to make a fool of herself—or worse, to admit to an emotion and then make her prove it by allowing him to seduce her.

"Loving a house isn't the same as loving a man," she stated simply, moving out of his embrace, heading for the stairs.

"Hold on, you haven't told me which bed you've chosen."

"Where's your bed?" she asked.

"Over there, near the windows." He smiled invitingly.

"Then that's mine, over there." She pointed clear across the loft to a bed near the corner.

Her shoulders were squared, her tone was brittle.

"Take it easy, Caren. Don't get so defensive. You came up here to relax and I'm not in the habit of forcing myself upon unwilling maidens. Now come on, I've got something especially spectacular to show you."

Marc led her down the stairs and out the door. The path led through the woods and the smell of autumn was thick in the air. Dappled shadows created little havens of dimness from the glare of the sun, and arbors were formed by the overhanging branches.

They walked side by side, each feeling comfortable in the other's presence. When Marc took her hand in his, she liked the feel of his long, artistic fingers against her own.

Deeper into the woods they walked, stopping to pick an exceptional leaf and stooping to inspect deer tracks. After ten minutes or so, the woods broke into a clearing where the sun was in full reign. And in the center of the clearing was a pond, green and still, reflecting the glory of the sky.

A touch on Caren's cheek brought her attention to Marc. He was lying beside her, watching her, his hand pressing now on the back of her neck, pulling her face down to his.

His kiss was gentle, light and feathery, insisting on little more than this brief contact. She felt herself yielding to him, allowing his lips to part hers, welcoming the intimate pressure. And then his arms were around her, holding her, pressing the length of her body against his own.

The warmth of the sun was on her back, but the fires between their bodies were hotter, consuming. Caren responded, answering his demand, creating demands of her own. Her lips trailed a pattern across his cheek, finding the place where his strong jutting jaw joined his neck. Her hands were in his thick, dark hair, tangling in it, running it through her fingers. All dimension of time was lost. There were only two in this world of reds and golds. Two people, alone, together.

In his embrace, she felt the hard, supple muscles of his arms. Her fingers traced along the wide, strong expanse of his chest; she felt his muscles ripple beneath her touch. His jacket was open; the warmth from him dispelled the chill air. The heady scent of his maleness was heightened by the cool, crisp autumn day. Their legs tangled, their hands sought to know each other, and always, their lips touched.

He pushed her backward, following, bending over her, molding her body to his. His mouth sought the pulse point at the base of her throat and lower, further, down between her breasts, igniting fires, dashing fears. Caren's arms held him, receiving him, offered herself to him.

With a barely audible groan, Marc lifted himself from her. His eyes were dark with unquenched passions, his mouth tight and grim. "Caren," he whispered, "you'll never know how lovely you are. You'll never know how much I want you."

Her eyes held his, dreamy, half-closed, like a doe's, in bashful surrender. Her lips, full and passion bruised, were slightly parted. Her hair tumbled about her head, coloring the forest floor with its brightness. Tenderly, his fingers traced a path from her cheek to her lips, touching them lightly, like a kiss. She shivered, trembling from unappeased passion and unquenched desire. No one, ever before, had aroused these feelings in her. No one, not ever, had made her lose control this way. Hot color flushed her cheeks. She had been absolutely brazen in her responses, practically wanton in her desires. Yet from the way Marc was smiling down into her upturned face, these qualities pleased him, aroused him. Why then did he stop?

"Come on, it's getting late and will be dark soon. We've got to get back to the house." Pulling himself to his feet, he grabbed her hand and helped her up beside him.

CHAPTER EIGHT

AFTER a dinner of steaks, done on the indoor smoke-less grill; fried potatoes, from which Caren abstained; and a crisp green salad, Marc and Caren washed dishes together. Night had fallen blackly, the surrounding woods yielding no light from the moon. The expanse of glass became dark mirrors against the darkness outside. But when Marc moved to the panel beside the front door and flipped a switch, outside spotlights flashed on, bringing the forest to life once again, creating murals of color and dimension as a backdrop.

The living-room fireplace roared to life and warmth with a brightly glowing fire and the built-in stereo system throbbed to Rimski-Korsakov's "Schehera-zade." The thick white carpet felt good against their bare feet as they sat on the floor and leaned back against the sofa, sipping at icy glasses of Amaretto.

Peace prevailed as they basked in one another's company, sharing small talk, and lighthearted humor. The fire shone in Marc's eyes, softening the chiseled lines in his face, flushing his cheeks to bronze. Caren settled back beside him, listening to the music, feeling it pulse through her, knowing it was Marc's nearness that quickened her heartbeat, not the symphony.

Marc refilled their glasses, the sweet liqueur cold and fiery against their lips. When he took his place beside her he draped his arm over her shoulder, drawing her closer, resting her head against his shoulder. After a moment, Caren realized he was looking at her, staring down at her, as though trying to memorize each and every line of her face. And when his mouth sought hers it was with a barely concealed passion. There was no attempt at tenderness as his lips ravished hers.

The music surged to a crescendo, rising with their passion, swelling with intensity. His tracings on her mouth were eloquent expressions of desire; her responses were stirring burning emotions. Locked in an embrace their longings were deep and spirited, sharing, giving, taking....

A sharp, heavy rapping sounded on the glass. At first they thought they imagined the intrusion, but the knocking continued. With a low, muttered curse, Marc drew away from her, seeking the source of this invasion.

"Marc, Marc, what are you doing in there? Marc! It's me, Moira! Is that girl in there with you?"

Caren's heart sank. Moira, again.

"Marc, do you hear me? I've got to see you! Marc!"

Opening the door, Marc admitted his assistant. "For crying out loud, Moira, how do you manage to find me? You must make it your life's work! What do you want?"

"Marc, is it my fault you refuse to have a phone here in the outback? Remote isn't quite the word for this place, 'isolated' and 'in the sticks' fit it much better." The tall, slim woman entered the living room and spied Caren sitting on the floor opposite the fireplace. "Actually, I've come for our little Miss Ainsley. Somehow some of those preliminary photos have been ruined. We'll have to reshoot them. A good thing we've two days left before she has to leave for Texas."

Caren's spirits sank. Standing, placing her glass on the coffee table, she faced the intruder. "I've given notice that I refuse to be disturbed until it's time to leave for Texas. I can't see how important a few photos are. Mr. Valenti must have thousands."

"That's just it, darling. Bill Valenti doesn't. They've been sent on to most of the places where you'll be doing personal appearances and shooting on location. These photos are special, black and white, for newspapers and magazines." Turning to Marc, she held her hands out in supplication. "Marc, you know we can't possibly use color photos for newspapers. They won't accept them, they don't show up in print. As for the magazine advertisements—" She shrugged.

Marc looked at Caren and seemed to deliberate. "She's right, Caren. We must have those black-and-whites and they can't successfully be made from color prints."

Caren drew in her breath, ready to do battle. "But Marc, you promised me these few days—" Her gaze fell on Moira's smirking face. She'd be willing to bet that those photos were destroyed for the same reason that Jacques had been instructed to sabotage her makeup—the same reason reporters at the preview got word that she was the Nightstar girl.

Caren looked again to Marc. Her heart fell. She could see he didn't want her to go back to the city to have the pictures taken.

"You had better get your things, Caren," Marc said tonelessly, his eyes never leaving her face.

ALL the way back to the city, Caren sat between Moira and Marc in the chauffeured limousine, silent. Over and over she thought of her day. It had been idyllic. Dinner had been an easy time together, quiet and friendly. Why did Moira have to ruin everything? Why?

Moira's eyes were on her, watchful, glaringly triumphant.

Caren blinked back tears, refusing to shed them in front of Marc's assistant. Her teeth bit into her lips to keep them from trembling. She leaned back against the seat, wishing she were somewhere, anywhere but here, under Moira's smug gaze. She sighed. Gone were her three days off. Instead she would be facing the camera again. And worse yet, facing an ovenful of dirty dishes.

THE WELCOME Caren received in Texas was worthy of royalty. Everything and everyone was at her beck and call. In her entourage traveled Jacques, Henri, and Bill Valenti. As a special surprise to Caren, because of her agreement to continue with the promotion and location tour on schedule, Marc Rayven had asked Maggie Bryant to accompany her as her companion. Everything was perfect, or should have been.

Maggie was a wonder. Her natural sense of orderliness helped Caren to arrive at appointments promptly, and aside from her professional help, Maggie was Caren's friend. She had never thought that she would be able to travel, to see the sights and meet all the glamorous people, especially not at company expense; however, because she was a widow, Maggie Bryant was free to travel. She had never had children, so her maternal instincts were focused on Caren.

As Caren lounged for a precious few minutes on the king-size bed in her elegant hotel suite, she scolded herself. *I should be counting my blessings!* The second half of the tour had been redesigned to include faraway places, foreign countries. Traveling to exotic lands was part of the American dream and Rayven Cosmetics wanted to capitalize on that dream. It had been surveyed as the American woman's fantasy and Marc was now making Nightstar an integral addition to that daydream. Here I am, she sighed, in a position most girls would envy, surrounded by friends and people who only wish the best for me, and instead I sit here fighting back tears. Why? Why?

The answer was disgustingly evident—Marc Rayven. Marc had been in touch with his production manager daily. He had even had conversations with Jacques and Henri after seeing the daily rushes that were messengered to him in New York by express. Even Maggie had been called to the phone to talk to the makeup mogul, but never Caren. She was the ignored member of the wandering tribe.

The personal-appearance tour, combined with location photography sessions, had begun in Texas. From there it had traveled to Los Angeles and San Francisco. But never, never a word from Marc Rayven.

She suspected he had been behind some of the ideas the production manager had created for the commercials. Clothing was being expressed to her from some of the most famous designers. From what Caren could gather, many designers were begging

Marc to allow them to create something for Caren to wear on camera. There was the linen suit from Halston; she had worn it in Los Angeles, at the filming in front of the Chinese Theatre; and at the Hollywood Bowl, she had posed in a Givenchy dream. San Francisco had demanded a Bill Blass silk classic as she wandered the hills. But always Bill Valenti's camera had caught her looking romantic and wistful.

Now here she was in Chicago with her little entourage and something was dreadfully wrong. Aside from the bitterness she was feeling concerning Marc Rayven and his beautiful and sophisticated assistant, something was going wrong with the shooting.

Bill Valenti was constantly in conference with Jacques and Henri, prodding them to try new makeup, new hairstyles. And still he wasn't happy with the results. Only an hour before, Jacques had come to Caren's room to talk with her.

The Frenchman had begun by telling her he considered himself her "Dutch Uncle." "Caren, I want you to feel you can talk to me. Something is eating at you and it's showing on camera. There's a coldness about you, a defensiveness, that wasn't there when we first began."

"I don't know what you mean, Jacques," she had answered honestly, not understanding what the Frenchman meant.

"I don't know either, Caren. You're still as sweet and charming as when I first met you, yet something is coming across on camera—"

Giving his typical Frenchman's shrug, he peered deeply at her. "*Chérie,* there are little lines of discontent and unhappiness that even the most artfully applied makeup cannot hide. May I be personal and ask if you are having problems in your love life?"

Caren laughed harshly. "What love life, Jacques? You never see anyone hanging around, do you? Really, I can't imagine what you're talking about. I try my best, it seems I'll have to try harder—"

"No, no, *chérie.* Trying harder is not the answer for that special look.... Ah, I'm being a foolish old man."

Now, stretched out on the satin coverlet on her lonely bed, Caren remembered the exchange and forced it out of her mind. Trying harder was the answer; she knew it, it had to be. She'd try to take better care of herself. Eat more, for one thing. She didn't like the gaunt look that was unbecoming to her. And for another, she'd try to rest more. How could a girl look romantic when she was dead on her feet?

As she glanced at her bedside clock, the ringing phone startled her. Seven o'clock. It must be Maggie calling to have dinner with her. But it wasn't Maggie's voice on the other end of the line.

"Caren? Marc here."

Marc! Oh, how she begrudged the lifting and soaring that took place in her heart just from hearing his voice. Hang on tight, she warned herself. He's probably calling to tell you how disappointed he's been in the daily rushes. "Hello, Mr. Rayven," she said simply, breath bated for what he would say.

"Have you had dinner yet?" His tone was casual, friendly, and close, so close she could have sworn he was calling from the next room.

"No…no, I haven't eaten yet. I was waiting for Maggie—"

"Maggie's having dinner with Bill Valenti and the rest of the crew. What about yourself?"

Now how did he know who Maggie was having dinner with? "I—I guess I'll have room service send something up…Mr. Rayven. Why are you calling me?"

"To have dinner, of course. I'm here in Chicago, right down the hall from you, as a matter of fact."

Down the hall! Her heart beat like a trip-hammer, thudding and thudding against her ribs, taking her breath away. Her tongue stuck to the roof of her mouth; words refused to come. She wanted to tell him she loved him…. No! No! She wanted to tell him to stay away, that she couldn't see him, that she was too tired. Instead, her silence committed her.

"Fine," Marc was saying, taking command as always. "I'll pick you up in a half hour. Unless, of course, you want to stick to your original plan. We could have dinner in your room—or mine, if you prefer."

Dinner? Here in this room, alone with him? No…no…

"I'll be ready in half an hour," she managed to sputter. No matter how tired she was, she'd drag herself out. If she must see him, it would be outside this room, where there were people, where she could defend herself against him.

Exactly one-half hour later a knock sounded on her door. A quick glance in the mirror at her Bill Blass silk suit and casual, free-flowing hairdo told her she was looking her best. After all, if it was good enough for the Nightstar commercial, it was good enough for dinner with Marc Rayven. She had already decided she wouldn't invite him into her room, and she had bathed and dressed in record time. She had actually been waiting for him for three whole minutes!

Picking up her slim handbag, she went to the door and opened it. There stood Marc and his good looks almost took her breath away. How was it that she hadn't remembered how handsome he was? Somehow, Caren felt she was losing her grip on things. In a disconcerted manner she flashed him an automatic smile and closed the door to her suite behind her. Darn, she hoped she had remembered to put her room key in her handbag. Well, she wasn't going to check for it now, not with Marc's glistening blue eyes watching her. That was a problem she would have to deal with later.

"You're lovely, Caren, as always. It's so good to see you again. Have you missed me?" His tone was soft, casual, intimate.

Of all the nerve, she thought, still smiling. He could have told her that *he'd* missed *her!* She parried his question. "Actually, I've got this boss who keeps me fairly busy," she said lightly, avoiding his eyes.

"Ummm. You're wearing Nightstar. You delight me—"

"What would you expect me to wear?" she answered caustically. "You did hire me to promote your product and that's what I do."

Marc seemed taken aback by her remark, but he quickly recovered. "Where would you like to have dinner? I'm a key member of the Playboy Club. Chicago is their national headquarters, you know. Or perhaps you'd enjoy something else?"

Playboy Club, indeed. How fitting, she thought nastily. There was no way she was going to sit through dinner and watch Marc ogle all those little bunnies. And some not so little, she thought as she glanced down at her own modest bosom. "I've heard so many nice things about Benihanas. It's not too far from here."

"Japanese food it is," he agreed, taking her arm and leading her to the elevators. "But I'll have to watch myself. Because of your hostility I'm afraid you'll take one of those cleavers the cooks use and bury it in my skull."

Caren laughed, a rousing, sincere laugh. Things were going to be fine. She just knew it.

Outside, the streets were decorated for the coming holidays. Red Santas and silver stars lined the streets, illuminated with power from the streetlamps. There was an air of Christmas and peace on earth in the lovely city. The wind off the lake was brisk and invigorating but not frigid or gusty. There was a calm permeating the atmosphere and it seemed to filter into Caren as well.

"Do you love Christmas?" he asked her. "You seem to be the kind of girl who does. Does your family mind it that you won't be with them this year?"

Caren shook her head. "No, there's really no family any longer. Mom and Dad are gone and I've sort of lost touch with aunts and uncles. But Christmas makes me feel all warm inside anyway. I remember the traditions my grandmother used to follow and then my own mother did the same. I try to keep them myself. Sometimes there doesn't seem much point—but I try."

"You always give everything your best shot, don't you?" Marc asked respectfully.

"I try!" Caren giggled, lengthening her stride to match his.

As they rounded a corner onto Michigan Boulevard, they found themselves in front of the John Hancock skyscraper. "Have you had time to go to the top of 'Big John'?" Caren shook her head. "Well, now's as good a time as any. I've never been either—" He quickened his steps, carrying her along with him, making her breathless.

The long elevator ride to the top of the skyscraper had its usual effect on her, and she felt as though her stomach had swung from her throat to her toes and had settled somewhere off kilter. She followed Marc out of the elevator and down the hall into the bar whose panoramic windows revealed the city below in all its glory.

As they stood near the glass, Caren could feel the building being buffeted by the winds off the lake; the sheer drop to the city below was frightening. But standing here with Marc, with his arm draped casually around her waist, she had never felt so safe and secure in all her life. Below they could see the bright red and green lights of Christmas decorations. Out on the lake marinas and small boats were lit, creating a string of glistening gems against the black waters. And the sky! Tonight the sky was clear and every star, millions of them, shone brightly in the special way they do in the winter sky.

No words were exchanged between them. No words were needed. The excitement and beauty of the city came alive for them in each other's presence. It was shared and cherished, a sight never to be forgotten.

"Caren, how would you like to have dinner here? I could make a reservation right now, and we could look at the city and watch the stars. Perhaps we could even find that nightstar you told me about at that first board meeting. Would you like that?"

Her smile was his answer.

Dinner was perfect, the service sublime and unobtrusive. Throughout the meal Marc told her of his boyhood, and they exchanged silly stories about when they were children. No mention of the company was made, no reference to the Nightstar campaign spoiled their celebratory mood.

It was with great reluctance that they stepped into the elevator and descended to street level. The wind had kicked up quite a bit so they ran back to the hotel, skipping down the street like children. Their cheeks were rosy and their toes were frozen by the time they arrived, to the amused glances of the doorman and the desk clerk.

In the lobby Marc pulled her over to the main desk and picked up the house phone. "Hot buttered rum for two. Room 1132. And make it quick."

It was a full minute before she realized that Marc had ordered the hot beverage for two! And in *her* room!

"You like hot toddies, don't you?" he asked as they stepped into the elevator.

"Huh?" She hadn't heard him, so engrossed in her thoughts was she.

"I asked you—" His arms came around her, softly, tenderly, pulling her against him, close, so close she could feel his breath upon her cheek. "Who do you love, Caren? Tell me, who do you love?"

Her answer was in her eyes, but she knew he couldn't see it because her eyes had closed as his mouth covered hers, possessing it, adoring it. When he released her, it was just as the elevator door opened and a man entered. Blushing, Caren lowered her head and waited for the lift to stop at the eleventh floor. They ran from the elevator, laughing and giggling at being caught in an embrace. Lightheartedly, Marc challenged her to a race down the hall and courteously allowed her to win.

Still laughing and breathless, she fumbled in her handbag for the key and waited while Marc opened the door.

"You really should leave," she told him after he had tuned in the radio to an all-music station. "I do have my job to consider and you know I have to look my best."

"Oh, yes, your job. I'm not sure they'll be shooting tomorrow. Valenti told me he was going to scout the city for a backdrop to shoot against. His assistants haven't come up with much, it seems."

"Marc, how about the top of the John Hancock building. It was beautiful there—"

"No." His answer was abrupt, almost stern.

"I—I just thought—"

"No," he told her as he gathered her in his arms. "That's our place. We discovered it together and I don't want it run in a commercial to promote some perfume. Tonight was too special—too perfect. Understand?"

Caren nodded, falling against him, offering her lips and also her heart.

Room service knocked and Marc ushered the waiter into the room. The buttered rum was soothing, warming after the cold Chicago weather. Room service had added an assortment of cheese straws and like greedy children they consumed them, and brushed the cracker crumbs off Caren's bed where they sat.

"What would you like to do tomorrow? We have the whole day."

"Tomorrow? But I thought you had to return to New York, and Maggie and I promised each other a shopping trip at the Water Tower Place."

The pleading look in his eyes persuaded her that there were more urgent needs to be filled.

"Can't you go with me instead of Maggie? Maggie will have you for the rest of the tour. We could do some Christmas shopping. I will need your expert advice, you know. There's the production crew, Maggie, Jacques, and Henri…. Say you will," he demanded, touching her neck just below her ear with his lips, nibbling softly, persuading.

"I'll call Maggie in the morning—"

Again she was swept into his arms. Again her world spun and tilted.

THE NEXT DAY was a blustery day of winter. Marc called for her at eleven and instructed her to wear slacks and dress warmly. Bundled into gray wool slacks with a bright red pullover, Caren slipped into the white rabbit coat that had been made for her as part of her campaign wardrobe. "You look terrific," Maggie complimented Caren as she searched for a pair of woolen gloves. "But you'll freeze if you wear those skimpy kidskin gloves. This is Chicago, Caren, and it's a whole lot closer to the North Pole than it appears on the map."

Caren laughed, excitement bubbling out of her. She found she was laughing quite a bit since Marc had taken her out the night before. Or was that just because there had been so little to make her happy until he arrived on the scene?

"Maggie, you're a wonder not to mind about me going shopping with Marc."

"Don't be silly," Maggie assured her. "I do most of my shopping for Christmas throughout the year. You know how it is, picking up little bargains on a typist's salary. Besides, I'm saving my money for when we go on tour. I love shopping in new stores and boutiques. I plan to return home with a king's ransom."

The tour...new cities...new shops and glittering boutiques... How could Caren have forgotten? She would be on location at Christmas time. And Marc would be in New York, no doubt. In New York with Moira over the holiday season. Suddenly crestfallen, Caren slumped down on the edge of the bed.

"What's the matter, honey? What's gotten into you? Aren't you feeling well?" Maggie asked solicitously, touching her fingertips to Caren's forehead.

"I'm fine, Maggie. Just a little homesick, I guess. To me Christmas means glitter and polish and snow and turkey and there won't be any of that where we're going. What I mean is it will be there, but it won't be the same as back home."

Maggie clucked and crooned, holding Caren in her arms. "To me Christmas means being with someone special. Someone who means more to you than anyone else in the world." She sighed so deeply that Caren pulled away and stared at her. Could it be possible that Maggie did have someone special and she had given that up to accompany Caren on the tour?

"Who's your someone special, Maggie? Anyone I know?"

"No, you wouldn't know him. I met him back in New York and we became very close. I'll miss him, but then I won't be all alone as he will. I'll have you and Bill and Jacques and Henri. My someone special is from England and all his family is there. Business reasons are keeping him in New York."

"Oh, Maggie, that's terrible! I don't want you to go on tour with me. I want you to go back to New York—"

"Don't be silly. The arrangements have all been made. Besides, Mr. Rayven is counting on me and I won't let him down." Maggie's voice was adamant. She would not tolerate an argument. Period.

There was no time for further discussion. Just as Maggie found Caren's bright red woolen gloves, Marc announced himself at the door. Breezing out to warnings to keep buttoned up, Caren literally danced out of the suite and down the hall; the only thing keeping her feet on the ground was the steadying influence of Marc's hand in hers.

The day was colder than either Marc or Maggie had predicted, but Caren reveled in it. The new Water Tower Place shopping mall was only blocks away from the Hancock skyscraper and Caren insisted they walk. They decided that after the shopping mall they would continue down Michigan Boulevard to the numerous art galleries and antique shops. Surely something appropriate could be found in one of those places for the very particular Jacques.

Inside the seven-storied shopping mall, Christmas

carols jubilantly rang out. People scurried from one store to another, jostling each other in a friendly manner and smiling, always smiling. The season was upon them and in their hearts.

At a jewelry store a gold cigarette case was purchased for Jacques. Caren, who could not afford anything so extravagant, settled on a pair of jade cuff links for Henri.

For Maggie, Caren found a simple gold chain from which was suspended a tiny gold three-dimensional box containing a mustard-seed grain for good luck. Marc added to Maggie's Christmas present by purchasing a slim gold watch, which was neat and tailored, just like Maggie herself.

At a leather-goods store Marc bought an English cowhide wallet for Bill Valenti and an exquisite attaché case for Henri in which he could carry all the tools of his trade.

The silversmith carried the perfect gifts for Caren to purchase for Jacques: an engraved mustache cup and a sterling money clip. For Bill Valenti, Caren spied a Norman Rockwell lithograph she just knew the photographer would like.

"Time for lunch, Caren," Marc said with authority. "My arms are breaking and I thought Santa Claus carried his own bag of goodies."

Marc led the way to an old English pub he had seen

on the third level. The Black Bull offered a delectable menu of luncheon entrées and they decided on thinly sliced beef and a crisp green salad.

As they were leaving, their pert blonde waitress pointedly studied Caren. Suddenly, recognition dawned upon her. "You're Caren Ainsley, the Nightstar girl, aren't you? I've asked my husband for a bottle of Nightstar for Christmas." The waitress's glance went to Marc and then back to Caren. "Now I'll know who put those stars in your eyes when I see you in magazines and on TV. I have to admit, those commercials are the most romantic advertising I've ever seen, and you're wonderful in them."

Caren's voice, when she spoke, was hesitant. "Thank...thank you. How nice of you to say so."

The blonde laughed and waved them a good-bye and a happy holiday. Outside the pub in the midst of the holiday shopping Marc pressed close up against Caren. "Am I?"

"Are you what?"

"Am I the reason you have stars in your eyes? Tell me," he whispered. "I want to hear you say it."

All around them people milled; strangers' eyes glanced at them speculatively. Not even before the cameras or on nationwide television had Caren felt so conspicuous and exposed. Marc held her fast, demanding that she tell him. Again, he repeated, "Tell me, Caren. Is it true? Am I the reason you have stars in your eyes?"

Color crept into Caren's face and Marc tipped up her chin, peering down at her. "That's all I wanted to know," he said huskily before covering her mouth with his own and making her oblivious to the fact that people were passing by and staring.

THE NEXT DAY Marc had to leave to go back to New York and he took Maggie Bryant with him at Caren's request. Just because she, Caren, was going to be away from the man she loved at Christmas, was no reason for Maggie to be away from the city and the friends she loved.

THE CREW finished up in Chicago and Bill Valenti and Jacques seemed especially pleased with the results of the shooting. Three days' shooting in Atlanta, Georgia, and another five days in the Caribbean.

Each day Marc called her, sometimes twice a day. Bill seemed ecstatic with her performance before the cameras, and Jacques wore a grin that said it all.

The plan was to leave for the Nevada desert the following morning. All the details had been handled by Marc personally. It was to be the next-to-last location before returning to New York to await the results of the first half of the campaign. A month or so for rest and relaxation and then they would tackle the foreign market with a lengthy tour. How excited Marc had been with his idea for the Nevada desert. He said it was a preview of things to come. His description of the Arabian hotel in the middle of the desert had made her breathless. Half old world and half new world. They would stay in the old part of the hotel with all the Eastern flavor and culture the owner refused to change.

"You'll think you're really in the Arabian desert, Caren," Marc had said with enthusiasm. "Even the shopping plaza was designed to resemble a mock Arabian bazaar. You're going to love it!" If he said she was going to love it she knew she would. Imagine someone with enough money to build an Arabian palace in the middle of the Nevada desert. She grinned when she recalled Marc's saying that commercialism had won out and the owner had been forced to add onto the palace—a more modern building that American guests desired.

The phone near her bed rang and Caren quickly snatched it up. It was Marc. It was always Marc. This time his voice was excited.

"I've done it! I've cleared my desk. I'll be joining you in Nevada for Christmas after all. Tell me you can't wait to see me."

It was a dream come true. Marc. Marc would meet her in Nevada. He was going to spend Christmas with her. "I can't wait," she bubbled happily into the phone. "Hurry," she whispered before she replaced the phone in its cradle.

CHAPTER NINE

CAREN blinked. Impossible was the only word that came to mind. How had Marc Rayven's crew made all this possible? It was a world apart from anything she had ever seen. It was unbelievable, but Eastern sights and sounds assaulted her senses. The costumes, the settings in the desert, were all ancient world. Harem pants, brocaded vests, glittering face veils, and pillows were everywhere. Hundreds of them, thousands of them, surrounded her. It was a make-believe world, compliments of Rayven Cosmetics and the expertise of Jacques, Bill, and many others.

Silken tents were constructed on the desert. There were even a few camels and goat herds to fill the background. Who had gotten them and from where were complete mysteries to Caren. Make-believe bazaars and temples were used as backdrops. And always, Marc sat on his stool just behind the camera, watching. Scenes were created in rapid-fire succession. Bill Valenti seemed very pleased with her work. Daily rushes were viewed and notes were taken on their editing. The world was a beautiful place; the work went well. And always, there was Marc—taking her around to see the sights and to give her a personal tour of the old palace-motel in the desert, taking her to dinners and pageants and to the real bazaar for endless shopping tours.

Caren knew she had never been so happy in her life and that happiness was Marc Rayven. But an icy wind blew across the desert late one afternoon when Moira Evans suddenly arrived. Caren's world seemed to crash down around her when Moira favored her with a deadly look. That one look told Caren that whatever excuse Moira had used to bring herself to Nevada was either trumped up or created especially for this purpose. The president's beautiful assistant was here to protect her territory—and that territory was labeled "Marc Rayven."

Dusk, her favorite time of day. Aimlessly, Caren strolled along the wide balcony of her hotel suite. This was her time, her private time of day to sit and contemplate the day's happenings. A time to relax, a time to ponder, and a time to make decisions. Gripping the balcony rail like a vise, she stared into the pearl-gray shadows of early evening. "I love Marc Rayven," she said to the stillness around her.

This stop in the Nevada desert was the next to last

in the ad campaign. When they finished shooting here on location, they would head for home to wait out the results of this first half of the tour.

If only she could be sure of Marc's feelings for her. True, he had kissed her as a man kisses the woman he loves, and true, he had murmured all the right words in response to her own husky whispers. Yet, he had said nothing that could be taken as a commitment. He had made no promise of what would be when the Nightstar campaign was over. And there was Moira Evans always lurking within eyesight and earshot.

Caren's eyes narrowed as she stared down into the courtyard beneath the balcony. The early twilight wove lacy patterns over ancient, gnarled trees that circled the small area. Marc! Moira! Unable to tear her eyes from the couple, Caren stared, willing her eyes to see clearly in the semidarkness. She shivered slightly in the evening air. What were they saying to each other? As she watched the couple, the lavender shadows deepened and lengthened, cloaking the small private garden in soft, caressing blackness. She was frightened.

Suddenly, the garden was bathed in a dim, yellowish glow from the apartments beneath her own. The silhouettes standing under the tree leaned toward each other and seemed to melt into oneness. Caren gasped and felt as though her heart were being ripped to shreds. It was a long embrace, each second doing more damage to her wounded heart. Then Moira's words, clear and distinct, wafted toward her in the cool evening, making her wish for a chasm to fall into.

Caren raced back into her apartment as though a devil chased at her heels. It was a game. It had been a game all along. Marc was playing a game to get what he wanted—and she was the loser. The cool, mocking words had seared her brain, penetrated her being. "You've succeeded, Marc. As Jacques said, the only thing missing was the 'look of love.' Now that you've succeeded in making Caren fall in love with you, you're going to have to come up with a way to extricate yourself gracefully. Little girls like Caren can be crushed so easily. Better to bruise her now than later since she thinks that all of this was serious on your part, Marc. We only have three days here and then home to New York. Start to wean her away from you now. She has to realize sooner or later that it was a trick. In time she'll forget about it—as the residuals come in from the commercials. Money, plenty of it, can work wonders. And to think we have you and Jacques to thank for making this the perfect campaign. I still can't believe that he was astute enough to come up with the idea that what was missing in Caren's eyes was the 'look of love,' or that you were magnanimous enough to cast aside your own feelings to make the little pigeon fall in love with you. I, for one, call that dedication above and beyond the call of duty. I understand better than anyone how far you'll go to make this company the number-one cosmetics firm in the country."

Silence. Caren sobbed into the scarlet pillow on the chaise. She shouldn't have stood there and listened; she hoped Marc and Moira were enjoying the little trick they had pulled on poor, unsuspecting Caren. How could they…how could he have done this to her? He certainly knew how naive she was.

Caren jumped up from the chaise and recklessly started to toss her clothing into the stack of suitcases with which she traveled. She gave no thought to wrinkles or the havoc she was creating. Shoes were dumped unceremoniously on top of sheer blouses, and tailored slacks found themselves tangled up with gossamer nighties. Her eye fell on a cut-glass decanter with the silver-and-gold medallion that represented the Nightstar perfume. Without a second thought she picked it up and threw it against the mosaic tiles on the floor. Minuscule shards of crystal flew into the air as the heady scent permeated the room. She stared at the sparkling slivers of glass as they settled on the tiles. Shattered, just as she was. It was over. In a split second she had destroyed Marc Rayven's perfume just as Moira's words had destroyed her.

She had to get out of here, out of this room, away from the heavy, cloying scent that was everywhere, making it impossible to breathe. The cool evening air would help her to get her thoughts together. Run, her mind shrieked. Run fast and hard and don't think. Without a backward glance, Caren flung open the door and raced down the corridor and then down the stairwell.

Everything smelled like the perfume that was soaking into the tiles in her room. It seemed to be all about her, in her hair, in her nostrils, in her mouth, and on her clothes. "I hate it, I hate it," she choked out over and over as she ran around the building into a formal garden. Then, she slowed down, picking her way carefully between the lush foliage.

She roamed the gardens from end to end for what seemed like hours, until, drying her tears on the hem of the colorful caftan she wore, Caren looked at her surroundings to see how far she had come. Tiny, twinkling lights from the hotel to the east told her she had come much farther than she intended. She was going to have a long walk back. Strangely enough, no thoughts for her safety entered her head. It seemed a peaceful, quiet place. She walked a short distance and sat down on a tile bench beneath a monstrous old tree.

Peaceful and sad, her tears dried, Caren kept up a running conversation with herself. "Am I sad for what was, what is, or what is not to be?" She could find no answers to her silent questions. Wearily, she rose and gathered the material of the caftan in her hand. Daintily, she picked her way through the garden. When something was over, it was over. You went on from there.

Tears pricked at her eyes as she continued to walk in the direction of the hotel. She gulped and swallowed hard. No more tears. The time for tears was over. Now it was time to be angry, gut angry for having been made a fool. How could he! No, that was wrong. How dare he!

Mentally, Caren ticked off the appointments on her schedule for the following day and the day after that. If she was careful, she could almost manage to stay away from Marc. Her free time would be taken up with complaints: it was too hot; she had a headache; the water was getting to her; she had stomachaches from the spicy food.

The lights from the hotel were closer now, just beyond the circle of trees that flanked the formal gardens. How strange this majestic hotel looked sitting here in the desert, half old world and half concrete and steel.

For a moment Caren was disoriented as she took in her surroundings. Now she appeared to be on the side of the original hotel, palace really—the west side. A glance at her watch told her a good three and a half hours had passed since she had stormed out of the hotel. She had missed dinner, and, of course, the inevitable cocktails beforehand with Moira, Jacques, and Marc. What had they thought when she hadn't shown up in the dining room? Marc had probably sent Moira to her room, and by now she would have reported the smashed bottle of scent and the disarray of the half-packed luggage. Caren turned, closing the iron gate behind her.

It was another world, a garden within a garden, manicured to perfection. She stopped. Surely, this oasis in the desert wasn't for the guests. Perhaps it belonged to the owners. She stood, puzzled as to what to call the area. It wasn't a room, and yet it wasn't a patio either. She moved closer, each step taking her back in time to the legends and the palaces of ancient Rome. Arcades were fastened along two sides of what looked like a room, and beneath each tiled and marble arch stood braziers that burned brightly to give both light and warmth. Long, low divans upholstered in marvelously rich fabrics lined the two walls. The floor beneath Caren's feet was carpeted in the most lush jewel-like colors of the rainbow; these created a translucent effect that made the floor covering appear thicker and more welcoming to the foot. Tapestries, which Caren recognized as coming from French looms, were hung from pedestals supporting figurines and statues of goddesses. The area had a furnished feeling that in no way detracted from the simple sweep of what she was sure was the finest in old-world architecture.

To the left was a pool fed by an outside stream, and

floating atop the blue-tinted water were rose petals and fragrant pomanders studded with spices. Upon closer examination, Caren discovered that a pit had been fashioned outside the perimeters of the pool, and within this pit were polished rocks heated by burning fragrant oil. Caren dipped her hand into the clear water and tested its temperature. Pleasantly warm, soothingly so. The continual runoff from the pool emptied itself into a trough that fell beneath the floor and ran to the outside garden. Never in her life had she imagined such luxury. Who had devised the mechanics of it? That person was a genius—a genius in his field as Marc Rayven was in the cosmetics industry. Now the moment was spoiled. She had allowed thoughts of Marc to creep into it. Now the beauty of this special place was shattered, ruined. How could she appreciate it when Marc Rayven was trampling roughshod over her heart and mind?

"So, you found it on your own," a quiet voice near her said.

Startled, Caren whirled and stood staring at Marc Rayven. Her heart leaped to her throat making it impossible to answer. She nodded.

"I was here many years ago, and when we checked in at the main desk, I specifically asked for this suite of rooms. I think this garden, this small oasis, is about the closest thing to perfection that a man could find.

All it needs is a woman to make it complete. Tell me, how do you like it?"

She couldn't have spoken if her life depended on it. She shrugged, aware of his nearness. Carefully, she backed off a step and then another one.

The silence between Marc and Caren continued, each alone with their thoughts, yet ever aware of the other's presence. The air was wine sweet and left Caren lightheaded. Still the silence continued, and when he reached out his hand and captured hers, they walked out into the chill night, hand in hand. Caren filled her lungs with the bracing air and felt a slight, pleasant buzz in her head. She looked up at him as they walked, conscious of his height, his maleness. His hand was warm on hers; her shoulder brushed his arm and tingled with the contact. They walked across the gardens, out onto the grassy knoll. Beneath the cover of the trees, hidden from the stars, they stopped. He took her in his arms and the universe clashed.

She had no will, no desire to stop him. She needed this as much as she needed to take another breath. Tomorrow was another day to make decisions.

His mouth became a part of hers, and her heart beat in a wild, broken rhythm without a pattern. They strained toward each other, caught up in the designs of the flesh as they toiled to join breath and spirit.

They tore at each other, each seeking that which the

other could give. There in the shadows of the trees, away from the prying light of the heavens, they devoured each other with their searching lips and hungry fingers.

It was Marc who gently extricated her from the circle of his arms. "Not here, not now," he said huskily.

To her ears the words were tortured, full of something that sounded like regret.

Marc was quiet for so long Caren didn't realize that she had been holding her breath, hardly daring to breathe until he spoke. She let her breath escape in a long sigh.

Marc's voice was carefully controlled, Caren thought. "I suppose what I'm really saying is that things aren't always what they appear to be. Things change, people change." Again there was a silence. Caren waited. "Tricks, for want of a better word, aren't always tricks, per se, like when we were children. From any experience, even betrayal, we learn and we grow." His voice was hesitant, less controlled, as if the words he chose were not to his liking.

Again Caren waited, a small knot of fear tightening in her stomach. The words swirled around her head, making her dizzy. They were words; anyone could say words. It was what the words meant that was important. She understood now and the words were his. He was admitting that he had betrayed her. He wasn't going to use her again and make a fool of her—not again.

"Do you understand what I just said?" Marc said quietly.

Caren stood up and deliberately moved away from the nest Marc had created beneath the tree. "I understand perfectly, Mr. Rayven. You used me to make a success of your company. You pretended to fall in love with me so that I would come across on camera with the 'look of love.' Well, you succeeded. I did fall in love with you. You boasted that you could turn me into a silk purse and you succeeded. Well, Mr. Rayven, I no longer want to be a silk purse. I like what I was. In fact, Mr. Rayven, I hate you from the top of your head to the bottom of your feet. But you're right about one thing—we do learn from each and every experience. You're nothing but a slick, conniving, dyed-in-the-wool phony. You…you…Lipstick King. Oh, and one last thing, from here on in, Mr. Rayven, you're on your own. I quit."

Marc's face was in the shadows but his eyes took on the glaze of rage. His fingers bit into her arm, squeezing, hurting. He was frightening her, making her want to run like a rabbit and hide away from him— away from his rage.

"Caren, listen to me!" It was an order.

She bristled, railing against her traitorous impulses. No, she told herself, no! She had listened enough already and where had it gotten her? To the deserts of

Nevada with nothing to show for it but a badly injured ego and a broken heart.

"No!" she protested, tearing her arm from his grip. "I've heard enough!"

He seized her again, shaking her till she thought she could hear her teeth rattle. "If you won't listen to explanations, then you'll listen to this! You have a contract, Miss Ainsley and it is not complete until you finish the next two days' shooting. And finish it you will! Not another word, do you understand?" he bellowed.

She understood. She understood *everything*.

CAREN glanced at the watch that lay next to an empty coffee cup on a stool. Two more hours and her contract was finished. Two more hours and she could pack it in and head for home. How she had gotten through the past forty-two hours was beyond her. Willpower, guts, stamina, call it what you will, she had delivered. And she had paid her dues in full. No one, and that included Marc Rayven, could say she had been anything but professional. She had bent but she hadn't broken under Rayven's steely gaze and sharp tongue. She had more than delivered. Jacques said she was as professional as they come. Henri had said he would be glad to work with her anytime, anyplace. Only Marc Rayven had remained silent, his eyes cold and hard. Now that it was down to the wire with only two more shots to finish one would think he would have the decency to at least congratulate her. Oh no, the perfume wizard was going to get every minute out of her if it killed her. What did he care as long as he made money and his campaign was successful?

"Bill, in the last two shots don't use the handbag. Too awkward." Marc Rayven shouted to be heard over the music that Jacques was playing in the background.

Caren's back stiffened. "Now just a minute, Mr. Rayven. I've done everything you wanted; I've followed orders. But the purse stays or you can get yourself another girl for the last two shots. It's my right," she said heatedly. At his perplexed look at her outburst she rushed on. "If anyone deserves to be photographed with a purse—a *silk* purse—it's me. Take it or leave it," she continued hotly.

Marc Rayven flinched and then stood. "You're absolutely right. Shoot it, and use the silk purse. Somehow, I hadn't thought you would have come so…prepared," he said, letting his eyes come to rest on a square of scarlet silk attached to a thin gold chain.

"That's been the problem all along. You never thought I could think on my own. I meant it when I said I want the purse in the shot," Caren said coolly.

"And I meant it when I told Bill to use the purse." Without another word he left her standing alone, more alone than she had ever been in her entire life.

It was over. Finished. Done. Quickly she gathered her things together and was off and running, her long legs pumping furiously. Her adrenaline flowed as if someone had tapped an underground spring. By the time she reached her apartment and locked the door securely, the phone was ringing. She fixed the black instrument with a steely gaze and shouted, "Ring all night for all I care!" Within minutes she'd finished her haphazard packing. She would leave on the first available plane.

Why did he have to beat around the bush? Why couldn't he just be man enough to come out and say he'd duped her, that he didn't love her and had only been pretending. If he had done that she would at least respect him for his honesty. After all, one person could not make another person love someone.

Her mouth was a grim, tight line as she fished in her bag for her airline ticket. Her hand was on the phone, ready to pick up the receiver, when it shrilled to life. She withdrew her hand as though a snake had lashed out at her. She stared at the ebony instrument with unblinking eyes, willing it to stop its insistent bid for attention. The moment it ceased to ring Caren picked up the phone and asked to be connected with the airport. Thirty-five minutes later she had a confirmed reservation for the following day at 6:00 p.m. It was over. She was going back home to her little two-room apartment. It was time to get on with her life—whatever that was and wherever it would lead her. Later, much later, she would decide about the second half of the tour.

A bath. Always take a warm, soothing bath and you will feel better. She had read that somewhere. Picking her way over the broken perfume decanter, Caren walked into the bathroom and turned on the gilt faucet. Water rushed into the tub creating a halo of steam that spiraled upward. She watched with clinical interest to see if the water pressure would change. Amazing—the torrent of water filled the tub within minutes. The phone shrilled again at the same time a loud rapping occurred at her door. Thank God for the old part of the palace-hotel where the doors were stout and some macho hero couldn't break it down with his manly perfumed shoulders.

When the phone stilled, Caren picked it up for the second time and spoke to the desk clerk. She enunciated slowly and clearly. "I don't want any calls put through to my room this evening." The moment she replaced the receiver, it clamored to life. So much for clear distinct instructions said in a firm, no-nonsense voice.

She felt confused, out of sorts. Where to go, what to do? She could go to the shopping center, the one fashioned like an old-world bazaar. She should have thought of that sooner. She could go there and while away her hours and be lost to anyone from Rayven Cosmetics.

The phone jangled again, jarring her nerves. It was Marc; she knew it. How long would it be before he decided to come pounding on her door? Before she could allow herself to be trapped in her room, forced to see him, hear him, she rushed out the door and slammed it shut behind her.

Caren realized too late that she was still dressed in her bright yellow silk caftan that was more loungewear than outdoor attire. Halfway down the long hallway she remembered that her key was locked in her room behind the door she had just slammed closed.

Too late. She wouldn't go down to the desk and explain so that she could get a spare key because she couldn't run the risk of encountering Marc Rayven. Not ever!

CHAPTER TEN

AN HOUR LATER Caren trudged into the desert shopping plaza. There were busy shoppers everywhere as she weaved her way among the throngs in the plaza bazaar. Suddenly she realized she was hungry. But she immediately remembered that she had no money with her. She shrugged; her stomach would have to wait. Each stall was more colorful than the next. The Christmas decorations made her feel sentimental as she followed a group of tourists. The smells were entrancing. One stall held every cheese imaginable while the one next to it was decorated with every exotic flower under the sun.

"Peaches! Peaches! Ripe and succulent peaches! Fit for a king! Firm and delicious! Peaches! Peaches!" The merchant held out a plump, pink peach as he stood before Caren. "Ah, lovely lady, see how firm and sweet they are. Their beauty is equaled by your own."

Caren shook her head. She turned her palms up to show she had no money with her.

"For you, lovely lady, it is a gift. Enjoy."

Caren accepted the peach reluctantly and thanked the vendor. She devoured the fruit, the thick, rich juice dribbling down her cheek. "Food fit for a god." She smiled at the merchant. He nodded his head as Caren continued with her progress down the narrow aisle.

Tired from all the walking she was doing, Caren leaned against a building and looked around her. Her eyes circled the milling throngs of holiday shoppers, coming to rest on a pair of laughing, dark eyes across the aisle from where she was standing. She became mesmerized, her breath catching in her throat.

For that one brief moment time stood still as she continued to return Marc Rayven's gaze. The hot sun was now a warm caress; the shrill cries of the vendors became soft words of nothingness. The vibrant colors whispered to her, and the hot, dry wind cloaked her softly. Her heart thumped madly in her breast. This couldn't be happening to her. After that humiliating scene in the garden last night she couldn't be standing here feeling this way. It was insane. She had to get away, she had to move, run. Run! Her mind ordered.

Suddenly, a babble of voices rang through the bazaar as a horde of children raced past the over-crowded stalls. Caren jumped out of the way and then quickly regained her composure. When she looked for Marc again, he was gone. Where was he? Climbing on a stool, she let her eyes rake the customers of the bazaar. He was nowhere about. He was gone! The sun was again a hot, brutal mantle of heat; the shrill cries of the merchants fell tumultuously on her ears and the persistent wind was torturous to her fair skin. She had to leave, to move before he found her. She managed somehow to fight her way through the jostling crowds to an area far removed from the bazaar.

She was angry, her momentary lapse back in the bazaar forgotten. Of course, he was looking for her. He couldn't let her get away from him. She was the goose that was laying the golden eggs. She was what was going to make him *numero uno,* right up there with Charles Revson. He'd probably even write a book about his experiences sometime and make her a fool in print. She knew she was thinking nasty, terrible things about the man she loved but she couldn't help it. She felt so ashamed to have fallen for his "line" that she felt almost physically sick.

If only she could go back to that pool and sink down into the cool wetness right up to her neck. She felt so hot and weary, so used and abused, that tears again threatened to erupt. Feeling sorry for herself wasn't going to get her anywhere. Midmorning and she still had to trek back to the hotel. What she had to do right now was put one foot in front of the other as fast as she could.

At best it was agonizing torture to walk along the desert road. The temperature, according to her perspiring brow, must be hovering somewhere around one hundred degrees. Her hair hung in limp, wet strands and plastered itself against her sweaty cheeks. Her neck felt stiff and the tiny particles of sand from the hot desert winds were sticking to her, making her itch. Hot, searing anger coursed through her. This discomfort was all Marc Rayven's fault.

The high-pitched whine of a desert jeep made her stop and turn. Well, what else had she expected? she wondered disgustedly. Of course, he would ride. Kings always rode and the stupid subjects walked. She squared her shoulders and continued to trudge down the road, only this time she walked on the side, leaving room for his jeep to pass. She was angry about her appearance, angry with the brutal heat, and angry with the man who was riding in the jeep, looking so cool and aloof. He was saying something. She ignored him.

"Only a fool walks in this heat. Get in and I'll take you back to the hotel. That's an order, Caren."

"Leave me alone."

"Get in before you suffer a heat stroke and I have to put you in a hospital. I won't tell you again. Get in!"

This time it was an iron command and Caren flinched. More anger surged through her. "Oh, sure, and then you can take a picture of me spraying Nightstar on myself in a hospital bed. Well, for your information, the only thing I'll be spraying from now on is disinfectant. To get rid of you, Mr. Rayven. Now, leave me alone." She was feeling lightheaded. It must be the anger she was feeling or maybe she was dehydrating. Not knowing anything about dehydration, it seemed as good a reason as any she could think of at the moment. "I'm getting in, but under protest," she said weakly.

"Look at your feet. Why are your toes bleeding?" Marc demanded.

Caren's head buzzed. He could ask the dumbest questions at the dumbest times. Talking seemed such an effort. "For a cosmetics rep, and I use the term lightly, you really are a mess, do you know that? My toes *aren't* bleeding; that's nail polish. Rayven Crimson Berry to be exact." Caren frowned; her voice sounded thick and her tongue felt swollen. "I thought you were offering me a ride, why are we sitting here?"

"I think you've about had it, Caren. The heat can do cruel things to a person. For God's sake if you wanted to go to the damned bazaar, why didn't you take the hotel shuttle or borrow the jeep for that matter?"

"Mr. Rayven, every time I listen to you I manage to get fouled up in some way. You did ask me to get in this jeep so you could drive me back to the hotel? That was some time ago. Are you going to drive or not?"

The jeep roared to life as Marc floored the gas pedal. Caren leaned back against the seat. Maybe she should catch forty winks and she wouldn't have to talk to him. Her last conscious thought as she drifted off was that her big toe was indeed bleeding. Maybe he wasn't so dumb after all.

The jeep hit a deep rut in the road and Caren's eyes flew open. Soon she would have a cold drink and be within the air-conditioned confines of her apartment. The rest would take care of itself. So what if she allowed him to transport her back to the palace-hotel? That was all she was conceding. She risked opening one eye and was chagrined to see mocking eyes staring down at her. Fool! she chided herself.

"You're exhausted, but I knew you weren't out of it. Stop pretending, Caren. It's time you and I had a talk and that's exactly what we're going to do as soon as we get back to the hotel. I'm going to throw you into the pool in my apartment and there's no way you're going to get out till you listen to me. Do you understand what I'm saying?"

"I'm not as stupid as you seem to think," Caren snapped. "That's what hurt the most. The fact that you thought I was so stupid I would fall for all of your tricks. Well, I'm wise to your antics now, so let's continue this ride in silence. There's nothing you can say to me that holds the least bit of interest. I told you I was finished and I meant it."

"Somehow I never thought of you as a quitter, Caren." The words were soft and full of regret.

Caren hardened her heart. "And," she said, a note of steel in her tone, "I didn't think you were a liar and a trickster. You know all the weasel words, don't you? You have all the traits of the consummate politician. You missed your calling. I'll bet you even kiss babies."

"You are the most stubborn, the most exasperating, the most—"

"I don't want to hear it. That's no more true than all the other things you've been saying about me," Caren interrupted.

"It's not important what you think, not any longer," Marc snapped back, his face furious, his hands tight on the steering wheel. "Okay, we're here. You're going to shut up even if I have to muzzle you. One false move on your part and you've bought it. Do I make myself clear?"

Caren gulped. He couldn't talk to her like this. Of all the insufferable nerve! "And don't get any funny ideas about carrying me. I can walk by myself. I am going to use your pool—alone."

Marc grinned as he waited for her to climb from the jeep. He was next to her, ready to reach for her arm. She jerked free of him and started to walk around the garden, intent only on jumping into the sparkling pool and submerging herself till she was cool and refreshed.

Marc's eyes were laughing as he watched her stand at the edge of the pool. "The way I see it, you have two choices. You can skinny-dip, as we say back home, or you can go in with that silk shirt you're wearing."

He was mocking her again. Did he think she was stupid enough to go about with nothing on beneath the yellow caftan? Evidently, by the leer in his eye, that was exactly what he did think.

"Go away! Go find Moira and tell her some lies like you told me. Make love to her and tell her she's the only woman in the whole world for you. Maybe she's dumb enough to fall for your line, but I don't think so. That one would want it in writing and in triplicate, a copy for her and one for her attorney. If you're lucky she might give you one."

Marc laughed, a great booming sound that seemed to come from his toes. She watched in horror as he slipped off his shoes and socks and started to unbutton his shirt. Her eyes widened as his hands fumbled with his belt. He wouldn't…he wasn't going…

Before she knew what was happening, he was in the water, a flash of bronze skin and then ripples. Had he… Was he down to the buff? She had closed her eyes momentarily, missing the fact that he was wearing swim trunks beneath his slacks. She also didn't notice the dark hand that snaked out over the rim of the pool. Her ankle was in a viselike grip and then she was tumbling into the water, the heavy caftan dragging her down. She struggled to the surface, sputtering and howling. "You…you…war-paint mogul. Stay away from me. How dare you get into this pool without… without…naked! I'll scream. Do you hear me? I'll scream!"

"Go ahead." Marc grinned as he leaned back against the sides of the pool. His dark eyes danced merrily. "I do think, though, we should even up the odds a little." Suddenly, his hand was at the neck of her caftan and the sound of the wet material being ripped was thunderously loud in the stillness that surrounded them. "Now, you won't want to get out for fear I'll see all of your womanly attributes, and I won't want to get out for fear you'll see all of my manly attributes. I think it's called a Mexican standoff."

"You're disgusting," Caren sputtered as she tried to wrap the wet cloth around her, covering her wet, revealing undergarments. He was beneath the water tugging at the material until it was free.

"Now, it's safe to say you're a water nymph. Or a mermaid."

"Where's your stinky perfume? I'm surprised you don't carry a bottle around your neck for emergencies like this," Caren said heatedly. "I'm warning you, stay away from me."

"You're thinking of Saint Bernards." Marc laughed. "You know, they carry brandy and save snowbound and frostbitten people."

"Well, I'm not snowbound and I'm not a nymph and I'm not a mermaid. I'm cool now and I want to get out of here. Turn around."

"Not on your life. I'm staying right here till you turn into a prune. I want to see what you'll look like when you get old. If I'm going to grow old with a woman, the least I should get is a sneak preview."

"Think again, Mr. Rayven. If that was supposed to be some kind of left-handed proposal, I'm rejecting the offer."

"You don't have a choice. As soon as we get back to New York, I plan to marry you."

"Stupid and dumb. I'm not marrying you. I could never again believe anything you told me. I wouldn't marry you if you were the last man on earth."

"If you stay here much longer, I will be. Just how many men do you think would put up with you? Not many," he said, answering his own question. "You should just see yourself. You're a mess. Only a man in love with you would think you look beautiful. And," he said, wagging a playful finger, "you aren't even wearing my perfume."

"Why should I? It stinks. Did I tell you it S-T-I-N-K-S?"

"Sure, but I didn't believe you. You see, you tell lies to suit your convenience. I thought a small wedding, a hundred or so guests. We could go to the Philippines to finish out the ad campaign and then I'll lock you up somewhere in some white cottage with a picket fence, and we'll have five kids, enough for a basketball team. I like basketball, did I ever tell you that?"

"No, and I'm not interested." She watched in horror as Marc trod water till he was next to her. With virginal modesty she crossed her arms over her breasts and tried to blend into the side of the pool.

"This is ridiculous, all of this game-playing. You know I love you. I've loved you since the first time I saw you in that board meeting. You are a bit of a sow's ear. They're words, Caren—they mean nothing. All the photographers, all of the makeup artists, can't make you something you're not. All they give you is a veneer that washes off. It's what's here," he said, touching her eyelids lightly. "It's what's here," he said tracing his finger down her neck to a place slightly below her breasts. "You fell in love with me long after I fell in love with you. It makes no difference what Moira or Jacques say. It's what *I* say and what *you* say that matters. I love you. That's the bottom line. The game is over now. It's up to you to decide what you want to do. But first, I think you should hear me out, Caren."

"No more lies, Marc. I don't want to hear them."

"I've never lied to you, Caren."

She looked into his eyes, felt herself held in his gaze, and she knew that whatever he would tell her would be truth. She dropped her eyes, quiet, waiting. She felt herself being taken into his arms; his lips were very near her ear, his voice barely more than a whisper.

"Caren, first I must tell you that it was no accident that Maggie Bryant asked you to cover the minutes of the board meeting. I'd noticed you for some time before that. I'd already formulated my plan for making you the Nightstar girl. Or at least I was determined to give it an all-American try. I didn't honestly know whether you'd work out or not. Sometimes, the most beautiful women can't project a camera. But I did know that I wanted someone with your qualities; a wholesomeness—Mom and apple pie…. You're what the girl next door grows up to be. To me, that's the finest thing any woman can achieve. That's why I didn't want a glossy high-fashion model. In fact, I wanted you to be the Nightstar girl so much that I didn't dare let my hopes be known. So I downplayed it, too much I'm afraid and even cruelly. I couldn't let anyone know how important you were. But Bill Valenti and Jacques began to suspect that day I barged in on that photo session and saw you with your wrapper dropped off your shoulders and the light playing off your silky skin…. I was jealous, protective—a fool."

Caren felt her heart beat a pace faster. He had said jealous…. "And because you didn't want anyone to know how important my being the Nightstar girl was you called me a sow's ear?" Caren asked, holding her breath for his answer.

"Exactly. Which leads me to Moira. I had no idea that she had tried to sabotage you with Jacques. And I now know that it was Moira who spilled the beans to the press at the film opening. I discovered it only recently. Moira and I go back a long way—all the way to college. I knew she was capable of some dirty tricks, but I never thought she'd stoop so low. Thankfully, Jacques saw his duty to the company, but only because he thinks the world of you, Caren. I've been wrong. I know it. For years I've allowed Moira to daydream about me and our relationship because I didn't think it serious enough to do anything about it. Moira was the best assistant a man could have—"

"Was?" Caren squeaked.

"Yes, was. Moira knew from the beginning how I felt about you, Caren, because I told her. Remember that night in your apartment when I stormed out on you? That was the night I told her. In fact, I thanked her later for calling when she did. I knew I loved you and I wanted you to have a chance to fall in love with me. I didn't want to do anything that would hurt that chance. But, damn it, woman, you are the most desirable, most loving, and giving—I almost lost control, almost took advantage of you. I'd been too used to getting what I wanted from a woman. I needed time to cool off and so—"

"There had never been anything between you and Moira?" Caren was surprised to find her voice so controlled, so level.

"Only in Moira's head, I'm afraid."

"But I overheard her with you in the garden beneath my hotel room. I saw you hold her—"

"I know what you heard and it was vicious and untrue."

"But I saw—"

"You saw me take her in my arms. I felt sorry for her. I had just told her the truth about how I really feel about you and that I was going to ask you to marry me. I had also just told her that I couldn't work with anyone who was so devious and caused so much pain. Especially when that pain and trickery was directed at the woman I love. And I do love you, Caren. More than words can say."

Splashing and frolicking like two children, they reveled in their newfound closeness. They were standing in waist-high water, and Caren's breasts were firm, their rosy crests erect and hard from the coolness of the pool. She saw Marc's eyes drift to them time and again, his pleasure evidenced by his sultry look.

Once he bent to grasp her knees and pull her down, the water closing over her head. Whooping for revenge, Caren splashed and tormented him by threatening to run from the pool.

Laughing, Marc captured her and threatened to dip her beneath the surface again. Screaming for mercy, Caren clung to him fiercely, her arms locked around his neck, her face pressed close to his. Suddenly time stopped, the birds were silent. Nothing and no one existed in the whole world, save the two of them—two lovers enraptured with each other and reveling in that private world that only those in love can enter.

Gently, he embraced her, cradling her head in one of his hands while the other supported her haunches. Backward, backward, he dipped her. Into her line of vision swept the treetops and the sky, which was darkening by the moment. Slowly, deliberately, he bent his head, beads of water shining on his dark hair. Closer and closer his mouth came to hers. Tighter and tighter became his hold on her, as if he were clinging to her, desperately cleaving to this moment of time, cherishing it, remembering it, burning it into his memory, searing it into his soul.

Caren knew in that moment, without a shred of doubt, that he would cherish her always. She, Caren, the woman she was; her soul, her mind, her body, not the facade in the Nightstar ads. Caren became his in that one gentle searching kiss, and she knew she could never belong to another.

"Not here, not now," Marc said huskily.

Caren smiled, understanding perfectly. Still, she felt compelled to ask, "When?"

"Later, beneath the first nightstar."

BEYOND TOMORROW

CHAPTER ONE

A SLATE GRAY evening sky accompanied by intermittent drizzles of a chill rain was characteristic of a bright July summer day in the resort community of Bar Harbor, Maine. The unrelenting drops fell into skips of puddles and flooded the gutters outside the low, one-story building at the far end of Main Street, staining the cedar shingles a muddy brown. It was nearing eight o'clock, a time when most of the businesses in town had closed for the day, but several lamps glowed from within, illuminating the mullioned windows and falling on the neatly lettered sign signifying "Andrews Realty."

Carly Andrews worked diligently at her desk, her soft, dark hair cloaking her delicate, patrician profile as she bent her head. The papers fluttered beneath her gracefully long fingers as she studied them, and they softly reflected the color of her azure-blue silk blouse. Long legs, clad in white linen slacks, crossed and uncrossed beneath the desk, and her shoeless feet habitually rubbed into the soft yellow pile carpeting. The entire office was tastefully furnished in muted pastel colors with bric-a-brac placed casually, but deliberately, on gleaming end tables. The whole effect was feminine and frilly, and Carly had often complained to her mother, whose taste the office reflected, that it was more like an eighteenth century boudoir than an efficient realty agency.

"It's a steal! A steal!" cried a raucous, ear-piercing voice. "No points! Mortgage!" the crackly voice continued to shout.

Carly cast a baleful eye in the parrot's direction and continued with her work. The parrot fluttered his green plumage and then tucked one foot under his wing.

"Quincy, go to sleep," Carly muttered in the bird's direction as she tilted the directoire lamp for better light. Lord, was she tired. What she didn't need right now was a talkative parrot.

"Darling, are you still at it? Tomorrow is another day. It's time we both went home and had some dinner. I'm sure the James couple will take the property." The elegant, pencil-slim woman patted her silver hair and pretended to scold. "All work and no play makes Jack a dull boy. We don't want that to happen to our Carly, do we, Quincy?" she cajoled the bird who was older than Methuselah and had been handed down through three generations of the Andrews family. There were times that Carly believed Quincy knew more secrets about the Andrews family and had more solid business sense locked up in his feathery little head than she would ever learn in a lifetime.

Carly put down her pencil and slumped in her high-backed chair. Her voice was patient when she spoke, as though she had had long years of practice, but it was also respectful and loving. "Mother, between you and Quincy I can't get anything done. First of all, I am not dull. Second, I had lunch at three-thirty and I'm not hungry right now. Third, I want to finish this contract this evening because I have a breakfast date with the Hollisters in the morning. I gave my word I'd have it ready for them. Why don't you go home? You've had a long day too and I know you're tired. And take this creature with you." She pointed her finger at the perch where Quincy spent most business days.

Melissa Andrews looked down at her daughter, a frown creasing her porcelain doll features. Her voice was slightly petulant when she replied, "Are you saying I have to eat alone? Sometimes, Carly, I think you do this deliberately."

Immediately, Carly was apologetic. Sometimes, she thought, things got to be too much for her and she became testy. Her tone softened.

"All right, if you insist on being maternal this evening, you can stop at the deli and get me a pastrami sandwich. I'll have it when I get home which should be within the hour."

Melissa placed her hands on her slim hips and clucked her tongue. "The deli is out of my way, darling. How about peanut butter and jelly? And a can of clam chowder? I declare, I positively envy your appetite and it never shows on your figure."

"Fine, Mother, peanut butter and jelly will be just fine. Skip the chowder. Don't forget to take Quincy with you. I'll be along soon."

"Carly, I can't take Quincy. He messes my upholstery. And," she added indignantly, "he flutters his wings when I stop for a light. People think I'm positively strange. You bring him with you," she directed, closing the front door behind her.

"Life is hell! War is hell! Squawk!" Quincy babbled to Melissa's departure.

"Now that you've almost exhausted your vocabulary, bird, why don't you go to sleep?" Carly snapped, throwing a cover over the bird's cage.

Ah, peace and quiet for a little while at least. She sighed deeply and propped her slim ankles on an open desk drawer. She leaned back in her chair and let her eyes scan the pages in front of her. All she really had to do was make a final check on her figures with the calculator and she could call it a night. Satisfied with the contract, Carly slid the pages into a folder and then stuffed it into her tote bag. Looking around the office, she had the feeling she was forgetting something. She shrugged. If she was, it would be a simple matter of returning to the office first thing in the morning before having breakfast with her clients. She knew she had done a fine job and the commission was going to be healthy. Time to go home to that peanut butter and jelly on toast.

Removing the throw from the bird's cage, she waited for the parrot to emerge and settle himself on her shoulder. Carly laughed as she bent beneath the desk to find her high-heeled sandals. She was laughing aloud at Quincy's antics as he nipped playfully and tickled her neck and ear. She emerged from her very unladylike position with her shoes in her hand in time to see a tall, muscular man and a high-cheekboned woman with an incredibly willowy figure enter her office. Carly blushed a brilliant crimson and moistened her dry lips. Quincy continued with his nudging and nipping.

The man's voice was brisk and cool, heavy with authority, but holding a warm note of graciousness. "Miss Andrews, I'm Adam Noble, and this is Simone Maddox."

The woman was stylishly dressed and perfectly coiffed, and succeeded in exuding poise and control from the tips of her scarlet painted fingers to the soles of her needle thin heeled shoes. From the looks of her finely arched brows and the slight, disdainful curl of her lip, it was evident that *she* would never be caught with her posterior in the air, groping beneath the furniture for her shoes. *And* with a shrill-mouthed bird flapping on her shoulder!

Carly nodded to acknowledge the introduction.

"I realize this is after business hours, but the door was open and your lights are on."

Simone Maddox pulled on Adam Noble's arm, "Don't be silly, Adam. No one in his right mind would turn away from a chance to do business with any of *the* Nobles." Her sharp glance rested on Carly, defying her to deny it.

Carly's jaw tightened. "You're correct, Mr. Noble, it is after business hours." They were all alike—the idle rich who came to Bar Harbor, Maine, to spend their summers while they waited expectantly for the new social season to open in the fall. Then they would flock to New York or London or Paris like mindless geese following an ancient migration route. But it was their haughty contempt of the Bar Harbor locals that so annoyed Carly. True, the little town did exist on the "summer people" trade and tourism, but it rankled her that they would take it for granted that she would stay after hours and then fall down on her knees just to serve one of the celebrated Nobles. "I'll be glad to discuss whatever it is you would like tomorrow during business hours. Shall I make an appointment for you?"

Carly's abrupt tone was not lost on the ravishing woman at Adam Noble's side.

"But, darling, you're just standing there with that…that…creature on your shoulder and holding your shoes. We really only want a few minutes of your time." While Simone Maddox's voice implored Carly to reconsider, her attitude made it clear she was unused to being denied.

"You've already had a few minutes of my time, and I'm late for an appointment. As I said, if you care to come back tomorrow, I'll make an appointment with you now. At that time you will have my undivided attention." Why was she behaving this way? Normally she wasn't rude. And why was her stomach churning like a windmill?

Adam Noble had the bluest eyes she had ever seen and they were staring right through her. From the look he was giving her, this must be some kind of first for him. People in Bar Harbor catered to the Nobles who accepted it as their due. Well, Carly Andrews didn't bow and scrape—to the Nobles or anyone else for that matter. It was clear Adam Noble didn't care for her abrupt rebuff, and it wasn't sitting well.

"My apologies, Miss Andrews. I just wanted to ask you about some property. If you aren't interested, I can go somewhere else."

"Life is hell! War is hell!" shouted Quincy as he left

Carly's shoulder and circled the room in a feather flap of wings and finally perched on the desk.

Carly bristled. "Perhaps you didn't hear me, Mr. Noble. I said I would be glad to discuss business with you tomorrow. If that doesn't interest you, then there's little I can do about it." Two rebuffs in one night. In the short span of a few minutes! Probably a new experience for him.

"She's not interested," Miss Maddox cooed. "Come, darling, we'll go to another agency. A place where people know the value of handling business for the Nobles."

An angry surge of adrenaline shot through Carly. It always came down to power and money. Walk softly and carry a big stick. Money was always the club. "Let's go, Quincy, time to go home." The parrot flew to her shoulder and settled himself.

"Miss Maddox, try Olsen Realty on Main Street. Mr. Olsen runs a very efficient business, when he's not out fishing. Now, if you'll excuse me, I really do have to leave."

Adam Noble moved almost imperceptibly so that he was standing directly in front of Carly. "My apologies, Miss Andrews, for assuming I didn't need an appointment. I'll call tomorrow, and perhaps we can set something up. And, Miss Andrews, don't you think you should put your shoes on? It's raining outside." He grinned, showing perfect white teeth. Miss Maddox giggled. Carly froze in her tracks.

"Good night to both of you," she managed to choke out. Adam Noble was staring at her and his blue gaze seemed to see much more, which made Carly uncomfortable.

To cover her confusion, Carly reached for Quincy and held him as the couple exited the office. Quickly, Carly lowered the shade on the front door and then locked it securely. She turned off the lights and left by the back door, her shoes still in her hand. The shock of the cold rain puddles made her gasp. It was a good thing her mother hadn't been around or she would be hearing about this for the next twenty years. Melissa Andrews' biggest moment in life would be to sell something to the Noble clan. Her mother had been wrong. Tonight, she had been anything but dull. Actually, she frowned, she had been downright obnoxious. She wasn't *that* tired. Would he come back to the office, and if he did, would Simone Maddox be with him? Adam Noble had a reputation for escorting elegant women and this one certainly was elegant.

THE ANDREWS' Cape Cod house looked warm and inviting after the chilly rain. The only thing Carly dreaded was her mother's habit of playing twenty questions when she arrived home. If she pretended to be tired, she just might be able to eat her sandwich and retire. She should be so lucky, she mused.

"Mummy dear, you look so ravishing," Carly laughed as she eyed the tissue wrapped hair and her mother's shiny face. "If your clients could see you now, what would they say?"

"They would say that I'm an indulgent mother. Look, I even put some pickles on your plate. Eat, before it gets cold."

"Mother, a peanut butter and jelly sandwich can't get cold and pickles come from the refrigerator. If that's the best you can do with your mothering, retire. Besides, I've been thinking, since we both hate housework and cooking, why don't we hire someone to come in for a few days a week? The agency is making enough money."

"I won't hear of it. I detest people prying and poking into my things. You wouldn't like it either, Carly. The answer is no. If you would find yourself a beau, you could dine out more often. Just look at you, Carly," Melissa said, forging ahead on her favorite subject. "You're as pretty as a picture, smart as a whip, you have a college degree, and you don't even have a boyfriend, much less a steady. You're twenty-three, Carly. Time is moving on and you know what they say about late starters."

"Can't you see that I'm a late bloomer, Mother? I

like my life the way it is. When and if the right man comes along, I'll know it. You don't want to become an interfering mother-in-law or a grandmother before your time. That's a fate worse than death, right?"

"I don't expect you to jump into anything, but for heaven's sake, Carly, you could at least get your feet wet."

"I did, Mother, I did," Carly said, at Melissa's puzzled look, as she thought of how she had gone barefoot in the rain puddles. "Never mind, it was a sort of joke."

"You're the prettiest girl in town and you know it. Just the other day Judge Noble was telling me he saw you out on the interstate, and he couldn't believe his eyes."

"The reason he couldn't believe his eyes was because I was changing a flat tire. He had his chauffeur stop to offer help but I was all finished."

"Well, he said you were the prettiest girl in town and those are his exact words. He also said he hoped Adam would look you up one of these days. The judge doesn't seem to care for the flashy women Adam has been squiring around. Adam is the catch of the season. And another thing," Melissa said, lowering her voice to a hushed whisper, "there's talk that Adam is going to run for the Senate. Aren't you going to say something?" Melissa demanded, annoyed at Carly's lack of enthusiasm.

"I'm sorry that the Noble clan doesn't interest me

as much as they do you, Mother. As far as I can see, all they do is throw their weight around and pretend they own the whole town. Adam and his brother Cayce are playboys, and the girls sit in the beauty shop and the spa all day. If you think that's a worthwhile life, then you're welcome to it. Society, Mother, is not all it's made out to be," Carly said tartly. She carried her plate to the sink and rinsed it. "I'm going to take a shower now and turn in. I have an early breakfast appointment. Good night, Mother." Instantly contrite over her tart tone to her mother, Carly turned and wrapped her arms around the slim woman. "Mom, you just have to stop trying to match me up with one of the rich men who vacation here. I'll find my own man when I'm ready. I'm happy, really I am. I know how you love the social set around here, and that's just fine for you. It's not fine for me."

"Oh, Carly, you haven't called me Mom since you were little. All right, all right, you live your life and I'll live mine. I'll cook Sunday dinner, how's that?"

"Fine, Mom. Now, let's hit the sack. We both have a busy day tomorrow."

"You go along, I'll lock up and turn off the lights," Melissa Andrews said with a hint of a tear in her eye. "Good night, Carly."

CHAPTER TWO

IT WAS three o'clock according to Carly's watch, and still Adam Noble hadn't made his promised call. Surely, he wouldn't just pop in again without an appointment, not after last night. Another half hour and they would close the agency until Monday morning. He had exactly thirty minutes to make his presence known, preferably without the seductive Simone Maddox in tow.

Carly turned back to her paperwork and the next time she looked at the square digital watch on her wrist, it read 3:58. The phone shrilled on her desk. Sighing, Carly picked it up. "Andrews Realty, may I help you?"

"Miss Andrews, this is Adam Noble." Carly swallowed and patted at her stomach to quiet the swarming butterflies. "I would like to make an appointment for the early part of next week. I'm here on vacation, so my time is my own. Make the appointment at your convenience."

"Just a moment, Mr. Noble, and let me see when

I'm free." Carly held the phone away from her ear and shuffled papers on her desk. She knew exactly what her schedule was for the next ten days. "Mr. Noble, I'm free Tuesday morning at eleven-thirty. Is that convenient for you?" Now, why had she said Tuesday instead of Monday? Monday was always a lost day in the real estate business. Nobody ever did anything on Mondays. Even Mr. Olsen didn't do business on Monday. Well, she was stuck with it now.

"Tuesday is fine with me. Would you care to have lunch with me?"

"Lunch would be fine, Mr. Noble." Why not? He probably plans to take it off his income tax, she thought snidely.

"Tuesday it is then. I'll pick you up at the office. Goodbye, Miss Andrews."

"Goodbye, Mr. Noble." They certainly were being polite with each other. She should take Quincy along just to aggravate him. Quincy would straighten him out in three seconds flat. What was wrong with her? Why did she feel she had to come out on top, to get the last word?

Why did she resent him so much? His whole family, for that matter. So, he was born with a silver spoon in his mouth. So what if he went to the best prep schools and the top-notch ivy league colleges? So what if he was tall and handsome? So what if she was jealous of all the slinky Simone Maddoxes? Did he ever work a day in his life? Did he ever do anything but drive a high-powered sports car and sail in one regatta after another, and when he was bored with that, jet off to Monte Carlo and the Riviera? Did she care? No way. The life of the idle rich would not play a part in her life. There was more to life than just breathing.

"Who was that on the phone, Carly?" Melissa asked as she prepared to lock up for the weekend.

"I made an appointment for Tuesday with a prospective client." No point in getting her mother all riled up. She planned to keep the name of her "new client" to herself for as long as possible. If she knew her mother, she would have Carly at the altar within three months, if not sooner.

The weekend passed in a blur. Carly played mixed doubles Saturday and dined at the club with a group of school friends, and on Sunday she brunched with one of her new clients who insisted they wanted to show their appreciation for the fine house Carly had found for them. Monday was maddeningly idle.

Tuesday morning dawned clear and bright as Carly made her way to the office. At the last minute she stopped at the Cottage Inn for a light breakfast. Normally, she just had orange juice and coffee, but today, she felt the need for something a little more substantial. She decided on a poached egg and an apricot danish.

As she drank her coffee, she took special pains not to slosh on her carefully selected outfit. She couldn't go to lunch with her "new client" with coffee and egg stains on her lilac shirt and beige skirt. The pastel of the lilac brought out the hidden blue lights in her ebony hair and did flattering things to her peaches-and-cream complexion. The traffic policeman at the intersection near the wharf had bestowed her an approving smile, and Carly knew she looked fresh and pretty. The day promised to be another hot one with the temperature reaching the high eighties, and with this prospect in mind, she had pulled her hair on top of her head and tied it with a bit of ribbon. A few stray curls escaped to frame her face and trim her long, graceful neck, enhancing her very feminine appearance.

Restlessly, she placed her coffee cup on its saucer and reached for her cotton crocheted handbag to pay her bill. Carly was ashamed of her rude and abrupt behavior toward Adam Noble and at lunch today she knew she must face up to it. In every sense of the word she knew that this was going to be a very long morning.

Somehow, Carly managed to fill in the time after breakfast by shuffling papers from one spot to the other. Melissa, sensing that all was not quite right in her daughter's life, tactfully said she was leaving the office to attend a political luncheon. Carly heaved a sigh of relief when she saw her mother's car leave the lot in back of the agency. Twice she yelled at Quincy who was babbling to himself because of neglect.

"You'd think this was a date or something," Carly muttered to the now sulky parrot. "I wonder if I look all right, not that he's going to notice." Carly frowned. She wondered what Adam Noble thought about freckles. The smattering across the bridge of her nose always bothered her. He probably wouldn't even notice.

A last quick look in her compact mirror and she was ready for anything and everything.

He was prompt; she had to give him that. He had appeared wearing finely tailored white slacks and an open necked shirt beneath a featherweight nautical blazer. A familiar style of dress for most of the Bar Harbor gentlemen who were lunching in town. In the evening most of the clubs demanded more formal dress.

"I thought we would go to the Whale and Porpoise if that's all right with you, Miss Andrews."

"That's fine with me," Carly volunteered.

Adam Noble held the door of the low-slung Mercedes sports coupe open for her. Carly jackknifed herself into the bucket seat and was surprised at the leg room the small car offered. Adam backed the car from the parking slot and drove effortlessly. He was a powerful man, almost as powerful as the car he was driving. Carly liked the fact that he was making small talk and so far had made no mention of the first meeting. If he was willing to start with a clean slate, then she could do the same. She had to admit that he was an impressive man. If only he wasn't such a playboy she might respect him more. Why couldn't he be doing something to earn a living? Such a waste. And where was the ravishing Simone? If only she could ask. But she would bite her tongue off before she did that.

"Here we are," Adam said, maneuvering the little car between two oversized sedans.

He was the perfect escort. He held open the door for her and helped her from the car, and then he held the door of the club open and bowed elaborately, a wide grin splitting his features. Carly grinned and curtsied.

The interior of the Whale and Porpoise was nautical from the entrance foyer to the back room with its fish nets and whaling hooks. The heavy round tables were bare except for place mats. A waitress deftly skirted the tables, holding a tray full of beer steins above her head. Carly liked the jaunty sailor caps the waitresses wore and the bell bottom trousers looked authentic.

Adam held her chair and immediately ordered beer, the Whale and Porpoise's only concession to liquid refreshment. The dark, German beer was just what Carly needed for her parched throat. She found herself admiring the way the heavy mug looked in Adam's strong, sun-bronzed hand. "I love this beer," Carly blurted suddenly.

"I do, too. Sometimes, I drop in here just for a drink. I've had beer the world over and this is by far the best. Unfortunately I have an appointment later on in the day, so I better get down to business. If you don't have any objection to talking while we eat."

"It's all right with me, Mr. Noble. Tell me what I can do for you," Carly said, drawing a small notebook and pen from her bag.

Adam Noble stared at her for a full minute before he replied and then it seemed to Carly he was unsure of what to say or else he changed his mind at the last second and was groping for a new thought. "If we're going to do business together, call me Adam. I believe your name is Carly."

Carly nodded.

"I'm interested in a home for myself. Something within a thirty mile radius of Bar Harbor."

"Mr....Adam, you have to start off by changing your wording a little. What you're looking for is a house. Only you can make it a home. Do you understand what I'm saying?"

"Perfectly." There was that strange expression on his face again, and his eyes were so dark, so deep, she felt she could drown in their depths. "I'm looking for a house. I would like a tennis court and a pool, if possible. If the property has neither, I'll still be interested if there's a possibility that I can have both a pool and court built. A fireplace is an absolute necessity. I want one in the family room and one in the master bedroom. I'll require plenty of closet space and a modern kitchen with every gadget that's ever been made. I like to cook."

"Do you really like to cook?" Carly asked in surprise.

"I enjoy it immensely. I'll tell you a secret if you promise never to tell. Did you ever hear of a restaurant in New York called Chez Martine?"

"I've heard of it, but I'm afraid that it's a little too expensive for me. I've heard that the food is magnificent, especially on the weekends."

Adam Noble's eyes danced. "That's because I'm the chef on the weekends. An old college buddy from Brooklyn owns the restaurant and I do private parties for him. Since I've closed my law office I find myself with extra time on my hands and I'm spending more and more of it at Chez Martine."

"That's wonderful!" Carly said exuberantly. "I'll save my money, and perhaps by the end of the summer, I'll be able to afford to dine in your restaurant."

"You'll have to let me know ahead of time so I can prepare something really special. I'll outdo myself," he said proudly. "Now, tell me, is there anything on the market that you think I might be interested in?"

"Offhand, several pieces of property come to mind. How many bedrooms and baths do you want? A one-car garage or two? Are you interested in buying furnishings or do you intend to decorate yourself?"

"At least four bedrooms. I plan to have a lot of kids someday. Same thing with the bathrooms. I'll have the place decorated myself. If it's a deal where the furnishings go with the house or it's a no sale, then I'll buy them. Two- or three-car garage. I have a lot of junk that I've managed to accumulate over the years."

Carly filled her page with scribbles and looked at Adam. "Why don't you just build the kind of house you want?"

"It wouldn't be the same. I want an old house that has seen life. I want old timber, not new green wood. I don't care for chrome and glass and aluminum siding. I want character and white birch trees. Hundreds of them. I want a lawn that has to be mowed, not manicured with a pair of scissors. I want leaves in the fall and buds in the spring. I need a space for a garden so I can grow my herbs. I have some now in small planters, but again, it's not the same. When can you let me know what's on the market?"

"How about tomorrow?"

"That's great, Carly."

"When would you want to move in, assuming that I have something that fits your needs?"

Adam's features closed and his lips tightened. "I'm not sure. You can handle the sale, and whatever time the closing is scheduled for is all right with me. I'm sorry I can't be more definite right now."

"How did you want to finance the property? How much do you want to put down and what's your price range?"

"If you find the right piece of property, money is no object. There's no need for financing. I'll be paying cash. Whatever you need for a deposit will be all right with me."

Carly grimaced. The comfort of money. "You are a most agreeable client, Adam."

Adam grinned. "I do try to please. I'm afraid we got off to a bad start the other night. I was sort of hoping you'd agree to have dinner with me this weekend. To make amends," he added hastily as he saw her hesitate.

"I'd like that, Adam."

"Fine, I'll pick you up Saturday night at seven. Now that our business seems to be taken care of, what do you say we enjoy our lunch and get to know one another? I think I'd like to know you better, Carly Andrews."

And I think I would like to know you better, Adam Noble, Carly said to herself. She smiled and speared a succulent shrimp. This was definitely one of her better days.

CHAPTER THREE

CARLY worked industriously the rest of the day poring over new listings. From there she delved into a list of properties she had been compiling over the past two years of possibilities. Possibilities which required a personal call to the homeowner on her part. This was the one part of real estate that she hated. Knocking on strange doors, asking people if they wanted to sell their houses, was not something she enjoyed. For some reason she took each no as a direct slap against her salesmanship. She knew she wasn't being realistic, but she couldn't help herself. Canvassing was the first rule of thumb for any successful real estate office.

Her dark eyes scanned the new listings a second time. They were all small clapboard houses with no real property to speak of. Adam Noble wouldn't be interested in any of them with the exception of one possibility, and it was slim at best.

Carly glanced at the office clock. If she hurried, she could call the owner and take a quick run out to

Orchard Lane and take a look at the twelve-room house that her mother had listed just a week ago. Melissa had a way of making a shack sound like the house of one's dreams. Her eyes scanned the printed form that listed the acreage of the property. It sounded good, certainly room enough for a pool and tennis court. Landscaped by a professional. Country kitchen. That should please Adam. A smile tugged at the corners of Carly's mouth. Adam. The name pleased her. The man himself intrigued her. Did she please him? Or was that interest he showed her at the restaurant merely courtesy on his part? Did she, for that matter, want his interest to be anything other than that?

"I think it's time to call it a day," her mother called from behind the real estate section of the paper she was scanning.

"It's all right with me, Mother. I think I'll take a ride out to the Barlow property you listed last week and take a look around. I think I might have a buyer for it. Actually, I should have said possible buyer. How much of this write-up is frosting, Mother? Is the place as good as it sounds?"

"Carly, for shame! It's everything I wrote down on the form. Of course, it needs some work," she added hastily at Carly's suspicious look.

"How much work, Mother? In terms of money, how much?" Carly asked tartly.

"Five, maybe seven thousand. Who can say? It depends on who is doing the buying and what they want to change," Melissa answered airily.

"Let me put it to you another way, Mother. If I was the one who was considering the purchase of this property, how much would I have to pay for improvements to make the house livable?"

"Darling, you have such plebeian tastes. You wouldn't change a thing. You adore all that rustic rusty nonsense."

"I guess that means the place is falling down," Carly snapped. "Now, why didn't you just tell me that in the beginning, and you could have saved us both aggravation."

"I'm not aggravated, darling. You're the one who is aggravated," Melissa said checking her makeup in a tiny compact. "You've been in this business enough to know you have to gild the lily a little. Go out and check it out yourself. It's a handyman's dream, and the price is…"

"Utterly ridiculous," Carly shot back, annoyed with her mother's airy words.

"Is it my fault that the Barlows want to retire to Paradise Island and run a charter fishing outfit? I didn't set the price, they did."

"You certainly didn't discourage them, did you?"

"Good heavens, no. After all, I would like the highest possible commission. Darling, properties like the Barlows' don't fall into your lap every day. Foresight is what's called for here on the part of the buyer."

"Foresight!" Carly exclaimed.

"Somewhere, some place, there is someone who is just waiting to see the Barlow property, and that someone will think it's the house of his dreams. I personally guarantee it."

Carly gave up and settled back in her chair. It didn't pay to argue with her mother. "Okay, I'll close up and see you later. I am going to call the Barlows and stop by on my way home. Don't wait dinner for me."

"I won't. I'm just going to pop a potpie into the microwave for myself and, darling," she called over her shoulder, "stretch that seven thousand to ten." The door closed behind her with a curt slam that set Carly's teeth on edge.

"Motheeerrr," Carly groaned aloud. The last comment told her she shouldn't even bother making the trip to the Barlows'. Still, she didn't have anything else to do so why not stop by? At least she could see with her own eyes what condition the property was in. If the Barlows had any kind of business acumen, they might be willing to make some improvements themselves to entice a buyer to meet their price. Paradise Island, no less, she sniffed to herself, deciding to cancel the whole idea. What she really wanted was to go home. Take off her shoes, relax in a hot tub. Slamming her desk drawer shut and covering her typewriter, she decided that was exactly what she would do.

A WRINKLED apple in one hand and her briefcase in the other, Carly headed for her room to draw that hot bath.

Submerged in the fragrant, steamy water, she let her mind wander back to her lunch with Adam Noble. He certainly was a handsome man, a powerful man with great magnetism. And she had been completely wrong about him. He did do more than just breathe. During their lunch he had told her that until recently he had held a position as a public defender and had maintained a small law practice. Since abandoning those projects he was now busy making contacts helpful toward a political career and learning the ins and outs of campaigning.

With his background and family connections he was a natural to run for the seat in the Senate. And she would bet her last dollar that he would win. People like Adam, who had his charisma, always came out on top. She would probably vote for him herself.

He hadn't actually told her why he wanted such a large house. Was he planning on getting married? The thought was disconcerting. She wasn't certain she liked the idea of knocking herself out to look for just the right house so he could share it with some other woman.

"Bells ringing! Bells ringing!" Quincy screeched as he fluttered into the bathroom and then out.

"I hear it, I hear it," Carly yelled as she stepped from the bath and wrapped herself in a lime-green terry robe. She dabbed at the perspiration on her forehead with her sleeve as she padded downstairs to the front door. Melissa must have forgotten her key as usual, or else she was too lazy to dig in her purse to find it. She caught sight of her hair piled in a topknot on her head in the foyer mirror as she opened the door. Quincy lighted on her shoulder and blended with the lime robe. "Life is hell! War is hell!" he babbled as Carly tried to shake him loose.

Carly's eyes widened. Oh, why me? Why now? Adam Noble stood framed in the doorway, Simone at his side.

There was a smile in his eyes as he stared at the girl in the doorway. "This will take but a moment. Late this afternoon a friend of mine told me the Newsome house is due to go up for sale in a few days. I thought if you went out there ahead of the other Realtors we might be able to work something out. I apologize for coming by, but I thought you might want to get an early start in the morning."

Carly swallowed hard, aware of how she must look compared to Simone Maddox who looked as though she had just stepped from the pages of the latest *Vogue* magazine.

"Fine, fine," she mumbled. "I'll look into it in the morning. Tha…thank you for stopping by to tell me."

"We thought you would be interested," Simone said coyly as she tightened her grip on Adam's arm. It was clear she felt she had nothing to fear from Carly in her lime green robe and perspiring face. "Your bird is adorable. Does he fly south in the winter?"

"Only if he has a reservation at the Fontainebleu," Carly snapped. Her tart tone went unnoticed by the woman who tugged at Adam's arm.

"We'll be late, darling, and you know how the judge gets upset if I don't play at least one game of chess with him before he retires for the night." She inclined her head in Carly's direction and tugged again on Adam's arm. He seemed about to say something and Carly waited. Instead, he smiled warmly, apologized again and walked into the darkness with his companion.

Carly closed the door and seethed with anger. It was *her* idea, Carly knew it; she could feel it. She was a witch. Somehow, she knew I'd be in this tacky robe, looking like a ragamuffin, and that's why she had him stop by. So he could compare. She snorted indignantly, what comparison? "You're right, Quincy, life is hell," she snarled as she made her way back upstairs.

At least part of her question was answered. The woman was right at home with the Noble family if she played chess with the judge every night. Was she staying in the Noble mansion? Was she engaged to Adam Noble? Prospective daughters-in-law would definitely play chess with a prospective father-in-law. Though Simone looked as though she didn't have a brain in her head. She also probably cheated or deliberately let the judge win so she could ingratiate herself within the family. She was a tricky one all right. Melissa would have seen through her in a minute and put her in her place. There was no doubt about it; she had been upstaged by an expert. Well, there was upstaging and there was upstaging. The next round would be hers, she would see to it.

Carly seethed and fumed the rest of the evening and only cooled down when she heard her mother's key in the lock. Then she dived beneath the covers and turned off the light. Her dreams were fitful, filled with ravishing-looking women chasing Adam Noble along the bay. She was not one of the parade of women. She was standing on the sidelines with tears streaming down her cheeks. Her mother was behind her waving a chessboard overhead, screeching that if she had only learned to play chess she could be one of the chasing women.

CARLY woke instantly. For a moment she felt disoriented and puzzled. She never woke before the alarm next to her bed shrilled. She knew something was about to happen, she didn't know how she knew, she just knew. When the phone next to her bed rang, she caught it on the first ring. "Hello," she said cautiously, stealing a peek at the clock near the phone. Five a.m.!

"Miss Andrews, this is Adam Noble. I apologize for calling at this ungodly hour, but I was wondering if you would be interested in viewing a sunrise with me. I know it's a bit early and that I woke you, and I do apologize."

Carly was stunned. View a sunrise with Adam Noble! And he apologized for waking her! Cool, she had to play it cool. "I'd like that very much, Mr. Noble."

"Would you really?" he asked in a surprised voice. "I debated calling you and then I said to myself, Carly looks like the kind of gal who likes to see a sunrise. I want to take you to a favorite spot of mine. I'll pick you up in ten minutes. Can you be ready?"

"It's no problem. I adore sunrises and sunsets. I'm always up at this time of day," Carly fibbed, "and, yes, I can be ready in ten minutes."

"Good, I'll be the guy in the red car, standing in front of your house. I'll see you in ten minutes then. And, Carly, you promised to call me Adam."

"I'll be waiting, Adam," Carly said happily into the phone.

A streak of lightning had nothing on Carly as she threw on her clothes and quickly washed and brushed her teeth. She was running a comb through her hair as she ran down the stairs. She was tapping her foot on the driveway when Adam Noble skidded to a stop. He leaned across the seat to open the door for her, and Carly slid into the bucket seat. She grinned. "I don't know why, but I feel as though I'm playing hooky or something."

Adam laughed, a full rich sound that delighted Carly. "It goes with getting up early and watching the sun come up. It's my favorite time of day. What's your favorite time of day, Carly?"

She wanted to say any time as long as you figure in the time span, but she didn't. "I think I like sunsets the best. Have you ever been to Key West?" At Adam's nod, she continued. "I'm not that well traveled, but I think that the Keys have the most gorgeous sunsets I've ever seen. There's a sort of peacefulness about viewing a sunset. It's the end of the day, that kind of thing," Carly finished lamely. She should have said she preferred sunrises.

Adam laughed again. "How did you like the Keys?"

"Fantastic," Carly exclaimed. "I took the tour through Ernest Hemingway's house. I don't think I would want to live there with the only water supply coming from that one pipe though. And that bridge! The less said about it the better."

Adam frowned. "Do you have some kind of fear about water?" Adam asked, a strange note in his voice.

"No, not really, why do you ask?"

There was a relieved note in Adam's tone. "Because I'm taking you for a ferry ride to see something special; at least, it's special to me. If we luck out and catch the first ferry, we'll make it to land just as the sun comes over the horizon."

"Where are we going?"

"To a special place as I said. It's no secret really. Everyone hereabouts knows that the Sinclaires have the most beautiful piece of property in these parts. Martha Sinclaire is my godmother and from the time I was a small boy that house was a second home to me. I even have my own set of keys," he said, pointing to the dashboard. "Hop out, we're here. Looks like we'll be the only passengers," Adam said cutting the engine.

Carly hopped out as she was told and was suddenly overcome with shyness when Adam took her hand in preparation to running toward the ferry. How warm and strong his hand felt. A sudden overwhelming sense of freedom coursed through her as she gripped his hand to show that she was aware of him and the closeness they were sharing.

Aside from the helmsman and pilot the ferry was desolate as it prepared for its initial run of the day across the bay. It serviced the small community of Deer Island and brought commuters over to the mainland where they worked. Later in the day two more trips would be made before the final voyage at nine o'clock. There would be an hour and a half layover at the island so Carly knew it would be after seven-thirty before she arrived back in Bar Harbor.

The ride on the ferry took nearly half an hour as they chugged across a metallic gray inlet of the bay over to Deer Island whose lush green grasses and gentle hills rose about the blue Atlantic and saved for itself a gull's eye view of the bluffs of Bar Harbor. Early morning sea birds, intent on finding breakfast, swooped and played in the eddies of wind created by the churning prop. Their voices were mournful and melodious, breaking the quiet of the new day just as they broke the gray of morning and the first light glinted off their outspread wings.

Adam led Carly from the ferry landing, tugging on her arm. "Hurry. Come on. We have to run. We just have a few minutes."

Carly nodded and started off on a sprint, glad she had worn blue jeans and sneakers. She ran beside the long-legged Adam and was winded by the time they reached a small rise at the end of the Sinclaires' property. Adam was breathing evenly and grinning at the same time. "City girl," he teased, as he turned her to face the eastern sky, standing behind her, his hands placed lightly on her shoulders.

It was a long moment before he spoke, and when he did, his tone was hushed. His lips were so near to her ear that Carly started. "When I watch the sun come up, I wish I was a writer, but I still don't think I could ever describe the mysteries or the colors of dawn."

"That's because you're trying to describe your emotions, not the colors."

Adam turned her around and looked down into her face, that strange, mysterious expression making shadows in his indigo eyes. His voice was husky when he spoke. "You're right, you're absolutely right. All these years I've wanted to describe what a sunrise from this spot on Deer Island was like, and I've never found the words."

Carly heard a kind of wonder and understanding in his tone, and it sent shivers up her spine. His hand tilted her chin upwards so she could look into the indigo depths of his eyes, and she saw herself reflected there. And deeper, much deeper, beyond the shadows and light, was an emotion that seemed to steal her breath away. Gently, he enfolded her in his arms, drawing her nearer, blocking out all awareness of beauty around them. He filled her gaze and became her world. And when his lips touched hers, it was softly, so softly, and she could have wondered if she were imagining that this was happening if it were not for the strong, un-yielding strength of his embrace and the stir of emotions and dizzy soaring of her heart.

As the sun crept over the horizon and shed its

golden light over them, Adam's lips warmed hers, igniting in her a desire she had never known she possessed. And she basked in that light, felt it reflected in her. Higher and higher, he took her with him, like the sun on its endless journey across the sky, bursting forth in celestial splendor until the fires within her blazed beside his own.

When he released her, she was lost, abandoned, cold, feeling as though the daylight had been stolen from her. But when she looked into his eyes once again, she saw the embers of a fire banked and glowing, ready to explode once again if she would only step into his arms. Struggling for control of her emotions, she murmured, "You're missing the sunrise, Adam." His name came so easily to her lips. The lips where the burning impression of his kiss still lingered.

Adam smiled, a rich, warm smile that made Carly smile in return. Suddenly, Adam threw back his head and laughed, the laugh that delighted Carly. "I guess you know we missed the sunrise. I brought you all the way out here to see a sunrise and we missed it." He looked at his watch. "All we have time for now is a walk through the gardens, and then I have to get back to town. I wish you could see the inside of the house, but it's impossible. Perhaps, another time."

"I'd like that, Adam. If the inside is anything like

the outside, I know why you love this place and it's special to you."

"You have no idea how special this place really is. My mother died when I was five years old. Martha Sinclaire was a surrogate mother to me. It seems I ferried over here every day of my life until I left for college. I think I would sell my soul to own this place; that's how much it means to me."

"Do you think they'll ever sell it?" Carly asked.

"There have been rumors that that is what they're planning. If it ever does go up for sale, I would buy it in a second."

"I'm sure that if the property ever does go on the market, you're the first person the Sinclaires will think of," Carly said in a consoling tone.

"Not likely, Carly. Malcolm Sinclaire and my father had a disagreement a few years back and haven't spoken a word since. I tried to be fair about the matter but found myself siding with my father. Malcolm has a tendency to be stiff-necked. He knows how fond I am of Martha, his wife. Him, too, for that matter. If this house ever does go on the market, Malcolm will do it through an agency. That's the way he does things. At that point I would have to be there, johnny-on-the-spot, that kind of thing. Fortunately, he hasn't allowed his pride to prompt him to forbid my seeing Martha but I'm afraid even that has become an uncomfortable situation for both of us. Martha is unbendingly loyal to her husband. Someday, I hope the situation will be rectified; until then, I'll just have to wait."

Carly giggled. "Adam Noble, you have nothing to worry about. My mother plays bridge with Martha Sinclaire, and if there's one thing you can say about my mother, she's johnny-on-the-spot when it comes to listing properties. I think it's safe to promise you first crack at the deal if it ever happens."

Adam sighed as he led Carly around the rock garden. "Anything else would always be second best. This is what I want—where I belong. I can't explain it any other way."

"You don't have to. I understand. You feel it's part of you, part of your childhood, your youth. Part of your life. You've come full circle now, and you want to put down your roots. It's understandable that you would come to the place that has made you the happiest."

Adam stopped in midstride and turned to face Carly. His face wore the same expression it had back on the atoll. "What you said, just now, it's true. I have come full circle."

Carly felt herself begin to tremble. Was he going to kiss her again? She swallowed hard as Adam's eyes bored into hers. "Did...did I say...say something wrong?" she asked in a tight little voice.

"On the contrary. You said something very right. Come, we have to get back. We'll come here again, I promise you that."

CHAPTER FOUR

CARLY spent the balance of the day in a near daze. She couldn't believe the moments she had spent with Adam on Deer Island. The kiss, the closeness, the wanting to learn more about him.

From time to time Melissa looked at her and shook her head. It was simply amazing how much busywork Carly could find when something was either troubling her or was going so well that she was afraid that her own personal "jinx" would rise and spoil it all.

Melissa's close scrutiny did not go unnoticed by Carly. Right now, this very second, her mother was dying to know more about her early morning trip with Adam Noble. How could she talk about it so soon when it was something she wanted to keep to herself and cherish? To hold it close like in her childhood days when she found a treasure she wanted to savor alone. Now wasn't the time to confide in Melissa.

Carly knew she was doing busywork by filling out forms, straightening out files, watering plants and emptying trash. Repeat phone calls to follow up work could also be classified as busywork. All of it contrived to keep her moving, to keep her from thinking. What she really wanted to do was to lean back in her chair and recapture the moments with Adam.

Melissa frowned, uncertain if she should speak to Carly. As the dreamy expression on her daughter's face brought a smile to her lips, she went back to her own tedious job of sorting through three months of bank statements.

The phone, when it rang, seemed to be muted and come from far away. Without wasted motion, she reached out for the receiver. "Andrews Realty."

"Carly, Adam. I realize this is short notice but I was wondering if you would like to take a ride out to the Fisherman for Maine lobster and sourdough biscuits."

Carly's arm tingled as she held the receiver to her ear. Just the sound of his voice did strange things to her. Her voice was nearly breathless when she replied. "I'd like that very much, Adam." Out of the corner of her eye she watched a smile play across Melissa's face. Good mother that she was, it was evident that for once she wasn't going to ask any questions.

"Good, I was hoping you'd say 'yes.' If it's all right with you, I'll pick you up at the office. All I ask is that you bring a hearty appetite with you. I understand that the smallest lobster is something close to three pounds.

And as you know, the biscuits are made on the hour and they're hot and dripping with butter."

Carly laughed. How deep his voice was, how sure and confident. Again, she felt the breathlessness coming over her. This was exactly the way she had felt when she was in the eighth grade and had a crush on the football hero of the junior high. Swallowing hard, she forced herself to relax. "I think I can promise that I'll have a very hearty appetite. You're talking about two of my favorite foods."

"Six o'clock then?"

There was a catch in her voice when she answered. "Fine."

"Carly?"

"Yes?"

"I'm not a very wordy person as you must have noticed this morning. I want you to know that I enjoyed missing the sunrise with you."

"Hmm," was all Carly could dare with Melissa hanging on every word. "Six o'clock then. I'll be ready and so will my appetite. That's a warning."

Adam chuckled. "That's all I ask. See you later."

Carly replaced the phone. It wasn't until moments later that she realized she hadn't said good-bye. A nervous giggle erupted in her throat. She felt lightheaded with the knowledge that in just a short time she would be sitting next to Adam. They would dine together and after that, as in true romantic fiction they would walk along the rocky strip of beach. It was almost one of the requirements of the Fisherman. Leisurely cocktails, gourmet salad bar and then the serious business of devouring the specialty of the house; Maine lobster and sourdough biscuits. The patrons were left with no other choice but to walk off the calories. It was standard fare for the patrons of the Fisherman and one or two of Carly's old friends had admitted that the intimate strolls along the beach had direct bearing on their engagements to the men of their choice.

"Going out, darling?" Melissa asked casually as she folded the hateful bank statements that refused to balance according to her records.

Carly couldn't help herself. A wide grin split her face. "Adam Noble invited me to dinner. He's picking me up at six."

"That's nice, Carly, have a nice time. Make certain he follows the tradition of the Fisherman and takes you for a walk along the beach."

"Mother, who said anything about going to the Fisherman?"

"You didn't have to. It's the nicest restaurant in town and where else would Adam Noble take you? I hear the smallest lobster is three pounds. Darling, whatever you do, don't eat the whole thing. It's so tacky to see women digging into a lobster the way men do. Try to be dainty. I'm not saying you're sloppy, Carly, it's just that you have to wear the bibs and the drawn butter does dribble. Your fingers get all messy and you constantly have to use those little wet cloths. Not ladylike at all." Melissa pursed her lips to show her disapproval. Even though she dearly loved fresh lobster she would never subject herself to wearing a bib in public or wiping her hands on what she called little wet pieces of paper.

"Oh, I will mother. Don't worry about me. I intend to dive into that lobster and I'll eat each and every morsel savoring it to the fullest. If I should look tacky I won't let it bother me. After all, the main purpose of going to the Fisherman is to indulge. I'm certain that Adam will be too busy savoring his to notice me. I know how to behave in public," Carly assured Melissa, "you did bring me up with all the proper manners."

Melissa preened at the compliment. She really had done a good job with Carly. Actually, the job must have worked out better than she had even suspected if Adam Noble was interested in her little girl. He had a reputation for dating only the most glamorous society girls. She sniffed. Carly could hold her own anywhere once she made up her mind to it. "Darling, just enjoy the evening. If you want to gorge, then do so, by all means."

"I intend to," Carly answered brightly. "Go along now and take care of Quincy. I can finish up here. I'll even go over those bank statements for you. Adam is picking me up here at the office so I might as well keep busy until he gets here."

"Carly, you are a darling child. I thought you'd never ask. I left the statements in the drawer for you. I never saw such a hodgepodge of numbers. Sometimes banks are so unreasonable. Now, you enjoy yourself and don't be late. Tomorrow is a working day." With an airy wave of her slender hand, Melissa was gone, her perfume lingering in the office.

Carly sighed. It was nice to be alone. She had an hour to kill before Adam picked her up. First, she would freshen up and apply some casual makeup for evening wear and then she would get down to the bank statements. In a way, it would be a welcome relief to really concentrate on something important. This way, she couldn't keep thinking about Adam and the morning sunrise.

Deftly, Carly applied fresh blusher to her high cheekbones. A slight smidgin of charcoal liner and just a dab of eye shadow. She stood back to see the effect. Just a trace more mascara and some lip gloss. Thank heavens she had dressed with extra care this morning after she had returned from Deer Island. Almost as if she had had a premonition of this evening. More like wishful thinking, she told herself.

The mulberry sheath with contrasting orchid belt set

off her slim figure to perfection. A golden expanse of leg flashed as the linenlike fabric parted at the knee. It was dressy, yet casual. She felt satisfied as she straightened the slim gold chain at her neck, her only concession to jewelry aside from the gold circlet on her wrist.

The only thing missing now was a dab of perfume behind each ear and again at the base of her throat. She searched through her purse and found the tiny vial of Balmain perfume she always carried with her for an occasion like this.

The door opened suddenly while Carly was frowning at her mother's penciled numbers. A look of exasperation crossed her pretty face. She was so engrossed in trying to decipher the figures Adam Noble had to speak twice before she heard him.

Quickly, she gathered up the statements into a neat pile and then shoved them into the drawer. The deep indigo eyes were making her feel strange again, washing her over with an almost uncontrollable desire to fling herself into his arms. "I really am sorry. I was so engrossed in what I was doing I didn't hear you come in." Thank goodness simple words could take the edge off her emotions.

He smiled to show he understood. Suddenly, she felt comfortable with him again, just like during the early morning hours they had spent together. The breathless tight feeling in her chest was gone. One smile from him and she felt like a new woman. The only woman, in Adam Noble's eyes.

The short ride to the Fisherman was made with small talk. Adam had a keen wit and Carly laughed as he expounded on some of his childhood exploits with his brother Cayce.

The interior of the Fisherman was dim. Wide lengths of fishnets hung from the open beams with starfish attached to the netting. Japanese floats sparkled, reflecting the light from the lanterns.

A stunning hostess in a trim sailor suit greeted Adam with a warm smile that embraced Carly at the same time. "Please follow me and watch your step. It's rather dim in here until you get used to the lighting."

Carly followed the hostess's sure-footed stride with Adam following. A hanging fishnet that made each booth private was parted for Carly to enter. As always, when coming to the Fisherman she marveled at the beauty of the pewter serviceware and the subtle gleam of the silver. The tiny hurricane lamp with its miniature candle danced in the slight breeze the fishnet made when closing. How intimate this setting was. How nice of Adam to suggest it.

Settling back into the softness of the leather booth Carly let her gaze lock with Adam's for a moment. It was impossible to feel so drawn to a man so quickly, she told herself, yet that was exactly what was happening. A strange, new emotion was kindled within her, a yearning, a kind of hunger, a hunger that all the Maine lobster in the world would never satisfy. A warm flush stained her cheeks as Adam gazed into her eyes. Just then, the waitress arrived for their cocktail order.

"A banana daiquiri," she said to Adam.

"I'll have Scotch on the rocks and a banana daiquiri for the lady."

How husky his voice was, how sensual. Damn, here she was letting her emotions and her attraction for the man run away with her again. She should come down to earth instead of sitting opposite him smiling into space.

"You're beautiful in the candlelight, Carly. I've been remiss in complimenting you. You look lovely this evening."

Carly blushed prettily. Compliments always threw her off her stride. But she remembered Melissa's advice. Turn the compliment around, accept it graciously. "Thank you, Adam. How nice of you to say so."

His voice had been sincere, warm and flattering. Interested. Was it possible that he was as attracted to her as she was toward him?

The drinks arrived. Noiselessly, the fishnet separated. Conversation was suspended as the glasses were placed in front of them. The waitress stepped back waiting for them to sample the drinks. Adam nodded his approval and looked at Carly who nodded. "Delicious," she said. Discreetly, the waitress withdrew, leaving them alone once again. Conversation was easy as they commented on the season, the various restaurants and the gaggle of tourists that invaded their habitat of Bar Harbor each year.

"I hate to move but I guess if we want to eat we're going to have to go into the dining room and choose our lobsters and tackle the salad bar. There's no hurry, but I warn you, I'm a starving man. Take pity on me, Carly. Finish your drink and follow me."

Once more the lacy netting parted and Adam stepped aside for Carly to make her way to the lobster trough. With great deliberation, Adam scrutinized each and every lobster that moved crankily in the swirling water. He finally selected one, saying it was an exemplary specimen and waited for Carly to make her choice. Satisfied that she had picked one to equal his own, he cupped her elbow in his hand and led her to the elaborately arranged salad bar.

Carly bypassed the standard garden vegetables and concentrated on the clams on the half shell, deviled crab and plump, pink shrimp. Adam followed suit adding only real bacon bits to his small helping of garden salad. Conversation was animated as they devoured the tender seafood. "Carly," Adam said suddenly, "is it possible for you to take the afternoon off tomorrow?" Not waiting for a reply, he rushed on.

"I'd like you to come out to the house for lunch and some fun. My brothers are all in town, which is a rarity in itself. We so rarely find ourselves under the same roof that when we do, it's cause for celebration. The judge, now that he's older, lives for these little get-togethers. What do you say, think you can arrange it?"

Carly was stunned. He was actually inviting her to his home to meet his family. Melissa always said that when a man took a girl home it meant he was interested in pursuing the relationship. "I don't see why not. I more or less got caught up with my work yesterday. I'd like to meet your family, Adam."

"That's good. It's settled then. I'll pick you up a little after noon. Wear old clothes and we'll make a day of it. Lunch is always very informal. As a matter of fact, you really need a long arm to leave the table with any food under your belt when everyone is home. Shyness is equated with starvation, around the Noble home. My brothers live to eat. Just like me," he smiled. "It might be a little tough for you to adjust to their exuberance but they all mean well. And children, I hope you're crazy about children because there's a herd of them around our place just now and we all think they're important enough to deserve all the attention they demand…." His voice was soft, even a little shy as he gazed at her. "I just wanted to warn you about what you're getting yourself into if you join the Noble clan for the afternoon. I guess I've done a good job of scaring you away."

Excitement gripped Carly. "I'm an only child. I remember growing up wishing I had a dozen brothers and sisters. I know I'll enjoy meeting your 'clan' as you call them. And thank you for inviting me. I'm looking forward to it. Casual clothes, right?"

"Right. Jeans and sneakers. A windbreaker in case the afternoon cools off. I hear a storm is brewing south of us. Trust me, I know at times I seem overpowering to you. Being the youngest of all my brothers I had to yell the loudest, fight the hardest and be the best to get any kind of notice at all. I guess I haven't really outgrown all those childhood traits. Not faults, just traits," he teased.

In that one moment Carly felt closer to him than she had in the time she had known him. How dear he was. How wonderful he made her feel just being with him and listening to him talk. He could recite nursery rhymes and she knew she would still think he was the most interesting man she had ever met. Her mind and heart soared with a new elation that was washing over her. A tiny niggle of apprehension tried to warn her; too quick, too fast. Slow down, Carly. Adam Noble was the big leagues. She was Carly Andrews, little league.

"It's nice to meet someone who isn't perfect. Wait, let me revise that. Nice to meet someone who admits to being imperfect," she teased.

"And you, Carly. What about you? What do you want out of life?"

"Oh, I don't know. I think I've been in some kind of holding pattern or at least, that's what my mother tells me. For now I'm doing a job that I like and doing it to the best of my ability. I like to think I take care of my mother and then there's Quincy who somehow or another got to be my sole responsibility. He does keep me hopping and at the same time he's great company. I guess that more or less sums up Carly Andrews and just in time. Here come our lobsters." Was she imagining it or did Adam seem disappointed? Whatever the expression was in his eyes, it was too short-lived to put a name to it.

"I've been waiting for this all day," Adam said gleefully as he allowed the waitress to attach an oversized paper bib with a large red lobster printed on the front around his neck. "Don't say it," he laughed as the waitress turned to Carly and shook out the folded bib. "Don't say how cute I look."

"I won't," Carly promised, "not unless you tell me first."

The waitress laughed saying, "Enjoy your dinner. If you want anything else, just press the buzzer at the side of the table."

Adam nodded as he turned the lobster around on his plate trying to decide if he should attack the claws or the tail first. His eyes danced with laughter as he watched Carly do the same thing. "You look like a little cherub sitting there."

Carly couldn't help it, she burst out laughing. "I was thinking you look like an overgrown baby waiting for his mother to tell him it's okay to dig in." They looked at each other, happy, contented, excited.

It was one of the most enjoyable evenings Carly had ever spent. While Adam paid the check she skipped off to the powder room to repair her makeup. Not wanting to delay the walk on the beach that she was certain was forthcoming, she made her way to the front of the restaurant that was jam-packed with diners who hadn't had the foresight to make a reservation. Adam's eyes seemed to light at the sight of her.

"What do you say to a walk along the beach?"

"I'll have to take my shoes off," Carly told him, looking down at her spike heeled shoes.

"So will I," he confided. "We'll walk along the mud flats. Away from the rocks. You can't eat at the Fisherman and not take your girl down to the beach. And you can't abandon a tradition as old as time itself."

"Fine, I get the message," Carly giggled as she slipped out of her thin heeled slippers. Gallantly, Adam reached for them and stuck one in each of his pockets. "Does that make you feel like Cinderella?"

"Of course. But I promise I don't turn into a

pumpkin at midnight. At the stroke of twelve I'm still Carly Andrews."

They held hands as they walked along the hard mud flats, the wet, dark brown sand seeping between their toes. Carly loved every minute of it. Adam seemed to be enjoying himself too. She had half expected that he would take her in his arms and kiss her. But he didn't, but Carly didn't mind. It was so nice just walking beside him, knowing he was content with her company. And there was still tomorrow to look forward to. He must like her a little at least, otherwise he wouldn't be taking her to meet his family.

"I think it's time to head back. The lighthouse is just ahead and we've come pretty far. I don't want to tire you out. You have a big day tomorrow."

"It is getting late," Carly agreed as she turned to start back in the direction from which they'd come. Adam slowed a moment and caught her in his arms. A sound erupted in Carly's throat and smothered as Adam's lips found hers. It was a light feathery kiss demanding nothing but accepting all she cared to give. She was shaken to her toes when he released her. They gazed at one another through the darkness and then walked on. Words weren't necessary. They continued their lazy, contented walk back to the concrete area where a small foot bath had been installed. Carly sat down on the slatted bench while Adam poured water over her feet and then toweled them with the coarse paper towels. Other couples were strolling the beach, lost in one another, walking hand in hand, just as she had done with Adam.

"And that's the end to one of the nicest evenings I've spent in a long time," Adam said as he led her to the parking lot. "You really have to commend me, I'll have you home on the stroke of midnight."

"How cavalier of you, sir," Carly quipped as she slid into the low-slung bucket seat.

The ride home was much too short for Carly. Adam walked her to the door and held out his hand for her key. He fitted it into the lock and swung the door open. He squeezed her hand gently for a moment and then turned to sprint down the flagstone walk. Carly could hear him whistling before he turned on the engine. She smiled into the darkness as she made her way up the staircase to her room. "And a good time was had by all," she said softly. "Especially by me."

CARLY awoke, completely aware of her surroundings. No morning grogginess for her. She knew exactly what day it was and what was on the agenda for her in the afternoon. Excitement raced through her veins as she headed for the shower. She lathered up briskly and washed her silky hair. After all, she did want to look her best even if she was going to wear jeans and sneakers.

Coffee was perking merrily and Quincy was sputtering as he flew about the kitchen in search of his breakfast. "Feed me, Carly. Carly is a good girl," he cackled as he buzzed the top of her head before lighting on top of the refrigerator. He swooped down on Melissa who banged her shin as she tried to evade him.

"Darling, just one morning can't we keep that bird in his cage until I've had my morning coffee? Just one morning of peace and quiet."

"Don't you want to hear about my evening, Mother?"

"By the expression on your face I don't have to ask," Melissa quipped. "You look like you not only had a pleasant evening but are aware that there are more evenings to come."

"I'm taking the afternoon off, Mother. Adam invited me to lunch since his brothers and sisters are in town. I knew you wouldn't mind. I really am caught up with the office work. I even took a stab at straightening out the bank statements. If you bring them home I'll do them before I go to bed."

"What more could a mother ask," Melissa retorted as she brought the coffee cup to her lips. "It never ceases to amaze me that a little caffeine can make the world right side up. Why aren't you drinking your coffee, Carly?"

"I will, Mother. Do you think it's strange that Adam invited me to meet his family?"

"Not at all, darling. Men do that when they're interested in a girl. At least they did in my day and I'm not all that old. I don't think times have changed all that much. I think it's grand."

"Don't you think I'll be out of place if Simone is there? After all, I'm not quite sure what the relationship is between her and Adam."

"Darling, that is not your problem. It's Adam's. I'm sure he wouldn't have invited you if something… something was going on between them. Take it from your mother, Carly. You have nothing to worry about. If anything, I would say that Simone should do the worrying."

Carly impulsively threw her arms around her mother. "Thanks, Mom, I really needed to hear that."

"Carly, never sell yourself short. Darling, you're real, not like some of those high-powered ambitious fashion-model types that parade around the Harbor during the summer. They fade like autumn leaves. What I'm saying, dear, is blood runs through your veins, not chlorophyll. Understand?"

"I know, Mother, but remember, you're prejudiced. Look, I'm not going to jump into anything. So far, this is nothing more than a pleasant time for me. I enjoy Adam's company. He seems to enjoy mine. If there's going to be more it will come, slow and natural. If it doesn't work out then I'll have had a few pleasant memories to store away for a rainy day."

"That's the perfect attitude to adopt, Carly," Melissa agreed with maternal pride. "I really did do a super job of raising you. Sometimes I'm so proud of you, like now, that I want to go outside and shout it to the world what a great girl I raised."

"They already know. Old Mr. Snyder tells me that all the time when he sees me mow the lawn. He said there aren't too many people who can cut the grass with a parrot perched on the grass catcher. Thanks for the compliment."

Carly watched the clock all morning. At eleven-thirty she retired to the powder room to change into jeans and sneakers. A lemon yellow sweat-shirt was her only concession to color.

Melissa stared at her and sighed. "For a minute there you looked like a fifteen-year-old heading for cheerleading practice. I think I just got misty-eyed. I just saw a flash of red pull up on the street. Enjoy yourself, Carly."

"I will, Mother. Hold down the fort. I'll see you sometime tonight. Can't promise when."

Melissa waved airily as Carly skipped out to the car.

"Don't tell me, you're a canary, right?" Adam teased, pointing to her yellow shirt.

"Thank you," Carly settled in beside him, offering

Adam a wry smile.

Not too much later, Carly found herself being introduced to Adam's brothers. Each shook her proffered hand and grinned the fabulous Noble grin as they welcomed her to the "clan." She felt welcomed and accepted by all of them. Their manner was easy and comfortable, like Adam's. The Noble women were busy with their children who played on the wide expanse of green lawn out back but they each came over to meet her and say hello.

It was Cayce who bid for her to be on his team for a rousing game of touch football. The judge and a solemn-faced Simone sat on the sidelines with glasses of carrot juice in their hands.

"Feint, Carly, that's it. Good girl! Swivel now! You've got it!" Brock yelled as Adam tackled her. Laughing, Carly fell to the ground only to reach out, grab the ball and run like lightning.

"This way, Carly! Wrong way, Carly! That's it, you've got it. Run! Run! Wow! Adam, did you see her run? Great stuff," Cayce called to her as she tumbled over the line that made the touchdown legitimate.

"Hey!" Carly complained playfully. "I thought this was touch ball. No tackling!"

"Not the way we Nobles play. We've got our own rules!"

"Believe him, Carly," Adam's sister Helen advised. "All the Nobles play by their own rules."

"You can play on my team anytime," Brock and Cayce said as they each put an arm around her. "Wherever you found her, Adam, don't lose her. We haven't won against your side since we've come home. Come on, you guys, get the lead out. We've got three more quarters to go."

Carly giggled as she assumed the three point stance. Her eyes were bright as she glared at Adam. He was the enemy. Adam glared back. Steve, Adam and Michael took off after Carly on a dead run. Janice and Lorraine closed off the ends. Carly pivoted and then swiveled, sailing the ball high in the air to Cayce who literally leaped into the air. He was off, down the lawn for a second touchdown.

"Where did you learn to do that?" Adam demanded good naturedly.

"Just dumb luck," she retorted.

"Adam, telephone!" the housekeeper called from the patio. "Do you want to take it in the house or shall I bring the phone out here?"

"Time!" Adam called loudly.

"Poor excuse, poor loser! Some people will do anything rather than lose a game," his brothers joked as Adam sprinted back into the palatial house. Moments later, he was back, a grim expression on his face.

"What's wrong?" the judge asked, his voice gruff with concern.

"That was Martha Sinclaire. She's down in Portland getting her check-up at the medical clinic and she heard the storm warning. She wants me to go out to Deer Island and secure the skiff. You know, the one she promised to give her grandson when he graduated next year. She was having some work done on it and it's tied up at the pier. Small craft warnings are up but I couldn't refuse. You know how I feel about Martha." The judge nodded.

"Sorry fellas, this isn't intentional. I'll take the launch and be back as soon as possible. Any volunteers?" he asked as he looked pointedly at Carly.

"I can't go, Adam, I'm not dressed for it and I do so hate to get salt spray in my hair. I really don't think it's safe to be out on the water during a storm."

"Simone," Adam said in a cold voice. "I didn't ask you to go."

"I'll go with you, Adam," Carly said softly. "I was born and raised around here and know these waters almost as well as you do. You'll need someone to handle the lines to bring the skiff around. I've done it before. If you want, I'll be glad to go." She looked around for a moment and thought it strange that none of his brothers had offered to help Adam. Then she saw the grins on their faces. If they thought it was dangerous they would have insisted on going. As it was, their acceptance of her on the playing field had now carried over into something else. They wouldn't interfere. Adam also seemed to agree, even seemed pleased at her suggestion, as though he had expected it.

"Let's go then. If Martha calls back, tell her I'm on my way. Okay, Dad?"

"Right, son. Just be careful now. These storms from the south can really sweep up. And fast."

"I didn't realize we were expecting a storm," Carly said. "Guess I was too busy trying to figure out which way to run with the ball."

Adam ran along beside her as he led her to the Noble dock where he kept the launch in a tumble-down boathouse. "You did okay in that game of touch. Shame you weren't on my side. I hate to husk corn and shuck clams. That's the losing team's job."

Carly laughed as she braced herself for the first surge of power on the launch. It whipped away from the wharf leaving a froth of water behind as they headed out for open water.

Looking off to the south the sky was already dark and gloomy. The wind was rising and whipped the water into white caps. Carly had every confidence in Adam's ability as a sailor and settled down low in her seat to get as much protection from the wind as possible. The bow of the boat took on the rising swells with steadiness. Deer Island seemed worlds away as the weather continued to close in on them.

Eight minutes from landfall the storm hit full force, driving water into the open cockpit. It took all of Adam's expertise to steer the sleek craft toward land. "A few more minutes, Carly. We'll be there. I didn't expect the front to hit so soon. I don't think we'll have any trouble though. Hang on, we'll make it!" His voice carried over the whistling wind.

Carly hung on for dear life, the life vest snug around her, a comforting weight. Wind and rain slashed against her as the boat sliced through the frothing swells.

"Deer Island dead ahead. Hunker down, Carly, stay down. God, I'm sorry I brought you along. Hang on, we'll follow land to the Sinclaire dock." Carly managed a glance at Adam's face and saw the tight, grim concentration there. It was a face that instilled confidence.

"There's the boat house," he called just when Carly thought she couldn't stand another minute of the downpour. "Don't let go, Carly, till I cut the engine."

She shivered as the sound of the engine died to silence. Her knuckles were sore and knotted from the grip she held on the rail. Quickly, she turned in preparation for disembarking. "Wait for me, I'll take the lines."

Fleet of foot, she jumped onto the dock and handled the lines as he worked the boat along the dock into the boat house. With the agility of a cat, he bounded to the bow and attached the hanging hook to the bowring. The stern lines attached, Adam jumped onto the walkway beside Carly and flicked the lever for the electric winch.

"Now for the skiff," Adam panted. "Think you can do it?"

Carly nodded, keeping silent. She was freezing, it was all she could do to keep her teeth from chattering.

"Good girl. Now watch the ropes, they're slippery and don't get your hands burned."

Rivers of rain washed down on them as they ran for the mooring holding the skiff. It was a light sailboat, only about twenty feet long and not too difficult to handle. Together, they walked the skiff around and directed it into the boathouse beside the launch. With quick, capable movements, Adam had it hanging from the rafters of the boathouse.

Carly was cold and weakening. She was so cold and tired she couldn't think. She just had to hold on, she told herself. And hold on she would. If only she could get out of the rain and put on some dry clothes. Adam said something about an overhead loft where they could dry off.

Every bone in her body trembling, Carly managed the rough wooden ladder that led to the loft above. She was stunned by what she saw when Adam lit the hurricane lamp on the mantel. It was a cozy one-room apartment complete with bath and wood-burning fireplace. Carly sank to the floor, every muscle in her body crying for relief.

"The bathroom's over there. You go first. There are some old beach coverups in the linen closet. While you're showering I'll build a fire and make us some coffee laced with brandy. Hurry up now before you collapse," Adam ordered in a firm voice.

Carly went off obediently. A hot shower, a fire, coffee with brandy. She was living under the right star after all.

The storm raged on as she stood under the bracing water. It continued while Adam showered and she watched the coffeepot bubble merrily. There was no sign of a let-up as they snuggled down before the dancing flames with the hot coffee mugs in their hands.

"This is unbelievable," Carly sighed. "I've heard of boathouses like this but I've never been in one."

"Martha uses it for a guesthouse sometimes. It's got all the modern conveniences, thank the Lord. By the way, don't worry about your mother worrying about you. While you were in the shower I radio-telephoned back to the mainland and Cayce will see to it that your mother is notified that you're safe and sound."

"You think of everything," Carly murmured. "You're really a very thoughtful man."

"And you're really a very pretty lady. Especially all scrubbed and cozy. I see you found something appropriate in the linen closet," he gestured toward the pale blue terry robe that had been her only choice besides skimpy bathing suits and lightweight short beach coverups.

Adam had found a pair of cutoff jeans and a ragtag tee shirt. Together they toasted their bare feet by the fire, each enjoying the warmth and companionship that going through an adventure forms between people.

"I suppose I should get up and see what's in the pantry. Getting hungry, Carly?"

"Umm. In a little bit. What's it doing outside? I can still hear the rain beating on the roof."

"Pretty nasty right about now, I suppose. Come on, let's have a look." He hefted her to her feet and together they went to the window and pulled back the gingham curtain.

The late afternoon light was gray, almost wintry, and the roiling seas were pounding the shore. "No telling how long it will last," Carly said thoughtfully.

"No telling," Adam said, his mouth surprisingly close to her ear. Like the force of nature outside that was the wild force with which he took her in his arms. His lips came crashing down on hers, holding them, tasting them, making them a part of his own. He held her close, so closely she felt she would never again draw a breath.

He put her away from him and looked deeply into her eyes. "You're very special, Carly. Too special for a casual affair. You're the kind of girl a man marries. And that makes you extra special. To me." His voice was husky with emotion, his indigo eyes serious, plunging the depths of hers. But his smile was tender and seemed to hold a secret meaning. "I like the way you respond to me, Carly Andrews, there's no doubting that you're my kind of woman."

Carly's cheeks tingled with the heat of a flush. "You said something about a food pantry...."

"Yes, in the kitchen area. Want to see what we can find? Then I challenge you to a marathon game of Monopoly." He took her back in his arms. "And then we can have some hot chocolate and sit by the fire and fall asleep in each other's arms."

As his lips touched hers, Carly thought that she had never heard another idea that she so eagerly agreed with.

CHAPTER FIVE

CARLY woke early. Dawn was now her favorite time of day since she had gone out to Deer Island with Adam, and she enjoyed it alone on the small balcony outside her bedroom window. The tiny alarm next to her bed read 6:10. The rosy hued skyline blended with the rising fog that curled and spiraled upward on the fresh sea breeze. The diamond-shaped dew drops on the close-clipped grass beneath her window shimmered and sparkled and would have been the envy of any Cartier or Tiffany jeweler.

It was a quiet time of day—a time to assess one's thinking, a time to make decisions when minds were clear and uncluttered. Not that she had decisions to make. Her life was so staid and orderly it made her sometimes feel stifled. Nothing ever happened, it seemed to Carly Andrews. She worked all day, ate dinner, washed her hair, watched television and then went to bed. The following day she would wake and do the same thing all over again. A neat, orderly, uncluttered life. Most of her friends had run off to New York to seek their fortunes. The others had married and moved away from Bar Harbor.

Carly drew a breath deep into her lungs and started her yoga exercises. She stayed with the exercises for a full thirty minutes and then showered. She felt good, felt a sense of excitement, and her adrenaline was flowing again. Amazing what an attractive man on the scene could do for a girl. A pity he was taken. Still, he wasn't married yet. If a girl had a mind to, she could fight for him. Melissa had drummed it into her head for years that anything worthwhile was worth fighting for. Could she compete with the luscious Simone and did she want to? What was there about the man, the sometime chef and possible senator that appealed to her? Obviously, he was handsome and sexy as sin itself. Some package, she mused, as she deftly applied makeup.

Carly stood back from the mirror to view her handiwork objectively. Perfect. It didn't look as though she had makeup on at all.

Adam Noble. It did have a certain ring to it. Adam Noble, attorney at law. Adam Noble, chef. Senator Adam Noble. Mrs. Adam Noble. Carly Noble! Whew! She had to stop this sort of thing. Adam Noble was spoken for. This was purely a business deal. The lunch, delightful as it had been, meant nothing to him. The fact that he stopped by meant nothing. And when he

saw her in her green robe with a parrot on her shoulder.
The less said the better. Carly winced remembering the
picture she must have made as she opened the door. On
the other hand, how often had Adam Noble knocked
on a girl's door only to have it opened by a girl in a lime
green robe with a parrot who shouted, "Life is hell! War
is hell!"? Not too often. Suddenly, she giggled. "What
you see, Mr. Noble, is what you get." She giggled again
as she wondered what his elegant companion would do
if Quincy ever lighted on her shoulders. Scream and
faint dead away no doubt. She chided herself as she
made her way to Melissa's messy kitchen.

Still, there was that hasty jaunt out to Deer Island
to see the sunrise. Carly's cheeks flushed brighter. He
had kissed her. She touched her fingers to her lips. No,
she was being silly. It just wasn't possible that she
could still feel the warmth of his mouth on hers.
Besides, Adam Noble must have kissed hundreds of
girls. Deer Island couldn't mean anything to him.
Could it? But what about all the other kisses? her heart
drummed the question. The moment in his arms when
the earth stood still and Adam had become the world.

Carly looked around the untidy kitchen and made up
her mind to do something about getting a housekeeper
of sorts. How in the world could Melissa make such a
mess heating one little potpie in a microwave oven?
Carly wrapped a butcher's apron over her white linen

suit and started to straighten the kitchen while her coffee perked. Orange rinds and ends of green vegetables were whisked into the garbage disposal. Odds and ends of dishes that held remnants of food that did not resemble a potpie went into the dishwasher. An electric broom whisked up all the crumbs and some of Quincy's crackers. A dishcloth that looked as though it belonged in some other war cleaned off the butcher block table. Now, she could eat her banana and have her coffee. But first she had to wake up Quincy and feed him.

"Hi. What's new?" the green bird cackled.

"Not much," Carly replied as she sipped at her instant coffee.

"Good girl," Quincy squawked as he flew wildly about the kitchen, finally lighting on top of the range hood.

"Give me one good reason why I should feed you. What do you ever do but make a mess? That's all you and Mom do, make messes that I have to clean up. Why can't you say, 'Carly's a pretty girl,' or better yet, 'Carly is a beautiful girl?' It's already been established that I'm a good girl so can we get on to bigger and better things?"

Quincy circled the kitchen and finally perched himself on Carly's arm. He looked at her with round beady eyes. "Life is hell!" he said clearly and distinctly.

"You got it, bird, it really is. But you know something? I think it's all going to change soon. Adam Noble is going to change it."

Carly looked around the kitchen. She set the coffee-pot to low so her mother would have hot coffee when she awoke. Next, she checked her handbag for her car keys and her wallet to be sure she had enough cash on her for the day. Gathering up her briefcase, Carly was startled to see a bleary eyed Melissa standing in the doorway.

"Coffee…" Melissa croaked hoarsely, groping for the nearest chair while Carly hurried for cup and coffeepot.

"Mother, you look awful…."

"Yes, don't I?" Melissa smiled. "It was a glorious party and I imagine I look much the same as you did after you spent the night in the storm with Adam Noble."

Carly blushed. "I've told you, Mother. Nothing happened…."

"I can see."

"What's that supposed to mean…? Oh, never mind. I don't want to hear it."

Melissa gulped her coffee. "I have some really inter-esting news," she said after a moment. "Martha Sin-claire told me they've decided to sell their house and move to a warmer climate. The winters are becoming too much for the poor soul…. Anyway, she stayed overnight at the Wilson's but Malcolm went home."

Carly's actions froze. The blood seemed to tingle through her veins. The Sinclaire property. On Deer Island. Adam's dream house! "Have they listed with anyone?"

"Not yet. I was hoping you'd go out there and sign it up." Slowly, Melissa was being restored to her usual bright-eyed self. "You don't have any appointments this morning, do you, darling?"

Carly held her breath. She'd cancel an appointment with the Queen of England to go out to Deer Island this morning. Quickly, she picked up the phone and called downtown to the marina, making arrangements with Will Rumley to take her out in the launch.

"I'll just stop by the office and pick up a listing agreement. Will Rumley says he'll take me out there around nine-thirty." Impulsively, she kissed Melissa on the cheek and dashed for the door, her feet barely touching the ground.

Carly was working on the agreement for the Sinclaire property when Simone Maddox opened the door clad in the briefest of shorts that displayed spectacular legs.

"Hello, I was just walking by and saw you come in. Would you have an emery board? I've chipped a nail." Simone held out a scarlet tipped hand.

"I think I've got one here in my desk...." Carly murmured, opening the lower left drawer and rummaging for the emery board.

"What's this?" Simone asked curiously, picking up the listing agreement and seeing the name and Deer Island.

"Isn't this the house that Adam always raves about?"

"Yes, it is," Carly confessed. "I'm going out there to see if I can get Mr. Sinclaire to list it with me."

"You don't mind if I come along, do you? I knew you wouldn't."

Carly watched Simone deftly file her chipped nail. Nobody looked that gorgeous so early in the morning, she thought sourly. Simone looked as though she had spent ten hours in a beauty salon or, at the very least, had six people put her together. Carly was as green as Quincy's emerald feathers with jealousy. She forced a polite tone in her voice when she replied, "It's a little too early to leave yet. I have some work I have to do right now. If you like, you can wait, or you can go to the Cottage Inn and have some coffee."

"Coffee!" Simone said in a horrified voice. "Coffee is full of caffeine and it gives you pimples. I only drink herbal tea. I never touch a thing or put anything in my stomach that isn't one hundred percent organic. People are killing themselves with rich food full of all sorts of additives, and they don't even know it."

"Really," Carly said flatly.

"Just the other day I was talking to Judge Noble about it, and I told him I would like to do a once a week television show to bring all this to the public's attention. Vitamins are important. Natural vitamins. The judge is looking into the matter for me. If you stop to think about it, I'm the perfect person for the job. Look at my clear skin and eyes. I mean I really live what I talk about."

"Commendable," Carly muttered as she shuffled papers on her desk.

"I think I will go to the Cottage Inn. I always carry my own tea bags with me. Perhaps they'll be gracious enough to give me some boiled water."

Carly nodded. "I'm sure of it. You go along and I'll be ready when you get back."

Simone smiled and closed the door behind her. Carly sighed heavily as she pushed the papers in front of her into the wide middle drawer.

It annoyed Carly that Adam Noble's companion was going to be going along to inspect the house. Why? Was she going to live in it with Adam? Would she have final approval? Whatever the reason, it shouldn't be making a difference to Carly but it was. The plain simple fact of the matter was she didn't like Simone Maddox, and she was also jealous of Simone's relationship with Adam Noble.

If Melissa knew about this, she would stand over her and cluck her tongue in a motherly way and say, "Poor baby, poor Carly." She wasn't a poor baby and she wasn't poor Carly. She would handle this. She had momentarily let herself get sidetracked by Adam Noble's good looks and exciting attention. She didn't have to resort to snatching, or rather trying to snatch, a man from some other woman. She had merely day-dreamed for a little while, but now her eyes were open and she would carry on—business as usual. Adam Noble and his friend were clients and that was all there was to it. Either she would make the sale or not. If not, Adam would go about his business and she would go about hers.

Carly's stomach lurched. If that was the way it was going to be, why did she feel this nauseous feeling in the pit of her stomach, and why was her heart fluttering like a trapped bird? Indigestion, she told herself, as she stuffed listing forms into her briefcase. That's what it was all right, she assured herself weakly, a good case of indigestion. A mint would cure it.

Promptly at nine-thirty Simone Maddox opened the door and waved to Carly. "I'm ready if you are."

"Come in. We'll go in my car to the dock. Will Rumley will be waiting on his launch to take us out to the island. That way we won't be hemmed in by the ferry schedule, if that's all right with you," Carly said coolly.

"That's fine with me," Simone answered just as coolly.

The trip to the island was made in silence, each girl intent on her own thoughts. From time to time Carly felt Simone's eyes boring into her and for some reason it pleased her. Was the beautiful woman concerned about Carly? Concerned that Adam might have some sort of feeling for her other than a professional one, or at worst, a mild flirtation.

Malcolm Sinclaire himself opened the door of the sprawling Tudor house. There was no other word for it but sprawling. Additions, Carly decided. Quickly, she explained why she was there so early in the morning.

"Well, I was thinking of listing the property with Clarence Olsen, but my wife seems to think his 'git up and go' got up and went. I don't think listing with your agency will be a problem. Seems to me my wife, Martha, belongs to some of the same clubs your mother does. Why don't you ladies take a look around and then we'll talk? We can have a brunch on the terrace if you have the time."

Carly smiled. She liked Malcolm Sinclaire immediately. And she knew he would give her the listing for the house. Melissa would go into orbit over it.

"Miss Maddox, why don't you take the upstairs and I'll stay down here? That way we won't influence each other with our comments." Simone nodded her agreement and immediately started up the long, winding staircase.

Malcolm Sinclaire whistled for a huge Irish setter and snapped a leash on the glossy animal. "Just make yourself at home. I'll just take this fellow for his morning walk and meet you back here on the terrace. If you have any questions, you can ask me then."

Carly wandered through the immaculately kept rooms on the ground floor. She realized the house was old, but it had been designed with an eye to the future. Tall, wide windows opened upon the incredible view outside the house. The front windows gave onto a sight of the sparkling blue bay, framed by tall, white birches. A gracious center hall was flanked on both sides by archways, each leading to a separate wing. On the right was a study-library, bookshelves climbing the oak paneled walls and surrounded by more windows. A room where even the pale, winter light would welcome you and encourage you to curl up on the chair nearest the Goliath fireplace to read. Underfoot, the floor was polished oak in a shade slightly darker than the walls, and it was covered with a rug of oriental design whose colors splashed and glowed in the streaming sunlight. Her eyes fell on the old-fashioned desk set between the two windows. Its dimensions were masculine, and its cherrywood gleamed from loving care. Instantly, a vision of Adam Noble sitting behind the desk flashed through her mind. She could almost see him, riffling through his papers and concentrating on a complicated law brief, only raising his head to smile at Carly as she brought him a cup of coffee. "This is insane," she muttered to herself. "I've got to stop thinking this way!"

Quickly, she hurried across the hall to the opposite

wing. This was the front parlor, decorated with gentle Queen Anne furnishings. Like the library, its proportions were huge, and a view of the bay winked through the windows. Hearing Simone's footsteps upstairs, Carly hurried on to complete her tour. Behind the parlor was the dining room, complete with fireplace and tall, corner hutches displaying the family china. But it was the sunlight that beckoned through a doorway that drew her into the kitchen. As soon as she stepped over the threshold, she felt as though she was bathed in light. A skylight! And beneath it various pots containing local ferns and wild flowers. Long counters surrounded the perimeters and work area, and just beyond was a bay window, looking out onto the herb garden and the lawns. An old-fashioned table covered with a gay print cloth was nestled in a corner created by the window, and Carly couldn't think of a nicer place to have a morning cup of coffee. But beyond the breakfast area was another sitting room that backed onto the library. This, she decided, was her favorite room. Glass-paned doors opened onto a patio leading down to the lawns and the tennis courts. Just over the tops of hedges, Carly saw the striped awnings of the cabana in the pool area, its cheerful red and white vibrant against the blue sky.

Backtracking through the kitchen, bathed in the sunshine from the skylight, Carly admired the hanging ferns in their wicker baskets and the old-fashioned brick and copper utensils. The butcher-block countertops, real butcher-block not the plastic substitute, appeared to have been freshly scoured. Fragrant bundles of herbs, tied in small bundles and hanging from the beams, delighted her. It was a dream of a kitchen. Now she knew why Adam Noble adored this place.

So far, there had not been one negative thing about her tour. The house was exquisite and well kept. Even the slate floor she was standing on looked as though it had just been scrubbed. There was no dust, no sign of a cobweb anywhere. The asking price must be astronomical. Adam Noble could afford it, no doubt. Lord, what she wouldn't give to live in a house like this. She didn't know a soul in the whole world who had a fireplace in the kitchen, complete with hearthside rocking chair and yellow cat. Double ovens, double freezers and a monstrous refrigerator with double doors. Everything a cook could want. Everything a woman would want, right down to the oversized dishwasher. Any woman in her right mind would snap this up in a minute if she had any kind of sense at all. It was going to be interesting to see what Simone Maddox thought of the place.

Speak of the devil, she mused. "How quaint," Simone said walking through the swinging doors which led from the dining room into the kitchen.

"I'll go upstairs now and you can tour down here," Carly said shortly.

"Go ahead. Nothing up there impressed me one way or the other. It's just a bunch of rooms with wallpaper. I hate wallpaper. And it's so isolated! I don't see how anyone could live here. Little wonder the Sinclaires want to sell. This place must have driven her crazy!"

Carly stood for a moment at the foot of the circular stairway and tried to remember what it reminded her of. Tara in *Gone With the Wind?* Whatever, it certainly was elegant with the thick burgundy carpeting. She didn't know why she was tiptoeing through the rooms or why she felt the need to whisper. Each bedroom, and there were five, was perfection down to the last detail. Again, there was no dust, no sign of a cobweb anywhere. Mahogany floors! Unbelievable! Fireplaces in every bedroom! If she owned this house, she would never sell it. Never! This was a house for a family. A house to give birth in and a house to die in. It was the closest thing to perfection Carly had ever seen. And each bedroom had its own bathroom whose color scheme matched the bedroom. Gorgeous, simply gorgeous. It was suddenly important, paramount, that Adam see it with her. He loved this place; she could feel it, sense it. Now she understood what he was talking about. She had to get to him before Simone did. To Simone this was just a house. Adam Noble at some time in his life would make it a home. If Simone shared it with him, it would forever remain a house. She didn't know how she knew, she just knew.

Carly sat down gingerly in a high-backed chair and closed her eyes, pretending that she belonged in the house. A sudden, overwhelming possessiveness coursed through her. She would fight to the death for a house like this. She would work her fingers to the bone to keep it just the way it was. Dream on, Carly Andrews. If she worked her whole life, she could never afford a house like this one. Her mind started to race. Should she call Adam Noble from here before Simone could get to him and tell him she didn't care for the house? Should she wait? Just how much influence did Simone Maddox have over Adam Noble? She would wait till she got back to the office. As soon as she dropped Simone off at her car, she would make the call to Adam. Providing Malcolm Sinclaire didn't change his mind. Even if he listed with another agency, she could still show the house since the Andrews Agency was a member of the Multiple Listing System. Childishly, she crossed her fingers and then her ankles.

Carly glanced at her watch. She didn't want Simone spending too much time with Malcolm Sinclaire. God only knew what she would say or what kind of ideas she would plant in his head. Surely she knew about the bad feeling between Mr. Sinclaire and the Nobles.

Taking a deep breath Carly raced down the curving staircase just in time to see Malcolm Sinclaire walk through the French doors with the Irish setter.

"All finished?" he called, a smile on his face.

Carly laughed. "Mr. Sinclaire, this is the most beautiful, gorgeous house I have ever seen in my whole life. How can you bear to part with it? Who keeps it in such excellent condition?"

"Whoa there, young lady. One question at a time. I'm pleased that you like the house. It's been in the family for well over a hundred years. Martha is in frail health this past year, and the doctor recommended a warm climate, so we'll be going south. Our three married children live in the Carolinas and we want to be close to them and our grandchildren. We have a man and woman who come in every couple of days to dust up and straighten any mess Martha and I might make. Now, does that answer all of your questions?"

"I guess so. Your wife must love this house very much. I can't imagine a woman in the world who wouldn't want to live here. I think I might be tempted to sell my soul for this house if such a thing were possible."

Malcolm Sinclaire laughed. "It's timber and nails. A few doodads here and there for decoration. It's the people who live in a house that make it a home. I've been thinking while I walked my dog, and I have no objection to listing the house with you."

Carly smiled brightly. "Thank you, Mr. Sinclaire. If you're ready, I'd like to talk terms and join you for that brunch you were talking about."

"Good, good," Malcolm Sinclaire said rubbing his hands together. "I just heard Mrs. Nelson's car in the driveway. She went into town for groceries. She leaves the car at the pier and takes the launch in. She's our part-time housekeeper, and I'm sure if the right people bought this place, she might be persuaded to stay on and work the hours she's been giving us. We've had her for over twenty years. She's a gem, and Martha and I wouldn't be able to get along without her. Come along now, and we'll tell her we want something fattening for lunch. That's the best kind of lunch, and I only get away with it when Martha isn't at home." Carly laughed and agreed. What indeed could be better than a fattening lunch? Simone would probably go up in smoke or give a dissertation on organic foods.

Lunch turned out to be a delicious noodle and mushroom casserole with herbs and dripping in a buttery white sauce. A crisp watercress salad and iced tea accompanied it, to Simone's delight.

The moment Simone started her organic tirade, Malcolm Sinclaire squelched her by telling her he liked garbage and was a junk-food junkie for fifty years, and he had no intention of stopping, and he was seventy years old and who was she to tell him that he was dying a slow death and didn't even know it? Simone closed her mouth with a snap and then proceeded to nibble on the watercress like a rabbit.

Carly finished her lunch, and the second the table was cleared she opened her briefcase and withdrew the standard forms which required Malcolm Sinclaire's signature. They discussed mortgages and points and the ridiculous amounts of money people were asking for their properties. They finally settled on what Malcolm called a fair and equitable price, and he signed on the dotted line. They shook hands warmly and firmly.

Simone remained quiet on the walk to the dock where they met Will Rumley for the trip back to town. She didn't utter a single word, but sat back on her seat, her eyes closed as though asleep. It suited Carly just fine.

CHAPTER SIX

A FEELING of dread settled over Carly as she maneuvered the car through traffic. She didn't like Simone Maddox's silence. She should be making some comments on the house. Why was she being so quiet and why did her perfect jaw look so tight and grim? Was it possible that Simone was a "bright lights city girl" and the house on the island was too far from what she would consider civilization? True, you needed a power boat or had to use the ferry, but Adam Noble must have known that when he asked her to see about the house. Evidently, it made no real difference to him. Simone Maddox was another story entirely.

Carly fidgeted behind the wheel as she stopped for a red light. She had to say something, break the silence, so she had some idea of the beautiful girl's thoughts. Ammunition to defend her own liking of the Sinclaire property.

"Simone, what did you think of the house? Does

your silence mean you didn't care for it?" Carly asked politely, dreading the answer.

Simone turned slightly in her seat and stared at Carly for a full minute before she replied. "As far as houses go, it was just another house. Personally, I prefer chrome and glass in the way of furniture. It was a little…woodsy for my taste, and of course, I detest the idea that you have to crawl into a boat to get on and off the island. The spray from the water makes my hair fall and my clothes damp. I don't think I would like having to wear a raincoat and carry an umbrella each time I wanted to go off somewhere. I don't think Adam will care for the place at all," she said coolly. Her eyes were veiled as she watched Carly for any reaction to her statement. Carly was not unaware of Simone's scrutiny, and her apprehension increased at Simone's cool words.

"Mr. Noble led me to believe this was exactly the sort of property he was looking for," Carly said quietly. "I'm sure I didn't misunderstand his instructions."

Simone tapped a long nail against her handbag as she continued to stare at Carly with veiled eyes. "Adam has a way of wanting something one day and forgetting about it the next. All of the Nobles are like that, but then I don't expect you travel in their circles so you really can't be expected to know how…how eccentric they are at times," Simone said knowledgeably.

A lump settled in Carly's stomach, and suddenly, she found it hard to breathe. She didn't believe a word Simone Maddox was saying. She wouldn't believe it until she heard Adam Noble say it. He wasn't indecisive. He had certainly given her the impression that he knew exactly what he wanted and would settle for nothing less. Adam Noble was a man who never "settled" as the saying went. Carly moistened her dry lips. She wouldn't have been that wrong in her judgment. Once she met him all her previous doubts concerning him and his family were swept away. Simone Maddox was wrong. Simone Maddox *had* to be wrong.

Carly parked the car behind the agency and climbed out. Simone waved and said, "Keep looking, I'm sure you'll turn up something that will appeal to *us*." Not missing the emphasis on the word "us," Carly watched as Simone climbed behind the wheel of the small Mercedes and roared off down the street.

She had been dismissed like a school child. Carly fumed and admitted that it wasn't the curt dismissal but the word "us" that set her teeth on edge.

Angrily she unlocked the back door of the agency and made a beeline for the phone. "Adam Noble, please," she said breathlessly to the voice at the other end of the phone.

"Mr. Noble is away and won't be back until the weekend. Would you care to leave a message?"

Carly frowned. Four days. "Is there any way I can get in touch with Mr. Noble? This is Carly Andrews from Andrews Realty. It really is important that I speak with him as soon as possible."

"I'm sorry, Miss Andrews, but Mr. Noble did not leave a number where he could be reached. Perhaps I could have Miss Maddox return your call if the matter is urgent."

Carly felt drained. "No, that won't be necessary. Just tell Mr. Noble I called and that I found a property for him and that I would appreciate it if he contacted me as soon as possible."

"I'll take care of it, Miss Andrews," the impersonal voice responded.

"Thank you," Carly muttered as she hung up the phone. She drummed her fingers on the desk top. Why hadn't Simone mentioned that Adam was out of town? For that matter, why hadn't Adam told her he expected to be away for a few days? Carly's excitement over the Sinclaire property sank, taking her into the doldrums of uncertainty. The answer to that last question was easy enough. He hadn't told her because he hadn't cared enough to tell her. She meant nothing to him. Plain and simple. All that talk in the boathouse the night of the storm about how special she was. It was just another way of saying he didn't want her. To Adam Noble, Carly Andrews was just a means to an end. Perhaps he

had heard a rumor that the Sinclaires were thinking of
selling. He wanted that house out on Deer Island and
she was in a position to know if and when it ever went
on the market. The surprise was that the Sinclaires had
decided to sell at this time. People like the Nobles
always seemed to have things fall into their laps.

She had an obligation as a professional Realtor. An
obligation to the Sinclaires as well as to Adam. Carly
determined that she would continue to try to contact
Adam. For the moment there was little else she could
do. After all, it wasn't as though a buyer for the high-
priced estate would fall out of the sky.

CARLY worked industriously for the balance of the
week. Each day she called the Noble residence, leaving
a message for Adam to return her calls. Each and every
time except for the first call, Simone managed somehow to always pick up the phone.

When she called on Saturday morning, confident
that Adam was home by now, Simone answered the
phone again and informed her that Adam was sailing
with his brothers. And yes, she would give him the
message and have him get back to her. Carly waited
all day in the office doing odd paperwork and when she
ran out of chores, she gave herself a manicure. She had
lunch sent in so she wouldn't miss his call. By four
o'clock she was so edgy, she thought she would

scream. She had to do something. Water the plants again that were already drowning. Clean the tiny-paned front door with Windex. She covered her type-writer, sharpened her pencils and put new refills in all the pens. The phone shrilled and she screamed at a friend to hang up because she was expecting an important phone call.

Excitement rose and ebbed like the tide in Carly's heart. One moment she imagined Adam's joy to find that the Sinclaire property could be his and then she believed that Adam did not really want the house after all. Suppose, which was more than likely, Simone already told him about the house. In which case, courtesy demanded that he at least call and tell her he wasn't interested.

The digital square on her wrist read five-forty. Who was fooling whom? Adam Noble wasn't going to call today or any other day for that matter. One more call. She would make one more call and then lock up and go home.

Carly dialed the now familiar number and waited. Simone Maddox answered, voice impatient. "I said I would give him the message and I have. He'll be in touch with you when he's free."

The connection was broken before Carly could do more than feel foolish.

"That does it," she muttered angrily. She bent over to remove her handbag from the desk drawer and then kicked the drawer shut with her foot. "You know what you can do, Mr. Noble, with your answering service. Well, I don't care if you don't want your 'dream house.' You can have some chrome and glass condominium with plastic plants for all I care. And you can eat TV dinners that Simone serves you straight from the microwave oven. You two deserve each other!"

AT HOME, Quincy greeted the distraught Carly with a wild flapping of his wings.

"Knock it off, Quincy. I'm in no mood for your antics tonight. Some people have no consideration. Do things like professional courtesy count to rich people? Not on your life!"

Carly sat down at the table after she made herself a cup of instant coffee. Tomorrow was Sunday and on Sundays whenever the Noble clan was in town, they always gathered in the park, rain or shine for a game of touch football. She would make it her business to be an interested observer. If it was the only way she could get to Adam then that's exactly what she'd do. All she had to do was look in a copy of today's local paper to see what other clan the Nobles would be playing and the time would be listed. Sunday morning excitement! Ha! she snorted, scanning the newsprint. Her eyes flew down the columns…. Mrs. Nebit from Providence R. I. was visiting her niece, Barbara

Smith…Cub Scout troop 77 was having a picnic at three o'clock…Mr. Hemple was in the hospital and receiving visitors now…Cathy Coolidge was vacationing in New York…the Hahn family had spent two weeks in the Great Smokey Mountains…Mr. Olsen and his son John had caught a six foot 220 pound cod off Kennebunkport…. Here it is. The Noble Clan vs. the Conrads…Sunday 10:00 a.m.

That settled, it was time to think about dinner. Carly opened the freezer and withdrew a roast. She peeled off the wrapper, seasoned it and shoved it into the microwave oven. Quickly, she scrubbed some yams. Next, tossed a salad and then set the table. Melissa should be home soon. Should she tell her mother about Adam wanting the Sinclaire property or not? Carly decided she had enough problems without adding Melissa's questions to the list. Melissa would want to know where Adam had been, why he hadn't told Carly, etc., etc., etc. Besides, nothing was happening so why get Melissa's hopes up?

Her kitchen duties under control, Carly took her coffee cup and walked out to the backyard to sit down under the apple tree.

Melissa Andrews shook Carly's shoulder. "Wake up, Carly, dinner's ready. You look so tired, I really hated to wake you but that beautiful roast shouldn't be allowed to go to waste."

"I was just dozing, Mother. I'm starved. Do you believe I actually dozed off sitting here? I haven't done that since I was a kid."

"You must have been tired," Melissa said fondly as she ruffled Carly's dark curls. "By the way, I have a buyer for the Sinclaire property. An architect. It's just what he wants. I'm taking him to see it Monday afternoon. I called Martha Sinclaire this afternoon, and she said she would leave the keys with us on Monday. They're leaving for South Carolina so they won't be underfoot when the house is shown. That house won't be on the market long, I can tell you that. And what a commission! Carly, I'm so proud of you."

Carly's stomach lurched. An architect from New York. Of all the rotten luck. If there was anyone in the whole world who would appreciate the Sinclaire house, it was an architect. I could strangle you, Simone Maddox, she fumed silently.

Carly rinsed her hands and sat down at the kitchen table. Melissa chattered non-stop as she removed the roast and transferred it to a platter. "The price is right and Mr. Dillon will have no problem with the down payment or securing a mortgage. I haven't taken him out there but he knows the house. He visited there once when he came to Bar Harbor. It's almost as if he told me what he wanted as a prospective buyer and then the Sinclaires' house was put on the market."

Carly sliced into her yam with a vengeance. "Are…are…what did you say his name was? Oh, yes, Dillon. Is he here now?"

"He's been here for a week trying to get in touch with Clarence Olsen. He finally came to me just as I was closing up this afternoon. I must have come into the office right after you left." Carly toyed with the yam and then swished the salad around her plate. The rare roast beef she ignored completely. If she forced herself to chew, she would choke to death. This definitely wasn't the time to go on to her eternal reward. Not till she evened up the score with Simone Maddox.

Melissa ate ravenously, saying she only "wanted to pick" because she was gaining too much weight. "For God's sake, Carly, isn't it about time you threw that record out? I can't stand it another minute," Melissa said, throwing her hands up in the air. "Quincy," she bellowed to be heard above the stereo, "turn that thing off."

"What do you want from him, Mother, he's just a dumb bird."

"If he's smart enough to turn it on, he's smart enough to turn it off," Melissa said, attacking another slice of roast beef that she "picked" at.

The silence was deafening.

"You see? Now, if you could just train him to say the right thing at the right time, maybe we could palm him off on someone. I can't stand that bird, Carly. And to think that was all your father left either of us. He's getting a bit salty. Too much television. Curb him, Carly, before it's too late," Melissa said wiping at her mouth. "You do the dishes, dear. I'm playing canasta with the girls this evening and I want to change. My turn next week."

Carly set about clearing the table and straightening the kitchen. Her chores finished, she settled herself in front of the television to watch one ridiculous show after another until it was time to retire for the night. Tomorrow was another day. A day in which, with any luck, she would come in contact with Adam Noble.

CHAPTER SEVEN

SUNDAY turned out to be an overcast day with chiffon gray clouds threatening to erupt any moment. Carly felt as depressed as the day around her. She snuggled down into the raincoat she wore and watched as the Noble clan and the Conrads squared off for a rousing game of touch football.

Carly squinted. Where was Simone? Foolish question. She was no fool. There was no doubt in Carly's mind that the other woman was ensconced in the Noble mansion, nibbling on carrot sticks while Carly was standing around waiting for an audience with Adam.

Adam, where was Adam? All four Noble brothers looked alike in their jeans and ragtag college shirts. There he was. A perfect specimen of fitness. You could tell by his loose stance and the easy way he hefted the pigskin he was holding. She didn't remember his hands being so big, so powerful looking. Was he ever going to look toward the bleachers? Not likely. Right now, it was the Nobles and Harvard versus the Conrads and Yale.

Despite herself, Carly found that she was getting caught up in the game, silently rooting for the Nobles. They were athletes, there was no doubt about it.

Time was called and both teams walked to their respective places. Now, look toward the bleachers, Carly silently willed Adam. She stared intently, praying he would notice her and wave to show he knew she was there. He seemed oblivious to anyone but his family and friends.

Carly tilted her head. Of all the rotten luck, it was raining. Would the game continue? She waited as the few observers in the bleachers packed up their gear and raised their umbrellas. If they all left, she would have to leave, too. The rain was coming down harder and the crowd was now running toward their cars.

Carly stood and tightened the belt of her raincoat. She fished around in her bag for a scarf and tied it around her dark head. Morosely, she climbed down from the bleachers and started to run to her car. In her hurry to get out of the driving rain she stepped into a hole and fell face forward. Embarrassed, she struggled to her feet, wiping ineffectually at her mud and grass stained raincoat. She was soaked and mortified as she fumbled in her bag for the car keys. She felt like crying. Why was everything going wrong? Nothing she did was right anymore. Nothing had been the same since she met Adam Noble. Her fingers found the metallic square the keys were attached to and she heaved a sigh of relief.

"One would almost think you were tired, from that mighty sigh," Adam Noble said, taking the keys from her and opening the car door. Carly gasped. How could he look so wonderful standing there in the rain with his hair plastered against his head? She smiled, fully expecting to see him return her effort. She sobered as she stared at the man. His eyes were cold and bleak, his jaw grim and tight. Even the knuckles of his hands were alabaster white as he clenched the door frame.

"Mr.... Adam," Carly said shakily, "I've been trying to get in touch with you all week. I think I found..."

"Mr. Noble will do just fine, Miss Andrews. Messages! I've received no messages from you. As a matter of fact," he said coldly, "I've had Simone call your office practically on the hour to see what was going on with regard to the Sinclaire property. When Simone told me the house was for sale you could imagine my excitement. And now do you know what she told me? She said Kyle Dillon is in town and he has first dibs on the property. Kyle is an old college buddy of mine and he told Simone at a party last evening. Tell me, Miss Andrews, how did that happen? Never mind, I already know. Your agency is representing him, according to Mac Sinclaire. Somehow," he continued in his frozen voice, "I didn't think of you as a wheeler-dealer. Don't call me, Miss Andrews, I'll call you," Adam said stalking away, his back stiff and straight.

Carly was stunned. How had this all happened? She climbed from the car and ran after him. "Wait! You don't understand," she shouted. "It's not the way you think!"

What was the use? He couldn't or wouldn't listen with the rain pounding the way it was. Of all the miserable luck. She knew the minute she stepped from bed that it was going to be a bad day. "Nuts!" she shouted to be heard over the pelting rain as she sloshed her way back to the car. "Nuts to you, Adam Noble, and nuts to you, Simone Maddox."

Carly tried to fit the key into the ignition with shaking hands. She succeeded on the fourth try as tears streamed down her cheeks. Why wasn't the stupid car starting? She turned the key again. Nothing. She waited and tried again. The battery. She had left her lights on somehow. She'd have to walk home. If she was lucky, she might get pneumonia and die and be put out of her misery.

The walk to the other side of town was an ordeal and Carly was exhausted when she opened the back door of her house. She kicked the door closed and then stepped out of her sodden shoes. "I hate him, he's insufferable, and that fast talking companion who answers his phone and delivers his messages. I hate liars and phonies, and Simone is all of those. And

Adam's a bore and a conceited ass in the bargain. Who does he think he is anyway? A Noble. Noble Adam. Phooey," Carly shouted angrily.

"Carly is pretty mad," Quincy sputtered as he flew into his cage and perched on the swinging bar.

"One more word out of you and I'm cutting off your licorice supply," Carly yelled as she struggled to remove her sodden raincoat.

"Carly's a good girl," Quincy muttered as he taunted the drenched girl. "Quincy is a good boy. Quincy is a very good boy."

"That's not going to get you any licorice, so just shut up." Carly tossed a towel over the cage and peeled off her slacks and shirt in preparation of throwing them, along with her raincoat, into the dryer.

The phone in the kitchen shrilled. She reached out and placed the receiver next to her ear. "Carly Andrews," she said quietly.

"Miss Andrews, this is Simone Maddox. I've been trying to reach you for ever so long. I thought you must have gone out of town or something."

"Or something," Carly muttered, disliking Simone more by the minute.

"I can't tell you how upset Adam is over the fact that Kyle Dillon is trying to buy the Sinclaire property. He's getting ready to leave now for New York, and I did so want to try your number one more time, so I can tell him how you do business. Tsk, tsk, tsk, and to think you're one of the town's own daughters. After all the trouble Adam went to to steer you to the property. He's very distraught. I just thought I should bring it to your attention."

Carly listened with unbelieving ears. She couldn't be hearing this conversation right. She must be missing something somewhere. She'd been had! Simone Maddox was devious and sneaky. And there wasn't a thing Carly could do about it.

"Miss Maddox," she said sweetly. "I know exactly what you're up to, and I can't say I blame you. Adam Noble is a very attractive man and he does have pots of money. A very winning combination. I'm extremely flattered that you seem to think I'm some sort of threat to you. And before I hang up, let me say that I do wish you luck in getting your own television show. I can't wait to turn you on so I can turn you off." Carly slammed down the phone so hard, she thought she cracked the receiver. Quincy was right. Life was hell!

"You deserve a licorice stick, Quincy. Sometimes you're right," Carly said removing the towel and sticking a raspberry licorice stick in Quincy's beak.

"A wheeler-dealer!" Now that hurt. She had to defend herself somehow. After all, she did live and work in this town and she had a reputation to consider. Of all the dirty, rotten tricks.

Carly stomped about the kitchen, shivering in her underwear as she seethed and fumed. Briskly, she rubbed at her arms as goose bumps broke out all over her. Lord, she was freezing. A shower, she would take a shower and then get into bed till she warmed up. As if she could ever be warm again.

Quincy was up to his tricks again. What was he babbling about? Carly turned on the shower full blast, and at that precise moment a knock sounded on the back door. Quincy stared at Adam Noble through the back door and then flew out of the kitchen in search of Carly.

AFTER a hastily eaten lunch that Monday afternoon, Carly was busily working at her desk, straightening out a contract for interested buyers. The slight tinkle of the bell over the door sounded, and it was a full moment before she could drag her thoughts away from the work before her until she looked up. There, standing before her, was a tall, muscularly built man staring down at her. For the moment little else about his physical appearance was communicated to her, so dazzled was she by his wide, ingenuous grin. In spite of herself Carly found she was smiling back and motioning him to have a seat opposite her desk.

A pearl-gray Stetson hat was balanced on a knee. In a voice softened by the merest hint of a drawl, he said, "I'm Kyle Dillon. I have an appointment with

Mrs. Andrews to see a house out near Straw Hill on Deer Island. I'm a little early, but where I come from a man never keeps a lady waiting. Our appointment was for two o'clock."

Carly's eyes flashed to the office clock. It was one fifty-nine. "I'm Carly Andrews, Mr. Dillon. Your appointment was with my mother. Right now she's in the back finishing her lunch. She'll be with you in a moment."

He was too big for the chair. All six feet of him and every inch of that rip cord muscle. Carly remembered her mother saying that Mr. Dillon was an architect. It hardly seemed possible that he could complete fine drawings with those big hands. Years of sun and wind were the only plausible explanation for his deep golden tan and the crinkles near his eyes told her he spent a lot of time laughing. She liked his deep chocolate eyes and the heavy fringe of lashes that any self-respecting girl would cry to have. He was a hunk, as the saying went, but the obvious humor in his face and his friendly attitude made Carly want to know him better in spite of the fact that he wanted to buy Adam's dream house. Considering Adam Noble's recent behavior, a girl should look out for herself. She definitely did not owe Adam Noble a thing.

"My mother told me you were from New York but your accent…"

"Ma'am, I'm from Dallas, Texas. I've been hanging my hat in New York for a while because I've been finishing up a job for a friend of mine. I'll be heading back to Texas just as soon as I check out this property to see my folks. I hope to live here six months of the year if things work out the way I plan. Now, tell me about you. What's a pretty girl like you doing hiding her light under a bushel in Bar Harbor? You look as though you were made for bright lights and the busy city."

Carly laughed. "I do like the bright lights of the city. I go into New York every so often to see some plays and check out the restaurants and do some Fifth Avenue shopping. But I always come back here, this is my home."

"I can relate to that, Ma'am." Kyle smiled.

"Mr. Dillon," Melissa Andrews said, walking into the room, "how nice to meet you at last. I see you've met my daughter. You're right on time. I like that in a man. Shows responsibility."

"I've been getting acquainted with Miss Andrews. You have a nice office here," Kyle said, looking at the window frames. "Sturdy building, built to last. Not like some of those cracker boxes I've seen at the other end of town. If there's one thing that will curl my lip, it's tract houses. I know, I know," he said holding up his hand at Melissa who was about to protest. "Someone has to design and build them because folks need places to live. I accept it, but I don't like it."

"Carly, call her Carly, everyone else does," Melissa said with a calculating look in her eye.

Carly winced. She could almost read Melissa's mind. Super jock, pots of money, lucrative profession that he took seriously and easy on the eye. Was he ever. She felt a giggle work its way up her throat and quickly suppressed it. She knew what was coming next even before Melissa spoke. So did Kyle Dillon from the look on his face. It was obvious that he liked the idea.

"Darling Carly, I just remembered that I have to take a spin out to see Daphne Winters. There's something wrong with the mortgage and her lawyer wants to see me. Why don't you be a real love and take Mr. Dillon out to the Sinclaire property for me? I peeked into your engagement book, and your afternoon is free. By the way," Melissa chirped, "are you by any chance going to the fish fry at the Bradshaw's?"

Kyle Dillon laughed. "You bet, I'm the guest of honor it seems. I've just finished a job for Mr. Bradshaw's new office building in Bangor. What about you two pretty ladies, are you going to be there?"

"I'm not, I have a political rally to attend, but Carly is going, aren't you, darling?"

"Mother, you're about as transparent as cellophane. Yes, Mr. Dillon, I was invited, and yes, I'm attending."

"Then perhaps you'll allow me to escort you. I'd like to get to know you better while I'm here."

Carly's heart fell to her shoes. How could she refuse this charming, eligible man? She couldn't. But, what was it going to do to her plans to seek out Adam Noble? Would Adam be there? Of course he would be there, even if he had to fly back from New York just for the fish fry. When the Bradshaws threw a fish fry, the whole state turned out, it seemed. It was rather like a command performance and one Carly was sure Simone Maddox wouldn't want to miss.

"That sounds…fine," Carly said quietly, to her mother's obvious approval.

"It's settled then. You're my date for the evening. You'll have to take me in hand—I'm just a poor little old country boy and not used to all of this razzle-dazzle."

Carly returned his grin. "Off the top of my head, Mr. Dillon, I'd say you were doing just fine. Everyone knows poor little old country boys grow up into dashing, handsome men who can handle anything."

"That's probably the nicest thing anyone has said to me in a long time." Kyle grinned, showing square, white teeth.

Melissa tossed the key ring to Carly who caught it deftly. "I guess we might as well be on our way then," Carly said quietly. Why was she feeling so disloyal? Why did she feel she was doing something sneaky by taking Kyle Dillon out to the Sinclaire property? She had done all that was humanly possible as far as Adam

Noble was concerned. A man's arms really could make you a prisoner and soft, passionate kisses could make you lose all perspective just as the romantic novels said. She shouldn't be thinking of that now. For now, she had to concentrate on Kyle Dillon by keeping up her end of the conversation and always remembering the business at hand.

Kyle turned out to be an easy conversationalist as they made the trip to the island. For the most part Carly listened and was surprised at how easy it was to be with this good-looking man. And the best part was he didn't have a Simone Maddox on his arm, and from the things he said there wasn't anyone like her in his background. No one was going to take this man down the garden path. Both of his feet were on the ground and his head, while pretty far up, was definitely not in the clouds. Straightforward and honest. Two of the most important traits in a man. And he had a delightful sense of humor. A winner. Then why did she feel as though she had lost something? Finding no answers, Carly smiled and linked her arm through Kyle's as they made their way up the path leading to the Sinclaire house.

"Carly, I've seen houses and I've seen houses. But this is one for the books. I'll buy it right now."

"But you haven't even seen the inside," Carly said forlornly.

"I don't have to. I know what I'm going to find when I get in there."

She shouldn't be feeling so dejected, so lost. Kyle's face wore a look of absolute rapture as he moved to view the house from different angles. He loved the house. Mr. and Mrs. Sinclaire would be pleased to sell this man their home. He loved it and would grow to love it more each day. Carly knew that in sight of six months the property would cease to be referred to as the Sinclaire property. He would make his presence known and felt, and it would be the Dillon property over on the island. Not the Noble property but the Dillon place. She choked a little as they continued toward the house.

If only his enthusiasm weren't so contagious. In spite of herself Carly was caught up in Kyle's delight over the small estate.

"I've been through the house, so I'll open the doors for you and you take the tour yourself. Browse and wander to your heart's content. I'll sit out here under the birch trees and think pleasant thoughts."

"Never mind the pleasant thoughts," Kyle said exuberantly. "Start the paper work. By the time we get back to the office I'll have the check ready and I'll sign on ye olde dotted line."

Carly's heart plummeted to her shoes. It was settled. She had no other choice. She couldn't stall, even if she wanted to. It wasn't fair to Kyle.

A LONG TIME later Kyle Dillon joined Carly under the birch trees. "This place is the closest thing to perfection I could ever hope to find," he said reverently. "There's little to change, little to fix. It's a small piece of paradise."

Carly gulped. It was definite now. Even if she had a faint, dim hope in the back of her mind, it was gone now. It was his, Kyle Dillon's house. The only thing that would hinder the sale now was the terms, and she knew that this man would sell his soul, leave no stone unturned, to get this property.

"I'm glad you like it," was all she could manage.

"Like it! Carly, I would give up everything I hold dear for this place. This is the kind of place that grabs you in the gut and never lets go. It's perfect for raising kids. Course, it needs a woman. But," he grinned, "one thing at a time. I want to live in this house, get to know it, and let it get to know me before I start thinking about things like sharing it with some woman." For the first time he seemed to notice Carly's quietness. "Is something wrong? Did I say something out of turn? Sometimes I can get carried away. I should think you'd be happy making a sale of this sort. Your agency should get a really nice commission off this."

"No, nothing's wrong," Carly forced a smile to her face. "Late night last night, guess I'm a little tired," she fibbed.

Kyle accepted her explanation totally. "What I don't understand," he said, lacing his sun-darkened hands across his knees, "is why no one else snapped up this property. The asking price is high but worth every penny. There's a lot of wealthy people around here and it doesn't make sense. Is there something you aren't telling me that I should know about this property?" There was a hint of concern in the big man's voice as he asked the question.

Carly quickly reassured him. "Of course not. The house was just officially listed and only went on the market. I did have a prospective buyer for the place. As a matter of fact, he was the one who steered me to the property and I managed to get the listing. Once I listed it I tried for a week to get hold of the man. None of my calls were returned."

Kyle laughed. "His loss is my gain and I can't say I'm disappointed. Is it someone from around here?"

"Yes, Adam Noble," Carly said quietly.

"Adam! You aren't kidding me are you?" Kyle asked in amazement. Not bothering to wait for a reply, he continued. "I went to college with Adam. We played football together and were on the same wrestling team. He's a nice guy. He's really going to be bent out of shape when he hears I beat him to the draw. That guy was always fast on his feet. And all because he didn't return phone calls." Kyle chuckled, a delighted, smug look on his face.

Carly didn't want to hear any more. Of all the rotten luck. By tomorrow everyone in town would know Kyle Dillon was buying the Sinclaire property. Adam would be at the fish fry along with Kyle. Carly groaned inwardly. And to make matters worse, she was Kyle's date. When you reached bottom, there was no place to go but back up. What she had to do now was act as though she hadn't done anything wrong. And she hadn't. It wasn't her fault. A pity Kyle's friend, Adam Noble, wouldn't look at it that way. She didn't have to feel defensive and on the brink of disaster. It was a straight-forward business deal. There hadn't been any double-dealing. Now, why had that phrase entered her mind? Because, she answered herself, that's what Adam Noble is going to think. Maybe she could plead a headache, the office would burn down, Quincy would get sick. Anything, so she wouldn't have to go to the party.

Coward! she rebelled. You didn't do anything, so why do you have to hide and pretend you did? Every-one is aboveboard.

"I hate to leave here. I could just sit here all day and stare at that house," Kyle said contentedly. "However, I have to get back, and the sooner I sign the papers, the sooner I'll feel as though I own this chunk of paradise. What do you say, pretty lady, are you ready to leave?"

Carly grinned. It was hard to stay depressed around Kyle Dillon. "As ready as I'll ever be. I love this place, too. It's so…so…perfect is the only word I can think of. If I owned this place, I would never part with it. It's the kind of house that goes with big families and down through generations. You're very fortunate that you can afford it, Kyle."

"Pretty lady, I'd work the rest of my life digging ditches if I had to for this house. I can feel it, it's part of me already. I'd never give it up."

"It looks like you won't have to as long as you meet the requirements." Carly smiled. "I think it's safe to say the Sinclaire property is yours."

"That's the second nicest thing I've heard in a long time." Kyle grinned, touching her cheek softly with the tip of his finger. Embarrassed by this little gesture of intimacy, Carly lowered her eyes, suddenly standing. Even before his arms came around her, holding her close to him, she had expected his embrace. And before his head lowered and his lips touched hers, she had known he would kiss her. And even before she had experienced that light caress, she had known he would be tender and gentle. Why then didn't her heart leap and why didn't she feel herself lost in the world of his arms? And why was she allowing his kiss a second time? Deeper, more demanding. It was a salve to her wounded pride. Had Adam wounded her so deeply that she needed to find solace and peace even if it meant turning to another man's arms? Whatever her reasons, she allowed it, wanted it.

At last Kyle Dillon broke away from the embrace. The expression on his face when he looked down at her was gentle and happy. Silently, he took her hand in his and led her to the quay where their launch was waiting.

CHAPTER EIGHT

MELISSA ANDREWS danced around the office the moment the door closed behind Kyle Dillon. "Do you know what the commission on that property is? If we don't sell a house for the next year, we're still in the black. Congratulations, Carly, you did a super job of selling the property," Melissa said enthusiastically.

"Mother, the property sold itself. I didn't have to open my mouth. He saw, he liked, he bought."

"Be that as it may," Melissa said airily, "I prefer to think of you as a super salesman, excuse me, salesperson. And, Carly, tomorrow at the party, Adam Noble and Kyle Dillon, and one of them is your date. I'm so proud of you. You know, Carly," she lowered her voice to a bare whisper, "if you played your cards right, you could play one against the other and who knows? Adam showed a great deal of interest in you before he left. What happened? You might come up with a winner after all. It's time for you to think seriously of getting married. You don't want to be an old maid, do you?"

"Mother, don't help. And for your information, Adam Noble is spoken for. Remember the beauty who trails after him?"

"See, see, you've given up already." Melissa pouted. "But you do have a point whether you realize it or not. She trails after him, there is a very big difference. And," she said loftily, "there's no ring on her finger so that makes anything else more than fair."

"Mother, please. I can do it myself. If I feel like it, that is," Carly said hastily.

"So far time has been just crawling or marching by, Carly. At your age it speeds up and literally races. If you get married, you can have Quincy."

"Mother, stop helping, and bribery in the form of Quincy is definitely no inducement. Any self-respecting man would run the other way if he found out I came with an interfering mother and tart-tongued parrot who is addicted to raspberry licorice sticks."

"Oh, Carly. You're just being difficult."

She wasn't being difficult; she just wanted to be left alone to ponder the day's happenings and what might happen tomorrow. She felt weak in the knees and her elbows hung limply, like a Raggedy Ann doll, just re-membering the feel of Kyle Dillon's arms. And the feel of his lips on hers. Delicious was the only word she could come up with. Her heart had fluttered like a wild bird when Kyle kissed her. She had been content when he released her from his embrace. Was that what she wanted, contentment? Was that what love was? Contentment would sooner or later turn to boredom. She had heard that often enough from aunts and girl friends who had gotten married right after school.

Adam Noble's embrace had been different. He had been masterful the way he drew her into his arms and held her prisoner. Her heart had literally pounded in her chest and her senses reeled till she thought she would faint. And the feel of his lips, gentle, yet demanding. And when he released her she was sorry, she wanted more, so much more. Had she been wrong, did Adam Noble's eyes promise more or was she deluding herself with wishful thinking?

She was getting a headache. Time to go home. Dwelling on the new man in her life and another who had entered and exited too quickly was not going to do a thing for her splitting head. Two aspirins and a hot shower might cure the ache in her head, but what about her heart?

"Darling," Melissa trilled, "I have a marvelous idea, stupendous, actually. What do you say to both of us going to the Chanticleer Chateau for dinner? My treat. We both deserve a rest from that microwave oven. We won't even have to go home to change. All either of us needs is a little fresh makeup and you could use a touch of color at the neck. Here," she said whipping a gossamer melon scarf from her handbag.

Carly shrugged. This was one of those times when it didn't pay to argue with Melissa and she did have a certain light in her eye. Why not? At least she would be spared a few hours in front of the boob tube. "All right, Mother, let me freshen up, and you're right about the scarf. Is it new?"

"Oh, Carly, I've been wearing it for months now. We'll really celebrate tonight. Let's get the works, surf and turf, and a magnificent dessert. We will throw caution to the winds and gorge to our hearts' delight. I deserve it," she said airily. "All week, I eat those dietetic killers and I really deserve this. So do you, darling. Tonight is ours. We'll hoot with the owls."

"If you hoot with the owls, you won't be able to soar with the eagles in the morning," Carly called tartly over her shoulder on the way to the powder room.

"Darling, I do not soar…ever. I glide, there is a difference," Melissa called to Carly's retreating back.

Melissa was at her best when she was going public and the Chanticleer was definitely public. Carly ordered white wine for herself and a Martini, extra dry, for her mother.

"Darling, brighten up, this is a happy occasion, and remember, it's tax deductible," Melissa said as she re-arranged the table accompaniments to suit herself.

"I should have known," Carly groaned.

"Known what? Oh, look, Carly, there's Mr. Dillon

at the bar. I thought he said he was going home? Should we ask him to join us? Carly, are you listening to me? Carly, as a mother, I feel I should say something. Mr. Dillon is a fascinating man. Now, as your mother, I wish to apprise you of something you overlooked. Mr. Dillon is a man of today. Do you know what I mean?"

Carly gulped at the wine and centered her gaze on her mother. "I'm not sure. Don't play cupid, Mother, I'm too old and so are you."

Melissa's face took on a maternal glow that she usually reserved for Christmas morning. "Darling, Mr. Dillon is a today man. His plans and ideals are for the present. Men like Kyle Dillon rarely build toward the future. I know what I'm talking about. It's not that he isn't steady or dependable, he is. He has things to do and places to go. He's an idea man who makes things happen. Today in Maine, tomorrow in Beirut. Do you understand what I'm saying?"

"Perfectly." And she did. "Mother, I just sold the man a piece of property. I have no intention of losing my heart to Mr. Dillon." How true, Carly thought. She couldn't lose her heart when she had already lost it to Adam Noble.

"Now, you take Adam Noble. Adam is a man of tomorrow. Adam knows where he's coming from and where he's going. His aims are set on the future. A girl couldn't do much better than Adam Noble. And it doesn't hurt to remember that Adam comes with gilt-edged securities."

"That does help, doesn't it?" Carly's sarcasm was wasted on Melissa who was waving her long arm in the direction of the bar.

"Be charming, Carly. Mr. Dillon is coming over here. Let's be hospitable and invite him to dinner. Charming, Carly, with a capital C," Melissa warned.

"Why not? It's tax deductible!" Again her sarcasm was lost on Melissa who was showering Kyle Dillon with her hundred-watt smile. In spite of herself Carly smiled, too. How could she be angry with Melissa?

"Mr. Dillon, what a pleasant surprise. Join us, please. We haven't ordered yet."

"If you're sure you wouldn't mind," Kyle said, looking directly at Carly.

The words were forced but Carly managed to get them past her tongue. "By all means, Mr. Dillon, join us."

"This is some kind of restaurant," Kyle drawled as he looked around the elegant dining room. His tone, as well as his gaze, was approving.

"It is the best restaurant around unless you want to go all the way into Bangor. It's a quiet night, but on weekends you need a reservation and then you wait at least an hour for a table. We like it, don't we, Carly?"

"Very much," Carly replied.

"I don't want either of you ladies to think I hang out in bars. It's just that I've been on a high since leaving your office and the Bradshaws are out for the evening. I was sort of left to fend for myself. Now I'm glad that I decided not to go to Bangor with them."

In spite of herself, Carly laughed at his winsome tone. He was putting Melissa on and she was eating it up, or was she?

"I'll join you on one condition." Carly and Melissa waited expectantly for the tall man to make his condition known. "That you allow me to pick up the check."

"I wouldn't hear of it," Melissa demurred. "After all, we did invite you."

"I insist," Kyle said firmly.

"I never argue with a man who insists." Melissa capitulated. "I do so love forceful men. My husband was like that—forceful and dynamic."

Carly almost choked on her drink. The only forceful thing her father had ever done was inherit Quincy, over Melissa's protests, and the only dynamic thing he had done was to marry Melissa. Douglas Andrews had been a scholar and a dreamer, a man of a thousand years ago, and Carly had loved him blindly, as had Melissa. If Melissa preferred to remember him as forceful and dynamic, so be it.

"I'm sorry I never got to meet him."

"I am, too, Mr. Dillon, I am, too." And then Carly

understood. It was Melissa's way of pointing out to Carly that her earlier statements concerning Kyle Dillon were true. He was a today man, her father was a man of yesterday. Dreamers. Adam Noble was a man of tomorrow and all the tomorrows beyond today.

"Tell me, Mr. Dillon…"

"Please, call me Kyle. Mr. Dillon is my father," Kyle interjected.

Melissa nodded. "Tell me, Kyle, how do you like Maine? Have you met any of our town fathers since you've been here?"

"Actually, I've been here many times. I used to come here on semester breaks with a friend of mine while I was in college. I spent a summer here my second year of college."

Melissa's eyes narrowed slightly. "Anyone we know?" she asked casually.

"Adam Noble and his family. Adam and I were roommates back in college."

"Really," Melissa said coolly. "Have you seen the Nobles since you've been here?"

"Not really. I called the manse several times and was told that Adam was out of town. I left my number, but he hasn't returned my calls. I wanted to see the judge before I left. We used to have some really rousing chess games. They're wonderful people. They opened their home to me and treated me as though I was one of their own. Hospitality like that I don't forget. Adam came with me to Texas on several Christmas vacations. He never could get the hang of riding a horse. Old Adam, he beat me out of everything but that. Just couldn't come to terms with a four-legged beast."

"What do you mean, he beat you out at everything?" Melissa asked softly.

"Well, Ma'am, Adam was always the best in everything. He didn't even have to work at it, it just came naturally. Book learning was a snap, sports were a natural, and when it came to the girls, well, Ma'am, they knew a winning combination when they saw it. I hear he's thinking of running for state senator, is that true?"

"As far as I know it is. He was born to politics as were all his family."

"I think you're right," Kyle said thoughtfully. "Senator, governor and, who knows, the White House. Anything is possible."

"What about you, Kyle, what are your plans for the future?" Carly asked.

"Right now, I have no plans beyond settling in to my new house once you ladies give me the right of way."

There was a tinge of anxiety in Carly's voice when she spoke. "You've definitely made up your mind then, this is the house you want?"

"Pretty lady, I signed those papers with just that

thought in mind. I still can't believe that house is going to be mine."

I can top that, Carly thought, I can't believe it either and I'm the one who sold it to him.

"I think it's time to order," Melissa said reaching for a menu the waiter was holding out to her. "I recommend the surf and turf, Kyle."

They gave their order and ordered another round of drinks.

Drinks wound their way into dinner and then dessert. Kyle proved to be not only an amusing dinner companion but a knowledgeable one. Carly enjoyed herself as did Melissa.

"Darling," Melissa said, addressing herself to her daughter. "Would you mind if I skipped dessert and joined the Zacharys? See, there they are over in the corner of the room. Adele hasn't been feeling up to par and I've been meaning to stop by and check on her. This is my chance. I'm sure neither of you young people will mind. Thank you for dinner, Kyle. You must permit Carly and myself to cook you a home-cooked dinner before you leave. We have this fantastic microwave oven which just does everything you tell it to do."

"I'd like that very much, Mrs. Andrews," Kyle said, rising to hold out Melissa's chair. Melissa nodded graciously as she wafted to the far corner of the room.

"I like your mother," Kyle said sincerely.

"I sort of like her myself. She doesn't exactly fit into the ordinary garden variety of mother, but I don't think I would want her any other way." Carly smiled.

"I can understand that. When I left for college, my dad took me aside and sort of whispered to me. What he was trying to tell me was to remember to write home to my mother and then he said, 'Son, your mother is the best friend you'll ever have.' He was right and I've never forgotten those words."

"I think I agree with your father, Kyle."

"You take Adam Noble now, his mother died when he was young and he was raised by his father and a whole parcel of maids and live-in help. Of course, there's all those brothers and sisters of his, but no one can make up for a mother. Adam took to my mother and she took to him. She always said Adam was a man, even when he was a young college student. She said I was a boy compared to him. I don't mind though, Mom is usually right."

Carly stared at the man across from her. He did mind; he minded terribly. She could sense it. Adam was a man and this tall person across from her was also a man in a different way, a man who lived and savored the present. How astute of Melissa to have seen it so quickly.

"Well, what shall we have for dessert?" Kyle asked, opening the menu.

"I think I'll pass."

"I was hoping you would say that. I don't think I could eat another bite. What do you say we take a nice long walk and work off all the damage that we've done?"

Carly straightened the scarf on her neck and picked up her handbag in preparation to leaving.

"Would you look at that!" Kyle exclaimed. Carly followed Kyle's gaze and swallowed hard. Adam Noble and Simone Maddox were making their way to the table. Even from this distance Adam's face wore a chiseled, cold, hard look. The word granite came to Carly's mind. It was too late now to try to tell him and explain how Kyle had won the Sinclaire property. Please don't invite them to sit down; please, she prayed silently as Kyle and Adam went through the back slapping routine that is so common to men.

"I would ask you to join us, but we were just leaving," Kyle said amiably. "You know Miss Andrews, don't you, Adam?"

The reply, when it came, was chips of ice carved from an iceberg. "Very well, as a matter of fact. You've met Simone, haven't you?"

"At a dinner party last week and before that two years ago in Monte Carlo, right?" Kyle grinned. "Don't you remember, Adam?"

"*You* remembered!" Simone trilled delightedly.

Darn. Two years ago in Monte Carlo! That meant Adam and Simone were a thing, an item, as the saying went. Two whole years! Carly's heart thudded sickeningly. She had to get out of here and fast before her emotions got the best of her. How gorgeous she was, how sophisticated. And the burnt orange caftan that would look like a rag on anyone else was perfection on the stunning Simone. Evidently Kyle thought so, too, the way he was ogling her.

"Miss Andrews, how nice to see you again." Simone's tone and the look in her eye clearly stated something else. Carly nodded, not trusting herself to speak. Instead she gave the melon scarf another hitch and stood up, not bothering to wait for someone to hold her chair.

"I'm ready when you are," Carly said coolly to Kyle, ignoring Adam Noble and his beautiful companion.

Carly walked around the side of the table and inadvertently brushed against Adam. When she realized how close she was to the man, she turned and stumbled. Strong arms caught her and held her the barest fraction of a second. Just long enough for Carly to stare deeply into the coldest eyes she had ever seen in her life.

"Are you all right, Carly?" Kyle asked with concern as he placed a firm, hard grip on Carly's trembling arm. "C'mon, let's get on with our walk. I feel all that drawn butter settling around my waistline, not to mention a whole loaf of garlic bread. Funny how the salad and the vegetables seem to go to your feet and everything else goes to the waist."

"It does seem that way," Carly smilingly agreed.

The walk, while not lengthy, was enjoyable. Carly strolled hand in hand with Kyle pointing out various points of interest to the architect's amusement. "I really think we should be getting back. Tomorrow is a work day for me and I want to be bright-eyed to do all the paperwork on the Sinclaire property," Carly said as an inducement to being taken home. Everything was such an effort. I should be enjoying myself and I am, to a degree. I just want to go home and think about Adam in the privacy and darkness of my room.

"Whatever you say, Carly. I really enjoyed this evening. I hope you did, too."

Carly's face wore a stricken look. Had she been that obvious? No, he was just making conversation. "Of course, I enjoyed it. You're a very easy person to be with. And I do want to thank you for dinner."

"It was my pleasure and I'd like to do it again, soon, real soon."

"I'm not hard to find." Carly smiled warmly.

The ride back to her house was pleasant with the car windows open and the soft music coming from the stereo system in the mile-long Cadillac. Kyle walked her to the door and waited while she fumbled with her key.

Carly's head and heart raced as if each were vying for the winning place. Please don't try to kiss me, please don't try, she repeated over and over to herself.

The door open, Carly turned to face Kyle who had backed off a step. "Good night, pretty lady. I'll be calling you." Without another word he turned on his heel and walked down the driveway to his waiting car.

SOMEHOW Carly managed to get through the night and the following day. Always her thoughts were on Adam. Melissa suggested they close the agency early so Carly could get a head start on getting ready for the Bradshaw's fish fry.

"Darling, you need scent from the skin out—bubble bath, bath oil, and then spray your entire body with the scent. You want to waft. Waft, Carly, as you move about. Scent is so important. It teases men. If you use a fragrance that is 'you,' anytime a man smells it he'll think of you even if it's being worn by some voluptuous femme fatale. Carly, you aren't paying attention," Melissa said irritably.

"Mother, stop helping," Carly said just as irritably. If there was one thing she didn't need right now, it was an observer while she dressed for the party. She resigned herself to Melissa's presence, spraying lavishly of the intoxicating scent.

"Good, perfect," Melissa chortled. "Now show me what you're wearing. Oh, Carly, you can't wear that! Don't you have something a little more…that shows off some skin…?"

"Mother, I'm not being auctioned off. What's wrong with this sun dress?"

Melissa pouted. "Nothing. Absolutely nothing, if you were going to a tenth-grade spring dance with a freckle-faced boy. I didn't realize they were still using dimity. It's tacky, Carly, and it won't do." Her voice was firm and held a no-nonsense ring to it. Carly trotted back to the closet and frowned.

Melissa tapped her foot impatiently as she watched her daughter move hangers in the large walk-in closet. "You irritate me beyond belief, Carly. You knew this party was coming up weeks ago. You also knew you would be attending and you should have been prepared."

"I was prepared till you started helping me. You should have told me I was a side of beef you wanted to sell off to the highest bidder," Carly snapped.

"You're an ungrateful daughter," Melissa retorted amiably. "I'm leaving. I know when I'm not needed. You just go right ahead and wear whatever tacky outfit that pleases you. I've done my best," she said dusting her hands together and exiting the room.

Carly heaved a sigh of relief. Now she could get on with her picking and choosing. Melissa was usually right. She did have a flair for fashion and what was right for special occasions. Just because it was a fish fry didn't mean the affair was casual dress. In fact, the Bradshaw affairs usually stopped just short of white tie and tails. She finally selected a sleeveless plum-colored silk dress, slit up both sides. The deep V of the neck should please even Melissa. Simple, elegant, and if the designer label meant anything, she would be as well turned out as Simone Maddox. The sexy three-inch heels with the two slim braids of leather across her toes would definitely add, not detract from the overall effect. No jewelry except the tiny gold and diamond earrings and the diamond snowflake on her hand. Necklaces and bracelets were a no-no as far as she was concerned. What with the high price of gold, every woman there would be dripping in the stuff. If one of them managed to fall into the pool, she would go straight to the bottom. Now in her opinion, *that* was tacky.

Quincy flew into the room and was immediately attracted to the brilliant baubles in Carly's ears. "Carly's a bad girl," he said, lighting on her shoulder, picking at the stones with his hooked beak.

"The only way you're going to get the fix you need, and by that I mean your daily quota of licorice, is to say that Carly is the most beautiful, the most ravishing, the most sexy girl in the world. You say that and you can have two sticks of licorice." Carly grinned as she tried to apply a light dusting of eye shadow to her upper lids.

The emerald bird ignored her as he zeroed in on her flashing finger as Carly's hand moved from the eye shadow to her eye. "Say it, you dumb bird, say that Carly is the most beautiful, the most ravishing, the most sexy girl in the whole world."

"Life is hell! War is hell!" the parrot cackled excitedly.

"You just might have a point at that." Carly giggled.

Carly stood back to survey her handiwork and was satisfied. She wasn't a Simone Maddox but she could definitely hold her own. "And, I even have a brain. What do you think of that, Quincy?"

"Let me see how you look," Melissa said, coming into the room. "My goodness, Carly, you do look…" she searched for the right word, "ravishing. Yes, you really look quite stunning," Melissa said sincerely as she watched her daughter twirl around for her benefit.

"Thank you for your help." Carly grinned. "Well, time to go. Are you certain you won't come along with me instead of the Zacharys? We can still call them and tell them of your change of plans."

"No, darling, I'll go to the fish fry with the Zacharys as planned. And what's more, I'll stay completely out of your way. That dress doesn't signify having a girl's mother hovering in the background."

Carly let out a sigh. "Okay, Mummy dearest, you'll see me…when you see me."

THE PARTY was off to a good start with people milling companionably about. Drinks and hors d'oeuvres on

large silver trays were circulating on the shoulders of
trim waiters in red jackets. The tantalizing aroma of
lobster boiling in huge caldrons at the end of the terrace
drew the crowd for inspection. Carly made chatter with
old friends and clients she had done business with, all
the while searching for some sign of Adam Noble. He
was nowhere in evidence, nor was Simone. No matter
where she moved or who she talked with, the topic of
conversation was Kyle Dillon and his purchase of the
Sinclaire property. A new man on the scene, and from
the looks of things, a rich and successful one. Eligible
bachelors were hard to come by in Bar Harbor.

She knew Adam and Simone had arrived an hour
later when all heads turned toward the entrance. Heads
always turned for the beautiful people. She was no different. She stared as did the others at the delightfully
outrageous gown Simone wore that stopped just short
of being obscene. All that good, clean living, Carly
thought tartly as she gazed at the dress that was parted
to the waist. She drew in her breath. Simone did have
a beautiful figure. The dress was so simple it had to
cost a king's ransom. And Adam, so casual in his suit
of white linen which showed off his marvelous
coppery tan. They looked like the perfect couple. They
were the perfect couple. Carly winced slightly as she
watched Simone link her arm possessively in Adam's
and smile winningly at those around her. Her small

maneuver clearly said to the men she was taken, and to any woman who might have faint ideas of capturing Adam, it meant "Hands off!"

Any man who could be maneuvered that easily wasn't worth it, Carly told herself as she smiled up at Kyle Dillon.

"He hasn't changed at all." Kyle grinned. "Wherever Adam Noble was or is, you can count on finding the most beautiful woman. They look perfectly matched."

"You sound as though you're discussing two pedigree bloodlines," Carly muttered.

Kyle frowned. He would never understand women. He raised an eyebrow in question at Carly's sudden anger but said nothing.

"You don't like Simone, do you?"

"I don't like her and I don't dislike her. Let's just say she's not one of my favorite people."

"Another logical answer. Tell me, Carly, could I ever be one of your favorite people?"

There was an intensity in the tall man's face that unnerved Carly. "I don't know, Kyle," she said, opting for honesty. No game playing for her.

Kyle took her by the arm and led her to the buffet table. "Now, let's have some frivolous party conversation."

"Oh, I do love frivolous conversation." Carly laughed, the infectious sound making those around the table smile. "You look so...so winsome and sort of wispy. It goes with frivolous conversation." Carly continued to laugh.

"I've been called a lot of things in my day but never wispy and winsome," Kyle said in mock anger. "Is it becoming on me?" he demanded.

"Quite," a cool voice answered. "It looks like our climate up here is agreeing with you."

Carly watched as the two men shook hands and then backed off a pace almost as if they were squaring off. They had been friends at one time, that was obvious, but now there was a strain. It was evident to Carly in Kyle's stiff back and in Adam Noble's narrowed gaze.

"I hear talk that you're going to run for state senator. You were born to politics. Didn't I always say you had the makings of the consummate politician?"

"That's what you said, all right," Adam said coolly. "I hear you're the famous architect who is designing the multibillion-dollar airport terminal on the West Coast."

"I don't know about the famous part, but I'm the one doing the designing. Adam, I can't tell you what a challenge it is. My moment of glory, so to speak."

Carly waited, hardly daring to breathe. Where was Simone? Out of the corner of her eye she saw a flash of tangerine silk and sighed. She was being well taken care of by a bevy of men with stupid looks on their faces. When were they going to mention the Sinclaire house? When was Adam going to acknowledge her presence? The tension between the two men was so thick she thought she would suffocate. Say it, say something, her mind ordered. No, more inane party conversation.

"How long will you be here, Kyle? I'd like to have you over to the house. I know the judge would like to see you. He's been following your career for the past several years." Adam's tone was cordial but still cool. Carly sensed that while he offered the invitation, he was hoping Kyle would turn it down.

"I called the house several times but was told you were out of town. I'm afraid I won't be able to take you up on it now. Give the judge my regards. To answer your question, I expect to be here another week or so before heading west. I have a little business to take care of and my hosts have plans for me or so they said. And this little lady here," he said placing his arm around Carly's shoulders, "is hopefully going to take up the slack and entertain me a little."

Adam stared at her, his eyes shards of ice. His mouth was a grim, tight line and Carly could see the stiff set of his shoulders. She smiled happily and thought she would explode with the effort it cost her. All she wanted to do was throw herself into Adam Noble's arms and tell him everything was a mistake. She wanted him to smother her with kisses and hold her in his arms and say it didn't matter, that he was going to make everything right. That's what she wanted.

If Adam Noble was experiencing any emotions, and if Carly was interpreting them correctly, all he wanted to do was strangle her. She couldn't remember ever seeing such hostility emanating from an individual before. Emanating from him and directed at her. Things are tough all over, Mr. Noble, Carly thought nastily. Why should she be subjected to the man's hostility? She had done her job and more if the truth were known. It wasn't her fault if Simone Maddox had a rope around his neck and had named herself his protector. If the delectable Simone wanted to run interference for Adam Noble, it was no concern of hers. Just say one word to me, Adam Noble, just one word, and I'll let you have it with both barrels.

Kyle noticed for the second time the hostility Adam was exuding and correctly surmised that the petite creature next to him was the reason. He grinned down at Carly and then winked. She smiled up at him and suggested in a husky whisper that they walk in the garden. As far as she was concerned, Adam Noble had been dismissed.

With a last scathing look in Carly's direction Adam headed toward the knot of men that surrounded the tangerine-clad figure of Simone Maddox.

"I hate tangerines. They're always sour and full of pits," Carly blurted to Kyle.

"I always thought they were sweet but kind of tangy. When I was a kid, I looked forward to getting them around Christmas."

"They're sour and full of pits. Take my word for it," Carly replied firmly.

Kyle grinned when he noticed the direction her gaze was taking. Come to think of it, he had had a sour one or two. His face continued to wear an amused expression as he led Carly to the garden.

"And where do you think you're going?" a shrill voice demanded. Kyle and Carly stopped in their tracks before Midge Bradshaw raised her voice a second time. "Carly," she continued to shrill, "release this man immediately! I want to show him off to the other guests. Later, you can have him."

Kyle raised his eyebrows and followed the tall heavyset form of Midge Bradshaw. "Don't worry, Carly, I'll find you if I have to set out with Midge's spaniels to track you down."

"You go along. I'll wait in the garden. Go ahead, I'll be fine, really. See, I have a drink and everything. I'll wait for you by the birch grove."

Carly sat for a long time with her untasted drink getting warmer by the moment. She kicked her shoes off and curled her feet under her on the soft chaise. It was so peaceful here in the darkness with the sounds of the party going full swing. She was dozing, on the brink of sleep, with the plastic tumbler about to slip from her hand. In her twilight sleep she felt the glass being removed from her limp hand. Kyle must have done his duty and come to find her. "I hate tangerines," she muttered.

"I never liked them myself, too many pits," replied a cool voice.

Carly was up off the chaise like a shot. "Who… what…"

"Your Lochinvar is over there with the ladies." Adam pointed toward a cluster of people at the far end of the pool. "I'm leaving now, but I couldn't go without telling you what I thought of your business practices. I've heard of scalping, but your tricks are about the most blatant I've ever seen used around here. You knew how much I wanted that property. I spilled my guts to you and this is how you repay me, by putting someone else onto the Sinclaire property. I trusted you to act on my behalf and you repay me by double-dealing with a friend of mine."

"Now, just a darn minute, Adam Noble…" Carly sputtered.

"No. Not another minute. I thought you were honest, that you had integrity and I hoped that you might…"

Carly didn't give him a chance to finish whatever he was about to say. Her eyes spewed fire as she stood to her full height, aware her spike heeled shoes were somewhere in the grass. "Look, Mr. Noble, if you want to attack me, Carly Andrews, that's fine. I'm sure I don't come anywhere close to that tangerine you had hanging on your arm. That's okay, I accept that. Don't you dare, don't you ever dare attack my business methods. I called your home every day, sometimes twice and left messages for you to call me. I did everything I could to make sure you got that property. Kyle Dillon had left messages for you and you didn't seem to get them, either. Why is it so unlikely that my messages were lost? Don't talk to me about business ethics. Take it up with that orange ball over there. And another thing, don't you ever speak to me again. Do you hear me? Not ever!" Tears glistened in her eyes as she bent to find her shoes. The dew on the freshly trimmed grass shimmered in the dim light from the Chinese lanterns but it was also slippery and she slid and nearly fell.

Strong arms reached for her and held her close. "Never is such a long time."

"Never is forever," Carly stated hotly. "I thought I told you never to speak to me again."

"That's what you said all right," Adam said as he brought his mouth closer to hers. "Is that what you really want?"

His wine-scented breath teased her senses as she fought with her emotions. The heady fragrance of his after-shave lotion made her head spin. What did she want? Who cared. Right now, all she wanted was to surrender to this powerful force that was holding her a prisoner. An invisible devil perched himself on her shoulder and she pulled away. "Do you really hate tangerines?"

"With a passion," Adam replied huskily. "Is there something about fruit you can't deal with, something I should know?" he teased as he bent his head again toward her mouth.

Carly moved even closer. "I can think of at least one other thing I would rather discuss right now," she murmured as his lips found hers.

Neither Carly nor Adam saw Kyle Dillon on the edge of the birch grove. They didn't see his shoulders slump, and if they had, it wouldn't have made a difference. They were one, lost in their moment of eternity.

Carly was shaken to her very toes with the intensity of the long kiss. Adam gently removed her from the circle of his arms and stared down at her, his face expressionless in the dim lantern light. He should be saying something, Carly thought wildly. How could he kiss her and hold her the way he had and not say something? What was wrong; why was he suddenly acting so…so indifferent? Did he think she went from man to man, kissing and then telling? Say something, don't look at me like that, she pleaded silently.

Adam's face remained inscrutable and he stared a moment longer before he walked away from her. Carly had never felt so alone in her life. Tears of frustration and longing rolled down her cheeks as she searched for her shoes. She couldn't put them on now, her feet were soaking wet from the dew on the grass. The best thing she could do now was make her way through the birch grove to the parking area and go home. I must have some invisible mark on me that says, "dump on Carly, she won't mind." Well, Carly did mind and Carly was angry. Angry at Adam Noble and angry with herself. And, yes, she was even angry with Kyle Dillon. Where was he? He had left her to go with Midge over two hours ago. The angry tears continued to roll unchecked down her cheeks as she made her way on bare feet to the parking lot. By the time she pulled into the driveway and parked behind Melissa's car the salty droplets were reduced to a mere trickle.

She was a wishy-washy female. And fickle as they come. She fell into his arms as though he were some warrior returning from slaying all the bad dragons of the world. How could he just leave her standing there with her heart in her eyes? In her bare feet no less, like some street urchin. How dare he kiss her like that! Who did he think he was anyway?

"Toy with my affections, will you?" she muttered

angrily as she slammed the refrigerator door shut, deciding there was nothing worth eating, nothing that would make her less angry with the tall, handsome man. And that…that…blueprint fanatic, where was he? He hadn't even shown up. Two hours he had left her in the birch grove! What did he think she was supposed to do for two whole hours? The word date must mean something else in Texas, Carly fumed as she stalked around the kitchen. Men! Put them in a paper bag, shake it up and they all came out the same. Male chauvinists, the lot of them. She didn't have to put up with either one of them. She was, after all, her own person, always had been.

Why was she tearing herself apart like this? Neither Adam Noble nor Kyle Dillon were worth the effort. Anything that caused this much emotional turmoil should be eliminated. How dare they treat her in such a shabby fashion!

She stomped up the stairs and down the hall to her room. Several hours later, Carly had just slipped her nightgown over her head when Melissa walked into the room. "Home so early?" she yawned elaborately. "Carly! What is that suitcase doing on your bed?" she demanded, now completely awake.

"I'm not running away, I'm just going someplace," Carly replied through clenched teeth.

"I'm glad to hear it. Would you mind telling me

where you're going and why? And what makes you think I would think you're running away?"

"Well, I'm not, so there. Don't help, Mother. I can take care of this myself."

"I can see that for myself. You must be planning on spending a lot of time in bed wherever you're going."

"No, I'm not going to spend a lot of time in bed. In fact, I may never sleep again. Why did you say that?" Carly asked as she continued to toss garments helter-skelter into her suitcase.

"So far," Melissa said ticking off items on her fingers, "you packed three pairs of pajamas, four night-gowns, two robes and three pairs of slippers. How's that for starters?" She yawned again and perched herself on the arm of a slipper chair covered in lavender velvet.

Carly looked baffled for a moment but quickly recovered. "I'm trying to decide which ones to take. I'll sort through later. This is just angry packing," she said defensively.

"I understand that perfectly," Melissa said nonchalantly. "Now, would you tell me why you're angry? So angry that you're running away, excuse me, going away?"

"I really don't want to talk about it. And don't think you're foisting that bird off on me, either. Where I'm going, they don't allow birds."

"Fine. Fine. Where are you going? I'm your mother. I have a perfect right to ask that question and a perfect right to expect some kind of an answer. Carly, this isn't like you at all! You've always been so…so stable. I'm the flighty one. You always had your feet on the ground. Dependable, if you know what I mean. This is so entirely out of character for you that I don't understand."

"Dump on me, too! Why not? Why should my own mother be expected to understand? Just dump on Carly, she won't mind. She's stable, dependable, and you can always count on her having her feet planted firmly on the ground. Well, let me tell you something. I'm tired of being stable and dependable. I only wanted to stick my head in the clouds and soar a little. I did that and look what happened to me," Carly blurted. "You know I have feelings and emotions just like everyone else. I hurt. I'm vulnerable. Why can't people see that? Why do I always have to be trampled on? What makes me different?"

Melissa was at a loss. "Carly, baby, tell me what happened. I don't know if I can help, but I'm here for whatever good I am."

"Oh, Mom," Carly sobbed throwing herself into Melissa's arms. "I goofed it all up and I was left high and dry, as the saying goes." She sniffed and dried her eyes on the sleeve of her nightgown. "I'm okay. We'll talk in the morning, okay? I just want to get into bed for now. Go to bed, Mom, I'm okay."

"If that's what you want, Carly," Melissa said, patting her daughter affectionately on the head. "If you need me or decide you want to talk, call me." She left the room in a swish, leaving in her wake the faint, elusive scent of night-blooming jasmine.

Carly slid beneath the covers and then pulled them up to her chin. She felt like sleeping with the light on. She didn't want to lie in the dark and imagine even darker thoughts. She slept eventually, her dreams filled with visions of herself mailing one letter after another, all the while listening for the phone to ring.

Carly woke exhausted when the alarm shrilled the start of a new day. Her head throbbed and her shoulders ached. Maybe she was coming down with the flu or some kind of virus. Come to think of it, she was overdue. She had gone through the entire winter without one case of the sniffles. She was getting sick, and if you were sick, you got to stay in bed. When you stayed in bed, you didn't have to go to work and see people. You didn't have to put on a brave front or make decisions. When you were sick, you got waited on hand and foot; your every need was seen to by someone else. The last thought was the one that made her slide from the bed. She could just see Melissa tying a thermos of hot tea around Quincy's neck for him to deliver because she didn't want to climb the steps. "It was a thought," she muttered to herself as she headed for the bathroom and her morning shower.

Stepping back into her room, she noticed the open suitcase on the floor at the foot of her bed. That was exactly what she should do. Go away somewhere, get her mind off the whole Sinclaire mess. Somewhere there was plenty of life and lots of diversion. New York.

Satisfied with her decision, she dressed with care and then quickly packed her bag and overnight case. She called the airline and charged a round-trip ticket on her American Express card. Now all she had to do was have some breakfast, give Quincy his licorice stick, kiss Melissa goodbye and take off.

CHAPTER NINE

BY USING superhuman effort Carly managed to while away two full weeks in the Big Apple. She stayed with her friend Jenny from college, alternating her time between shopping, luncheons with old friends, and partaking occasionally of an intimate dinner with still older boyfriends who professed they were glad to see her and asked how long would she be in town. She gave vague answers to what she thought was their obvious relief. She was past tense in more ways than one. She might as well go home. She had wanted to get Adam Noble out of her system and it wasn't working. You can't run away from your problems, she told herself over and over as she packed her bag for the return to Bar Harbor.

She had run away when she left Melissa two weeks before. In her heart of hearts she knew the only reason she chose New York as her destination was that she hoped in some way she would be walking down the street and accidentally bump into Adam Noble. It always happened that way in the movies and the place was always New York City. It was time to go home and she hadn't seen Adam at all.

Carly glanced at her watch. She still had time if she really wanted to see Adam. She could even delay her flight till tomorrow morning if she had a mind to. Chez Martine. That was where Adam said he did his gourmet cooking on weekends. This was the weekend. Why not? She had told him she was going to try out the restaurant when she got to New York again. Why not tonight? Why not indeed? But Adam had said he catered private parties. Well, there was only one way to find out and that was to go the restaurant. Before she could change her mind, Carly pulled out the heavy Manhattan directory and riffled through the pages. Chez Martine, East Fifty-second Street, between First and Second Avenues. All she needed was a taxi and some money.

The square black phone on the tiny table in the foyer drew her eye. Perhaps she should call for a reservation. And while she was at the phone, she might as well call the airline and change her reservation for the following morning.

"Chez Martine," a warm, friendly voice with a hint of a foreign accent announced.

"I'd like to make a reservation, please."

"Your name please, and how many in your party?"

"Carly Andrews. I'll be dining alone."

"And what time would you like your reservation?"

Carly glanced at her watch. Thirty minutes by cab at the most. "Eight o'clock will be fine."

"Your reservation is confirmed, Miss Andrews. Thank you for calling Chez Martine."

Carly looked at the phone as she replaced the receiver in the cradle. She dreaded the thought of eating alone in a popular New York restaurant especially at the height of the dinner hour that was a usual hour for dinner dating. Much as she hated the feeling of being conspicuous she would suffer through the experience in the hopes that she would see Adam Noble. For an instant her heart fell. Maybe Adam wouldn't be there. Perhaps she was planning all this for nothing.

Refusing to face that possibility, she made a quick call to the airline and her plane reservation was changed and rebooked by an obliging computer. Now all she had to do was open her suitcase and take out one of the new dresses she had bought during one of her shopping sprees.

An hour later Carly was dressed in a raspberry silk dress and ready to go. She looked pretty and for the first time in two weeks she felt pretty, more like the Carly Andrews of old. Amazing what the thought of seeing the man in your life could do for your spirits. There was no point in denying, even to herself, that she was in love with Adam Noble. For all the good it's going to do me, she thought unhappily as she climbed into the rear seat of a Checker Cab.

It was a basement restaurant, like so many in the city, and from the appearance, it was one that catered to intimate dining. It would be dim with the candles on the tables and there would be romantic couples seated in nooks surrounded by foliage. Her stomach started to churn as she opened the door and walked into the dimly-lit room that held a large, circular bar. She blinked and tried to focus her eyes.

The hostess was tall and model-thin. She made her way to Carly smiling a welcome. It seemed to Carly that all eyes were on her as she was motioned toward a tall podium holding an open reservation book. "Name please."

"Carly Andrews. I'm dining alone." Now why had she said that? Any fool could see that she was alone. Carly tried to stifle her defensiveness. She was here in this place eating alone by her own choice. If she felt out of place and conspicuous that was her own problem, no one else's.

"This way please." Carly followed the hostess and wondered fleetingly how she could stay so thin and work in a restaurant.

"Here you are," the hostess said, indicating a tiny table set back in a dark corner of the room. It was next to the kitchen and beside the dish and utensil counter.

She had read in several women's magazines that restaurants as a general policy seated solitary diners somewhere off to the side. This was especially true if the solitary diner was a woman. For the moment, she was grateful. The table's proximity to the kitchen was just what she wanted and it would also serve to make her feel less conspicuous.

The wine list was brought and Carly scanned it quickly, ordering the house white wine. A glass carafe was placed before her and the amenable waiter poured her the first glass. He held out a menu in a heavy burgundy folder with a long golden tassel dangling at the end. Carly again scanned the printed words, trying to decide what to order.

"If I may make a suggestion," the waiter said softly. "Chez Martine is most fortunate to have on the weekends a fabulous chef. Today his specialty is Osso Bucco à l'orange and roulade de veau Florentin."

He was here, in the kitchen. Adam Noble was really here. Out there, just beyond the door, only yards away. "Fine, the Florentin please," she decided, her eyes straying to the kitchen door. Whatever it was she was sure she would love it.

Carly's meal arrived and was served to her with what she could only call reverence. It was apparent that Adam's reputation as a chef was held with great respect even with the waiters.

She was aghast at the huge platter of food the waiter was placing in front of her. Even though she was hungry and eager to taste Adam's cuisine she couldn't possibly make a dent in the amount served to her. The New England Patriots Football team combined with the Boston Bruins hockey team would have been hard pressed to eat what was on the platter. She glanced in askance at the waiter who suddenly seemed decidedly uncomfortable. She risked another glance, this time around the room. The other diners seemed to have normal portions.

Another quick glance at the waiter and Carly saw he was smiling in the direction of the kitchen door. Turning, she caught sight of Adam's laughing face looking back at her through the round glass window. Within a split second, he was gone.

Adam Noble was trying to make a fool of her, embarrassing her in front of the other patrons. Trying to remain calm, she waited for the waiter to serve her a portion of the veal on her plate. Instead, and looking quite uncomfortable about it, he removed her service plate and placed the huge platter in front of her. Squelching down the urge to get up and run away, Carly instead picked up her fork and tasted the tempting dish. The delicious food stuck in her throat and tasted like sawdust to her palate. She knew the food was expertly prepared but somehow she had great difficulty swallowing it. Adam had purposely set out to make her feel foolish. Well, she would treat him in kind.

She raised her index finger slightly and the waiter appeared as if by magic. Carly moistened her lips and motioned for him to lean closer. In a voice barely above a whisper she said, "I really hate to complain but this is overspiced and overdone. Please return it to the chef and ask him to make me a salad. Lemon dressing, please."

The waiter blanched. "You…you want me to take all of this back…and…"

"Yes. I do," Carly said simply, her tone soft, ladylike and yet authoritative.

"Yes, a salad. Lemon dressing." Solemnly, he removed the huge platter from the table and made his way into the kitchen.

She sat there resolutely, little quivers of apprehension dancing through her veins. She told herself she should pay her bill and leave. Now. Before the waiter relayed her criticisms to Adam. The sound of an angry crash reverberated through the room and its source was the kitchen. Again Carly wished she had the courage to get up and leave before Adam himself came into the dining room to strangle her. She knew he took an artist's pride in his culinary techniques.

Again the waiter returned, looking shaken and harried. He placed the salad before her. Suddenly, Adam himself appeared opposite her and seated himself at the table. "You ordered it, now eat it. And to set the matter straight, the veal was neither over-spiced nor overdone. Do you understand?"

"Perfectly, Mr. Noble. You're telling me it's per-fectly all right for you to criticize my business prac-tices but it isn't all right for me to do the same."

Adam ignored her words. "Eat," was all he said.

Carly was about to obey him when something inside her rebelled. She signaled to the waiter and asked for her check. The poor hapless man looked first at Adam and then at Carly.

"You're beautiful when you're angry," Adam said quietly. "You're always beautiful. Apologize to me for your comments concerning my food."

"Apologize!" she gasped, hating the smile that was already forming on her lips. "Do you really think I'm beautiful?"

"Of course you are. You might operate your business a little on the shady side but you're still beau-tiful. Apologize."

"No. You apologize to me for what you said about my business ethics."

"Impossible," came the sharp reply.

Carly looked at the nervous waiter. "My check, please."

"I'll take care of it," Adam offered, "it's the least I can do seeing how dissatisfied you were with the meal." He fixed his indigo eyes on her and the flame from the candlelight seemed to burn within them. He was angry, terribly angry, Carly could see it in the tight set of his jaw and his unblinking gaze.

Gathering her purse and scarf she hastily stood up, wanting only to get away from Adam, away from Chez Martine, before she burst into tears. How could he be so unbending? Did he think it was only by pure chance that she had come to Chez Martine? Couldn't he see that it had only been to see him again, hopefully to patch up the misunderstanding between them?

Literally running from the restaurant, she found herself wandering aimlessly down the street, knowing she shouldn't be walking alone at this time of night but not caring. How could she love such an obstinate single-minded person the way she loved Adam? Regardless of how she could, she did love him. And now, nothing would ever come of it. For whatever it had been it was over.

A car pulled alongside of her and the door opened. "Get in," was the curt order. "You really should know better than to wander around alone at this time of night."

Adam's voice was stern, sharp. Carly obeyed, never considering to do otherwise. Her heart beat in sudden raps against her rib cage. Folding herself into the sports car she had no sooner slammed the door shut when he spun away from the curb. In the close confines of the car her shoulder was almost touching his and daring a glance at his stony profile and tightly set mouth that conveyed his anger, she drew closer to the door.

"Where to?" Adam asked curtly.

"Aren't you supposed to be on duty at the restaurant?" she asked in turn.

"Everything is prepared—they only have to serve it. Where to?"

Carly gave him the address and leaned back in her seat. She stared straight ahead, not daring a second look in his direction, not wanting to witness his anger. From time to time she felt rather than saw him turn in her direction; felt his gaze piercing her. She felt confused, neither knowing what to do or what to say. They continued to ride in silence and Carly thought her heart would break. She wanted that gentle, attentive, easy-to-be-with Adam she had come to know in Bar Harbor before the situation with the Sinclaire property had erupted.

The car came to a smooth stop at the curb outside Jenny's apartment house. "Thank you for the ride," Carly muttered.

"My pleasure," was the abrupt reply.

"I'm sorry," she whispered.

"It's late, Miss Andrews, you'd better get inside. I'll wait here until I see that you're safely indoors." His voice was flat, nearly as emotionless as the expression on his face.

It was all she could do to whisper a husky, "Good night, Adam." Had she been mistaken or had he said, "Good night, Carly"? And his voice had seemed soft, void of annoyance.

She would never know for certain because she had already begun to slam the door shut when he answered and she couldn't bring herself to open it again on the chance she had been wrong.

Almost the instant the outside apartment door closed behind her she heard the sound of his car pulling away; the powerful sound of the engine drowning out her stricken sob.

Desolate, inconsolable, she pressed her face against the glass pane and stared out into the night. "Good night, Adam," she whispered again. "Goodbye."

CHAPTER TEN

THE NEXT MORNING Carly lay quietly in bed in the guest room of Jenny's apartment, listening as her hostess readied herself for an early tennis date. Jenny had been marvelous. Instinctively, she had included Carly in some of her plans, taking her out, introducing her to new people, but Jenny had also realized that Carly had a need to be alone some of the time and this was graciously allowed. Much as Carly was fond of Jenny, she couldn't face her this morning. If Jenny should return from her tennis date before Carly left for the airport, their goodbyes would be said then. If not, the free and easy Jenny wouldn't be upset by a phone call from Bar Harbor.

Carly rolled over on her side, appreciating the quiet of the cozy guest room. Her cheek felt hot against the pillow as she recalled the evening before in the restaurant with Adam. Misery, misery! Why couldn't she be as cool as a cucumber and carry things off the way other women seemed to do? All poise and stature. Oh no, not good old Carly. No, she was all big feet and trembling fingers.

Outside her closed door Carly heard Jenny whisper a faint "Good morning" and "I'll see you later after tennis." Carly couldn't bring herself to answer, preferring that Jenny think she was still asleep. After the snick of the lock hitting home on the front door sounded, Carly reluctantly threw back the covers and planted her feet firmly on the floor. She couldn't allow herself to lie abed and hide from the world. After all, truth to tell, it was really only Adam Noble that she wanted to hide from. Outside her window were the muffled sounds of light traffic. Saturday morning in New York City was a place of slowed paces and gleeful shopping. Business had ceased for the week and, wonder of wonders, it was almost possible to get a cab just by standing on a corner and waving an indecisive finger. Not like during the rest of the week when you practically had to throw yourself into the rush of traffic and pray the cab would stop before it ran over you.

After brushing her teeth and running a brush through her crackling dark hair, she padded out to the minuscule kitchen in search of a cup of coffee. The electric percolator hissed quietly and puffed out fragrant streams of brew. When she found the milk in the fridge, it was well on its way to sour. Sighing,

Carly poured herself a mug of coffee, added an ice cube to cool it down, and sipped carefully. It tasted flat without the milk. Just as flat as the rest of her life would be without Adam Noble to sweeten it. Grimacing at the thought, yet unconsciously squaring her shoulders for courage, she pushed the thought aside and went into the expansive living room to peer out into the street.

A sporty black Corvette screeched to a halt in front of the apartment building and, even as she watched, Adam Noble unfolded his lean length from behind the wheel.

Adam! Here! What did he want? She wouldn't open the door. She would pretend that she'd already left for home. There was no way he could know that she was still in Jenny's apartment, hiding like a child from the bogeyman. There was no way on earth that she was going to open that door. No way!

Trembling, Carly moved toward her bedroom, the furthest place away from the front door. She would stay there until he went away. Then she would get her gear together and take a cab to the airport. He'd never find her, never again. She would hide, hide away from Adam Noble. Hide, and the rest of her life would be dark and without light. The light from Adam's smile.

Suddenly Carly stopped, frozen, thoughts rolling,

heart pounding. No! She was through hiding. She couldn't hide for the rest of her life. Sooner or later she would have to face him, and now was as good a time as any.

Brazenly, she stalked back toward the front door. She ran a peremptory hand through her hair and tightened the belt of her robe. Swinging open the front door, she stood against it, prepared for battle, relishing the thought of it. For once and for all, she was going to take Adam Noble head on.

The sound of the buzzer sounded through the apartment. Steeling her voice to keep it from quivering, she answered the ancient intercom.

"Yes?" she answered into the small microphone.

"Carly? That you? It's me, Adam." Was that a note of uncertainty she heard in his voice? Was it possible that the stalwart Mr. Noble was actually uneasy about his uninvited visit?

"Yes?" she answered again; this time with more confidence.

"I want to see you. Can I come up?"

Carly's finger hesitated over the electronic button that would unlock the door downstairs and admit him. Deliberately, she punched her finger onto the button. A few seconds later she heard the rapid sound of his steps on the stairs. When he at last rounded the landing, he found her leaning against the doorjamb, arms folded across her chest, an expression of resignation on her face.

"Morning!" he said brightly, ignoring the thinly veiled hostility in her eyes.

Carly nodded, knowing that if she spoke her voice would waver and crack and once again he would have her at a disadvantage.

"Smells like coffee. Could I have some?" The boyish smile that touched his lips and lighted his eyes sent a pang of tenderness through her heart. No, she must stop this. Adam Noble was not a little boy begging for a cookie. He was a grown man who was very much in control of seeing his needs and desires filled. Instantly, she remembered the feel of his lips against hers, the way his arms enfolded her, keeping her for his own, protecting her from the world.

Before she lost her control and allowed him to see the vulnerability in her eyes, she turned her back and walked to the kitchen, hearing him enter the apartment and close the door behind him.

She had expected him to wait for her in the living room, so when she turned to the counter where the electric percolator steamed, she was shocked and unnerved to find him standing close behind her.

"Do you always do that?" she asked, annoyed.

"Do what?"

"Creep up on women that way."

"Only when they're as lovely as you and have the morning roses on their cheeks." He gazed down at her, captivating her with the ingenuousness of his smile.

"And do you always think a woman is going to fall for that line of blarney?"

"Most times," he said softly. "Especially when it's true."

"Well, not this woman!" Carly warned. Abruptly, she turned her back on him and poured the dark brew into a mug, filling another for herself.

Taking the mug from her, he winked conspiratorially. "Ah, the first hemlock of the day. Smells delicious. Did you make it?"

"No, I didn't make it. And if you've come to remind me what a fool I made of myself last night, you just may be wishing that *was* poison in that mug."

The look he gave her was startled, shocked and surprised that she would even think of him being so ungentlemanly. Carly had to hand it to Adam. Whatever the situation, he would charm his way out of it.

"Adam, did anyone ever tell you that your career in politics would be brilliant?" She had meant it as a gibe, but he took it seriously.

"As a matter of fact, yes. But it's always nice to hear it."

Together they laughed, enjoying the teasing and the unusual form of camaraderie they shared.

After several sips of coffee, Carly turned to him again. "Suppose you tell me just why you are here?"

"To take you home."

"Home! I've already made airline reservations."

"Cancel."

"I couldn't do that. I had intended to be home by late this afternoon and that's just what I'm going to do."

"Cancel. Please?" The honesty of his gaze penetrated Carly's determination.

"Why? It seems senseless to drive all the way to Bar Harbor. That's almost an eight hour trip. I could be there by plane in a little over an hour…."

"Stop fighting it, Carly. I want to spend some time with you. It's been a long time…cancel," he ended with authority as though he weren't used to having his requests and decisions ignored.

For a long moment Carly found herself looking into his eyes, questioning the expression she found there. That he was perfectly serious was evident. "Adam… really, my reservations have been confirmed. I was planning on returning to Bar Harbor yesterday, only…" Instantly, she realized she had given herself away. Now he knew that she had put off returning to Maine in order to seek him out at the restaurant. Angry with herself, Carly heard herself say, "You're just looking for someone to keep you company on the drive home. I'm as good as anyone, is that it?"

"Wrong." He frowned.

"Why don't you get Simone to fly down to New York? She'd be more than happy to drive all the way back to Maine with you and have you all to herself." As soon as she uttered the words, she realized how juvenile they sounded. She had to stop herself from clamping her hands over her mouth. Now he knew about her jealousy.

"If I wanted Simone, she would be with me right this very moment and I wouldn't be standing here scuffing my shoes together like a schoolboy getting a lecture from his teacher. Now, I ask you once more and I won't again. Will you accompany me back to Bar Harbor?"

"And if I say no?"

"If you say no, then you'll be traveling all the way back to Maine in the scruffy robe you're wearing." At her look of shock, he laughed. "That's right. I'll pick you up right off your feet and carry out to my car. And don't think anyone on the street will save you from abduction. This is the Big Apple, remember, not little Bar Harbor where everybody's business is everybody else's. Down here, no one wants to get involved."

"You wouldn't," she dared him, carefully placing her coffee mug on the counter, prepared to run away from him. This was a side of Adam she had never seen before, a side of him she didn't know how to deal with. Something in his voice warned her that he meant every word he had spoken.

"Oh, wouldn't I?" A glint shone in his eyes, a smile played around his lips.

"You're incredible!" Carly protested. "You have the effrontery to come in here and…and… threaten me!"

"And you had the effrontery to come into the restaurant and criticize my cooking! Seems as though we're two of a kind, Carly. Now hurry up and get your things together. And don't overdress. Jeans will do. I intend for us to take in a little sightseeing on our drive back."

"I will not! I have no intentions of going anywhere with you, Adam Noble, so you can get that idea right out of your foolish head." Carly crossed her arms over her chest and slowly tapped her foot on the worn tile floor.

In an elaborate gesture, Adam lifted his arm, pulled back the sleeve of his fine knit sport shirt and looked at his watch. "I'll give you three seconds to get to your room and dress. One…two…"

"No way!" Carly shouted. "There's no way you're going to come in here and give me orders! I'm a big girl now, Mr. Noble, or hadn't you noticed?" Her tone was snide, her lip was curled, her cheeks blazed with anger.

"Believe me, I've noticed, Carly." The softness of his tone was disarming, bringing further heat to her cheeks. "Shall we begin again?" he asked looking at his wrist watch. "One…two…"

"Ooh! You insufferable, egotistical…" Unable to control herself, she pushed him, nearly knocking him off his feet, leaving him swaying for balance against the apartment's small refrigerator.

Quicker than she would have thought possible, he regained his balance and flew after her, grasping her arm, pulling her backward, tumbling with her onto the carpeted floor of the living room.

"Adam! Let me go!" She struggled. "Let me go, right now!"

He pinned her beneath his weight, holding her arms over her head, looking down into her face, so close that she could feel his breath upon her cheek. Their gazes locked and held. Slowly the anger ebbed out of Carly's bones. Slowly, with each heart beat, anger was replaced with a yearning, a yearning to have his head bend to hers, to have his lips touch hers.

As Adam's eyes met hers, she felt herself falling into the depths of emotion, melting into him, allowing him to see her unmasked feelings, the desire for something outside herself.

As though in a dream, Adam's struggles ceased. His grip tightened, but this time it was with a strange brand of gentleness. Softly, his mouth claimed hers and his kiss deepened and became intense and swept her along with its persuasion.

Slowly, her arms circled his neck, her mouth yielded up to his and his tender, teasing touches. She heard him murmur her name against her ear, and when he lifted his head to look into her eyes, she could see desire ablaze there, a raw hunger that she knew was beyond her power to control.

"Adam!" she began to protest, but he misunderstood her cry for one of passion instead of one of protest.

His arms seized her, his lips found her throat, the V of her robe, the promising swell where her breasts began to rise.

He was wicked; he was tender; he excited her senses and commanded her pulses. She was his prisoner; he was her prey. She could not escape his loving, his strength. He kissed and caressed her, robbing her of her will, awakening in her a responsive fire that, unleashed, could consume them both.

Carly exerted weak protests against his chest, his arms, pushing, fighting to have him release her. Desire told her to surrender to his arms, his lips. Passion whispered and throbbed at his every touch, telling her that he alone could lead her to the heights of fulfillment and topple her into the realm of sensuality. Common sense pounded at the small portion of her reality that was not filled with Adam Noble.

"No…no…!" she begged, using the last of her strength to wriggle out from under him, knowing that if strength should fail, she would lose herself in the desire he aroused in her.

"Adam, no…"

Slowly, tenderly, he released her from his embrace. Patterns of emotions played about his face. His voice, when he spoke, was warm, husky, simmering with barely achieved control. "Carly." That was all, just her name. With a display of reluctance, he climbed to his feet and pulled her upright to stand in the circle of his arms. "Now, will you please get dressed and drive back to Bar Harbor with me? Tell me what airline; I'll cancel your reservation."

As though through a dream, she told him. Beneath his spell she was without a will of her own. She knew she would do as he asked. Do it and love doing it. Within, her heart sang. Of course she would drive back to Maine with Adam. Was there ever really any doubt?

ONWARD, onward, the road curved before them. Interstate 95 unfurled before them, dancing them through New York State, Connecticut, the few miles of Rhode Island and Massachusetts. At last, they left the Interstate for the more picturesque Route 1 just on the far side of Bath, Maine.

The day was still young, young enough for Carly to still feel the imprint of Adam's arms tight around her and the firebrand of his kiss on her lips. She wondered if the remembrance would ever leave her, to fade away like so many other memories. Somehow, she doubted it. She would mark this day as a milestone in her life.

From now on it would always be "before the day that Adam kissed me," or "after the day in Jenny's apartment when Adam kissed me," or even "the same year that Adam made me feel like a woman."

The radio sang softly and Adam and Carly noted the bewitching names of the tiny hamlets through which they passed. Wicasset, Damariscotta, Friendship, old names, salty with the sea, foreign names reminiscent of farms and fertile fields.

And as they drove, they talked of many things. Mostly, Carly was content to lean back against the soft leather of the Corvette as the vehicle hugged the ground and whizzed them along and listen to the deep sounds of Adam's voice. He spoke of his deep love for his family, of his rambunctious brothers and keen-minded father, the judge. He told her of his love for this state of Maine and his concern for its people. One day, soon, she wouldn't be surprised to see his name on the ballot for State Senator.

With each sentence he spoke, Carly was imbued with an understanding of just how much family and citizenship meant to Adam. His eyes were toward the future, his feet planted very firmly in the present. In all truth, Melissa had been right about him. He was a man for tomorrow and beyond.

Her thoughts touched lightly on thoughts of Kyle. A man for the here and now. Somehow he could always make the most advantage of today and devil take the hindmost. Like his craft of architecture, Kyle built his life on accomplishments today—building for the present and looking forward to the next city and the next building. Roots were not a part of Kyle's vocabulary.

Roots. Generations. Dynasty. These were words with which Adam was fully familiar. They were the touchstones of his life and his reason for being. Building for the future. Security for his family, with always an eye to the world that family would inherit.

"We're coming into Rockland, Carly. What say we stop for a late lunch?" His voice broke into her thoughts.

"Umm. I'm starved."

"Well, I know just the remedy for that condition." Adam smiled. "I know where we can get the best hot dogs this side of Coney Island."

Carly laughed. "Don't tell me you have a penchant for hot dogs, not after all your bragging about being a gourmet cook!"

"Ouch! Well, the secret's out."

"Hot dogs it is. Now, don't tell me, let me guess. We're going down to the public landing, right? And there's this little old man with a heavy French accent who sells steaming hot franks and ice-cold orange pop."

Adam laughed, the sound filling the interior of the automobile. "You've been here before."

"World traveler that I am, how could I not?"

Like a capricious breeze, the Corvette swung around the curves and descended steeply down a gravel track to the harbor on Penobscot Bay and to Pepe's hot dog stand.

The afternoon sun shone off the waters like a ransom in gold. The hot dogs were incredibly hot, the orange pop refreshingly cold and like two children with treasure, Adam and Carly absconded with the goods and walked the length of the public pier, munching and sipping.

In the distance, the outline of Vinalhaven Island could be discerned. The blue waters of the bay were salted with white sailing boats, their mainmasts seeming to scrape the sky, their brilliant sails creating a carnival of color.

"It's a little chunk of God's country, Carly. The water is so calm and peaceful, but we both know what it can be during a storm."

Carly nodded her agreement. "There are times I really don't know which I prefer, this calm or a good roiling storm. There's something about the power and force that excites me." Suddenly, Carly's cheeks pinkened. Wasn't that part of Adam's charm for her? His power, his force, and yet the appealing other side of him—his gentleness and tenderness.

"Funny how when people think of Maine they imagine windswept rocks and boiling sea beating surf against the beach. That's only true in the southernmost part of our state. The further north one goes, the shore-line becomes expansive bays dotted with islands where the trees reach down to the water and the land palisades into cliffs."

"But there's no denying our twelve foot tides, Adam, when the shore can become a shelf of mudland…."

"Ah! But otherwise, who would be able to harvest clams and beachcomb…?"

"Do you always see an advantage to everything?" Carly asked, a twinkle in her eye.

"Why not? I'm not exactly the cockeyed optimist, but there is usually something good about every situation. Take the house on Deer Island, for instance."

As soon as he mentioned the island, Carly stiffened. She didn't want to go into a broad explanation of why the house seemed to be sold out from under him. Not here, not now.

Adam shrugged. "If it wasn't meant to be, then it won't be. Besides, if I'm not missing my bet, it won't be long before Kyle finds his fancies going in other directions and the house might just be mine some day, after all."

Carly sighed in relief. There was a lot of truth in what Adam said. "Kyle told me he thought the house just perfect the way it is. I don't believe he's planning any major renovations."

"Kyle always did have an eye for perfection," he

said, his voice closer to her ear than she had expected. She was startled, but not dismayed, to find herself wrapped in his tender embrace, his lips tracing a pattern from her ear to her cheek. He released her as quickly as he had embraced her and Carly felt bereft when he removed his arms.

"Look." He pointed to the water and to a sailing vessel tacking into port. "It's the *Victory Chimes,* the loveliest boat to sail these waters. She cruises the Maine coast and takes on passengers who work as her crew. I've always wanted to book passage but somehow I've never found the time."

"Oh, Adam, have you really? So have I! I've heard people talk about it and I fell in love with the idea."

"So have I," Adam agreed, a strangely intimate light in his eyes as he gazed at her. "I've fallen in love…with the idea." He pulled his gaze away from hers, gazing out to the horizon once again.

A heat spread through Carly, touching her breasts, her lips, her cheeks. Her heart beat a rapid tattoo, pounding, threatening to erupt from her chest. Was it possible, had Adam meant what she thought…? No, silly. You're reading into his words, she chastised herself. When Adam has something to say, he says it. Period. Besides, with the inimitable Simone Maddox waiting in the wings, she mustn't hope for more than a companionable ride back to the Harbor. A kiss was a kiss, it wasn't a commitment for life, she reminded herself. Yet, there was so much more. So much emotion and yearning… Don't, she warned. It was a kiss, not a promise. Period.

She was aware that Adam had taken her hand in his and was leading her back up the pier. He seemed mesmerized by the loveliness of the scene before him and was certainly in no hurry to go back to the sports car and make a hasty end to their journey. Bar Harbor was just a little over two hours away. They could have arrived well before evening, but Adam seemed disinclined.

Without asking if she was agreeable, he led her on a circuitous tour of the town. Behaving like tourists, they drove to the Ureneff Tuberous Begonia Garden where they marveled at the blossoms and plants and raced down the grassy slopes to where the sunken garden was displayed against an overwhelming natural setting of pines and birches and ferns.

They traveled to the Farnsworth Library and Art Museum for firsthand appreciation of the works of Andrew and James Wyeth. And finally on to the Farnsworth Homestead and its nineteenth-century Victorian mansion with its fabulous carriage house display of sleighs, wagons and smithy shop.

Their day in Rockland wouldn't be complete without a stop at the Shore Village Museum on

Limerock Street where they viewed over a thousand artifacts relating to early Coast Guard and Lighthouse service history.

Through each exhibit, throughout the whole day, Adam kept Carly's hand in his complete possession. As she walked beside him, she was captivated by his easy, graceful walk and the sheer height of the man. With Adam beside her she felt protected from the world. And when she glanced up at him, it was always to find him smiling down at her, his eyes twinkling, his darkly handsome head framed against the scrubbed blue of the sky.

Each step was light and easy—painless, despite the amount of walking. She believed she could walk the world around if Adam were beside her.

With a pang of regret to have their idyllic afternoon come to an end, Carly settled back against the soft leather seat of the Corvette and watched Adam take command of the machine. Before backing out of his parking space near the wharf, he turned to her, a long, searching light in his eyes. A gentle finger brushed a strand of hair away from her cheek, and although he remained silent, Carly felt his meaning. He was as pained to have the day come to an end as she was.

A few minutes later they were breezing along on Route 1 heading north. To home. Where everything was the same as it had always been and would always be. The real estate business, Melissa, Quincy…Simone Maddox and Adam's unavailability. Refusing to spoil the day by dwelling on the empty void that lay ahead, Carly began humming to the tune on the radio.

Adam's deep voice joined hers and they simultaneously broke into song. Their camaraderie was easy, the gentle part of friendship. It was difficult to believe that only this morning Adam's power had overwhelmed her, that he had ignored her protests and had wrestled her to the floor to hold her and kiss her and arouse a deep, sensual need in her that she had only suspected was there but which had never really surfaced before.

The late sun was shining in the window over Adam's left shoulder. She turned to look at him, his aristocratic profile outlined in gold. The dark hair near the nape of his neck cried for a trim, and it curled with a will of its own around his ears. Strong and firm, his jaw gave authority to his handsomeness, a masculinity that was definitive. His long legs stretched out casually before him as he worked the gas and clutch with ease. But it was his hands that she found herself gazing at time and again. Strong hands, capable hands. Flexible and well formed. The tiny hairs on his knuckles became golden in the light. Adam's hands that had held her, touched her, delicately yet with a demanding possession. Hands that could be gentle or arousing.

Adam's hands that could trace delicate patterns of ecstasy or could quell a storm of anger.

"Bucksport is coming up. Hungry?" Adam's voice broke her out of her fascinations. "Should be dinner time by the time we arrive. Ready for an early supper?"

Carly laughed merrily. How easily Adam could slip in and out of local custom. Back in New York the term would have been dinner. Now only hours and miles away, he slipped into local jargon, referring to the evening meal as supper.

"Ever been to Jed Prouty's?"

"Once," Carly answered, remembering the quiet atmosphere of the old tavern with its romantic candlelight.

"Prouty's it is, then."

"Adam, no. Really, I'm hardly dressed for the occasion," she mourned, looking down at her jeans and tennis shoes.

"Both of us have suitcases in the trunk," he offered the remedy.

"And where will we change? In the restroom of the corner gas station?"

"I had something a little better than the gas station in mind." Before she knew it, he was angling the car off the road and pulling into the drive of the Jed Prouty Motel. Carly's eyes widened and her throat constricted, choking off her breath. Her heart plummeted to somewhere below her belt. How could he? After this wonderful, idyllic day. How could he? Her mind raced, her mouth refused to form the words, and before she could speak, Adam had stopped the car at the front office and hurried inside.

Sitting alone in the sports car, Carly wanted to bolt. To run. This wasn't what she wanted. If Adam thought that she was going to share a room, share his bed…disappointment welled within her. Despite the attraction between them, she was just not that kind of girl. Call it old-fashioned, call it prudery, even call it stupidity…he had no right to assume that she would gladly jump into his bed.

Suddenly, her hand was on the door latch. Then she swung her feet out and she was outside, outside and ready to run. The fresh breeze off the Penobscot River cooled her flaming cheeks, but there was little that could cool her rising anger. Her luggage. She'd be damned if she'd let him take off with her luggage. Her eyes fell on the ignition where the keys dangled. Hurriedly, she reached for them, searching through them for what she felt would be the key to the trunk. Hands shaking, she managed to fit the correct key into the lock. Her eyes fell on her bags and she struggled to lift them out of the cramped trunk quarters. Suddenly, she heard his voice behind her. "Let me help you, Carly."

She turned on him, ready for battle, and found him

standing with a wide grin on his face. And in his hands were two sets of room keys.

"Both rooms face on the river," he informed her, seemingly oblivious to the turmoil his hasty stop into the motel had caused her.

"Both rooms?" she asked, wanting to be certain she understood.

"Doesn't that please you? I could change…"

"No, no," she breathed, smiling again, overjoyed that Adam had not assumed she would share his room. "The river is perfect."

"Let's get going then. I made reservations at the tavern for eight. That should give us time to prowl around and see a little bit of the town. What there is of it, anyway," he joked.

Joy soared in her heart and she silently cursed herself for having so little faith in Adam. Then her heart gave a little tug. Was it really consideration for her that had prompted Adam to obtain two rooms or was it because he really had no designs on her, that she didn't arouse in him the same feeling he excited in her?

Uncertainly, Carly followed Adam into the main lobby while a bellman carted their bags to the elevator. The bellman unlocked her room first and Adam followed him inside, checking to see that everything was to his satisfaction. He glanced inside the room, checking the lights and for clean towels. He picked up the bedside phone, checking for a dial tone and automatically snapped on the radio-TV to be certain all was in working order.

The uniformed bellman opened the drapes and turned on the air conditioner, instructing Carly as to its use. The nights were already growing quite cool even though it was only the end of summer, he explained, and showed her how to operate the heating unit.

Adam was at the door, checking the locks and the bolt, and seeing that all was satisfactory, he gave her a wink and told her he'd see her in an hour. "I'm right down the hall, Room 411. Call me when you're ready."

EXACTLY one hour later, freshly showered and coiffed, and wearing a soft silver-gray silk dress, Carly telephoned Adam's room. He answered almost immediately and the sound of his voice so close to her ear sent tingles down her spine.

One minute later, there was his knock on her door. Sweeping up her tiny purse, she stepped out of the doorway and right into Adam's arms.

His kiss was light, yet proprietorial, and Carly melted into the light of approval she saw there in his eyes. "You're a marvel, Carly. Always beautiful and always on time." There was a note of intimacy in his voice, a possessiveness in his touch, as he held her arm, leading her to the elevator.

"Do you like your room?"

"Oh, yes. The view of the river is magnificent. But not so spectacular as the view from…" she stopped herself.

"Deer Island," he finished for her.

Carly turned to him and looked up into his face which had become suddenly stony and intractable. He had told her that losing the house on Deer Island no longer upset him, but seeing the change in him this way, Carly knew better.

If she had expected her careless choice of words to throw a pall over the rest of their evening, she was wrong. Adam wasn't the kind of man who dwelled on disappointments. By the time he led her out to the car, he was laughing and joking with her once again.

"We have over an hour before our reservation," he told her. "If you'd rather, we can go across the road to the tavern and wait at the bar or we could take a spin through Bucksport and discover."

"Discover is the word of the day," she answered, liking the smile in his eyes when she agreed.

"I was talking to the bellman as he opened my room," Adam told her. "I pretended we were tourists and were totally unfamiliar with Maine. He told me about an old cemetery just down the road that's a favorite with visitors. Want to go?"

"Cemeteries aren't exactly my thing, but sure, why not?"

The engine purred its response to the starter, and within minutes they were parking on the road beside an area completely surrounded by a high iron fence behind which old tombstones rebuked their neglect.

"Anyone I should know buried here?" Carly asked as she followed Adam through the gates into the cemetery.

"No one we'd want to know, I'm sure. We're looking for the tombstone of Jonathan Buck, the town's founder. He was a judge who was prominent in the New England witch trials. It's believed that he condemned an innocent woman to the burning stake for lewdness and that his grave marker is indelibly stained with the imprint of a woman's leg."

"You're right. No one I'd like to know," she answered, peering at the worn inscriptions on the aged stones.

"Over here, Carly. I've found it!"

Carly stepped lightly across the clumps of grass and rocky ground to where Adam called her. There before her, was a tall, granite obelisk standing as straight as the day it had been installed. The face of it bore the name of Jonathan Buck, and on its gray exterior was the undeniable dark stain which looked remarkably like a woman's leg. "Ooh, it's enough to give me the shivers...." She shuddered. "How's that old song go? 'He Done Her Wrong!'"

"Or, 'Hell hath no fury...'"

Her attention was diverted and Adam stopped in

midsentence. Off to the right, several feet away, lay a tombstone bearing the inscription, "Henry Schneider" and several feet away from that stood another, smaller and of unpolished stone, "His Wife."

Carly was unaccountably saddened and yet there was a spur of rage within her. Adam followed her gaze and instantly realized her feelings. Henry Schneider's stone bore dates of the early 1700's. It had been made of polished granite and, while of simple design, it was apparent that it had been made by a craftsman while the other stone was rough hewn and was crumbling from the effects of wind and weather.

Carly bent to touch Henry's stone. "Look here, Adam. Look at the dates. He was sixty years old when he died, and it's quite apparent that the stone was erected before his death. See how the first date denoting his birth and the hyphen following it are carved deeply and with a sharp wedge? The year of his death is clearly not as deeply inscribed and the numerals are larger."

Adam frowned, following Carly's train of thought perfectly. It wasn't unusual, when upon the death of someone in the family, to have a headstone erected for oneself, leaving blank only the date of death. Old Henry Schneider, it would seem, had buried his wife, erected the insignificant headstone for her, and purchased a much more elaborate one for himself.

"Oh, Adam, I feel so sad for her," Carly mourned, looking at the crumbling stone. "It doesn't even tell her name or the dates or anything. It only says, 'His Wife.' As though she had no identity beyond that. He didn't even have it read, 'His Good Wife.' Nothing. It might just as well have said, 'His Dog.'"

Adam hunkered down beside Carly, his fingertips gently tracing the lettering on the old gravemarker. "Poor Mrs. Schneider. We can only hope this isn't indicative of the life she led."

Suddenly, Adam bounded to his feet. Surprised, Carly watched him stride through the gates of the cemetery and out onto the highway, disappearing from her view.

"Adam? Adam? Where are you going?" she called after him.

"Out here, Carly. Come and help me!"

She followed the sound of his voice, puzzled at his sudden departure. When she found him, it was in the tall weeds at the side of the road where bright blooms of wildflowers grew. Adam was working with his pocket knife, gathering a bouquet of blossoms.

"Adam, you're wonderful!" she gasped, running to help him, holding out her arms for the bunches of flowers he handed her. Together they picked and chose, arranging a pretty bouquet for Mrs. Schneider's grave.

While Adam stood by, Carly placed the blossoms in front of the headstone, tenderly handling the fragile blooms. When she was finished, Adam reached down and plucked a flower from the many and tucked it into Carly's curls. "Mrs. Schneider would like you to have it," he told her, kissing her lightly on the tip of her nose.

As Adam walked her back to the car, Carly couldn't help thinking that Adam Noble's wife would never be an insignificant part of his life like poor Mrs. Schneider. Adam's wife would always come first in his life, not a possession. And he would expect his wife to take part in his life, to be his helpmate. Carly brought her musings up short. She wouldn't, she mustn't, ever think of herself in that role. Adam had done nothing, said nothing, to commit himself to her. And with Simone Maddox in the wings, he never would. Simone was the kind of woman who would be politically advantageous to have as a wife. Not she, Carly, who didn't know the latest fashionable labels to wear on her clothes or the newest, rising young artist. Simone had contacts and her family connections could help Adam in his political career. While Carly had only the vaguest knowledge of politics and her only dealings with the arts were the ones to get her office walls painted.

"Why so glum, Carly?" Adam asked and there it was again, that faintly intimate note when he spoke her name. It was as though he liked to say "Carly." As though her name came easily to him and rolled off his lips.

"Not so glum, Adam. I've just been reminding myself of a few truths."

"Not all women are like the unfortunate Mrs. Schneider, Carly." He touched her hand, squeezing it. "And all men aren't like old Henry, either. Take me, for example." He laughed, his eyes twinkling merrily. "I'd be certain to have the largest, grandest grave-marker ever erected for *my* wife!"

"You beast!" Carly shrieked, pummeling him on the arm as they entered the motel parking lot where they would walk across the road to the famous Jed Prouty Tavern. "Are you really so certain that you'd outlive your wife? Not planning on being a Bluebeard, are you?"

"Yup," he teased as they walked across the wide front porch of the old stagecoach run stopping place, "I fully intend to kill her with love."

He laughed when he said it but there was a serious note hiding behind his jocularity—something that set Carly's pulses racing, but she couldn't dwell on it to reason it out because Adam was showing her pictures and portraits of some of the famous guests who had once frequented the tavern. She gazed up into the stern visages of Presidents Van Buren and Stonewall Jackson and William Henry Harrison and John Tyler as Adam directed, but it was his face she wanted to look at, his eyes that held the mystery for her.

For a moment he turned to her and looked down at

her and there was unspeakable tenderness in his voice. "I'm having a great time, Carly. I hope you are, too."

Before she could answer that this was the most special time she had ever spent in her life, the hostess entered from the dining room and showed them to their table.

UPON leaving the old tavern after an excellent dinner of Maine lobster and prime rib, Adam glanced at his watch as they were crossing the parking lot to the motel. "It's after eleven. Not late by New York standards but certainly too close to the witching hour here in Maine."

Carly felt forlorn and bereft. She never wanted this night to end. She wanted their closeness and the magic to go on forever.

Outside her door Adam took her in his arms. She felt the beating of his heart against her own, and the breath seemed to leave her body. His embrace was warm, possessive, and his kiss was hot, mystical. She offered him her mouth, answering his demand, feeding his passion. When he at last released her, it was reluctantly because of voices down the hall. His eyes shone down upon her and she was tempted to reach up to brush a lock of dark hair from his brow. "Get a good night's sleep, Carly. Good night."

HOURS LATER, after what seemed an interminable time falling asleep, the phone at her bedside table rang, jarring her awake. Groping for the receiver in the dark, her fingers made contact and she brought the phone to her ear. Adam's soft, intimate voice snapped her eyes open.

"Carly?"

"Umm?"

"I'm sorry, I shouldn't have wakened you, go back to sleep."

"Huh? No, Adam…what is it?" Why was Adam calling her? His voice didn't sound as though he'd slept. Was he having as much difficulty sleeping as she had had? Was it because he had lain awake thinking of her as she had of him? The tempo of her pulse quickened.

"Well…" he seemed hesitant. "I couldn't sleep. I decided to take a walk outside and I wandered out in back of the motel by the river. Go back to sleep, honey. I'm a jerk for waking you."

"No. You were walking by the river and what?"

"Hell. It's the trout! They're running!" His voice quickened and filled with a little boy's excitement that was contagious. "I asked the desk clerk about fishing gear and he kindly offered to lend us his. What do you say, Carly? What kind of angler are you?"

"Just give me two minutes and I'll be down in a flash!"

"Great! I'm at the check-in desk."

Carly bounced out of bed. If Adam wanted to share his adventure with her, she wasn't going to refuse. If Adam wanted to go fishing at…she glanced at her watch…three in the morning, then fish she would. Everything was wonderful with Adam Noble, everything…everything.

Jeans, an old pullover, a quick tug of the brush through her hair and she was ready to go. Remembering to pocket her room key, she pressed the button to the elevator, couldn't wait, and headed for the stairs, racing down them, blood pounding, running to Adam.

When she achieved the front desk, he caught her in his arms and swung her around, to the amusement of the desk clerk. "You're terrific, Carly. Come on, I've got everything."

Her tennis shoes were soundless on the tarmac surrounding the motel and made for easy footing on the steep, weakly lit incline that led down to the mud flat and the Penobscot River.

The water was inky black and faintly redolent of oil, but in the feeble light from the back of the building, iridescent flashes of color and light could be seen in the shallows.

"Shh!" Adam put his finger to his lips. "Trout are really skittish this time of year and any sound will spook them. Look at that, did you ever see so many? They've come in at the high tide to feed. Want to lay a bet as to who'll get the biggest?"

Devilment and competition spurred Carly. "And what's the prize?"

"Winner take all," Adam whispered.

Carly wasn't certain what she was getting herself into, but she nodded her head, agreeing.

"Come on, then. The clerk even gave me some bait. I'll bait your hook for you."

"Oh, no, you won't. My dad and I used to go fishing all the time. He said he wouldn't fish with a woman who was afraid of her own bait."

"A wise man, your father, a wise man."

Hunkering down, Adam and Carly prepared their hooks. Standing at the water's edge, they both cast in. Almost immediately, the bait was taken, the lines rushing out of the spools, the snap of fin and tail turning the water white.

Adam reeled his catch in easily, the trout's fury no match against his strength. He held it up, the light shimmering off its white belly. "You'll have to go some to best this one, it must be four pounds!"

"For your information, Mr. Noble," Carly grunted with exertion, "that's Moby Dick out there on the end of my line."

Her fish played out more line, forcing Carly to step into the inky water up past her ankles. Again and again she leaned backward, struggling to reel it in. Again and again the fish snapped at the end of the line, making

Carly believe she would never be able to play it in. The lightweight rod bent almost in two when at last she had fought it into the water's edge.

"Whew!" Adam breathed with astonishment when he saw the size of the trout. "Well, the night's not over. Ready for another try?"

"You bet."

For the next several hours they followed the path of the feeding trout, walking down the mudflats farther and farther away from the motel. The bait was fresh, the fish eager and their harvest was bountiful.

Their excursion had taken them out onto a natural rock jetty where Adam declared himself the winner. The last trout he had reeled in was the granddaddy of them all, and Carly agreed to his win, too exhausted to continue.

Adam dropped down onto the rocks beside her, wiping the vestiges of water and bait from his hands onto his old jeans. Leaning back on his elbow, he surveyed the sky. "This is the second time we're seeing daybreak together, Carly."

There it was again, the way he said her name. His voice almost seemed to soften, its rich basso tones lighten, as though he were whispering an endearment. "If I remember correctly, we didn't see much of that sunrise, did we?"

Carly's nerves tingled as she remembered that first

kiss. Every kiss with Adam seemed to be a first kiss, heady and intoxicating, filling her world, her senses.

Adam looked across the river to the sprinkling of far off islands glistening like jewels as the break of day illuminated them. It was almost as though she could read his thoughts. He was thinking about Deer Island and the Sinclaire house.

"Adam, about the Sinclaire house…"

"What about it?" His voice was casual enough but there was something beneath it, some bitter core.

"I really did try to contact you. Somehow, you never received any messages."

"Did you, Carly?"

"Don't you believe me? No, I can see you don't."

"What I can't believe is how I never received any messages. That home was my dream home, exactly the place I would want to live, raise children… I have no reason to believe…"

"That I really tried to get in touch with you," Carly interrupted, not allowing him to complete his sentence.

"No…I…"

Again she cut him off, rising to her feet, standing over him. "Yours is not the only integrity that can be offended, Mr. Noble! I, too, lay great store in my reputation and credibility!" Her voice was rising, broaching on a shriek.

"Carly, you don't understand…."

"Oh, I understand, all right. I understand that you

think I'm a liar. That I double-dealt you. That I stole the house out right from under you and sold it to Kyle Dillon. Let me go, Adam." She shrugged out of his reach when he extended his arms to her. "I can't bear to be near you. No...no..."

He was moving in on her, following her across the rocks. He captured her, holding her tightly, abating her struggles to be set free. He gripped her head, holding it still for his kiss, his mouth moving over hers, demanding, hurting....

"Let me go!" she cried, pushing him away, taking advantage of his unsteady footing. "I don't want to see you again! Stay away from me. You offend me!"

"Carly, don't be silly. You never let me finish what I was saying...." There was hurt in his eyes but also a kind of arrogance too. As if she should push her feelings aside and believe whatever he had to say, as though he expected her to believe him.

"At least let me drive you home to Bar Harbor...."

"Forget it. I'll make it home on my own. I'll hitch-hike, rent a car...a bicycle! Anything! And don't bother paying for my room. I'll pay for it myself...." Turning, she ran back to shore, each moment expecting Adam to catch up with her, to force her to be with him. Instead, Adam stood on the jetty, shoulders slumped, the fishing gear he would have to return to the desk clerk lying abandoned at his feet.

Later, after she was in her room, a tap sounded at the door. "Carly, it's me, Adam."

"Go away," she cried, choking back the tears. "I don't want to hear anything you have to say…why should you want to talk to a liar?"

"It's not that way, you never let me finish…."

"Go away, Mr. Noble, before I have to call the police and tell them you're harassing me. It might blot your burgeoning political career. Go away!"

There was a silence on the other side of the door.

Afraid to move, even afraid to cry for fear of being heard through the door, Carly buried her face in the pillow and choked back her tears and rage. Why? Why had he come to Jenny's apartment? Why had he given her an idyllic day, rife with romance, with tender touches and passion-filled kisses if he thought her a liar? Had he somehow expected her to foul up the deal for Kyle Dillon? Mess it up so Kyle wouldn't want the house so he, Adam, could have it? She was in the position to be uniquely useful to him in that capacity….

"No, no, no!" she sobbed, stifling the sound in her pillow.

CHECKOUT was one o'clock and when Carly finally dried her tears and washed her face, it was after ten. She had to get moving. A quick call to the desk clerk informed her that a public bus stopped at the corner near the motel and traveled on to Bar Harbor. Her transportation home wouldn't be difficult. After writing down the time of the bus's arrival, Carly asked in a meek voice, "Has Mr. Noble checked out yet?"

"Yes, Miss, over an hour ago. He left a message for you at the desk, telling me I should give it to you. And, by the way, your bill has been paid...."

Carly didn't want to hear anything else and clicked the phone down into its receiver.

CHAPTER ELEVEN

CARLY climbed down from the high bus step and waited for the driver to retrieve her luggage from the storage space under the vehicle. She glanced around expecting, yet fearing, that Adam Noble would drive up in his sporty car. When she saw that he wasn't anywhere around, she breathed a sigh of relief.

Things were going to be bad enough explaining to Melissa the delay of her arrival home. She should have been home by air shuttle yesterday. Now, here she was, arriving a day late and by bus.

Melissa could read Carly like a book and she would know in a minute that whatever the problem was her daughter hadn't solved it. Then she would cluck and hover the way mothers do when they're worried about their children.

The bus station was only a few blocks from the office and Carly staggered under the weight of her luggage with each step.

The little bell over the door rang as Carly entered the

cool of the office. Melissa did all the motherly things Carly expected. She kissed her only daughter resoundingly and babbled nonstop for fifteen minutes. She went in the order of priorities. Quincy was off his feed; the microwave oven wasn't working and she was near to starving; the sump pump in the basement only works for you, Carly, and what did you do to it; the basement is flooded and why don't we eat out from now on.

Carly winced. "Mother, Quincy is off his feed because he's molting. The microwave isn't broken. I pulled the plug during the electrical storm we had before I left, and as long as there's peanut butter and jelly, you'll never starve. The sump pump only works if you turn it on." Sometimes, especially now, she felt as though she was the mother and Melissa was the daughter. She waited, hardly daring to breathe, for Melissa to continue.

"I'm glad you're back. Not that I couldn't handle things, but this office is so quiet without you. I was going to bring Quincy in, but I can't stand it when those green feathers fly all over."

It was like pulling teeth without novocaine. "How's business?" Carly asked bravely.

"Hectic. Terrible. Nothing is going right. The bank didn't approve the Simpsons' mortgage, the closing went off on the Brackett place with only a few minor problems, and the lawyer for the Ryans misplaced their escrow check and can't find it, so the closing was postponed till he does find it. Mrs. Ryan is in the hospital under sedation and her husband is threatening to sue everyone in sight. The Sinclaires are now making noises like they don't want to sell after all. Martha thinks they might have been just a bit hasty. Kyle Dillon is on the verge of a nervous breakdown. By the way, Carly, he called here several times. The messages are still on the machine. I spoke to him once myself. And," she said, her dark eyes twinkling merrily, "guess who else called you?"

Carly's heart thundered in her chest so loud, she thought for sure Melissa would hear it. Please let her say it was Adam Noble, she pleaded silently. He would have arrived in Bar Harbor early this morning.

"Well, aren't you going to guess?" Melissa chirped happily.

"Mother, I'm too old and too tired right now to play games. Just tell me who called."

"Adam Noble, that's who. He sounded upset. Can you imagine, can you even begin to imagine how I felt when I said I didn't know when you were coming home? Your very own mother not knowing. And then I had to tell Kyle Dillon the same thing. Carly," Melissa said taking a deep breath, "is Adam Noble the reason you went off like a scalded cat?"

"Mother, don't help, don't give me any advice, and above all, don't ask questions. Not now."

"Darling, you asked me how business was. I told you. Is it my fault things haven't been going right? I'm so worried about Quincy, Carly. Are you sure he shouldn't go to the vet? He's not even eating his licorice."

She had done it again. Every time Melissa stuck her foot in her mouth, she used Quincy to get it out. "You're probably right to be concerned, Mother. I think he should go to the vet."

"Good girl. You can take him. You are going home to take your bags aren't you? I'm going over to see Martha and try to make some sense out of this mess. She did say they were selling, and the agreement was signed properly by all parties. Kyle Dillon is within his rights to sue if he has a mind to. I'll see you later. By the way, how was New York?"

"Simply paradise, Mother."

"Good," Melissa said hastily. "See you… whenever."

Carly heaved a sigh of relief. Melissa was so…she made her tired was what she did. Fifteen minutes of her nonstop prattle was enough to make Carly long for earplugs and a safe haven somewhere in the wilds of Canada. If she could bottle her energy, she would make a fortune. Carly sighed again. She might as well go home to check on things and come back later in the day to catch up. Now that Melissa knew she was home she would be off for days at a time, leaving Carly to take care of things. Practicable, dependable, feet on the ground, Carly would see to things. She sniffed and brushed a tear from the corner of her eye. No more tears. That was a promise she had made to herself on the bus ride home. She would never cry over a man again. She would save her tears for something really important, like when Quincy was placed in a foster home.

The emerald bird met Carly at the back door, jabbering just as Melissa had done. Feathers of all sizes were floating everywhere.

"Hi, Quincy. This place is a dump because your feathers are making a mess. But as you can see, I'm back. Molting sure takes all the starch out of you. If you keep it up, you're going to be the skinniest bird around. Want some licorice?"

Quincy flew into his cage and settled himself on his perch carefully tucking his head into his wing. Poor thing, I should have his problems. Quickly, before the green bird could change his mind, she tossed the cover over the cage and then set about cleaning up the carpet of shamrock-colored feathers. The feathers in the trash, Carly plugged in the microwave oven and tested it. Perfect. Melissa could bake her TV dinners till the end of time. She flicked the switch at the top of the basement stairs and heard the sump pump roar to life. Her house in order, so to speak, Carly mounted the stairs to her room. She unpacked, taking her time as she unfolded each article and then hung it carefully on a scented hanger. She was disappointed when she finished. Only a half hour had gone by. Why and how had she become so conscious of time? She had never been a clock-watcher for that matter. It was depressing. Suddenly, she was a lot of things she had never been before.

Carly slumped down in the lavender slipper chair and massaged her temples. She shouldn't be tired but she was. Bone tired. Weary to her soul of this boring life she was leading. There had to be more, much more. There just had to be. Who was it that had said, "Life is what you make it"? Obviously, someone far more intelligent than she was. Or else that person had more guts than she did.

She was getting nowhere sitting here contemplating the state of what passed for her life. She had to get up, go to the office and make something happen. Ha! She slung her shoulder strap bag over her shoulder and drove back to the office.

Carly poured something that looked like a combination of instant cocoa and coffee into a cup and looked at it. She wondered vaguely how long Melissa had let it sit there and if it were two weeks old. She carefully set the cup down when she thought she saw something move in the thick liquid. She was sorting through the messages when the phone rang. Should she answer it or should she let the machine take the call?

She hated to hear a phone go unanswered. "Hello," she said briskly. Silence. "Hello," she said a second time.

"Carly? This is Adam Noble. I was shocked to hear your voice, that's why I hesitated for a second. How are you, Carly?"

"I'm just fine…Mr. Noble." She wouldn't ask him how he was because she didn't care how he was.

Another silence. Ah, he picked up on the Mr. Noble. "I called earlier to see if you made it home all right. I left a message with your mother."

Carly smiled to herself. He had left a message. Amazing. "Really?"

"Are you telling me you didn't get my message?" Adam asked, annoyance creeping into his voice.

"No. You're the one who doesn't get messages. My mother told me you called."

"If you received my message, why didn't you return my call?"

"Mr. Noble, it might surprise you, but I have other clients who keep abreast of their business dealings and know what their priorities are. I do business my way. You handle yours any way you see fit. Actually, there was no reason for me to return your call."

There was a deep chuckle on the other end of the line. "You sound hostile, Miss Andrews. I thought we had made excellent progress the last time we were together."

Carly felt the devil imp perch itself on her shoulder.

"Is that what you thought." It was a statement rather than a question. "Please get to the point."

"Do I have to have a point? Can't I just call you for the sake of calling? Just to chat and hear your voice?"

"Why don't you practice that line on someone else? You're taking up my time, Mr. Noble. What do you want?"

The amused voice that had turned to annoyance was now cold and brisk. "I want to hear from you why you sold the Sinclaire property to Kyle Dillon. I want to know what he promised you to steal it out from under me and I don't want any lies. Just a few simple facts, Miss Andrews."

"Of all the insufferable, arrogant…I don't have to listen to you. How dare you talk to me like that? I think you better clean up your act, Mr. Noble. When and if you do, call me, and if I feel like talking to you, I will and if I don't, I won't. And let me say now the latter is more likely than the former. Goodbye, Mr. Noble!" Carly slammed the phone back in the cradle so hard she thought it would crack. Immediately the white instrument shrilled. Seething inwardly, Carly flicked the switch to the answering machine to On and leaned back in her chair. Who did he think he was? How dare he address her in such a manner? Maybe Simone Maddox permitted it, but she, Carly didn't have to put up with it.

More angry than hurt, Carly closed the office. It would be just like wealthy Adam Noble to come storming into the office and strangle her. If she went home, she at least had a fighting chance. She had enough. She was a capable person. Hadn't she taken care of Melissa and Quincy after Dad died? And she had done it well. She wasn't flighty and irresponsible. She took her responsibilities seriously and acted on them to the best of her ability. She didn't like her business methods or her integrity questioned. She didn't like it and she wouldn't stand for it.

Carly careened into the driveway and was out of her car as soon as the engine was cut. She raced into the house and locked and then bolted the door.

Carly sat in the kitchen waiting for Adam Noble. She was so sure he would come to the house just to rail her again that she kept her eyes glued to the multipaned glass on the back door. An hour passed and then two. The coffeepot was empty and Quincy hadn't moved a feather. Carly snorted indignantly. Just when she thought she had the arrogant man figured out, he went and threw her a curve. She wished he would have come storming up the driveway spewing fire just so she could tell him he was trespassing and to get out of her life. She deserved the ecstasy of telling him what she thought of him to his face. She would live with the agony later. If she sat here much longer, she would take root. He wasn't coming and she better make up her mind to that fact. Whatever nebulous strand there was between them was broken. It was time to put romance out of her life and to get back to business. Determinedly, she began to count on her fingers the most important duties awaiting her. Suddenly it came to her. Kyle! She hadn't even played back the messages he had left for her. How could she have forgotten? "It's all your fault, Quincy," she snapped irritably. Again the green bird ignored her. "Men!"

Since the microwave oven was working, Carly tossed a potpie into a glass dish and set the timer. She ate it without tasting the cardboard crust and the semi-hard vegetables. Who cared if she died from frozen food? Time to adjourn into the living room and the boob tube. She sat with her eyes glued to the set, aware only of the vibrant colors moving before her.

Melissa came through the front door like the proverbial whirlwind. "I pulled your chestnut out of the fire. Carly, are you listening to me? Martha Sinclaire is over her attack of the jitters and the property is still up for sale. All we have to do is call Kyle Dillon and we're back in business. Carly! Did you hear a word I said? What's wrong with you? Did you cook anything for dinner? Did you take Quincy to the vet? How is the poor thing? Carly, when are you going to call Kyle Dillon? Do you want the man to have a nervous breakdown?"

Carly yawned. "Mother, I did not take Quincy to the vet. He's sleeping. No, I did not cook dinner, but I did steal one of your potpies and I even ate it. I will call Kyle Dillon first thing in the morning. And whatever in the world makes you think I'm not happy?" She stretched her lips into a grimace. "See, I'm happy. I'm also happy that Martha Sinclaire decided to sell after all. You're a born salesperson, or how about con person? What did you say to her to make her change her mind?"

"Dear child," Melissa said loftily, "I merely pointed out to her the error of her ways. Besides, anyone can sway Martha Sinclaire. She's a mother and she wants to be near her children. I'd do the same thing if you got married and moved away. When do you think you'll take the step, Carly?"

"Never from the looks of things," Carly retorted morosely. "A lot you care if I get married. All you want is to get rid of Quincy and have that stupid microwave oven to yourself. Well, I'm trenching in and you might as well make up your mind that you're stuck with me."

"Carly, I would give you such a beautiful wedding. With the commission from the Sinclaire property, you can even have a dowry."

"You're forgetting one thing, Mother. In order to get married there has to be a man on the scene. And I don't need a dowry."

"You're probably right. Dowries are passé now. You did leave me a potpie, didn't you?"

"If I'm not mistaken, I left you sixteen chicken, eleven turkey and seven beef pies. Take your pick or eat one of each. Don't forget to put them into a glass dish."

"I know how to use that oven, I'm not addlepated like you seem to think," Melissa said huffily.

"They're fattening," Carly said gleefully, aware that Melissa counted calories constantly.

CARLY woke with the phone shrilling in her ear, demanding and insistent. "Hello," she muttered groggily.

"Carly? That you? It's me, Adam."

The sound of his voice reverberated through her like shock waves. The alarm on her nightside table stated that it was 5:17. Words refused to form in her throat.

"Carly," he began softly, "I remembered you like sunrises so I assumed you would be awake. You were, weren't you?" he challenged.

"Hardly," she croaked. "Look, Adam, if you're calling to upbraid me again about the Sinclaire property I don't want to hear it. Thank you for calling. Goodbye." The phone fell from her fingers and bull's-eyed into the cradle.

Carly fumed. The nerve of him to call at this hour and harass me. Tossing back the covers she swung her feet to the floor and stomped off to the bathroom.

There was no sense trying to go back to sleep, she was too angry.

Twisting the water faucets on viciously, the shower raged, spewing steam into the room. Showering quickly and toweling dry, she quickly went to her closet and selected at random a sleek navy blue skirt. A tailored white shirt and her blue blazer would do for the day.

She sat at her vanity table and applied a scant amount of makeup that included blusher, mascara and lip gloss. A tug of the brush through her hair and she picked up her purse and was out the door.

Quincy greeted her with a loud squawk as she flew through the living room and out the back door to the garage. There was no way, no way on God's sweet earth that she was going to hang around the house and make herself available for any more of Adam's accusations.

The tires screeched as she made the turn at the corner. Bar Harbor was still sleeping. The streets were void of traffic, and milk bottles and newspapers sat untouched on front porches. Aside from Adam Noble, Carly felt as though she were the only person awake in the whole world.

Making a left onto Main Street, she automatically headed for the office. She was about to park when she realized that aside from her home, Adam would certainly try to contact her here. Again her foot pressed the accelerator and she sped off. Her route took her past the dock where the ferry stood sentinel. The ferry that had taken Adam and herself out to Deer Island.

There was the Fisherman where she had had dinner with Adam. The Coffee Shop, the marina, the park where the Nobles played their regular Sunday touch football game. Everything, everywhere, reminded her of places and times with Adam.

Tears blurred her vision as her circuitous route took her around the town. The Coffee Shop was still closed. By a glance at her watch it was only 6:07. Too early for business; too late for a future with Adam.

Swiftly, she pulled into a parking space in front of the office. If Adam wanted to track her down he would, whether or not she went to the office. She needed to be someplace that would put her on her own ground. Somewhere familiar, somewhere safe.

No sooner had Carly stepped out of her car and smoothed her skirt than she saw him, standing across the street, watching the office. Her first impulse was to jump back in the car and run, but it went against her grain. However much she didn't want to hear any more of his accusations, she was going to stand and face them. Then, she would turn on her heel like the lady she was, and walk away. Clean and simple. Once and for all.

She stood her ground, facing him, daring him to cross the street and approach her. Her dark eyes held a challenge, one that he couldn't refuse.

Adam stood, moving his long, lean frame from the side of the building. His dark hair glinted with blue lights in the early morning light. The sun was climbing the sky, lighting the town with its red-gold hues. The white boating denims he wore hugged his body, accentuating the trim length of his legs. A soft blue pullover that she knew, even from this distance, did wonderful things for his eyes, topped his slacks. He moved toward her, unhurried and determined. Almost like a cat stalking a bird.

As he drew nearer she saw the grim set of his face, the tightening of his jaw, the way his well-defined brows were drawn into a frown.

Her heart fluttered within her, her pulses raced and yet she stood, ready to do battle. He came nearer, near enough to touch. "You hung up on me, Carly. I wanted to talk to you. I must talk to you."

Carly froze him with a forbidding look. Sticking to her resolve, she deliberately turned on her heel and walked away. Instantly, his arm shot out to grasp her. "Stand still. I have to talk to you."

Defensively, she pulled away, still walking, her back to him. He touched her again. "Carly…"

Without realizing it, Carly's footsteps quickened, still he was right behind her, reaching out for her. "Carly…I have to talk to you."

"No!" Carly shouted, "I've heard enough. You've

said too much already." The last words were nearly a sob and like a child, she placed her hands over her ears and began to run. Places passed before her in a blur. Her feet pounded the pavement as she tried to escape. Why wouldn't he take no for an answer? Why must he pursue her this way? There was nothing she could say that would make him believe that she hadn't deliberately, for some unknown reason, engineered to sell the Sinclaire property to Kyle instead of to him. She had been insulted enough and she wasn't having any more of it.

Suddenly, a viselike grip closed around her arm, pulling her backward and right into his arms. "Now you *are* going to listen to me, and right now." As he held firmly to her arm with one hand he reached for her bag with the other. "I assume the keys to your office are in here," he said, hot anger in his tone. "I don't intend to let you get away from me until you've heard what I have to say."

Roughly, unalterably, he pulled her along the street back to the office. Resolutely, she followed. Protests were beyond her. She was helpless. There was nothing else to do but submit to him, listen to his accusations for one more time. Hopefully, it would be for the last time.

Digging through her bag, Adam came up with her keys. He tossed them at her. "Open it," he gestured to the locked office door. Obediently, she found the key and inserted it into the lock. Almost before she could withdraw the key, Adam pushed the door open and pulled her inside.

"Now you're going to sit there and listen to what I have to say," he said gruffly, pushing her into a chair.

"I don't want to listen to you. Every time you say something it's insulting. I've had enough, can't you see that?"

"Be quiet. Don't say a word until you've heard me out."

"No, I won't be quiet. If you have something to get off your chest, go tell it to someone who'll listen. Go tell it to Simone."

"What has Simone got to do with this? No, don't answer. Let me tell you. I don't know what you ever thought was between Simone and myself but let me tell you it just isn't so. Simone was here in Bar Harbor at the invitation of my father. Not mine."

"Very interesting. If it's true," Carly heard herself say, her anger matching Adam's.

"Of course it's true. Why would you think otherwise?" he demanded.

"Any fool could see the designs Simone drew on you."

"That's just it, Carly, they were her designs, not mine. As a matter of fact, she's not even here in the Harbor any longer. She left without a word to anyone while I was in New York."

For the first time Carly seemed to hear what Adam

was saying and she was brought up short and found herself speechless. Simone was gone. Adam never had intentions of marrying her.... Suddenly she thought of a remark Kyle had made at the fish fry. "What girl wouldn't have designs on a man if she'd been seeing him for two years."

"What? Woman, where do you get your crazy ideas?"

Carly pulled herself to her feet despite Adam's glare and proximity. "From Kyle Dillon. At the fish fry he said he had met the two of you in Monte Carlo two years ago! That's where! And if you think I'm going to sit here another minute and talk about Simone..."

Adam grasped her shoulders, pulling her against him. She beat at his chest with small, tightly clasped fists. Her pummeling was ineffectual against his strength.

"I only happened to run into Simone two years ago in Monte Carlo. I've only seen her once or twice before she accepted the judge's invitation to Bar Harbor. Seems my dad thinks it's time I settled down and took a wife. And speaking of which, I've decided my father is right." His eyes burned into hers, making her already pounding heart beat faster. His hands came up and closed over the back of her head, lifting her hair, touching the delicate sensitive skin behind her ears. His mouth came crashing down on hers and she found she was incapable of movement, helpless against him. "I love you, Carly. I love you."

Carly couldn't believe her ears. Adam's voice was husky with emotion, and so close to her, close enough that she felt his breath upon her cheek. Again his lips found hers in a searing, passionate kiss that obliterated the world and demanded an answering response in her. When he drew away from her he looked down into her eyes. "I called you this morning because I *did* want to talk to you about the Sinclaire property. Now, now, let me finish. I started to tell you in Bucksport but you didn't give me a chance. I wanted to tell you that the house doesn't matter."

Carly heard her own indrawn breath. She waited, frozen with anticipation. "That's just a house," she heard Adam say. "I've already discovered that home is where the heart is, Carly, and you're my heart. Anywhere you are is my home. Marry me, Carly, tell me you love me."

Carly's mind was a whirlwind of confusion. He loved her. Even though he believed she had double-dealt him with the Sinclaire property. He loved her! She should be happy, she was happy, if only they didn't have this doubt between them.

"Say you will, Carly," Adam whispered, mistaking her silence for indecision.

Carly sank back against the desk, her hand falling on the buttons of her telephone answering machine. Suddenly, the sound of Kyle Dillon's voice filled the office, startling both Carly and Adam.

"Carly, I hate talking into these machines but I've no other choice. I'll make this quick. I'm going to South America. You won't believe this but I'm going to design a whole entire city! Me! Can you believe it? About that house. I'm afraid I'm not going to be able to buy it after all. I hate to disappoint the Sinclaires but there's nothing I can do about it. If I have to lose the deposit, so be it. Get me off the hook, Carly. From the look of things it's a five-year project. More to tell you. I'll call back."

Carly and Adam looked at each other in disbelief. The house, the Sinclaire house was available. Adam's dream house.

Deliberately, Adam leaned forward and pressed the button to listen to the next message. It was Kyle again.

"Carly, I know you always wanted Adam to have the house. So tell him it's his. I had a little heart-to-heart talk with Simone and after a few drinks she let it slip out how she detoured your telephone messages from Adam. It seems she wasn't looking forward to a quiet life in Maine, and you were too much competition. At any rate, after I put the fear of God in her and threatened to mention to Adam how a little scheming filly had duped him, it was easy to convince Simone to see the sights of South America with me. As for Adam, don't worry, Carly, he'll come around. In fact, I wouldn't mind a bit if you called your firstborn after me…. Wish me luck, Carly. Goodbye."

Kyle's message was so unexpected that Carly could only sit in her chair, thoroughly stunned by the news. Hesitantly she looked up into Adam's eyes expectantly. He was looking down at her, a strange light glowing in his eyes. His arms opened and she stepped into them, knowing she would never want to leave them.

"Carly, can you ever forgive me?" he whispered, the remorse etched clearly on his face. "What a fool I was. I believed Simone implicitly when she denied that you'd ever tried to get in touch with me. And then when Kyle… Can you ever forgive me? I should have known to trust my instincts. I kept telling myself that I should believe you but my pigheadedness kept getting in the way. All I knew was how much I wanted the Sinclaire house and…"

"Shh!" Carly intoned. She placed her fingers against his lips briefly, then slipped her arms about his waist. "I should have trusted my instincts too. I knew you weren't the kind of man to dangle two women on a string at the same time. Even when you explained about Simone…"

It was Adam's turn to hush Carly. But instead of touching a finger to her lips he silenced her with his own.